I've travelled the world twice over,
Met the famous: saints and sinners,
Poets and artists, kings and queens,
Old stars and hopeful beginners,
I've been where no-one's been before,
Learned secrets from writers and cooks
All with one library ticket
To the wonderful world of books.

© JANICE JAMES.

CLOSE TO YOU

Amanda Blake is only too happy to take care of her friends' holiday cottage complex while they're away. Though it is off season, she doesn't mind being on her own — it will give her the opportunity to put behind her the memories of a disastrous relationship . . . Sheila Malborne has no reason to suppose today will be any different from any other Saturday. She awaits her son Ewan's arrival with relaxed anticipation, even though she wonders why his girlfriend Amanda isn't coming too. Sheila thinks she knows her son — but by Sunday, Ewan has become a killer . . .

Books by Tim Wilson
Published by The House of Ulverscroft:

MASTER OF MORHOLM
ROSES IN DECEMBER
HESTER VERNEY
PURGATORY

TIM WILSON

CLOSE TO YOU

Complete and Unabridged

CHARNWOOD
Leicester

First published in Great Britain in 1994 by
Headline Book Publishing Plc
London

First Charnwood Edition
published 1996
by arrangement with
Headline Book Publishing Limited
a division of
Hodder Headline Plc
London

British Library CIP Data

Wilson, Tim, 1962 –
    Close to you.—Large print ed.—
Charnwood library series
1. English fiction—20th century
I. Title
823.9′14 [F]

ISBN 0–7089–8894–6

Published by
F. A. Thorpe (Publishing) Ltd.
Anstey, Leicestershire
Set by Words & Graphics Ltd.
Anstey, Leicestershire
Printed and bound in Great Britain by
T. J. Press (Padstow) Ltd., Padstow, Cornwall

This book is printed on acid-free paper

UPPER BOCKHAM, NORTH NORFOLK

Cromer 7 miles, Norwich and the Broads 20 miles

AN EXCEPTIONAL, SELF-CATERING HOLIDAY COTTAGE COMPLEX WITH SUPERB LEISURE FACILITIES, A SPACIOUS PRIVATE HOUSE, SET IN ATTRACTIVE PRIVATE GARDENS AND WOODED GROUNDS, A SHORT WALK FROM SHINGLE BEACH.

INCLUDING:

8 SELF-CONTAINED COTTAGES, FULLY FURNISHED AND EQUIPPED TO THE HIGHEST STANDARDS, VARYING FROM 1 TO 3 BEDROOM UNITS.

RESIDENTIAL FARMHOUSE WITH 4 BEDROOMS, 3 RECEPTION + FARMHOUSE KITCHEN, LAUNDRY/BOILER ROOM.

LEISURE COMPLEX FEATURING HEATED INDOOR POOL, GYMNASIUM, SAUNA, JACUZZI AND GAMES ROOM.

FOR SALE FREEHOLD

SOLE AGENTS: MORPETH & NETTLETON,
              25 TOMBGATE,
              NORWICH,
              NORFOLK

1

Saturday 17 October

"AND listen, Amanda, if anything goes wrong . . . Hell, is that the phone again? I don't believe it. I mean, I really don't believe this is happening . . . "

Alix Pennington in a tizzy was a sight to see. Blonde mane tossing as she whipped her head round at the sound of the phone, she threw her passport into the air with a despairing gesture, crossed her eyes in a comic grimace just as she used to when a sixth-form Lothario with a face like a plate of baked beans targeted her across the disco floor, and accelerated out of the room like a tennis player chasing a drop-shot, leaving behind a twang of expensive perfume.

"Hello . . . ? Oh, hi! Yes, long time no hear . . . Listen, I can't talk long, things are just totally crazy here at the moment — we're going away today . . . Yeah, Florence . . . Well, you know, we need the break . . . Yes, flight's in three hours, so everything's pretty hectic . . . No, it's really lucky actually, Amanda's going to look after the place — Amanda Blake, you wouldn't know her, I was at school with her . . . "

Amanda retrieved the passport from the floor and placed it on top of Alix's handbag, smiling to herself. 'Going away' — that was very Alix. People like the Penningtons didn't 'go

3

on holiday'. Even the last-minute panic was — well, there was something *right* about it. The panic of people who wouldn't really leave anything important behind no matter how late they were with their packing; the panic of people who would never miss their flight even if their Range Rover left three of its wheels scattered across the motorway. A theatrical panic, if you wanted to be unkind about it. In the dozen years she had known her, Amanda had often felt that Alix must have been issued with a manual at an early age, a secret manual that was distributed to all the successful people of the world, and that gave detailed instructions on how to handle every experience from cradle to grave. Because Alix had never put a foot wrong in life, and nor was it possible to imagine her doing so. The same went for Ben, the ideal match she had unerringly located: the manual-owners must have some cabbalistic sign by which they recognized each other. And somewhere in the manual there must have been a section on how to go frantic while still looking like a million dollars.

Unkind again, Amanda reproached herself. For one of the many astonishing things about Alix and Ben Pennington was that they were very nice people. It was just that when she was with them she had a feeling that they were not quite real — or else *she* wasn't. Ben had been a money-juggler at various giant companies, the sort whose cryptic names gave you no idea what they did or made; but now at thirty-six he was something she only vaguely understood — some kind of independent consultant, occasionally zooming off around Europe to troubleshoot for other cryptically named companies. What she did know was that he really didn't need to do it. Even the purchase of this place seemed to have been no more a big deal to the Penningtons than the purchase of a secondhand car would have been to Amanda.

And this place was amazing. She had been here before, but she had still been struck, on arriving this morning, by the size of it. It was like owning a village.

Ben came in from loading the car. He had a cashmere sweater knotted round his neck. He was what paperback romancers described as lean. They would have called him chiselled, too, and for once the word would have been appropriate: his cheekbones could have sliced bacon. Apparently ulcers were eating him from within like a shoal of piranha, but he looked as fit as an Olympic swimmer.

"Not again," he said when he heard Alix on the phone, and in a louder voice: "Darling, we're going to have to get a move on."

"Is there anything I could be doing?" said Amanda, feeling rather a spare part.

Ben shook his head. "Everything's under control," he said with a wry smile. "Listen, we really appreciate you coming to look after the place for us. It was pretty short notice. I hope it hasn't put you out."

"No, no problem."

"A bit later in the year and we'd probably have had no bookings, and we could have just closed the whole place up for a week." Ben hefted the last two suitcases. "We'll give you a call from the hotel, but there shouldn't be any problems. All three families that are coming this week are regulars — none of the awkward squad."

"Do you get that sort?"

"You'd be surprised. Banging on the door complaining the ping-pong balls in the games room are all squashed. Or pinching the loo rolls. Anyway, thanks again."

"Glad to help," Amanda said. Well, not glad exactly, but she didn't mind. After all, she owed them one. When she had had that bad time back in the early summer they had let her hole up here for a fortnight, refusing to accept payment for the cottage she had stayed in, treating her with kindness and tact. A cold compress for emotional bruises: it had helped a lot. She had used up the last of her year's holiday in coming to look after the complex this week, and her boss wasn't too pleased about the short notice, but it was a fair enough price to pay.

Ben went out with the cases. Amanda washed the coffee cups, wiping down the sink and worktop with excessive care. It wasn't just that she was in someone else's home; the kitchen was so state-of-the-art that it seemed mildly shocking to sully it with suds. It was a farmhouse kitchen, insofar as it was part of an authentic farmhouse and it had about an acre of tiled floor, but an Italian designer would have felt more at home in it than Farmer Giles.

Alix was back. "Amanda, I'm *sorry* about that. God, people pick this morning of all mornings to

6

ring . . . " An abacus of pottery bracelets rattled along her arms as she threw her hands up in exasperation. "I mean, I haven't heard from Paula for practically *centuries* and then she decides to ring just when everything's in total chaos . . . Come on, Alix. Calm down. Deep breaths." She smiled at Amanda, as if seeing her for the first time. "Hey, you're looking *well*."

"Am I?" said Amanda, bemused.

Alix nodded emphatically. "Miles better than last time . . . well, you know. Oh, bums, I wish we could have had a really good chin-wag, but there's no time as per usual. Listen, when we get back, yeah? I'll send Ben off somewhere, and we can have a bottle of wine and you can spill the beans."

"OK, we'll do that," Amanda said, smiling. She would have asked what particular beans she was to spill, but she knew very well. *Relationships,* for want of a better word, were what people wanted to hear about. It did faintly irritate her sometimes that this was the only part of your life that was supposed to be of any interest or importance. You've just had a head transplant? Oh. You've got a new job as the queen's official food-taster? Oh. You've learned the violin and you're appearing next week at the Albert Hall with the LSO? Oh . . . but who are you *seeing*?

Exaggerated, of course. And it was natural that Alix, at least, should be curious. After all, the last time they had seen each other was when Amanda had been in full flight from a bad relationship (no, for 'bad' read '*disastrous*') and there had been no pretending that *that* wasn't an important thing in her life. Worse luck.

"Now where was I? Passport, right. Got it. Oh, Ben, did you remember to pack your tablets?"

"We've remembered everything," said the returning Ben, "except to give Amanda the keys."

"Keys, right." Alix produced a ring of keys weighty enough for a Dickensian gaoler. "OK, Amanda, these are for the cottages — they've got the names marked on them. These with LC on them, they're for the leisure complex. This one's the garage. This one's the padlock for the henhouse. And these are the house keys, front door, back door, side door, french windows. This one's the laundry room: we lock it because it's separate and once we found one of the guests had wandered in there and started doing their washing because they thought it was like a launderette, can you believe that? Anyway, they're all marked. Just mind you don't do your back in carrying them around. In summer we usually lock the leisure complex about eleven, but now you can just close it any time before you go to bed. Now what else . . . ? List, didn't I write out a list, Ben?"

"Yes," said Ben, who was perching on a stool and looking like something out of a mail-order catalogue, "it's on the pinboard, and you went through it with Amanda earlier."

Alix poked out her tongue at him. "Let me just whip through it again with you, Amanda," she said, looping her hair back behind a perfectly shaped ear. The cheek and jaw that joined on

8

to it were perfectly shaped, too — in fact the whole ensemble was flawless. I'm not jealous, Amanda thought. Well, all right, maybe I am a little jealous, but surely it isn't fair that people should have looks *and* money?

"OK, keys, done that," Alix said, holding up the list with the faint, displeased frown of someone reading their own handwriting. "Alan, that's the maintenance man, he only comes in during the week, but his phone number's here if you need him. He lives up in the village. There shouldn't be any problems — we had the filtration systems for the pool serviced not long ago so it'll all just tick over. Sue, you know her, of course, she'll be in at eleven today. She'll be here all week, and she knows the place inside out, so I'm sure she'll be able to help if there are any problems. The other cleaner comes weekday afternoons, not very reliably, I'm afraid. I think she's got boyfriend trouble. Hens — OK, you know where the food is. Mind when you open the gate to the pen at night, Clara's very nippy at getting out and it's hell trying to fetch her back again."

"And if you hear a fox, turn on all the exterior lights," Ben said, "that should get rid of it."

"You've got a fox round here?"

"Comes down from the woods. It's had two of the hens. I took a shot at it one night, but frankly I couldn't hit a barn door, and I really didn't fancy killing it," Ben said. "So much for the unsentimental countryman."

"OK, guests," went on Alix. "The Lloyds and the Holmses and that other couple, I can never

9

remember their name, they left first thing this morning. What *is* their name? Anyway, I call them the Aliens, I mean, they are *seriously* weird. God knows what state that cottage is in. Pentagrams on the floor, probably."

"Alix, really," Ben laughed, "just because she doesn't shave her legs."

"It's not just that, Ben, she *hennas* them. Anyway. They've all gone, and that just leaves the Bushells in Dairy Cottage — they should be leaving about lunchtime. They'll drop the key off here — you know where the guest key board is. Then it's all quiet on the western front until the Howards get here. They should arrive this evening. They always have Honeysuckle Cottage; they've been coming here since before we took the place over. Really nice people — "

"If you like cheese," murmured Ben.

" — and once they're here, that'll be it for today and you can go to bed whenever you like. There are only two more bookings and they won't be arriving till tomorrow. Dove Cottage and Seashell Cottage. They've all paid up in advance so no problem there. Then it should be plain sailing for the rest of the week. The Rayburn, I've shown you how that works. There's plenty of wood in the woodshed if you want a fire. Now food . . . " Alix opened the refrigerator and looked into it doubtfully. "I hope we've got enough in . . . "

"Alix, really, you shouldn't have got all that," Amanda said, gazing with a sort of anguished greed at what looked like the entire stock of a large delicatessen. *You are not going to pig*

10

out, do you hear? said her mind sternly, while her taste buds cried, *Try me! Just try me!*

"Oh, this is just snack stuff," said Alix. "The main event's in the deep-freeze. Oh, Ben! I knew there was something."

She pointed at the wine-rack which contained, horror of horrors, only three bottles.

"Bugger," said Ben, examining them. "We've left you pretty short here, Amanda. There isn't even a decent hock. Hell, I'm sorry, I should have remembered . . . "

The unreal feeling struck Amanda again. They genuinely felt they were rather making her slum it because they hadn't got in a full selection of wines for the week's meals . . . She didn't know what to say. Certainly she thought it best not to mention that her experience of wine went no further than buying the odd bottle of Leap-frog Milk and swigging the lot in front of the TV. "Really," she got out, "you've done me proud, honestly, I shan't be able to squeeze through the door by the end of the week."

"Well, if you're sure . . . We'll give you the number of our hotel, of course, so that if anything does go wrong — "

"Alix," Amanda said, "nothing's going to go wrong. Now go and enjoy yourself and forget about it all."

"Right. Right. Stop worry-gutting, Alix," said Alix, patting herself on the top of her head. "Well, I think that's everything, isn't it, Ben?"

"Will you get in the car?" Ben said, rattling the keys menacingly at her.

"I'm ready, I'm ready," Alix said, stowing her

passport in her bag. "Well, thanks for stepping into the breach, Amanda . . . Now, are you *sure* you're going to be all right for a week here on your own?"

"Well, there's going to be plenty of people around."

"Yes, but I mean . . . we thought you might bring Nick. We did say you were welcome to. I'm longing to meet him."

"Oh, well, he's got this awkward shift pattern at work, so — you know — it's difficult," said Amanda, shrugging uncomfortably. "He might be able to come down for the day next weekend."

But he could have got the time off to spend the week here with her. It was just that they had drawn back from the brink of something so committed as a holiday together, even a sort-of-working holiday like this. Because once you took holidays together you were that dreaded composite beast: a Couple. Getting Serious. And you'd be wearing matching sweatshirts and holding hands in the shopping mall before you knew it.

Ridiculous maybe. After all, she had spent last night at Nick's flat, even though they had solemnly agreed that she ought to spend the night at her place, as she needed to be up early to drive the eighty-odd miles to Upper Bockham. Back to her own place in the evening, pack, early night with the Horlicks, fresh for the journey in the morning: that had been the plan. Instead of which she had ended up knocking them back in Nick's local, sleeping at Nick's — and not doing much sleeping either — and having to hurtle blearily out of his flat at six am. to get back to her place and start throwing whatever came to hand into suitcases. So if that wasn't the behaviour of people who were getting serious, what was?

All right, point taken. But it wasn't that simple, not for her. Not after last time.

"Anyway," she went on, seeing Alix's speculative look, "I like being on my own, really. I can do lots of reading and polish up the old banjo — it's lovely and quiet here. Really, I'm quite looking forward to it. So don't worry about that."

So she liked being on her own, did she? Was that why at twenty-six she was still in a flat-share instead of going domestically solo? Was that why she had fled from her parents' village home to the city practically as soon as her last school uniform was put away? Was that why she had embarked on a new relationship a few months after the break-up of one that should have put her off for life? And was that why she was contemplating this week of comparative solitude in the back of beyond with very mixed feelings?

But then perhaps this week would give her a chance to think, and to answer those same questions in her mind.

"Well, my darling," Ben said, "Amanda won't be spending the week on her own at this rate. Because I'm going to leave you with her and go off to sunny Tuscany by myself if you don't get in that car pronto."

"I hate it when they get macho, don't you?"

13

Alix said to Amanda, reaching out and giving her a peck on the cheek. "Take care then. We'll see you next Sunday. And we'll phone. And if anything does go wr — "

"Don't say it!" said Amanda. "Go, go, go!"

"Right. Schtum. Going."

Amanda followed them out, helped to dissuade Alix from pausing to say goodbye to the hens, and stood waving as the laden Range Rover drew out of the yard, up the sloping service road, past the leisure complex, past the guest cottages, and out of the gateway on to the country road. And as it was lost to view behind the high hedgerows, with a last well-bred toot from the horn, Amanda suffered a reaction that also brought with it a flash of long-lost, inconsequential memory. A memory of her parents going off shopping one day when she was a child: she had decided to stay at home, but at the last moment she had for some reason changed her mind, and had run out just too late to see the car disappearing down the street. Somehow that sight had produced a terrible desolation in her; she had run some way down the street fruitlessly calling out, "Wait!", and had gone back to the house sobbing with misery. She certainly did not feel like sobbing now, but something of the same panic flared up in her as Alix and Ben's car hummed out of sight, something inside that protested, *Wait! Stop! Don't leave me here alone!*

Which was pretty stupid, she told herself when for the past hour she had been secretly wishing they would go. That didn't sound very

14

nice, especially when it was their house — she didn't mean it like that; it was just that she had felt curiously in the way. She was here as a house-sitter — or house-and-holiday-cottage-complex-sitter, to be exact — and she couldn't be that until they had gone. And in spite of Alix's copious lists and detailed instructions, and her own assurances that everything would be fine, she wanted to go over the whole kit and caboodle thoroughly and methodically on her own and get all her duties firmly established in her mind. She wanted to know where she was. For one thing, this place was not a responsibility to be undertaken lightly, not for her at any rate; and that was something that Alix and Ben probably did not fully realize. Because they lived in a world of six-figure sums, a world in which wealth was breathed instead of air, a world in which ownership of such a property as this was normal — and they tended to assume that everyone else did. Whereas Amanda, in surroundings like these, was out of her league. It was like being given some fabulously expensive and fragile antique to hold: your immediate and overmastering thought would be, *My God I might drop it what if I drop it!?*

Not that she really expected to burn Upper Bockham to the ground or flood it or otherwise perform some spectacular act of carelessness. But while the Penningtons were used to having the responsibility of megabucks-worth of real-estate, she was not; and if it meant being a little obsessive for a while, and checking every

15

electrical socket and window-lock and leaving herself admonishing Post-it notes all over the place, then that was a fair enough price to pay for peace of mind. The scenario that featured Alix and Ben getting out of the car clutching their duty-free to be confronted by a pile of charred ruins and an apologetic Amanda Blake saying, 'I had a spot of trouble', might be extremely unlikely, but she was going to make damn sure it stayed that way.

"Hope for the best and expect the worst," as her grandma used to say. Someone else used to say that too . . . But she didn't want to think about that. She turned quickly and went back inside.

Strong black coffee first: she had quit smoking a year ago, but she still needed to jump-start herself with caffeine periodically through the day. She prowled about the intergalactic farmhouse kitchen, looking for gizmos that might explode or overheat or otherwise betray her. Stopping to glance at the cork pinboard on the wall, she was surprised and then touched to see a photograph of herself there, taken, she reckoned, a decade ago when she was sixteen. Alix and herself and a couple of other schoolfriends grinned red-eyed into the flash at some forgotten party, against a background of someone's parents' flowery wallpaper. She could almost smell the Cinzano and the cider and the hair-gel that made such satisfying spikes but turned you into something resembling a squashed hedgehog when you lifted your head from the pillow the next morning. It was surprising to see the photo there because she didn't think of Alix and herself as that close. They had been friends at school, but even then the trajectories of their future lives had been pointing in widely diverging directions. Alix knew exactly where she was going — and she went there: university, London, PA job at a cosmetics company and, ultimately, the arms of Ben Pennington, whose arc had risen to meet hers. Amanda didn't consider herself anybody's failure — and these days you could count yourself lucky if you weren't sipping soup in a night-shelter — but where Alix was concerned she, like most of their contemporaries, could only stand and watch as the Girl Most Likely To had ascended into orbit.

And yet the two of them had kept in touch. They had kept in touch the way people always said they were going to and seldom did. They might meet up only twice a year, but they did meet up, and always found plenty to say to each other. They inhabited different worlds, and each had little real comprehension of the way the other lived — hence Alix's assumption that Amanda would not be fazed by being entrusted with a property worth her whole lifetime's salary. Hence, too, Alix and Ben's amiable vagueness about Amanda's job; when they asked her about it she was always reminded of the queen touring a factory. But somehow it didn't matter. They still got on well. There was a lot to be said for being slightly less than bosom friends; you didn't get that overheated tension that went with all close relationships. And when Amanda had

had that bad time in the early summer, Alix had offered just the right degree of solicitude combined with practical help.

Yes, there was a lot to be said for people not being *too* close. And she had said it all right, that summer, after Ewan. Said it mainly to herself in the protective shell of solitude into which she had withdrawn, but said it with complete conviction. No more involvement. No more entanglement. No more mess. Looking at the other photographs on the pinboard — the snapshots of Alix and Ben in various exotic locations, on beaches, on balconies, arms around each other, smiling, laughing, and always together, together, together — she recalled the indignant perplexity that such sights had caused in her during that time. Happy loving couples. Didn't they see what a destructive fraud it all was?

Part of her still felt that way, or wanted to. But something else had intervened, and that something was Nick.

She looked at the wall-clock. Ten-forty. It was crazy, but having been apart from him for less than five hours she had a strong urge to ring him up.

She couldn't, anyway. His shift started at ten, he would be at work.

But he did have an answering machine, presented to him by one of his wide-boy brothers — best not to inquire where it had come from. So she could ring and leave him a message. Just something to say that she had got to Upper Bockham safely, and that Alix and

Ben had set off and that she hoped he had a good day at work, and . . .

And what? That she missed him? True enough. That she wished she was with him? True again. And that she loved him . . . ?

Ah, yes. She was very much afraid that that was true too. But she hesitated to open that particular Pandora's box, after last time.

"I'll ring later," she told herself. She spoke out loud, partly for the reassurance of hearing a human voice. The country quiet had enfolded her from the moment the Range Rover was out of earshot, and it was that country quiet that she relished least about this coming week.

She stood for a moment and listened. No traffic noise. The sea was close, if not quite as close as the brochures for the complex claimed, but she couldn't hear it. There was fragmentary birdsong, and a faint low crooning from the henhouse. And then, from the direction of the cottages: the sound of a car door — ah, life! No doubt the last family, at Dairy Cottage, loading the car up and getting ready to leave.

You think this is quiet, a pessimistic part of her piped up. *Just wait till the night-time.*

Well, if any of the coming guests started partying and cranking up what her mother called rasta-blasters after eleven, they certainly wouldn't get any complaints from the proprietor's house. She would probably be flinging the windows open to cop an earful of delicious noise.

You exaggerate, Amanda — I've told you that a billion trillion times, as Lisa, her flatmate, would say. This was the north Norfolk coast, not the Gobi desert. There would be *some* traffic on the narrow climbing road that ran past the gates; after all, follow it inland a mile or so and you came to the village which, with typical rustic obtuseness, was called Lower Bockham because it was higher up.

But in between, piped up the voice of the doom-merchant again, *in between it's all wooded, those peculiar Norfolk coastal woods, and they'll block everything out at night and it's going to be so dark . . .*

All right, so she would turn the external lights on. And anyhow: why was she getting so het up about a little rural remoteness? There would be people here, in the guest cottages. Those sandy woods contained nothing more dangerous than the odd rabbit; it wasn't as if Bigfoot was going to come stomping down and start pounding his hairy fists on the double glazing.

But it wasn't just the quietness of the Penningtons' rural retreat, alien though that was to her tastes; it was what that quietness reminded her of. Wasn't that it? The reminder of her parents' house in the dismal fenland village, the house she had always hated?

Yes, that house. Where there was no traffic noise. Where Mark's photograph stood in its heavy silver frame on the sideboard, and his forever boyish face looked out from it at a house he had never seen in life. The house Amanda could not think of as home, even though it had been because of her that they had moved out to it from the city. Because she hadn't saved Mark.

Quiet house, hideously quiet house. Her father, subdued and morose, slumped in front of the TV with the sound on low. The distant mutter of a combine harvester. Mark's smiling face, imprisoned in a photograph, forever silent.

And it was still the same when she went back there now to visit; except, of course, time had done its work, and her parents were more cheerful and talkative, and the photograph had lost much of its power to hurt. Yet that terrible velvety quietness seemed to her to lie at the back of everything there, like an unspoken reproach . . .

Amanda clicked the radio on. Radio Four, like a chummy, broad-minded Nonconformist minister, immediately abolished the silence, burbling out from cunningly concealed speakers. If the quiet got her down, she would have noise. Simple as that. She briskly continued her inspection of the kitchen, familiarizing herself with everything that could possibly break or go wrong. Actually, none of the gadgetry looked as if it would; it was all of the obedient sort that went *plunk* and *ting* and turned itself off. She realized she had been thinking in terms of her own place, where the spin-dryer chased you round the room and the iron sent up smoke signals.

"Fretting about nothing," she said. "It'll be a doddle." The sane sound of the radio lifted her. It was tuning her ears to that damned quiet that had given her the heebie-jeebies for a minute, and brought the dark thoughts crawling up from whatever mental cellar they lived in. Well, they could just get back down there. Because she wasn't that sort of person: the blue meanies were not her style.

Or they never had been, until Ewan. And that was the trouble with relationships (that awful word!): they threw your identity into the melting-pot. Finishing with Ewan had been like rediscovering her true self. And she was going to make damn sure she held on to that true self. Perhaps that was why she found herself being so cautious with Nick — so as not to jeopardize again what she had lost last time.

No sign of that so far, though. No feeling of being dragged down into a psychological quicksand. In fact, they were always laughing.

She leaned her elbows on the breakfast bar, remembering last night, remembering the way she and Nick had laughed together. She did not know she had gone into a daze until the knocking at the front door jerked her out of it.

"Hello. Mrs Bushell. We're off now. Key." The woman on the doorstep looked gloomy. The car waiting in the drive behind her contained a cross-looking husband and two children who were crying because they were going home, or because they were having to sit together in the back seat, or simply because they were acting on the usual orders from Children's HQ to make life as intolerable for adults as possible.

"Oh, thank you." Amanda took the proffered key. "Hope you had a nice time."

The woman gave her a pained smile. "Don't get married," she said. "Just don't ever get married."

"Well, I — I wasn't planning to," Amanda stammered.

"Ha! Neither was I! I was planning to be a fashion designer, can you believe that?" The woman's voice went up, through gritted teeth, and cracked on the last word like a snapping guitar string. Behind her the car horn sounded impatiently. She closed her eyes a moment and took a deep breath.

"OK," she said. "Give our regards to Mr and Mrs Pennington."

"I'll do that. Have a — have a good journey home." As soon as it was out, Amanda realized it sounded almost sarcastic in the circumstances, but the woman merely nodded tightly, as if she couldn't trust herself to speak, and returned with a sort of rigid glide to the car.

Amanda hung the key on the board in the kitchen, listening to the Bushells' car driving away. When she felt the same flicker of panic as when Alix and Ben had left —

you're alone now, really alone

— she marched through to the sitting room and confronted her reflection in the antique mirror that hung there.

"Listen, sunshine," she said to herself. "You and me are going to have to spend a lot of time together this week. So stop being a pain in the arse, all right? If you can't spend a bit of time on your own, then you're a sad case, that's all I can say. Christ, remember when you were going out with Ewan? You used to long to get away and be on your own. And don't say this is different, and this place gives you the

23

creeps. Because that's rubbish." She stopped to examine herself more closely. Boy, she looked weird. (OK, more weird than usual.) Yet what was different about her? Same dark hair, cut shoulder-length — surprising she had any left considering what she used to do to it at the time of that photo on the pinboard. Same face, whose qualities were for her summed up for ever in her grandmother's remark: "I suppose she's sort of got quite a pretty face in a way." Same eyes, brown according to her passport, but at the moment looking the colour of eyes that had torn themselves open at six and stared into the ugly mug of a champion-heavyweight hangover.

No, nothing was changed. (That nose that just sat there in the middle of her face, and didn't look aquiline or pert or distinguished or any of the things noses should do, was still there, goddamnit.) It was just her altered surroundings that made her look different — this gilt-framed mirror and the rectangle of reflected elegance in which it enclosed her.

"No, you're still the same," she said. "I know you, all right. And you're thinking of ringing Nick again, aren't you? Pathetic. What is it with you two, joined at the hip? Remember last time."

Well, she was not likely to forget. But that, thank God, was all over now: behind her, fixed as firmly in the past as that long-ago teenage party pinned up on the corkboard.

As for ringing Nick, she could do that after six tonight, when he got home from work. It was silly, the idea of ringing to leave a message

24

on his answering machine. It was just plain silly. It was as corny as writing I LOVE YOU in lipstick on the bathroom mirror.

No. She would leave it till after six. Just because you were in love didn't mean you had to go completely off your head.

2

AFTER Amanda left his flat at six that morning, Nick groped his way back to the bed. He didn't need to get into it; his head, feeling like a cannonball, simply toppled him face forward. He slept for another two and a half hours, but it seemed to him only two minutes before he was seized by those symptoms of cardiac arrest that meant he was being jolted awake by his clock-radio.

He silenced the squawking machine with a wild bash and, before sleep could grab him again, rolled off the sagging block of extruded foam that was the sofa-bed. It was called a sofa-bed because it was equally uncomfortable as sofa or bed, ha-ha. He blinked owlishly about him at the studio flat. There was something not right about it. Then he remembered. It was because Amanda was no longer in it. She had had to leave early this morning, to get to that place in Norfolk.

And now he wouldn't see her for a week! If there was anything that could make getting up with a hangover on a Saturday morning to go to work even worse, it was that knowledge.

"Damn," he said feebly.

And hello, there was more. A noise that he thought for a moment was the clock-radio bursting into life again quickly resolved itself into the familiar sound of Monty having a laughing

26

fit. Monty was a weird bearded sleazeball with a voice like a hyena who lived in the flat across the corridor and was visited by unhappy-looking youths in the small hours. They knocked and sometimes Monty let them in and sometimes he yelled, "FARK off" in his psycho-Cockney counter-tenor. The sound of his laughter first thing was not exactly likely to make you feel glad to be alive.

What Nick saw on the floor by the bed, however, was. It was an earring of Amanda's, and the wave of lyrical reminiscence that it produced carried him into the kitchen and dreamily through the process of making tea. Sipping, he stared through the kitchen window without seeing — not that there was much to see. He was on the ground floor, at the rear of the block, and from here the view consisted of a high grass embankment strewn with litter and planted with broken sticks. The sticks were young trees, but they had been vandalized almost as soon as they were in the ground. Beyond that were the breezeblock pagodas and grey roofs of township housing, built in the 1970s by the city's development corporation in Legoland style and not wearing well. Rottweiler-and-satellite-dish country. As Nick poured his second cup of tea, a super-woofer music system started up somewhere in the block, pumping bass through the wall like blood through arteries.

A rough area. Not rough in the old-fashioned, Cockney-sparrer, hearts-of-gold, ducking-and-diving, spirit-of-the-Blitz way. It was rough in a bleaker, unmistakably modern fashion. Even

27

its disaffected gestures were hand-me-down, fag-ends of old ideas. The drug culture was a dull sixties repro stripped of its Huxleyite pretensions. The light-fingered youths who haunted the car-parks in reversed baseball caps were never going to grow up to be the Krays. The faded punks who scrawled anarchy signs on the underpass walls were chiefly interested in competing for ownership of the most terrifying dog.

And yet Nick was lucky to have this flat, and he knew it. He was an auxiliary nurse at a residential home for the adult mentally handicapped, and the pay was so lousy that local authority housing was his only option. Or, to put it another way, his career structure did not permit him a stake in the property-owning democracy. And the city boasted worse estates than this, conceived in hope and reduced to white-trash dumping-grounds that seemed to decay visibly before the eyes as if on time-lapse film.

He was doing the work he wanted to do; if he had let bitterness get a hold of him he would have fallen apart, so he didn't let it. And if ever there was a time when he was inclined to say that God was in his heaven and all was right with the world, it was now, because he was going out with Amanda Blake and he thought Amanda Blake was the best thing since sliced bread. Amanda Blake was the best thing to happen to him since — well, since his parents had bought him that Scalectrix set when he was a kid, and remembering how he had felt about that Scalectrix set it wasn't such a strange comparison. Waking up in the night and having to re-convince yourself that it was true, going around with a feeling of suppressed exultation like a hot coal in your chest; stuff like that.

Stuff like that, which he hesitated to tell her. Oh, he wanted to, very much; at heart he was something of a romantic, or a sucker for the slop-bucket, whichever way you wanted to put it. But their relationship was just too low-key for that as yet; too guarded.

And he did understand. He understood that Amanda's last relationship had been the sort of disaster that could put you off for life. She had said very little about it and indeed preferred to avoid the subject — they didn't go in for those long résumés of their respective pasts, which was another symptom of their caution — but he could read between the lines. And in many ways it was fine by him. He tended to be reserved himself. If people thought of him as laid-back that was OK, but really it was a sort of self-preservation born of his upbringing in a large, rackety, claustrophobic family — an environment in which any vulnerably projecting parts of personality soon got knocked off. He had had to mark out a sort of private space for himself, an emotional threshold; access beyond that was strictly by invitation only. He would have been no good in the sixties, he thought. Finding himself in the middle of a love-in he would have given an embarrassed cough and then, as the saying went, made his excuses and left.

So it suited him that this thing they had together didn't have to run on high-octane fuel. It suited them both. Why, then, did he find himself fretting a little, just now and then?

He reached for the cornflake box, but his stomach sternly vetoed the idea. Skip that. He ran a bath, shaving and brushing his teeth in the meantime and listening to Monty whooping it up. Did he have company? Difficult to tell, he sometimes laughed on his own. It was obvious what brought those glum striplings in grunge and high-tops to his door, but whether Monty was on it himself or was simply a Simon-Pure headcase was debatable.

Another reminder of Amanda met Nick's eye as he bent to test the bathwater: a pair of her tights on the floor, forgotten in her haste this morning. A balled-up pair of tights was not the most aesthetically pleasing object in the world, but it could seem so, when you'd got it bad.

And he had got it bad, he ruefully admitted as he poached himself in the scaldingly hot water that was the block's chief amenity. No two ways about it. And that was why he experienced those little nibblings of doubt. For while they both laughingly dismissed the business of Getting Serious, he knew he was serious. And some little insecure Jonah in his mind whispered that perhaps she wasn't. Perhaps he had got it all wrong, and what he took to be a refreshing and thoroughly adult way of going about things was really her kind way of saying, *Don't get any ideas*.

"Oh, you plonker," he said, towelling lobster

flesh and hunting for clean clothes. Everything was fine, and so he had to invent problems, wasn't that about the size of it? Yes, it surely was. What a prat.

In the living-cum-bedroom, stumbling into his trousers, he noticed the piece of paper propped up on the bookshelf. Exact details of how to get to Upper Bockham: Amanda had written them out the other night, when they had talked about his driving down there to join her for the day next weekend. Again, a sensible arrangement, not pushing it too far. But now another doubtful voice spoke up: supposing it was *him* who had been too cool? Supposing he had got the signals all wrong, and what she had been hoping he would say was, 'Sod that, I'll get time off, we'll spend the whole week there together'? — and now she was sitting alone in the back of beyond thinking he wasn't really serious about her?

Come on, he told himself you can't have it both ways. One of those voices had to be wrong, at least.

He looked at the clock. He ought to be making tracks for work; but there was just time to give her a ring, if he wanted. She would certainly be there by now and the number was in that little book by the phone. Simple.

He was moving towards the phone when he was stopped by a word. It was probably suggested by the way his shirt felt on his just-bathed skin: the word was *clingy*. He vividly remembered Amanda using that word, mentioning her last relationship: indeed, that was about as much as she had ever said about

31

it, but the one word, and the intonation she had given it, had spoken volumes. *Clingy*.

Phoning when she would only just have got there herself was clingy, surely. It had clingy written all over it.

He darted back into the bathroom, dragged a comb through his still-damp hair, darted out again and grabbed his jacket and keys, and was out of the flat before either of the bleating voices could make him change his mind. He locked his door, which like the rest was a duck-egg blue, presumably chosen for maximum clash with the orange corridor walls. It was ironic that the place where he lived, rather than the place where he worked, was the one that looked and smelt institutional. On the way out to the security door he passed the community room, a grey vault of plastic chairs completely unused except by a middle-aged West Indian man called George, who called out his customary greeting to Nick: "A'riiight!" George, who spent his life staring out of the window at the car-park, was part of a government eugenics programme called 'Care in the Community'. Or, as it was known in Nick's profession, 'Nutters on the Streets'.

It was mild for October, but blustery. The car-park was alive with miniature cyclones of fast-food styrofoam. Nick registered the usual faint surprise that his car was still here, and with all four wheels intact. As he got in he sighed. Usually he didn't mind working on a Saturday: with his shifts the weekend didn't mean much. But today he just didn't want to be doing this. He wanted to be . . . Well, never mind.

Clingy — remember?

He started the car.

Of course, ringing Amanda when he got home from work this evening was a different matter. Yes, that was different entirely. He could do it as soon as he got in — ring, hear her voice again, run up a big phone bill talking a load of delightful nonsense with her . . . It was a good thought. His mind was full of it as he pulled out of the car-park, and so he did not even notice the man sitting in the parked car there, watching him go.

3

THE Bushells gone, Amanda was in sole possession of Upper Bockham until the cleaner arrived. She was monarch of all she surveyed, and she hoped she wasn't showing inverted jealousy when she concluded that she wouldn't swap places with the Penningtons for anything.

There was no denying the beauty of the spot. Woods, pasture and lanes brought you to the gates: go a little further down through more woods and lanes and you reached the sea. Most of the buildings were attractive too. Directly on your right as you came through the gateway were the holiday cottages, a horseshoe-shaped block around a courtyard — farm outbuildings originally — all as pretty and authentic-looking as you liked with their knobbly flint walls and red, pantiled roofs. Follow the service road down and you came to the leisure complex — a large new purpose-built building which, with its pebble-facing and pitched roof tried desperately to look like a converted barn and nearly succeeded. To the rear of it, and overlooked by one wing of the cottages, were two stream-fed ponds. Turn left at the leisure complex and you came to the farmhouse itself, well screened by trees, an L-shaped building with its back turned to the rest of the complex, garages and outhouses forming another courtyard with it.

The house had been made over, but tastefully, very tastefully: the deep casement windows had not been replaced by bland sheets of glass, nor the warped old doors by mock-Georgian ones with elaborate knockers; its connections with farming might be reduced to a few pet hens and a herb garden, but the utmost respect had been paid to its origins.

And inside it was as a dream. The farmhouse kitchen that was about the size of Nick's whole flat was the least of it. The carpets in the sitting room and the dining room were so thick Amanda expected to leave footprints. The sitting-room fireplace made laughable those 'stone fireplaces' that estate agents always made such a feature of. The beams were most definitely not the sort you adorned with plastic horse-brasses. As for the furnishings, Amanda didn't know where such things were bought — probably Alix's manual directed her — but it sure as hell wasn't your average out-of-town superstore. If she had to put a name to the style, she supposed she would call it a country-ethnic-contemporary mix. Or else just plain rich. A hi-fi lurked in an alcove. It looked small and delicate, and would probably take the roof off. The collection of CDs baffled her. How could you *have* that many CDs, when they had only been around a decade? The bedroom they had given her seemed to her almost decadent in its pandering to the comforts of the flesh, as did the en-suite bathroom with its panelled corner bath and its panoply of oils and unguents. Her wrinkled soap-bag and battered hairbrush looked like the personal effects of a squatting tramp.

So, you're not envious at all, then? Not a bit?

Of course she was. The place was the ultimate des. res. But she couldn't imagine herself living in it. And not just because country life was a non-starter with her anyway; she wouldn't fancy having a holiday village in her back garden. Sure, the cottages were well separated from the house, and she knew from her own stay in one of them that summer how upmarket they were. Butlin's they weren't. Nor the Bates motel, come to that. But there just seemed something unhomely about having a succession of strangers close at hand.

And that didn't make sense, because that was precisely what she liked about living in the city. The comfort of strangers. She had never understood why the word 'stranger' carried such a negative, even sinister charge. The truly bad bummers in your life, the rained-on parades and pissed-on picnics, seldom had anything to do with strangers. If it was hell you were after, she thought, try intimacy for size.

No, she was over that. Ewan was just a bad memory, mercifully fading. Being here at Bockham had revived it a little, because it was here that she had come five months ago, to escape the awful aftermath of the End of the Affair and to — terrible phrase — get her head together. Though for once, not an inexact phrase, as she had felt at the time as if her head were in imminent danger of flying

36

explosively apart like something from a video nasty.

Ah yes, she remembered it well. She remembered, too, making a solemn vow at that time: no more of men. If she was not exactly going to take the veil, she was going to give her evenings to macramé or some such blameless and solitary pursuit. And indeed, it was with a view to taking up her interests again that she had enrolled for the guitar lessons. And thus met Nick. She didn't know whether the irony was sharpened or blunted by the fact that this time it was turning out so well.

Oh, and by the way, she told herself as she finished her fire-hazard reconnaissance of the farmhouse, *you're not going to ring him yet. OK?*

She had just looked at the clock and remembered that Sue the cleaner was due at eleven when the knocking came at the back door. Pretending she was not glad of company already, she went to open it.

"One and a half for the stalls, please," Sue said. "Hope you don't mind me bringen him. That'll only be for an hour, then his dad'll be round to pick him up — called out on a job this mornen. Nowhere else to park him at the moment."

"Of course not. The more the merrier. Hi, Jamie. It's nice to see you again."

"Hell-oo," the small boy at Sue's side said in soft, shy Norfolk.

"And hello to you again!" said Sue, beaming. "Alix told me that'd be you coming to hold the

37

fort. How you keepen? You're looking well."

"I'm very well, thanks. And you?"

"*Fat*," said Sue, taking off her coat and hanging it in the hall. She wore her overall underneath. "Look at that. Last time I saw an arse like that, it was pullen a waggon. I don't know what I'm going to do about it."

"Sue, you are not fat!"

"That's not what that weighen machine in Boots reckon. Half a stun overweight, it reckon. Pilen it on, I am. John say to me in bed last night, Sue, he say, I can't get over you, I'm going to have to get up and go round. But I just can't seem to take it off. This new girl we got cleanen weekdays, she say you want to try liposuction. I say lipo-what? She say they stick this machine on you and it suck the fat out. She've had it done on her brains, I reckon. You know them log-burnen stoves in the cottages? I only found her looking for the switch last week. Dozy piece. Couldn't find her arse with both hands. They got off all right this mornen, then?"

"Eventually. It was touch and go. Would you like a coffee or something?"

"I shan't get up again if I sit down. Best get stuck in."

"What about you, Jamie? There're cans of Coke in the fridge, or — well, there's everything, really."

"Ooh, could I have a can of Coke, please?"

Norfolk children could reconcile you to the whole tribe, Amanda thought, fetching the Coke. Round where Nick lived, the boys of Jamie's age were setting light to cats and loudly asking every passing female whether she took it in the mouth.

"All the grockles gone, have they?" Sue said.

"The what?"

"Grockles. Visitors."

"Oh! yes. All empty till this evening. I suppose *I* was a grockle last time I was here, wasn't I?"

"Oh, everybody's a grockle far as some Norfolk people are concerned. Give you a funny look if you come from the next village. Right, cottages first. Shall I take his lordship with me?"

"Well, I tell you what — I've got to feed the hens. Would you like to help me do that, Jamie? We can go down to the ponds and feed the ducks as well. Then we'll bring you some coffee."

Sue gave a thumbs up. "That'll do me. Be good, now, Jims."

Amanda was glad to see Sue Gibson again. When she had stayed here in the summer she had struck up an immediate friendship with the cleaner, despite her feeling then that she didn't want to see or speak to anyone. Sue, a pretty trim black-eyed woman of thirty-five, droll and forthright, had broken down her defences without even trying. Amanda had even found herself confiding her troubles to her, pouring out the whole miserable story; perhaps because Sue was an outsider, remote from it all, but perhaps also because she radiated pure sanity, in contrast to a situation that had become more

39

than a little crazy. She had got to know Jamie then, too, and Sue's husband John, spending a day with them on the beach. John was an electrician, and as friendly and straightforward as his wife: they lived up in the village, one of the few remaining Norfolk-born families in a little flint hamlet that had been much gentrified. They were nice people. Just the fact of them had done much to heal Amanda then: it *was* possible, after all, for people to go through life without tearing each other apart.

Sue went off to fetch her cleaning materials from the laundry room, which was separated from the house by a covered brick passage adjoining the kitchen. Jamie followed Amanda outside to feed the hens.

"You've had a birthday since I last saw you, haven't you, Jamie?" Amanda said: she remembered him looking forward to it.

"Yes. I'm eight now."

"What did you get for your birthday?"

"A Game Boy."

"Did you? That's nice," Amanda said vaguely. At work she had a reasonably harmonious relationship with a VDU, but the computerized world of the modern child was beyond her. She remembered a friend of her schooldays possessing a gadget that plugged into the TV and produced an extremely elementary tennis game featuring two straight lines and a moving spot of light: she could imagine the howls of derision *that* would draw from Jamie's generation. Jamie's interest in gadgetry, however, went beyond what was dictated by playground fashion, as Sue had

40

told her. It gave him a real buzz to be allowed to press the programme buttons on the washing machine, or set the central heating thermostat. He was either going to grow up into a genius techno-whiz, Amanda thought, or into one of those irritating men who insisted on trying to mend your broken toaster and ended up destroying it completely.

"And I got T-shirts from my nanna," Jamie added, plainly feeling he should mention this out of loyalty, but looking less than thrilled about it. Eight wasn't too young to be a style victim, Amanda knew, and she had seen plenty of designer rats who were comparing labels when they were scarcely old enough to read them; but that bug had yet to bite Jamie, if it was going to at all. At the moment he was your standard-issue post-war small boy, who put on whatever clothes were by his bed — in this case jeans and a pullover with the washing-instruction label sticking out at the back in time-honoured small-boy fashion — and had an own-brand haircut. And he looked much nicer that way, Amanda thought, than if he was got up like a miniature version of a cover-hunk from *GQ* magazine. He looked like a boy who would read comics, and watch *Dumbo* without sneering, and jump down the last four stairs.

He looked, in fact, like Mark. Mark as he was.

Mark as he would always be.

(Thanks to you, Amanda . . .)

"You're at middle school now, I should think, aren't you?" she said hurriedly, shaking off the

41

darkness. And thought: why do we always ask kids about school, that most god-awful aspect of their lives, which they would much rather forget when they're not there?

Jamie nodded, with an eloquent look. "My teacher's called Mrs Murgatroyd," he offered.

"Is she? I had a teacher called Miss Tinkler," she said, and got a laugh in return.

"There's a boy in our class," Jamie said in a sudden urgent burst of confidence, "and he stuck his foot out when Mrs Murgatroyd was walking past, his name's Daniel Rush, and she tripped over, she nearly hurt herself and her sandals came off. And he say to her he didn't do that on purpose but I reckon he did because he said about it afterwards and when he stand at the teacher's desk when she mark his book he stick his fingers up behind her head like that." Jamie demonstrated.

"Naughty boy," Amanda said. But remembering some of the old dragons who had taught her, and picturing them shedding their Dr Scholls as they took a pearler on to the parquet, she could not suppress a smile. Jamie caught it from her; soon they were giggling.

"Yes, I know," she said, opening the door of the shed where the chicken-feed was kept, "but it's still naughty." And again, she thought: why does every adult have to play the moral card with children? Listen to us, kids. We invented the snuff movie and the neutron bomb. We know what we're talking about.

The henhouse was in a large wire enclosure alongside the double garage. Amanda slipped inside quickly, ushering Jamie before her, mindful of Alix's warning; but just now the hens were less interested in making a jailbreak than in the food. They went crazy as only hens can at the rattle of the corn in the bowls. Amanda probed the warm straw inside the henhouse, but there were no eggs.

"Mr Pennington says there's a fox around," she said. "Have to watch out for him at nights." Behind the outhouses was a large rambling garden, bounded by a wall and old mossy trees. Beyond that there was a steep grassy bank leading up to the road, and, beyond that, pasture mounted up to the encircling woods, which looked a smoky, secretive blue in the autumn light. Amanda gazed at this prospect, imagining the fox holed up somewhere in those woods, waiting for darkness "Do you ever see foxes, Jamie?"

"We do sometimes," said Jamie, who was kneeling on the grass and studying the hens as they bobbed their scaly heads into the bowls. "Our next-door neighbour, he saw a fox going through his dustbin one night. You just hear them mostly. That sound sort of like coughing."

"And owls?"

"Oh, yes," said Jamie unconcernedly. "Most nights. You know how they're supposed to go 'Tu-whit, tu-whoo,' well they don't. They go like this." He made a sharp screeching noise, so convincing that the hens paused in their troughing and looked more alarmed and birdbrained than ever.

"Fancy that," Amanda said. She tried to sound casual, but casual was not how she felt. She was picturing herself lying alone in bed tonight and hearing that shriek outside. All right, so it would only be an owl, but she didn't think it would be a whole lot of fun hearing it, all the same. Even in her parents' satellite-village home, oppressive as she found it, you were spared that sort of thing. It was all prairie-farming back there, just miles of pesticide-saturated fields, modern as the microchip, and the last owl had probably jumped the twig fifty years ago. Eighty-odd miles was all that separated this stretch of coast from her stamping-ground on the edge of the Midlands, but it was a different world. This stretch of coast was a strange place. Beautiful, but strange. The woods that clothed it gave way here and there to colourful swathes of heath and gorse and sudden, stunning perspectives of salt marsh, with glimpses of a ghostly grey sea. Some of those back-roads you had to hit to get to Bockham really seemed to be going nowhere — just gradually disappearing under a shifting quilt of blown sand — and then an ancient flint church the size of a pyramid would loom up out of the ground. And in spite of colonization by what used to be called yuppies, the population density still seemed comparable with that of the Australian outback.

So she had better prepare herself for coughing foxes, screeching owls, and whatever else raw nature had in store for her when the lights went out.

44

"Do you like living in the country, Jamie?" she asked the boy.

"I don't mind," he replied phlegmatically. "I wish there was more shops. You live in Nottingham, don't you?"

"Billingham," she said. "Same sort of place." Large, light-industrial, nondescript, and blessedly built-up and full of people.

"Is there a lot of shops there?"

"Yes, plenty. There are two great big indoor shopping centres." She refused to say 'malls', as you were supposed to nowadays. You couldn't even pronounce that word without sounding American.

"Coo," Jamie said. "Is there a McDonald's?"

"Yep. Two. One a drive-in, one in town. And a Burger King, and a Chicken Shack."

"Pizza places?"

"Millions."

"Is there a Toys-R-Us?" Jamie said, very wistful.

"Great big one. And Littlewood's and Menzies and Lewis's and all the lot." Everything, she might have added, except a little individuality. But then she had a feeling she would be longing for a dose of soulless consumerism by the end of this week.

"Coo," said Jamie again.

"But of course it's all no good if you haven't got any money," she said. Seeing Jamie's face, she thought how nice it would be if she could whisk him off and take him round those (*not malls*) shopping centres. Treat him. Especially at Christmas, when they decorated the places so

45

lavishly you just had to admire.

(Except it's not really Jamie you want to treat, is it? It's Mark. It's Mark by proxy . . . And there's another thing they've got there that they haven't got here. Traffic. Lots of heavy traffic.)

"Anyway," she said, "there's no sea there. No beaches. No fresh air."

"And the football team's rubbish," Jamie said, with a devilish look.

"Oy, you," she said, making as if to throw the feed-bucket at him. "You like hospital food, do you?"

Stopping off at the house for some bread — wholemeal granary, natch, in bite-size pieces, specially set aside for the ducks by Alix — they went down to the ponds. While the ducks brunched on their high-fibre freebie, Jamie, his first shyness gone, laboriously related to Amanda something that was bothering him at school. There was this girl called Julie, and he sat next to her on the bus sometimes, and she had written his name on her pencil-case, and now some of the other boys were saying that Julie was his girlfriend, and she wasn't, he didn't want a girlfriend, it was silly . . .

Amanda listened with unfeigned sympathy. All the nasty, niggling idiocy of school came back to her through Jamie's halting words. Of course it was no use him denying that Julie was his 'girlfriend'. At that age if a boy merely refrained from putting grass down a girl's knickers or giving her a chinese burn whenever she was in reach, then as far as his peers were concerned

46

she was his girlfriend. And she remembered how strangely upsetting it was to have these emotions attributed to you, emotions you didn't even understand, let alone feel. When she was at junior school there had been a boy called Simon with whom she had suddenly found her name jeeringly coupled. Two pre-pubescent torturesses had scrawled SIMONS YOUR BOYFIEND all over her new duffel-bag, and the sight of it had sent her into floods of helpless, bewildered tears.

BOYFIEND, for heaven's sake. The little cows couldn't even spell it right. Of course, it was a long time ago. If she saw those girls now, after all these years, she wouldn't bear a grudge. She would have a laugh about it with them. And then she would get the bitches in a good headlock and punch the shit out of them.

"Well, you don't want to take any notice of them, Jamie. Just ignore them," she told him. Grown-up advice: — easy to give, hard to take. "You see, they only do it because they want to see you upset. But if you just laugh at them, then they'll see it's not working, and they'll stop. Laugh at them, because they're the silly ones."

"She's not my girlfriend, see," said Jamie, absently chewing a piece of duck-bread. "I don't want a girlfriend." He looked at Amanda in appeal. "I don't *ever* want a girlfriend."

"Well, you don't have to. It's up to you. You don't have to do anything you don't want to."

This seemed to reassure him. Again, she remembered as a child making a similar protestation herself, with the sexes transposed, but there was no need to mention that. It was

47

just a pity he had to peek into that particular can of worms at an age when what really made your palms go damp and your heart beat faster was a new bike or being allowed to stay up and watch *Robocop*.

But then what chance had you got of escaping it? Turn on the radio and someone was gasping about 'lerve' to whatever was the current beat. Turn on the TV and even the commercials tried to flog you coffee by involving you in a voyeuristic affair. Open a newspaper — love lives of the famous, or who's shafting who. Pick up a book — well, Amanda was a fan of horror novels, but even there she often found herself giving an exasperated sigh as the dreaded Love Interest hove into view. It was the modern obsession: we had 'lerve' the way the Middle Ages had religion.

And OK, maybe she was something of a hypocrite, as witness the dither she was in over Nick. But still. Still and all. At least she had begun to be aware of it. At least she had begun to see that life could be more than just a game of romantic musical-chairs, a frantic scramble for a partner. You could make too much of it.

Look at Ewan.

No thanks. I'd rather not look in that particular direction if it's all the same to you. That episode has gone down the rubbish-chute and been carted away, thank God.

"Have you got a boyfriend?" Jamie asked.

"Hey, you, wind your neck in."

"What's that mean?"

"It means don't be so nosy," she said, but

jokingly. He wasn't being: he just had that quality, rare in children as in adults, of not talking about himself all the time. "Yes, I have."

"What's his name?"

"Nick Foster," Amanda said. And as an absurd pleasure just in saying the name rippled through her, she thought: oh, so this is the woman who was just deploring our contemporary obsession with 'lerve', is it? *She'd* be the one writing his name on her pencil-case next. NICK FOSTER IS MY BOYFIEND.

Just then the sun found a way through the ragged clouds of October. The effect was like turning up the colour on the TV. The pond became a dance of light, the old trees overhanging the water confessed their golden decay, the red pantiles on the cottage roofs blazed. Really, Amanda thought, appreciating the scene, you are an ungrateful cow. Plenty of people would give their right arm to spend a week here. In fact numerous people did give, if not their right arms, then umpteen hundred pounds for the privilege of spending a week here. So think on, as her grandmother used to say.

"OK, ducks," she said. "That's your lot. Back to eating waterweed or whatever it is. What *do* ducks eat?"

"Count Duckula eats rice pudding," Jamie said informatively. "I've got a Count Duckula that glows in the dark."

"I don't know, kids today. When I was your age all I got in my stocking was an apple and an orange."

Jamie chortled. "My dad says that. And I asked Nanna and she say no he never, he got spoilt rotten."

After a detour to the swings and slide on the lawn behind the leisure centre, Jamie swinging and sliding with a dutiful air as if he wasn't exactly bursting to do this but felt he ought to, they went on up to the cottages, locating Sue by the sound of her Vax. She was in Dairy Cottage, and indignant.

"Look at that," she said, indicating the sitting-room carpet. "That's pizza, that is. All trodden in. All over the shop."

"Mushroom and pepperoni," Jamie said, examining the evidence.

"All right, Sherlock Holmes. Whatever it is, it make me wonder about these people. I haven't even looked in the bathroom yet. Mind boggles."

"Will it mark?" Amanda said.

"Well, this here machine get most things up. If there's any damage I leave a chit for Alix, and they get on to them. I seen worse than this. You wouldn't believe the state these places get left in sometimes." She made an expressive can't-tell-you-in-front-of-the-children face, and Amanda's mind did a little boggling of its own.

"Can I have a little go?" said Jamie, on whom the hi-tech vacuum cleaner seemed to exert a powerful fascination.

"You're welcome, sweetheart," Sue said, relinquishing the machine. "Gadget-mad," she said to Amanda as they watched the boy sweeping, his brow creased in concentration.

50

"Mind you, that's a nice sight to see, isn't it? He'll make somebody a good husband some day. John, he don't even know how the microwave works, and him a sparks. He think he's the Galloping Gourmet if he takes the chips out of the newspaper."

"Well, according to Jamie," Amanda said under cover of the vacuum noise, "he's not going to be anybody's husband."

"They all say that. And on that subject — " she darted Amanda an impish glance — "how's things with you nowadays? I know I should mind my own business, but I can't, you see. Nose like Pinocchio. You were in a bit of a pickle last time I saw you."

"Oh, it all came out in the wash, like you said it would . . . Isn't that John?"

A van had drawn up in the courtyard. Jamie abandoned the vacuum and ran out to his father. "You can tell me all about it when we've got rid of their lordships," Sue said with a wink before they followed the boy outside.

John Gibson was a giant man of amazing fairness, with eyebrows like ears of wheat. He was a Viking who spoke in a voice gentler than a purr.

"Dad, I've been doing the vacuuming," Jamie told him.

"Have you, by crikey."

"All two minutes of it," Sue said. "You weren't long, love."

"Nothing to it. Daft buggers had overloaded the socket. Three freezers-full of food thawed out, so somebody's going to be eating a lot of

51

fish fingers this weekend . . . How you diddling, gel?" to Amanda. "You the boss this week, are you? You want to watch this one here. Count the spoons after she've gone. She've got me into trouble before."

"That make us even, then," Sue said.

John's laugh was even softer than his voice. "Right," he said, "I'll take Fred Fanackapan off your hands, then. Git on the bus, Gus. You can help me pick my horses."

"Don't pick the ones with long ears this time," Sue said. "John, you know how long that shepherd's pie wants heating, don't you?"

"Till it's hot, I reckon."

"And open a tin of beans with it. I'll be done at three — don't fall asleep in front of the telly and forget."

"I'll wake him up," said Jamie from the front seat of the van, which he clearly thought the most desirable spot in the universe.

"Bye, Jamie," Amanda said, "see you again."

"You'll have to come over to ours for a drink one night this week, duck," John said, folding himself into the driver's seat. "You'll go off your trolley stuck here on your own."

"Thanks, I'd love that."

"Not if he make you try his home brew you won't," Sue said. "Cheer-oo!"

"Coffee break," Amanda said when they had gone.

"Goo on, you twisted my arm."

Sue inspected Amanda's guitar while she made coffee in the farmhouse kitchen. "Nice-looken thing. Shall I ask the daft question?"

"Can I play it? Well, I thought I could. I mean, I taught myself to strum a few chords when I was in my teens. But I always wanted to learn classical guitar properly. So I finally started taking lessons a couple of months back, and it's like starting all over again. I'd been putting my left hand in the wrong position all this time, for one thing. You're supposed to just put your thumb at the back of the neck like this, whereas I was gripping the whole thing like a tennis racket. But you're never too old to learn, anyway. I mean, there's one old lady in the class who's seventy-eight and just taking it up for the first time. Her hands are a bit stiff, but she's managing. That's Nick's grandma, she's a real character . . . " She glanced over at Sue, who was now seated at the table regarding her with her chin cupped in her hand and one eyebrow raised. "Nick — he's — he's this bloke I'm going out with."

Not altering her position, merely narrowing her eyes, Sue said, "Mmmyee-es?" like Bugs Bunny answering the door to Elmer Fudd.

"All right." Amanda threw up her hands. "It's a fair cop, I plead guilty. I know I said — that last time I was here — I know I said I was never going to go out with anyone again, and I really meant it, but — oh, it just happened . . . "

Sue burst out laughing. "Well, anybody'd think I was going to send you to stand out in the corridor! That's good news, not bad!"

"Well . . . " Amanda laughed too. "You know what I mean . . . After last time . . . "

"What, you're supposed to become a nun,

53

just because the last fellah you went out with turned out to be a pillock and give you a hard time? Get out of it! That's just what I wanted to hear. The state you were in last time, I was afraid he'd buggered you up for good."

"So was I," Amanda said, with a momentary feeling as if she had been brushed by cobwebs. A clingy feeling.

"So," Sue said, hunkering down over her coffee and cigarette, enjoying herself, "you've picked a good 'un this time, you reckon?"

"I — I reckon."

"What's he do? Airline pilot? One of Major's millions?"

"He's an auxiliary nurse. He works at a residential home in Billingham, looking after mentally handicapped people." The idea of a man being a nurse did not, she was glad to see, throw Sue as it still did some nineties Neanderthals. Nick said if he had a pound for every wedge-skulled rugby player who had made a crack about him looking sexy in the uniform he could buy a yacht, or even pay his water bill. "It was through the guitar lessons that I met him. He takes his grandma to the college and back in his car. We got in the habit of going for a drink after the lessons . . . "

"With grandma as chaperon," said Sue.

"With grandma as chaperon. And that's how it started. Like I say, it wasn't meant to happen. I was out of that game for good, I thought. It was just one of those things that . . . steal over you."

"That's nice. That's the best way. I'd known

John for ages, you know, just to say hello to, before we started going out. In fact, I always thought his name was Brian, for some reason. And I called him Brian all through our first three dates and he was too shy to put me right . . . Well, I'm glad about that. Last time I saw you I thought, that gel hasn't half been through the mill, I hope she bounces back. I should think he's on shift-work with that job, isn't he?"

"Yes, it's a bit difficult sometimes, because I only work nine to five."

"D'you know, I've forgotten where it is you work."

"Don't worry, it's very forgettable. Land Registry. Not the sort of job that sticks in the mind. Not like Postman Pat or Fireman Sam. I don't think there'll ever be a character called Civil Servant Amanda . . . But anyway, we manage. I mean, we don't want to live in each other's pockets — you know, push it too far too soon."

"Makes sense . . . So he cooled off at last, did he? The other one? Him-as-was? Cheerful Charlie? The one who couldn't take no for an answer?"

"Eventually," Amanda said. She had mastered the trick of speaking lightly about that business, but she still couldn't think lightly of it. No sir. In her mind it still lay as heavy as a lorry-driver's breakfast. "He got the message in the end, and I stopped hearing from him." A memory popped up — a memory of the man from Interflora ringing her doorbell for the fifth time in a week. "You're popular, love," he'd remarked. The bouquets had piled up in the kitchen, ghastly as wreaths. She had stopped reading the enclosed cards after the second one. ALWAYS. EWAN.

Past. Finished. She gave the memory the bum's rush. And if there were any more like that hanging around hoping to get their foot in the mental door, they could get lost. It was bad enough living through that time, let alone having it repeat on her like fried onions.

"What finally convinced him?" said Sue.

Amanda shrugged. "I suppose he just came to his senses. Flogging a dead horse. Anyway, Lisa — she's my flatmate, she was such a help, standing him off when he kept coming round — Lisa's seen him around with another girl now, so that must have had something to do with it. Hallelujah!" *Poor cow, whoever she is,* she thought but did not say.

"That's typical, that is. After all that hassle he give you."

"Well, I'm just glad it's settled. I mean, it was ridiculous. I'm not exactly Cindy Crawford."

"There's no understanding men," Sue said. "We might think we do, but we never can, not really. Never get on their wavelength. You know why? Because they think through their pricks. Pardon my French, but they do. Ninety per cent of them. And we're supposed to be the unreasonable ones. Make you laugh, don't it? Git a bit tetchy because you're on the rag, and they act all superior and tell you to calm down because that's only your hormones.

And yet they're the ones who go through life like zombies doing everything their balls tell them to."

Amanda laughed. True enough; yet not really the whole truth in regard to Ewan. If it had simply been a case of permanent panhandle, she thought, it might in a way have been easier. They all tended to overestimate the capabilities of the old beef bayonet anyway. No, it was not the chronic hots that made a man flatly refuse to accept that a relationship was over and go to the lengths that Ewan had gone to. That was something different. For a little while there it had seemed more like . . . well, it had seemed like obsession.

Well, thank God he had seen sense at last, and had found someone else now. She genuinely wished them well. It might work out: some relationships did, some didn't. Theirs just hadn't — a simple fact — but getting Ewan to face it had been hell. At least that wasn't her responsibility any more.

"Go on, say it," Sue said.

"Say what?"

"That your Nick's not like that. Slave to his doodah and all the rest of it. Course he isn't. Neither's my John. We got to believe some men are different, else we'd never let them anywhere near us."

"True. I suppose I do believe that. Perhaps you have to catch them young. I think your Jamie's going to grow up to be a nice fellow."

"You've only seen him on his best behaviour. No, he's turning out all right. I wouldn't mind having another if it comes out anything similar, specially now we got our money straight. You got any brothers or sisters?"

"No," Amanda said, "just me."

As a girl she had broken her ankle falling off her bike; and even now, completely healed as it was, she could not twist it or put undue pressure on it without feeling just the faintest ghost of the old pain. Not so much a pain, in fact, as a reminder of the pain. And so it was with that question about brothers and sisters. She had trained herself to answer it easily, but she could not train away that twinge, that reminder of the pain.

"Well," Sue set down her empty mug, "back to the grindstone."

"I'll come and help you."

"No need for that, but you can keep me company." Sue got up. "We'll see what state the grockles have left the sheets in."

"Ah, is that what you couldn't tell me when Jamie was around?" Amanda grinned.

"Well, I don't know if I can describe them sheets even now, not without turnen both our stomachs. Let's just say, if you used that much wallpaper paste when you were decoraten, you'd end up with a pretty small room."

"Oh, Sue, gross!"

"I know. Strippen the bed was like folden up a load of ole cardboard. Christ on a bike, I thought, somebody's having a job to sit down this mornen." She looked with pleasure at Amanda's helplessly laughing face as they came out of the house into the fitful sunlight.

"Well, gel, I'm glad everything's turned out all right for you. When you come here back in June I thought you looked — well, hunted. That's the only word I can think of for it. Hunted."

4

S HEILA MALBORNE loved Saturdays.
No work, for one thing. It was true that she sometimes had free days in the week: it was as a supply teacher that she had made her late return to the profession, and as a supply teacher you worked when you were needed. But the point was, when you woke up on a Saturday you *knew* that you were not, under any circumstances, going to have to take charge of a classroom full of budding delinquents who had not a thought in their heads except where their next tube of glue was coming from.

For another, Saturdays had a nice bright feeling about them, especially where she lived now, on a busy road close to the centre of Billingham. She could walk into town in the morning and do a little shopping and thread her way through the Saturday crowds and feel she was part of life but not oppressively entangled in it. The day had an entirely different atmosphere from Sunday, which was a dull brown drowsy vacancy, a hole at the end of the week.

And what was more, it was on Saturdays that she was most vividly conscious of not being married any more. The old Saturdays, the Saturdays before her divorce, had been devoted to certain rituals, and her husband would as soon have shaved his head and turned Buddhist as alter the rituals in the slightest particular. There was the drive into Billingham from the farm, punctuated with much cursing of the traffic; there was the bad-tempered jostling around Marks and Spencer's, with more cursing and a lot of references to the price of things and how the unions were to blame; there was the invariable pot of tea and vanilla slice in Lewis's before the drive back; there was the invariable Saturday lunch of chops; and there was the invariable Saturday evening in front of the TV with its invariable tirade about the licence fee and the Lefties in charge at the BBC; and there was the invariable Saturday early night with its thirty-nine seconds of headboard-rattling exertion followed after an interval of a further thirty seconds by the first of the rasping snores that would continue unbroken until Sunday morning.

Those old Saturdays were the distilled essence of the awfulness of marriage. Because the two of them were together — all the time. Even now, eight years after they had parted, she could still taste that sour flavour. And no matter what happened on her new Saturdays — even if it rained buckets and her car broke down and her maisonette was burgled and then set alight and reduced to a charred shell — even then, she knew she could console herself by thinking, "Well, at least I am not married!"

But she liked Saturdays too because of a little ritual of her own, and one which showed, she supposed, that something good had come out of her marriage.

You shouldn't have a favourite child, no

61

doubt. But she didn't see how it could be otherwise, in her case. The two younger boys were variations on the theme of their father, with whom they were on excellent terms: one married to a yes-woman and already developing a paunch as if in imitation of her pregnancies, the other at Agricultural College and driving a car with a YOUNG FARMERS DO IT IN WELLIES sticker in the back window. Whereas the eldest had always disliked that narrow-minded world of tweed and manure and had cut himself off from it as soon as he was able. Indeed, it was partly his disaffection that had awakened her to her own, and prompted her to do something about it.

So it was with her eldest son that she had the closest relationship — probably, indeed, the closest relationship in her life nowadays. She was an attractive and elegant woman, but she had been thoroughly inoculated against sexual relationships. She had managed to make new friends since her divorce — not easy, after all those years of connubial incarceration in the middle of a ploughed field — but none that she cared to let get too close. Her son was her number one, her best friend, and she liked it that way. And she liked above all their Saturdays, when he came to her for lunch. They had a bottle of wine, they had lots of talk. And if one of them were not in a particularly talkative mood, it didn't matter. They could still be at ease with each other; there would be none of those huffs and recriminations that couples were plagued by. It was an ideal relationship.

So this Saturday, which Sheila Malborne had no reason to suppose would be any different from any other Saturday in her pleasantly remodelled life, she uncorked the wine and checked the moussaka in the oven and mixed the salad and waited for Ewan's arrival with relaxed anticipation.

It would be just Ewan on his own again today — not his girlfriend. It was perhaps because she had spent the first forty years of her life in a stifling world of received ideas, which she had not completely succeeded in shedding, that Mrs Malborne had expected to resent the intrusion of a girlfriend into this comfortable set-up. That was the agony-column cliché. But experience proved otherwise. She found she liked the girlfriend: she liked having the two of them to lunch now and then. Of course she wouldn't have advised anyone, son or stranger, to enter into any so-called loving relationship whatsoever if they could possibly avoid it, for the simple reason that it was like signing up for an extended course of mental torture. Or, to be blunt about it, it was like putting your tits in the mangle and turning the handle. But she was realistic enough to know that the mating game wasn't going to stop, any more than the moon was going to fall out of the sky, or the Americans elect a president who was neither a lecher nor a pinhead. When the hormones kicked in, the brains shorted out, end of story. It was regrettable that people seemed to think they couldn't live alone and be fulfilled, but that was the way of it. If they wanted to get themselves involved in that emotional mess, that was their business.

And she did like the girl — a friendly open sort with no side to her. Sheila felt just a twinge of envy at her freedom, as she did with most women of that age, remembering how she herself had been married at twenty-three and already pinned into her role like a mounted butterfly: the conventional, home-making, village-Women's-Institute, Rotary-Club-dinner-and-dance young farmer's wife (*gentleman* farmer, as her pompous shit of a husband had insisted on styling himself — presumably that meant one who wasn't particularly good at farming). She had been naive, naive even for the dog-and-pony Middle England in which she had been brought up. She had thought Ted Malborne was the bee's knees, and he turned out to be a horse's arse, a mistake for which she paid for twenty years. So she could not help the faint envy she felt at the sight of these bright young women who would never — it was just written all over them — get themselves caught like that and find themselves at forty realizing they had thrown their lives down the pan.

Well, at least Sheila had got out of it, late but not too late. It hadn't been easy, breaking away. The boys had been in their teens, and only Ewan had been unquestioning in his acceptance. The other two had been resentful. They resented the fact that their mother was going to do something other than be their mother — that useful piece of household furniture in between the cooker and the washing-machine. Pink yeoman cheeks flushing, they had spoken accusingly of breaking up the family, when what they meant was there would be no freshly ironed shirts any more. It had been hard, too, moving into the city alone, relaunching the teaching career that had been aborted by her marriage, learning to live as an individual. People's attitudes didn't help — that general assumption that being single is a temporary state, an aberration, not a choice. She might be sitting pretty now, but it had been a struggle, and a struggle without allies — with the single exception of her eldest son Ewan.

Sheila poured herself a glass of wine and fed the midi hi-fi with a CD of Schubert. Music was another thing she and Ewan had in common, though again she had only really found it out during her new life. Marriage had smothered all that: her own interests had been squashed by the dead weight of enforced mutuality. Ewan helped to guide her, though her tastes favoured the restrained more than did his; Wagner and Richard Strauss were what he loved: the grand gesture, the epic emotion. She sat and listened, almost totally relaxed . . .

Almost.

There's always something. Not a terrific piece of wisdom for half a century's experience, but at least it had the merit of being true. And the something in this case was a faint concern, a tiny hair in the soup of her contentment, about Ewan.

Nothing she could put her finger on, but it didn't need to be. She had always been sensitive to variations in Ewan's emotional temperature.

65

Probably all mothers were, but in this case it went a little deeper. The evidence only amounted to a certain preoccupation and constraint that she had noticed in him lately; and that in turn might only be evidence of one of Ewan's moods. He just hit a low sometimes, with no reference to his external circumstances, and when he did it was best to let him work his way out of it himself.

But there were other times, of course, when the problem was more than just an attack of the glums — when the problem was something real, full-grown, camped on the doorstep and not about to go away. And if that was the case, she hoped he would let her in on it rather than just brood. So far he had always done so, in the end; the business of dropping out of university, for example. She didn't know how much agony of mind that had cost him, but she did know that the landlady of his digs had one night found him wandering around her backyard in the small hours, weeping and clutching a half-empty bottle of gin, because she had rung to tell her. Fear of disappointing everyone, of course, especially just at that time, with the divorce going through, and good news in short supply. And it *had* been disappointing: Sheila believed in education, and Ewan had brains and talent, even if they had always promised more than they delivered. She had never pretended to like his decision to drop out in his first year, because it was a waste: it raised the spectre of her own past mistakes. But what mattered was that she was on his side — or, in the awful contemporary jargon, she 'supported' him.

She had made that clear to him. And she hoped she had made it clear that she would always do so, no matter what. She remembered how frightening his landlady's phone call had been — that image of her son lost in some private darkness. He must always tell her if he found himself in such a situation again, and tell her without fear of being judged.

It was true that the course of his life had not matched up to her hopes for him. The tendency to throw in his hand had marked it throughout. After dropping out of university and moving to Billingham with her, he had been offered a very promising job with a large local newspaper group, but just when she thought he was settled, he had left that too, over some personal disagreement. Someone less fond of him than Sheila would have said he had drifted since then. But if the job he now had, in catering at one of the city's hospitals, was not exactly what she had envisaged for him, it was at least a job, that scarcest of modern commodities. He had a nice little flat of his own. And now there was the girlfriend, who was a delightful young woman and about whom he seemed to be serious. So as long as he was happy, Sheila was happy.

And damn it, her feelings told her that he wasn't.

She went into the kitchen to check the moussaka again, and as she bent to look in the oven she heard the front door open. *Ah, good, he's here*, she thought — she always left the door unlatched on their Saturdays so he could let himself in — and then, as she straightened up from the oven, a second thought came to her. She didn't know where it had come from, she had never once had such a thought since she had started living alone. The thought was, *What if that isn't Ewan? What if someone else has just walked in?*

She pulled her hands out of the oven glove, which seemed to cling unpleasantly to her fingers. The thought was ridiculous — and just because he had closed the front door behind him without calling out hello . . .

"Ewan?" she said.

The wistful lilt of Schubert's *Octet* continued in the living room. Footsteps approached down the hall.

"Ewan?" she said, more sharply.

"Who were you expecting, your fancy man?"

She tried not to be too obvious about letting out her pent breath as Ewan appeared in the kitchen doorway, looking mildly puzzled.

"Wasn't sure I heard the door," she said quickly. "Listening to the music."

Ewan cocked an ear. "Old Mr Syphilis himself."

"They all had it in those days, dear. Pour yourself a glass of wine, this is nearly ready."

She felt foolish about her sudden attack of the creeps, but Ewan didn't seem to notice anything amiss. He ambled about the kitchen, wine-glass in hand, nibbling at bits of salad. While she got out plates and began dishing up she observed him: motherhood gave you eyes in the back of your head as compensation for the stretchmarks. Yes, she thought, there was something wrong. But how wrong, she didn't know. When they were eighteen, it was all too physically visible, like veins beneath the skin — which was one of the awful things about being eighteen. But a twenty-eight-year-old body kept its secrets better.

"Had a phone call from Dad the other day," Ewan said.

"How is he?"

"Oh, the usual. Says the NUAW is going to bankrupt him. Or was it the EC?"

"It wouldn't be his own incompetence, of course," Sheila said, though without real rancour. Her husband was a dead letter for her now. Even hearing that the woman from the village who came to do for him was now doing rather more than just wield the Ajax had produced no stronger reaction in her than a mild murmur of, "Poor cow."

"'This is a good time to concentrate on getting your domestic life just the way you want it. Monday's New Moon points to a new beginning, and something that you've long been hoping for is coming your way. But remember to look before you leap.'" Ewan was reading out from the pad by the phone. It was the dial-a-horoscope she had consulted earlier.

"You'd be amazed how right they are, you know," she said defensively.

"They should be, for two quid a minute."

"It's not that much. Come and eat."

Ewan ate, but absently. Sheila felt he wouldn't have known whether it was moussaka or locusts *flambé*. He was making short work of the wine, though, tipping it down his throat in jerks the way drunks did in old movies.

That wasn't like him, Sheila thought. Something was up.

"How's work?" she said brightly.

"Thrilling as ever. You?"

"Oh, I had to fill in at Stanley Road primary this week. Not my favourite place by any means. Stanley-knife primary, as we call it. I caught one of the little angels with a card listing those awful sex-line telephone numbers. Each one with a descriptive title. 'Lipstick on your dipstick' is the one that lingers in the mind."

She was glad to see Ewan laugh, though the laugh was curt. "Well," he said, reaching for the wine bottle, "at least they're in touch with reality, instead of being fed on Janet and bloody John."

"Oh, Ewan, that's not *all* of reality."

"Isn't it?" He raised his eyes to hers. Such very blue eyes, she thought. His father's best feature. Only good feature, in fact. Ewan had turned out much more handsome. Though she wished he would take a little more care of himself: he hadn't shaved properly, and that blond hair hadn't seen a comb lately. The little-boy-lost look, of course — women were fibbers if they said they didn't find it attractive. Preferable, anyway, to these oily Chippendales or Heppelwhites or whatever they called themselves, who would be forever at the

Immac and never letting you get near the mirror.

"Well, isn't it?" he repeated. Such blue eyes. And all of a sudden she could not read them, and was slightly alarmed.

"Don't be cynical, dear," she said. "Anyway, we don't have Janet and John any more. That went out before you were at school."

"Mm. I seem to remember two little brats called Topsy and Tim. Much the same. 'Topsy and Tim go swimming.' 'Topsy and Tim have a party.' It was never 'Topsy and Tim try acid and get touched up by Grandpa'."

The Schubert had come to an end. Ewan sprang up from the table and put on another CD. Sheila recognized it at once: the Prelude and Liebestod from *Tristan and Isolde*.

"You old Wagnerian, you," she said, but he did not respond. He poured the last of the wine while the luscious harmonies fell from the air like overripe fruit.

"Doing some overtime next week," he offered suddenly. "Emilio, the Spanish bloke who works at our place, he's off on holiday. Two weeks back in his beloved fatherland. He pissed me off going on about it so much that I gave him a mouthful. Well, not really a mouthful. I just asked him if he'd be joining in any of those traditional pastimes — like throwing donkeys off churches or pulling the heads off geese — that have made his country such a byword for thoughtfulness and compassion all over the world."

So perhaps that was it, Sheila thought.

71

Trouble at work. She knew Ewan could be very scathing. "There's been a bit of a bad atmosphere, then, I take it," she said.

Ewan closed his eyes for a moment as the music swelled. When he opened them again they seemed bluer than ever. "You know what he said — it was so funny — he said, 'You're doing in my head, stop giving me GHB in the earhole'. GHB, for Christ's sake." Ewan burst into loud laughter. Excessive laughter, Sheila thought. It wasn't like him.

But then did she really know what he was like, even though he was her son? Did she really? The question came from nowhere, and she experienced a moment of inexplicable terror as she was forced to answer herself: *No.*

"How's Amanda?" she said.

"She's fine." Ewan chased a last sliver of aubergine round his plate.

"You haven't brought her to lunch for ages," Sheila said. "Must be several months now."

"Is it?" Ewan said. "Well, like I said, she was doing this course in the summer, for work, and what with one thing and another . . . "

"Yes, of course. But you know she's welcome, don't you? Any time."

"Yes. Thanks, Mum."

A feeling of pure protective sympathy sprang up in her. She wouldn't keep fishing like this; if he and Amanda were going through a bad patch, which seemed highly likely, then it was none of her business. She was prepared to wait, if he wanted to tell her. In the past they had sometimes sat up all night talking,

72

slowly digging down to the root of something. She rather enjoyed it.

"There's some cheesecake in the fridge if you'd like," she said.

"Thanks, I'm full."

"An elegant sufficiency," she said, removing the plates with a chuckle. That was what her husband used to say when he finished his meal. As far as she could remember, he had said it every single day for twenty-odd years. Ah, wedded bliss. And people wondered how you could bear to live alone.

"We went to a concert at the cathedral last week," Ewan said.

"Sorry?" she said from the kitchen.

"Me and Amanda. The London Mozart Players."

"Oh! Was it good?"

She came back into the living room. Ewan had turned the hi-fi up and was gazing out of the window.

"It's very loud, Ewan," she said.

"Just a minute."

It was the climax of the piece, Isolde's love-death. The huge surges of sound pressed at the walls of the room, too rich, too overpowering for its light decor and slim furniture. She liked this music, but just now it made her a little queasy. It was like drowning in cream.

"Never one for the understatement, old Wagner, was he?" she said as the final cadence died away. She was hoping to draw him into one of his spirited defences — it was fun to argue the toss with him — but he merely continued to stare out of the window in a sort of bleak abstraction. The light behind him shone through his crumpled shirt, which looked as if it had been slept in. He had lost weight, she saw.

"Have you done any painting lately?" she asked him.

He stirred, as if coming out of his trance. "No point," he said.

"Why not?"

He gave her an impatient look. "I'm never going to be Renoir, Mum. Or even Beryl Cook. I'm just an amateur with no training; it's just a hobby. And it's rather pathetic."

"Well, I wish I could paint like you. It must be very satisfying."

"If you're not going to be the absolute best at something, there's no point in bothering with it, so I don't," he said, white-lipped.

Suddenly Sheila felt with a strange urgency that she could not simply wait for him to tell her what was wrong in his own good time. Though it was not her style, she was going to have to ask him straight out.

"Ewan, dear . . . "

She stopped as she glimpsed something through the slit in his shirt-cuff. She drew closer to him. "What . . . whatever have you done to your arm?"

"Oh, that." He undid the cuff and pulled the sleeve back. "Had a disagreement with the deep-fryer at work."

"My God . . . did you get it treated?" A patch of his forearm the size of a five-pound note looked like something from a Hammer horror, the skin shiny and blistered and dreadfully tight.

"It's nothing much." He studied it a moment, then suddenly thrust it towards her face like a little boy with a creepy-crawly. "Blaah!"

"Ewan, don't."

His grin faded. "It's only flesh," he said rapidly. "All matter is an illusion. Who was it who proved that?"

"Somebody very silly, whoever it was. Really, a hospital as well, you'd think they'd have proper safety regulations . . . "

"Bishop Berkeley," he said. "The non-existence of matter. And Dr Johnson said 'I refute it thus', kicking a large stone so that he rebounded from it. There. A mine of useless information. Mum, what *is* the matter? You're looking at me as if I didn't blow my nose properly. Ha, do you remember that time when Dad ate that lettuce and it had a caterpillar on it and it was crawling down his neck and he didn't know? We were all bursting ourselves trying not to laugh."

She smiled reluctantly. "You just look as if you haven't been sleeping well or something."

"Oh, like the proverbial log, me." He moved restively away from her.

"If the job's getting you down . . . "

"Yes?" He looked at her expectantly. "If the job's getting me down, what?"

She shrugged. "What I mean is, whatever's getting you down . . . " She had a sensation of being pressed against opaque glass, unable to see in.

"Nothing's getting me down, Mum. 'The world is so full of a number of things, I'm sure we should all be as happy as kings.' Who wrote that?"

"Kipling?"

"Robert Louis Stevenson. And then he dropped dead of a brain haemorrhage. Funny old game, isn't it?" he said with savage blandness.

Stop it, Ewan, she wanted to cry. *Stop fending me off.* And yet what could she do, in truth? He was a grown man. Whatever ailed him, she had no sticking-plasters for it. Perhaps that realization, not the shadows under his eyes and the brittleness in his speech, was what was giving her the panicky feeling at her heart.

And besides, he said there was nothing wrong, and she should respect that. It was a basic human right to give an account of yourself and not have it questioned.

It was just that she knew he was lying.

"I always thought Stevenson was consumptive," she found herself saying.

"Oh, they all were. It was that or the clap. Even Oscar Wilde had a dose. Funny old game again. Each age gets the disease it deserves. The Victorians were riddled with syph because they turned prostitution into a national industry. The Middle Ages got the plague because they'd all got their eyes fixed on the next world and didn't care how dirty they were in this. We get AIDS because we sleep around instead of bothering with a permanent relationship."

He spoke so fast she could barely follow him. "That's an . . . interesting theory," she said. "I'll try and think of an exception to it while I put the coffee on."

"Don't bother." He suddenly gave her his gentlest, most boyish smile. "I mean, don't bother with coffee for me, Mum. Sorry. I've got to get going."

"Oh, so soon?" She didn't want him to go, but not simply because she didn't want to lose his company. Today she felt oddly uneasy about letting him out of her sight. "Stay for some coffee."

He was shaking his head, frowning. "I can't . . . I'm meeting Amanda."

"Oh — well, in that case . . . "

The boyish smile came back for a brief encore. "Sorry, Mum. You know how it is. All's fair in love and war."

"Oh, yes, I know," she said, just relieved to see that smile; and only when he had gone did it occur to her that that was the strangest of all the things he had said.

5

"RIGHT, then, my old flower, I'll leave you on your tod now," Sue said.

The time had gone quickly for Amanda, helping Sue clean the cottages and launder the mercifully unimpregnated sheets, chatting and laughing as they went along: she could hardly believe it when she had looked at her watch and it had said three.

But three it was, and here was Sue putting on her coat in the hall of the farmhouse, and there was John's van with Jamie in the front drawing up outside.

"I'll see you Monday then," Amanda said, hoping she didn't sound as mournful as she felt. Perhaps she did, because Sue stopped and said, "Unless you fancy popping up to ours tonight. We usually have a drink and a video. You're more than welcome."

"I — well, I might take you up on that. Thanks. Oh, damn, wait though, there's this couple, the Howards, they're supposed to be arriving this evening. I shall have to be here to give them the key and everything. It depends when they turn up."

"Well, see how it goes. Drop round any time. It's number two, Middle Road. You can't miss it: it's the only house in the village without a Volvo in front of it."

"Thanks, Sue. Have a nice weekend if I don't see you."

She waved from the door. The noise of the van's engine diminished to a mosquito whine. At last the mosquito died.

Alone.

"'Alone — and yet ali-ive!'" Amanda sang in exaggerated contralto, heading for the kitchen. "'Oh, sepulchre! My soul is still my body's pri-son-er!'" *The Mikado*, that was. Remarkable, Holmes.

"Name all the Gilbert and Sullivan operettas in order," she instructed herself. "*Thespis, Trial by Jury, The Sorcerer, HMS Pinafore, The Pirates of Penzance, Patience, Iolanthe, The Mikado, Ruddigore, The Yeomen of the Guard, The Gondoliers, Utopia Limited, The Grand Duke.*"

No, there was one missing. What the devil was it? Not that she was a devoted fan of G & S, though she had seen them all as a child because her aunt was a member of Billingham Amateur Operatic Society, but it was the sort of thing you had to know if you were a trivia quiz fiend, as she was. Or had been, anyway. She had to admit there was the teeniest bad vibette attached to the subject of trivia quizzes now, because it was at one of those that she had met Him-as-was, as Sue had called him. Charity Quiz Night, Land Registry v. District Hospital. She'd nearly cried off that night because she had a stinking cold: a friend from work was willing to take her place on the team. But in the end, probably because she didn't want to be one of those people who

79

treat a cold as a combination of a body cast and the Black Death, she had gone. And that, as it turned out, had been one of the Bad Moves of the century.

No, unfair. She didn't regret ever meeting Ewan, did she? It was just one of those things that didn't work out. Besides, if you wanted to you could go ferreting back through your whole life uncovering moments that changed your life: wrong decisions, traumatizing experiences. It was a thing that Ewan's mother had been big on — inferiority complexes, self-analysis, slaying the dragons, the whole psychobabble bit. Ma Malborne could probably trace everything back to how many plastic ducks you had on your pram if you gave her the chance. The drawback was, Amanda thought, that you disappeared up your own arse in the process.

Pinafore, Penzance, Patience . . . What was that other one that began with P? This was going to keep her awake tonight, if the owls and the foxes didn't.

That awful quiet was seeping back again. Amanda switched on the portable TV on the breakfast bar, found an old British movie with various thoroughbred thesps trying to talk common and sounding curiously like Australians, and turned her mind to food. When in doubt, pig out. Talking to Sue she had forgotten that she hadn't eaten since early this morning, and now her stomach was sending up distress signals. Three hours till Nick would be home; a bout of frenzy-feeding should fill a good chunk of that time. She consulted the freezer in the utility room. The question of whether she could wait for a roast became academic as she realized the joint of beef she was holding was actually a steak. Could she really eat this? It was the sort of steak Tom and Jerry dangled in front of Spike the bulldog.

Yes she could. And chips and mushrooms too, you betcha. She set to work, blessing Alix and Ben and conjuring cooking smells that were gastronomic pornography. The whole thing reminded her of the time when she was at last too old (or too moodily adolescent) to accompany her parents on holiday, and for the first time had stayed at home while they caramelized in Benidorm. Forget your multiple orgasms — nothing could ever equal the pleasure experienced by a moody adolescent having the house to herself. She had eaten chips every day that week, sometimes for both dinner and tea. She had lolled in front of the TV in T-shirt and knickers, drinking cans of Coke that she didn't have to decant into a glass, watching Wimbledon and hooting at the German players' curious backdated Euro-haircuts. And to conclude the week's entertainment, she got blitzed on vodka and Russchian with a troika of schoolfriends and was violently sick before she could reach the toilet. It didn't matter. Not even parking a tiger all over her mother's bathroom set, not even the frantic cleaning up of the following morning with a pair of hands that felt like autumn leaves, could spoil the magic. And only someone who had forgotten what it was like to be a teenager could fail to understand that at the same time she loved her parents very much and was glad to see them back.

"Honest, Glad, I — I've never bin so heppy." "Well, I'm heppy too, Joe — course I em." The posh cockneys on the TV were moving into a clinch, and the girl was going to get herself a handful of brilliantine that would lubricate the engine of an artic. Amanda heaped her plate, torn between guilt and greed. "You're the best gel in the world, Glad," Joe said, extricating, himself from her lipstick. "You're the one for me — for always."

"Get out of it," Amanda addressed them, munching. "You'll be at each other's throats in six months."

Cynical, very. Was that what she really believed? She certainly didn't want to. Especially where she and Nick were concerned. And probably that was why she was holding back a little. Fear of the let-down. The higher you climbed, the further you had to fall.

Bloated, she atoned for her gluttony by making herself wash up immediately, then turned off the TV and moved into the sitting room with her guitar and sheet-music. An hour's practice, not counting the time it took to retune the instrument.

Tuning was a pain, but it didn't normally make her feel this glum. Was pigging out like sex, inducing melancholy when it was over? Not that she had ever experienced post-coital gloom herself. (She had felt pretty depressed *during*, but never *after*.) Or was it just the solitude getting to her again? Against the reinstated quiet, the plucked notes of the guitar sounded very forlorn. The last scant beams of afternoon sunlight were creeping through the french windows to stretch themselves and die on the sumptuous carpet. Human life seemed far away.

It wasn't just that, though, was it? She was suffering a delayed reaction from being with Jamie. When he was around the memories had kept just beneath the surface, but they wouldn't stay down once she was alone.

She almost wished she hadn't seem him — not here, not today, with no hustling city distraction to prevent her mind from settling, and with the strangeness of her situation making her feel unfortified, vulnerable. But it wasn't the poor kid's fault that he reminded her of Mark. Probably any nice, average, scruffy eight-year-old boy would have had the same effect. That was the trouble. What had been lost on that hot tarmacked road fourteen years ago was as everyday as it was unique and irreplaceable.

She struck a soft chord on the tuned guitar, unconsciously shifting her left thumb to the proscribed position on the neck. The chord was a bright C-major, but it didn't alter the minor key of her thoughts.

The odd thing was she couldn't remember what sweet she had been eating. She knew that she had been chewing something as she walked home from school that day. But no sweet she had ever tasted since had brought back a rush of dreadful association, no packet glimpsed in a shop had rung a doleful bell. It was odd because everything else about that afternoon was printed on her memory with the sharp boldness of a deep woodcut. The fierce heat and light of a precocious June, the glitter of mica in the pavements, the musty, tired smell of exhaust fumes. The weight of her school bag on her shoulder, the tinny jingle of an ice-cream van that played 'Lili Marlene'. And the crumpled dampness of the letter that Mark kept showing her.

It was a letter from school — one of those mimeographed form-letters that began 'Dear Parent' and always smelt inky. It was about a trip to Warwick Castle. Mark was excited. Would Mum and Dad let him go? Everybody would be going. Would they let him go? He kept flourishing the sweat-marked letter in front of Amanda, dancing round her, his plimsolls squeaking on the hot pavement, asking her what she thought.

"I don't know, I should think so. You'll have to ask them when we get home."

"Well, come on, then, hurry up!"

"Oh, hold your horses, will you . . . ?"

She could replay the scene as often as she liked, alert for its nuances, but she could never deny to herself that she had spoken crossly to him that afternoon. She was irritable with the heat; and she was, besides, twelve and Mark was eight, and the tolerance of twelve-year-old sisters for eight-year-old brothers is not unlimited. She had tripped and skinned her knees playing the dreaded netball that afternoon, and they hurt. They hurt too much for her to run, as Mark kept urging her to do. And so she had been tetchy with him. Nothing much, nothing that didn't go on in the happiest of families practically every day; she honestly doubted whether he had taken any notice of it. But still, in view of what was about to happen, it was an abomination.

Their home was two streets away. It was in the older part of Billingham, the long straight streets of late-Victorian housing crowded in between the railway and the city centre. A new ring-road had cut a lot of that district off now, and some of it had even been pedestrianized or made access-only. But in those days those long straight streets named after Liberal politicians and local dignitaries were still main arteries of traffic.

And she and Mark were used to it. They had grown up with that pounding traffic; they coexisted with it as young rabbits coexisted with foxes and weasels. They were, literally, streetwise. But Mark was excited that day. He wanted to get home and show their parents the letter. So he had started to run on ahead, and she had let him. And because he was excited, when he got to their road, the road you had to cross to get to the corner post office their parents kept, he ran out without looking.

And where was Amanda? Lagging along behind. Too far behind to stop him running out across the road without looking. Too far behind to see what happened.

But she heard the noise it made.

She remembered, too, with perfect clarity, the faces of the two people who got out of the car that was skewed to a stop in the middle of the road with a twin curve of skid-marks scored on the melting tarmac behind it. Somehow she even knew about them; somehow she knew that the man and the woman running round to the front of the car with faces frozen and stretched in anguish were not a couple, that they were just work colleagues or something like that. A lift home, chatting about the boss or the office party. And suddenly a little boy was on the bonnet of the car.

She remembered too that there was a low, crying noise, a sort of crooning, coming from the huddled figure on the tarmac, and that through the shocked paralysis of her brain had shot the wild mad hope, *He'll be all right he's making a noise so he'll be all right.* And she remembered too — she could see it now — the bright checked pattern on the blanket that Mrs Sears, who lived in the house opposite and had seen the accident from her window, came running out bearing in her arms like a great, flapping flag.

And she remembered the faces of her mother and father, as they too came running, out of the shop where they had been working and had heard the screech and bump and had not known what it was that they had heard or what it would mean for them. Her father was wearing his slippers, as he often did when he was behind the counter: she remembered that too.

The policeman who spoke to her, asking about what had happened: she remembered his young pink face, and she remembered babbling about the letter, it was important that she tell him about the letter, you see he had this letter . . .

And then there was the comic. It was probably the comic that she remembered with the most hallucinatory clarity of all. She and her parents came back home in the evening from the hospital where Mark had died of his injuries, and there was his weekly comic lying on the coffee table in the living room. It was a Disney comic and on the brightly coloured cover were Donald Duck and his South American friends José Carioca and Panchito, riding on a flying carpet.

Amanda's fingers mechanically played scales, softly.

It was the sight of the comic that had set her off. She hadn't cried until then. The comic lying where Mark had left it that morning brought it all out like a poisoned sickness that went on and on. And with it the desperate need for an absolution that her parents, for all their assurances, could never give her, that no one could ever give her. *I should have stopped him — I should have saved him* . . .

And yet she couldn't remember the sweets that she had been eating on the way home. She could only recall that, whatever had been in her mouth she had spat out in a retching jolt at the sight of the skewed car and the running people and the pool of blood standing up on the surface of the road like bright oil.

People talked about rebuilding their lives after tragedies. Those sad brave couples who had seen their child ripped to rags by dogs that would never hurt anyone or wasted by one of God's more cunning diseases, sitting together on the sofa before the ghoul eye of the TV camera, gripping each other's hands and talking about rebuilding their lives. And probably they meant it. But you couldn't do it, not really. Everything was maimed. In the case of Amanda's family, the rebuilding had included leaving the post office in the city and taking over the one in the scrubby village five miles out. It was the road, of course. The busy road that had taken Mark: they couldn't stay near that. And probably there was some buried notion of the country as refuge, the place that healed as opposed to the city that killed. But granted that they couldn't have stayed where they were, their new life offered nothing redeeming. Amanda's parents fitted into the new community, they spoke approvingly of the quiet and the fresh air, they grew vegetables, they ran stalls at village fêtes. And all the time they pretended they were doing these things by choice. They skated over the unbearable knowledge that they wouldn't have been doing any of these things, that they wouldn't be here at all, if it wasn't for Mark's death. Mark's death determined everything. It *was* everything.

As for Amanda, she was miserable there, had hated the place from the very first minute. But far from protesting, outwardly or inwardly, she had accepted the unhappiness as no more than her due. Because of . . . Well, it didn't need to be put in words. And it never was, except once. Her father's grief, for a long time afterwards, would periodically bear black fruit in the shape of fits of fierce and bitter despondency in which the world was his enemy; and in one such mood, when Amanda's bicycle had been stolen outside a shop in town, he had turned on her and cried: "You should have taken better care of it! That's typical of you! You should have taken proper care of Mark as well, but you didn't, did you?"

There was never such an outburst again, of course. That way lay chaos. But there didn't need to be.

Her father trusted to time, no doubt, to undo what had been done when he spoke those words. And time did repair the family, in a way. The bitterness was slowly ploughed under. Meanwhile, Amanda kept her own counsel. The thing was out: it was there, for always. Like the fact of your own mortality, it was a thing that once acknowledged could never be unacknowledged. You had to, in the fullest sense of the phrase, live with it. It wasn't necessary to give it a name like guilt or whatever. For Amanda it was just The Thing, The Thing that had come into her life when she was twelve and lay there like an ugly, scaly, slumbering beast.

And when she saw a boy like Jamie, the beast stirred and wakened. There was no guarding against it.

Or rather, there was, but it did not work all the time. The safeguard was the chemistry of her own personality, which tended to be light-hearted rather than melancholic. She was not, God forbid, what people called a 'fun person' — she always grimaced when she read those lonely-hearts advertisements in which women proclaimed themselves 'bubbly', as if they didn't realize that any man in his right mind would run screaming at such a description — but her shoulders set more naturally into the careless shrug than the defeated slump. She preferred a good laugh to a good cry any day of the week.

And yet that wasn't the whole story. She had heard someone interviewed on the radio say that yes, he was a workaholic, but the reason he was a workaholic was that he was temperamentally lazy — if he didn't flog himself he wouldn't go at all; and she had recognized something similar to her own position in that. She had to cultivate her good humour because she knew that the blackness was waiting for her if she let it in. It didn't happen very often. It tended to strike, naturally enough, when she visited her parents in their potato-patch retreat; it tended to strike if she was alone a lot, away from friends, away from the familiar. (And boy, had it struck now, she thought.) But while it was infrequent, when it did come it was very dark indeed: a pit that had no bottom.

Cue the amateur psychologists, who would wag their heads and say, in so many words, that Mark was at the bottom of that pit.

Well, up yours, amateur psychologists. Experience had given her a strong aversion to that breed. If there was one thing worse than a man who tried to put his hand up your skirt, it was a man who tried to put his hands in your head.

Her fingers tightened, and she struck a loud, harsh discord. "Bastard," she said aloud, and breathed out heavily. It was good to say it. Even through all that had happened, all the pestering and recrimination and emotional blackmail that had brought her within an ace of going to law and getting a harassment injunction against him and incidentally within an ace of a nervous breakdown — even through all that, she had never really cursed Ewan as she had just done so satisfyingly. She had thought, *This man won't leave me alone, what can I do?*; she had thought, *This man is driving me crazy, what have I done?* Most damagingly, she had thought, *It must be my fault, it must be me.* She had thought all those things, instead of thinking, *Why doesn't this little shit just go and screw himself?*

But of course he had wanted her to think those troubled, guilt-laden thoughts. Amateur psychologists might talk hogwash, but when it came to using that stuff against you they were no amateurs. Ewan certainly hadn't been. Guilt was his speciality. He'd have had her believing everything was her fault, right down to the hole in the ozone layer, if she hadn't come to her senses.

"Never give anything of yourself away," her grandad, a crusty curmudgeon kept on a short leash by Grandma, had once said to her, "because people can use it against you." Wise words, Grandad. But difficult to put into practice unless lifelong celibacy was your bag. Get close to someone, and things inevitably came out. The trick was, of course, to be a good picker. And not to open up the locked cupboards of your soul to someone who would peer into them hoping to spot an edged weapon that he could use when things got rough. Who would fasten on to your weaknesses like a piglet on a teat. Step forward, Mr Ewan Malborne.

That, at least, was her own fault. She had picked a wrong 'un. And perhaps it was no use protesting, as women innumerable had done down the ages, that 'he seemed so nice'. You didn't have to be Andrea Dworkin to know that men, like market-traders, kept the nice stuff on top, while underneath might well be a heap of crap. You found that out early, and bore it in mind in all your future dealings with them. And yet Ewan really *had* seemed so nice. Kind, funny, interesting, gentle, the whole bit. Nor could she say that they didn't have anything in common. The trouble was, the area that they did have in common was the area of her life that she liked least. The dark area. There were some men who could find your clitoris and some who couldn't locate it with signposts and guides on mules; and similarly there were some men, it seemed, who could put their fingers unerringly on your unhappy-spot and massage it till you hollered.

So Grandad was right. Give something of yourself away — at least to someone like Ewan — and you were handing him a psychological Kalashnikov. And that was her one overwhelming regret about the affair with Ewan: the fact that she had told him about Mark. She couldn't protect her little brother in life, and even in death she had betrayed him, turned him into a counter in the dismal mind-games of a resentful lover. The only excuse she could offer was that she hadn't meant to. It had been one of those evenings that Ewan loved — soul-baring into the small hours in a fug of booze and dodgy philosophy. Sloshed and vulnerable, enwrapped in that peculiar atmosphere of navel-gazing intensity that Ewan fostered, she had poured it out.

And how gently understanding he had been, receiving her confidence as if it were a precious gift. Which it certainly was, in its value to him. He had kept it nice and safe while they were still together, polishing it up, ready for use. And then, when the relationship hit the rocks, out it had come. In one of those last wretched confrontations during which she had tried to impress on him, in three languages with subtitles and diagrams, that their relationship was absolutely and completely over, he had suddenly played the suicide card. If you don't let me continue to make your life a misery, I'll top myself — that was the gist. He had used it before. But this time there was a twist.

"I'll do it," he threatened. "And then you'll have *two* lives on your conscience."

She had asked him to leave then — in the sense that bouncers and Mafia bodyguards asked people to leave. But the very violence of her reaction had told its tale. He had found the place where she bled. And he knew it.

She had wept long. The tears were for herself of course, but also for Mark. She had made a hostage of his memory. Failed him twice.

She was by then beyond surprise that Ewan should suppose such swingeing hurtfulness

93

would further his cause. The End of the Affair was not the time for sweet reason; and besides, at that stage Ewan and reason had already parted company. He was just thrashing and flailing.

And yet . . . The really grim aspect of that time, the part that had made her temporarily feel that the only sane people in the world were monks and nuns, was the fact that Ewan really seemed to think there was a way back for him. That even such emotional butcheries as that crack about Mark's death were testimonies of devotion which would finally prove irresistible. As if a double-glazing salesman, instead of just putting his foot in the door, should kick the door down, wreck the house, pee on the carpet, strangle the budgie, and then still expect you to say, Yes please, I'll have full sealed double-glazing and a couple of patio doors.

Amanda's fingers moved aimlessly on the fretboard now, picking out fragments of tunes, a musical doodling. She didn't want to think about Ewan, but with the melancholy mood upon her it was inevitable that she would. Ewan and gloom went together like eggs and bacon.

It was difficult to realize that she had only gone out with him for five months. It seemed much longer. They had met at the beginning of the year, and were breaking up by the time spring had sprung. But of course, it was that awful epilogue that made the whole business seem to go on and on like Texas. And even those five months together, viewed in retrospect, were a long hangover after a short drunk. The warning signs had appeared pretty early. You could put it in general terms and say that you began to find him possessive and manipulative, that a depressing morbidity began to show through that gentle surface, that you slowly realized that temperamentally the two of you were like chalk and cheese . . . but in truth the decline presented itself to the memory as a series of clear steps, vivid and concrete.

For example:

She found herself knowing exactly what he was going to say at any given time.

She found herself unconsciously tidying up after he had left her place, as if to erase the fact of his presence.

The question, "What shall we do tonight?" kept recurring.

The answer, "I don't mind", kept recurring.

Whenever she was alone with him she felt a strange compulsion to examine her fingers.

Certain characteristic turns of phrase of his began to irritate her beyond endurance.

They watched amusing TV shows together without laughing.

She became strongly aware of how fond she was of her friends.

She sometimes let the telephone ring without answering it.

They had laborious, exhausting disagreements over neutral and entirely trivial topics like the system of library fines.

They drank too much without ever getting tipsy.

She felt curiously awkward about calling him by name.

95

She kept frowning into the mirror and contemplating a complete change of image.

They folded their arms a lot.

He kept presenting her with what the shops called 'Greetings gifts': miniature teddy-bears, keyrings, gonks.

They accused each other of being in a funny mood.

And each often couldn't quite catch what the other had said.

They feigned sleep.

She somehow dreaded her birthday . . .

But what the hell, anybody could write the script from here on in. It was the oldest story in the world. Cro-Magnon Man and Cro-Magnon Woman had probably lain on the cave floor amongst the mammoth droppings facing different ways and grunting, "No, nothing's the matter." It just happened. It was rotten, but it was nothing exceptional.

Except in Ewan's eyes. Dear God, in Ewan's eyes it was Armageddon.

Sure, a break-up was always messy. You couldn't finish a relationship and not expect a few loose ends. What you didn't expect was weeks of hassle, of pleading and threats, of phone calls every hour of the day and night, of hammerings at the door in the small hours, of rambling, incoherent letters with every post, of deliveries of extravagant bunches of flowers, of being unable to step out of the office at lunchtime without him waiting there, baleful-faced, to buttonhole you . . .

Well, she could do without recalling the grisly

details. With luck, good old repression would eventually erase them altogether. Suffice it to say that, when it was at its worst, back in June, she had been on the point of going to a solicitor; and then had come Alix's offer of a Norfolk cottage bolthole, a fortnight's respite. She had jumped at it. It was a palliative, of course, not a cure: knowing Ewan, she had not expected her absence for a mere fortnight to cool him off. She had been quite prepared, indeed, to return to Billingham to find him camped on her doorstep holding up a placard that said, WHERE DID WE GO WRONG? And so it turned out, if not quite literally. The day after she had returned from her sanity-restoring fortnight, the phone calls had begun again.

But they didn't last long. Somehow, at last, Ewan had accepted that it was over: somehow at last, Ewan had got the message; the message that she couldn't have made clearer with skywriting. Finally, he had left her alone.

If it wasn't disrespectful to say so, she knew then how people had felt on VE Day.

And then, as the summer went on, she heard from Lisa that he was going out with another girl, a girl who worked at the same factory as Lisa. And that was the equivalent of VJ Day, if you liked.

But relieved as she was, she couldn't help wondering if the girl knew what she was letting herself in for. Because, after going out with Ewan for a while, Amanda had felt herself to be descending into a depressive underworld: stifling, lightless, labyrinthine. And what was worse, she almost mistook it for the real world. Until she came to her senses she didn't find it odd that he liked talking about his funeral — who he would want to be there and what music he would have played. Or that he paid an excessive attention to those junk questionnaires and surveys in *Cosmo* and the like: the ones in which a jaded sub-editor invented a few statistics about how many sexual partners the average woman had, or how often she fantasized while making love that it was Daniel Day-Lewis or Kevin Costner or the Pope on the other end of the tummy-banana instead of boring old hubby with his press-up technique and undesigned stubble. Or that any accidental mention of a male from her past — who could anyway be counted on the fingers of one hand and still leave room for a couple of rings — produced in him a curt, "I don't want to know", followed after an interval of brooding by an in-depth interrogation, as if to establish that she wasn't carrying even the smallest of torches for someone about whom she had forgotten everything except the dandruff on his school blazer. Or that he threw a wobbly if they had to mix with other people when they were together rather than be utterly and everlastingly alone, just the two of them.

"It's because I don't want to share you," he explained. It was after one such incident, indeed, that the scales fell from Amanda's eyes. By chance they had met up with a few of her friends in the pub: Ewan was in one of his impossible moods, and after glowering round at everyone and swallowing a succession of drinks in silence, he had abruptly stood up and walked out.

That, of course, should have been the moment when she hurried after him, darling darling what's wrong, and abjectly apologized for the fact that he was in a foul mood. Instead, she stayed put. She realized all at once that she was much happier with her friends than with him. If ever there was a moment when she had known that they must finish, the equivalent of a neon sign flashing, NOT WORKING NOT WORKING GET OUT OF IT, that was it.

Of course, even then there had been a few last guilt-ridden obstacles to overcome in her own mind. Was it her? Was she the reason for their misery? Did she bring out the worst in him? Stuff like that. Dear God. And they called sado-masochists perverts. When all they were doing was translating into physical terms what anybody who ever bought a Valentine or made a date was letting themselves in for.

Ah well. It was the unknown new girlfriend's problem now, not hers.

The sunstripes on the carpet were longer and thinner. Amanda looked at the clock. Four-thirty. The Attack of the Killer Memories had certainly used up the time, though at the expense of leaving her spirits as low as a Sumo wrestler's gusset.

Think good thoughts, Amanda. She hummed and strummed 'My Favourite Things', but Julie Andrews and seven brats in dirndl nightwear hardly counted as a good thought. Actually,

99

thinking of your favourite things was a lousy way of cheering yourself up. You were more likely to end up bawling your head off.

No, she knew a better way of shaking off the blue devils: and sod what the clock said, she was going to do it now.

She parked the guitar with a *boing* and made for the phone. Punched Nick's number. She knew of course she would hear an answerphone message, but it still gave her heart a momentary jolt when his voice came on, as if he were actually there.

"Hello, sorry I'm not in at the moment. Please leave your message after the tone and I'll get back to you." The voice had a slightly embarrassed inflection; as he had confided to Amanda, Nick felt rather silly having an answering machine, as if he were some sort of big-shot. It was a typical gift from those chancy brothers of his, who had the barrowboy fixation with technology and who still talked to him in masses of arcane detail about their latest wedge-shaped cars — *motors*, rather — as if they could never quite believe that it was all Greek to him. In fact, the answerphone had come in handy, the handicapped homes often needing to get in touch with him for emergency overtime. And in this case it had turned out very handy indeed, Amanda thought.

"Hello, Nick. Er — it's only me. Amanda, I mean . . . " Great start. Some day, presumably, the human race would accustom itself to using answering machines, and not sound like maundering idiots when required to speak into them. "I just thought I'd give you a ring and . . . say hello so that you'd . . . " So that you'd what? Hear my voice as soon as you got in, isn't that a treat for you? Modesty itself, dear. "So that you'd — know I'd got here and everything. Hope you had a good day at work. It's a bummer having to work Saturdays, isn't it? Well, I mean, for you, I don't think this counts as work what I'm doing. I feel like I've walked on to a set for *Dynasty*. Well, not *Dynasty*, because that's tacky, and this place is just so, well, tasteful I suppose you'd have to say. Luxurious anyway. And the food Alix and Ben left me, I'm making such a pig of myself. They got off OK this morning, by the way. God, it's seemed like such a long day already." She pictured the answerphone in Nick's flat, next to his permanently expiring cheese-plant, light blinking on as it stored up her words. A wish to be in that flat right now instead of here went through her like a bolt from a crossbow. "Actually it's pretty lonely here — well, you know, it's lovely, but it's so remote and quiet. You never hear a sound, that's what I can't get over. Here — I'll stop wittering a minute and you just listen."

She paused and held the receiver out to register the silence of Upper Bockham. At that moment the cockerel in the chicken-pen outside chose to let fly with an outstandingly ill-timed "cock-a-doodle-do". Amanda, after the first startled jolt, burst out laughing. "Well," she went on into the receiver, "I suppose you heard that — no, look, apart from mixed-up cockerels,

101

it really is quiet, honestly . . . God, I can't believe that happened. I suppose it must mean something very countrified and important when that happens. Like it's going to rain or the sheep are going to get sheep-rot or something."

As she spoke, something shifted in the dusty attic of her mind: A-Level English, and *Tess of the D'Urbervilles*. There had been something in that book about a cock crowing in the afternoon, hadn't there? She seemed to remember her male fellow-pupils squeezing the words 'an afternoon cock' for every last drop of innuendo. The dust on the memory of that book was too thick for her to be precise, but she was pretty sure that if old Hardy was pulling the strings, the misfiring rooster meant something nasty was about to happen. *That bodes ill*, her grandma would say; and, even as she used to cringe at the old lady's Starkadder language — 'bodes ill', for goodness' sake — Amanda had always found that the phrase gave her a curious unpleasant shiver in spite of herself. And the same shiver touched her now.

"Anyway," she resumed hurriedly, "here I am, better get used to it. You must be thinking what an ungrateful cow, there she is sitting pretty and here's me just getting home from work and having to listen to her waffling on. No, it is lovely here, but I just wish — well, I wish you were here with me." Whoops. That was rather gushy . . .

But what the hell, she *did* wish he was here, didn't she? Yes. Yes indeed. In fact, she could just imagine him sitting in that armchair over there, with his dark, compact, keeping-his-thoughts-to-himself look, which was at the same time somewhat boyish, as if his status as the youngest of that big boisterous family was for ever imprinted on him. In fact she could imagine more than him sitting in that armchair. She could imagine stampeding upstairs with him and acting quite unmanageable and riotous in that paddock-sized guest bed.

However. It was said now, gushy or not, clingy or not. And maybe it would scare Nick off and all the rest of it, but she didn't really think so. *Let's face it, Amanda, when you hold back and go all cautious about this relationship, what you're really saying to yourself is that you don't want to be like Ewan, isn't it? You're afraid of going over the top, because not so long ago you escaped a relationship with a man who went so far over the top he practically hit the stratosphere.*

True enough. And she shouldn't let such a fear disable her; whatever happened, she wasn't going to end up like Ewan. Because while she was facing things, she might as well face the fact that Ewan had been, not to put too fine a point upon it, a bit of a nutter.

A new thought, or newly arrived-at anyway: probably a last barrier of guilt had prevented her getting to it before now. But now she had got there, and she hoisted her flag.

"Anyway, I'd better let you get on and have some tea, I know you'll be starving when you get in. And Nick, don't eat those Value Burgers,

I'm sure they're dodgy." Nick was a mildly compulsive bargain-hunter, even at the risk of his stomach. "By the way, you can't think of a Gilbert and Sullivan opera that starts with P that isn't *Pirates of Penzance*, *HMS Pinafore* or *Patience*, can you? It's driving me mad." Worth a try, though it was hardly Nick's bag; anything operatic tended to make him look as if he were suffering from acute indigestion. As if he had eaten Value Burgers, in fact. "Right, I really will shut up now. You've got the number — give me a ring any time. Or I'll ring you. Bye, duck . . . This tape will self-destruct in five seconds."

She put the receiver down and grimaced at herself. That last burst of flippancy hadn't been at all what she had intended. She had intended to go the whole self-revealing hog and sign off with 'I love you', and even, ye gods, a smacking kiss right in the mouthpiece. "Chicken," she reproached herself.

And on the subject of chicken, she hoped old Foghorn Leghorn out there wasn't going to make a habit of those fluffed alarm-calls. If he could do it at four-thirty in the afternoon, there was nothing to stop him dropping one of his farmyard clangers at two in the morning. What with owls and foxes, enough was enough already.

Amanda dug in her jeans pocket for change, placed a pound coin by the phone. She knew Alix and Ben would try to refuse such things — they would look troubled, as if she had asked them whether she could scrub their floors for pin-money — but she preferred to make the effort.

She wandered over to the french windows and looked out at the embrowned and dusky garden being eaten up by shadow. The sun was tangled in the encircling woods; the horizon was a slow fire.

Well, whatever that cock-crow had meant, the bird had apparently said his piece: that silence was back, a heavy yet somehow suspended silence, like some ponderous roof held up by the slimmest of pillars. She seemed to feel it lowering over her, almost bowing her shoulders. She wondered when the Howards would arrive. Maybe she could go over to the cottages and check that Honeysuckle Cottage was all ready for them; though she and Sue had thoroughly prepared it this afternoon.

She switched on the TV, which was as slim as a placemat, with the remote control. A word would soon have to be invented, she thought, for operating a TV with a remote control. To zap, maybe. Or, better, to telezap. Only football results, but it was better than the silence.

She sat down.

She wished she could remember the name of that damned Gilbert and Sullivan opera.

She wished she could remember what that afternoon cockcrow meant.

6

EVERY person you saw, he thought as he waited at the traffic lights, was the result of an act of sexual intercourse.

Every single human being you met or spoke to or passed in the street was the direct visual evidence of a complete sexual act, as direct as a dribble of semen on the sheets or a slimy phallus or swollen dripping vulva or encrusted pubic hairs.

And yet what hypocrisy about it. The prune-faced bitch who lived next door to his mother was always going on about her wonderful son who was a doctor (and thus by implication not a failure and a disappointment). My son this and my son that. My son's going on holiday to Senegal next week, as she primped her lace curtains. My son's bought a new car, as she fussed over her Pekinese. And every time she mentioned him she was effectively proclaiming that one night thirty-odd years ago she opened her legs.

Hypocrisy. Lies, lies, lies.

He swung the car into a side-street and parked. The wine he had had at lunch had worn off, and he wondered about taking a swig from the flask in the glove compartment. A woman walking along the pavement glanced over her shoulder at him. He decided against it.

He got out of the car, stretched, sniffed the sick Saturday air. Rows of terraced houses, some covered with plastic stone-cladding, as if stupidity wasn't enough and they had to thrust it in your face.

He turned into the main road, which vibrated with maddened traffic. Cambridge Road, one of old Billingham's main thoroughfares, chopped up now into smaller portions by flyovers and parkways. This part of it was a parade of single-fronted shops and take-aways, weirdly assorted. Zorba's Kebab House next to a dingy old greengrocer's with dead wasps in the window. Ron's Plaice the chippie next to Private Lives, a sex shop full of dusty dildoes and shrinkwrapped scan mags. Cromwell Power Tools next to Nancy's Needlecraft. Saturday afternoon, but still there were grilles and bars everywhere, as if it were the haunt of wild beasts.

The terminal grimness of a rotting world. But for him this place had associations, and the associations transformed it.

At the end of the row was a big corner pub in mock-Tudor. Mock-mock-Tudor, if anything. The Prince of Wales. It opened all day Saturday, and from the doorway came a stale waft like a drunkard's belch. Men in capped-sleeve T-shirts circled a pool table, toting cues like rifles.

Associations. They transformed this place, for him.

He went in. He ordered a double vodka and stood at the bar drinking it. A noise like a strimmer punctuated with orgasm heartbeats blared from the jukebox; the sort of music they

107

would play in concentration camps to cover up the screams.

Associations, though. Vivid memories. He could even remember which table they had sat at. There, in the bay window with the shit-beige curtains. He gazed. The man sitting there now, a human-pitbull crossbreed bruised with tattoos, looked up from the tabloid toilet paper that he was trying to read without moving his lips. Their eyes met. They stared. At last it was the walking tattoo who dropped his eyes, coughing and turning to a fresh page of his bonehead comic.

But he was scarcely aware of it anyway. He swallowed the vodka, transfixed by another memory. The quiz machine. There had been a quiz machine in the corner, and later in the evening they had played it together and won the ten-pound jackpot. They made a dynamite team on the quiz machine. The perfect team.

The machine was gone now. They had had their day: too many people won on them too often.

The perfect team.

He ordered another vodka, single this time; he was driving.

Their first proper date. Its every moment was imprinted on this place, woven into the pattern on the flock wallpaper, carved on the phoney timber of the bar. They said that if you could find a way to play back a potter's wheel, it would reveal all the sounds ever heard in the potter's workshop. This place was the same, for him. It was a great recording machine, and what it played back was that evening they had spent together. There were many such recorders around the city, for him.

They had never come back here. Today was the first time he had been back — this day of replaying old memories.

Had she been back here? he wondered.

Had she been here with *him*, perhaps?

Fiery comets raced across his mind.

He slammed down his empty glass and left the pub.

Outside, the traffic noises assaulted him. Din, everywhere. Whirls of dust went for his eyes.

He didn't go back to his car. He carried on walking, because there were more associations further along the road. Here there was a junction with the parkway, and you had to cross a footbridge to get to the next amputated limb of Cambridge Road. He climbed the steps of the footbridge, slapped by wind. At the top he stopped and leaned on the railing, looking out across the city. To the left, a new retail park, brute bunkers that looked like detention centres, with the bright paintbox lettering on the roofs as the sinister finishing touch of deception. To the right, a corrugated streetscape, fetid with human lives, interrupted only by a playing field where men in shorts flailed and kicked and sweated and charged at each other, as if a lunatic asylum had been lifted up like a doll's house to reveal them.

But it had been night when they had come up here, the two of them, after the pub, and had stood on this spot, leaning on this railing.

They had talked, for ages. And below them the city had been like a jewel-box.

He looked down at the thrumming cars, chasing each other's tails, getting nowhere. The delusion that if you moved fast enough, you were alive.

Acid rose in his throat. Vodka on top of the wine, and that heavy lunch.

That lunch. His mother hadn't meant it, of course. But her questions had inflamed the wound.

Inflamed it. For Jesus' sake, they had torn the wound wide open, stretched its bleeding traumatized mouth and rubbed salt into the quivering naked tissue until the blood ran and the nerve-endings screamed. They had done such things to the wound that he just wasn't going to be able to bear it any longer.

Especially with what he now knew for certain. About *him*.

He looked up. A few yards along, leaning on the railing, were a pair of teenagers. Both boy and girl had long straggly hair and outfits of leprous suede and corduroy. Nit-comb chic. His arm was round her neck, and her hand rested on his rabbity buttocks. What enchanted evening had seen the start of that great romance? Across what crowded room had those two strangers seen each other? Perhaps their pusher had made the introductions, and they had shared their stash before he wafted her off to bedsitland for a glamorous shag on the infested bedspread?

They glanced over at him.

110

"What do you think you're looking at?" he asked.

The girl looked away, but the boy raised his eyebrows. "Pardon me for living," he said through his hair.

"Say again?"

The boy looked at him and flushed. His girlfriend was moving on, tugging at his sleeve. "Nothing," the boy mumbled.

"We can always have a chat if you like," he said, turning to face them. "If that's what you want. Yes? Is it?"

The scrofulous couple hurried away, the boy glancing back once over his shoulder but avoiding eye-contact.

Poor little dears. When they got back to their rathole they'd probably need an extra shot of whatever narcotic substances they happened to have in, just to help them get over the shock of meeting a little cold reality.

He turned back to his gazing and his memories, but it was spoiled now. The sight of even such nomarks as those two had set the wound throbbing more agonizingly. How did they manage it? What did that Neolithic manikin have to offer? Tenderness, sincerity, devotion? A telescopic prick? Perhaps that was it. Perhaps that was all women were interested in really: as long as you could summon up a cucumber in your trousers at the drop of a hat, they were happy. Never mind tenderness and sincerity and devotion. They didn't want to feel loved and cherished and needed; they wanted to

111

feel a pair of balls banging against their arse.

His fingers tightened on the railing until the peeling paint splintered under his fingernails. No: not her. She was different. They *had* been different together. They had been — well, meant for each other.

Yes, meant for each other. Even when it all seemed to be over, he had remained convinced of that. Just because she couldn't see it didn't alter the fact. And then maybe some day . . .

Except now it was all changed. Because of what he now knew for certain. And what he now knew seemed to suggest that she was like that after all.

And did she straddle *him*, the latest flame? Did she climb on top of him and straddle him, her hair hanging down?

Did she?

Did she?

The comets scored their trail of rage across his mind. Flaking paint dug into his cuticles.

Did she?

Did she?

With a gasp he wrenched himself away from the railing and set off at a run down the steps of the footbridge.

Did she . . . ?

Once in the car he unscrewed the hip-flask and took a shuddering drink and then closed his eyes for some moments, trying to banish the taunting images that capered across his mind. He breathed deeply, opened his eyes at last, saw the twitch of a curtain in a window across the street. Just some nosy old bitch with a face like a dog's arse. He glared, and she dodged out of sight.

Someone in a nearby garage was using an electric drill. The shrill whine of it rose and then rose again, as if some new, undreamt-of extremities of pain were being reached. The sound ground and gnawed at him, as everything did.

You know she's welcome, don't you . . . ? Any time . . . His mother's words would not leave him. Coming on top of his new knowledge they were fire, acid, napalm. The hot ache of his arm where he had splashed it with boiling fat — carelessly, indifferently, almost gladly — was nothing in comparison.

He replaced the flask in the glove compartment, wiped his lips.

He was going to have to do something. If he did nothing, he would implode, combust, suffer some terrible cataclysm of self that would rip him and the world into a million pieces.

He started the engine. He didn't have to make any conscious decision about where he was going to go. The place itself pulled him. It spoke, and he obeyed.

Seven or eight minutes driving along the busy parkways brought him to the place. He parked the car in the same space it had occupied this morning. The same space it had occupied all night, while he had sat huddled inside, smoking. Smoking, and looking at the two cars parked side by side at the other end. Looking at the block of flats, the hideous heap of new-town building-blocks set down in its green no-man's-land. Looking, and thinking.

And knowing.

Neither of the two cars were here now, of course. He had watched hers drive away very early that morning. Why so early? Didn't the latest flame have a bathroom, if she wanted to sluice his spunk out of her? Though perhaps she didn't anyway. Perhaps she wanted to keep it up there. Or perhaps they were just so relaxed and sure of each other that she could come and go any time.

It didn't matter. All that mattered was that he had watched them go in together last night, and he had watched them leave, she at six, he at a quarter to ten, this morning. And maybe he was stupid — maybe he was stupid, for example, to think that love and devotion meant something in this world — but as far as he could see, that meant that they had spent the night together.

Yes, they had. They had spent the night together, in the latest flame's ticky-tacky flat out here in Smurfland.

The knowledge. The unbearable knowledge.

It was not the first time he had been here. It was a couple of weeks ago that he had first successfully followed her here after she had left work. Since their break-up he had got into the habit of following her whenever he could — waiting near her office car-park, sometimes waiting in a side-street near her home. You were limited, of course, in what you could do; it wouldn't do to be seen, because she might not understand, and get upset. Towards the end —

no not the end

— she had talked about getting a harassment injunction against him and things like that. It was only talk, of course; but still, he didn't want to upset her, and if she realized he was following her she might take it the wrong way. When all he wanted was to be close to her. Watch over her, really. Like the song: 'Someone to Watch Over Me'. She used to play that on the guitar . . . And so he had to be careful, discreet. And more often than not he lost her in the traffic. But that time a couple of weeks ago he had managed to keep her car in sight all the way here. And had managed to park in the road outside the block, and watch her go in.

And from that moment it had been this place that had been the focus of his attention. She had no friends or relatives in this part of Billingham as far as he knew — and he knew her well, he knew her better than *anybody* — but he had been prepared to give her the benefit of the doubt. And so he had haunted this place, observing her visits.

And then he had seen them together, one evening, leaving the block by the main doors and turning down an alleyway that led to some blighted shopping centre with a plastic pub attached. They had been laughing. She, and the dark-haired young-looking guy he had seen getting in and out of a rusty Cortina in the car-park.

That was who she came to see, then. He was the one.

And yet, that first time he had seen them

115

together, the knowledge had still not been certain. They had been laughing, but not linking arms, not touching. Just friends, perhaps. It was possible. He *wanted* to believe the best of her.

But the terrible knowledge had drawn closer. He had seen them here together again, a few days later, and the dark guy had touched her shoulder. And then a few days after that, when he was parked round the corner from her flat and thinking about her, the rustbucket Cortina had swung into the street and parked just a few spaces down from him and the dark guy had got out, whistling, and made his way towards her place; and a few minutes later he had seen the two of them in his wing-mirror, crossing the road towards town, arm in arm . . .

And still he had fought the truth away. Until last night. When he had watched them go into the block together, laughing, drunk. And waited. Waited all night. Thinking of them in there, together. Knowing.

All through the lunch with his mother the new knowledge had been like a silent screaming inside him. A knowledge he could not share even with her. She had seemed concerned about him, troubled, but that was probably because he looked groggy from lack of sleep. Not that he felt he wanted to sleep, ever. Not with this knowledge inside him. Driven deep and hard and burning inside him, making him want to gasp and thrash, just as the dark guy's cock must have driven into her last night and made her gasp and thrash and call his name . . .

He got out of the car, closed the door, stood

116

leaning against it for a moment looking at the block of flats: a great, breezeblock wendy-house. The ground shuddered slightly with the vibration from the parkway on the other side of the grass banks.

He could have borne it. It was hell, but he really could have borne it, if he hadn't found out that she had started going with another man. Thinking about her after the breakup had been bad enough — but thinking about her *with someone else* . . .

He closed his lips together tightly, began to walk towards the main door of the building.

An intercom-security block: there was a whole column of names and buzzers alongside the door. He stood scanning them. He didn't know what he was hoping to achieve. He didn't know the guy's name, and even if he did . . .

A pair of eyes was watching him through the glass of the door. A mouth framed words.

He stepped back as the door opened.

"A-riiight?"

The elderly black man in the sagging cardigan stood smiling at him, holding the door open.

"Hi."

"You wanna press a button," the man said, gesturing. "You press a button, they speak to you through the thing. You know?"

"Oh, right," he said. "It's OK actually, I — "

"Who you want? Maybe I know him. I know everybody. My name's George."

"Hi," he said again, shaking the offered hand. "No, it's OK, it's just — well, I've forgotten his

117

name, he drives an old grey Cortina, young guy, dark hair — apparently he was supposed to be selling his car, and I was interested . . . "

"You want Nick. I know him. I know Nick. Number twelve. I think he's out. He go to work this morning, I see him go. A nurse, he works crazy hours. You know?"

"Oh, well, in that case — "

"You want to try anyhow? Come in, I let you in. Try anyhow."

He hesitated. "OK. Thanks."

The lobby smelt of floor polish and disinfectant. It smelt like school when someone had been sick and the caretaker had cleaned it up. It smelt like failed urban living, the despairing admission that there are too many of us, not enough money, not enough room. There was a row of lockers for mail, a blank noticeboard, and a metal-framed table with a solitary trainer on it.

"Down the end. That's where he lives. The end one. Try knocking. But I think he working, I see him go this morning." George was shuffling alongside him. "Try anyhow. Maybe leave him a note. Write a note and put it under the door. You know?"

"Yes, right, that's a good idea . . . "

He stood before the mould-blue door of number twelve, raised his hand to knock.

What the hell was he doing?

Knocking at his door.

The one she was seeing. The one she was . . .

But it didn't matter. He had seen him leave himself, this morning, and the rustbucket Cortina wasn't in the car-park now. So, like

118

George said, he was surely at work, this Nick.

Nick. His name. He knew his name now, and he didn't know how it made him feel — better or worse . . .

Worse worse worse she calls him by that name she speaks that name fondly she whispers it she tightens her legs around him and calls NICK OH NICK OH NICK . . .

His knuckles were smarting: he had been knocking hard without being aware of it. George beside him was shaking his head.

"Uh-uh. Nobody there. He gone to work. You want to leave him a note? Write a note and put it under his door. Or I'll give it to him. I'll give him a note for you when he gets back."

"Er, no, thanks all the same, but I think I'll just call round later."

"You sure? I'll give him a message, I don't mind . . . "

George followed him back down the corridor to the outer door, shuffling and waffling, reluctant to let him go. "I got some paper upstairs . . . you want to leave a note, I got some paper . . . " The old guy was going to die fairly soon; it was written all over him. He was going to die soon, and his life had been shit, and he was starting to realize it — that was written all over him too. And so he wanted people near him all the time so he didn't have to think about it and start screaming.

"It's all right. I'll come back later. Thanks for your help."

He was out, cutting off George's last maundering words, heading for his car. He

119

got in, snatched out the hip-flask, took a long, burning swig.

Nick.

Nick the nurse. So what had Nick the nurse got to offer her apart from his lousy development-corporation flat which he apparently turfed her out of at six in the morning after he had finished shagging her to within an inch of her life? Did he offer her unquestioning, single-minded, wholehearted love? Did he offer devotion? Did he know the meaning of the word?

Did he know every inch of her skin did she let him touch her did she straddle him with her hair hanging down

did she

did she

did she . . . ?

He closed his eyes.

Number twelve. To the left, right at the end.

He opened his eyes, studied the block of flats.

He got out of the car again, opened the boot, rummaged in his toolbox.

The rear of the block epitomized the wrong-headed design of these places. Communal areas, they would call this scarred wasteland. Dog-fouled grass, condoms, gluebags. Steep banks leading up to the pounding flyover, notionally screened by trees that had never been allowed to grow. Communal areas for a place that had no community. He passed the rows of windows, hung with the tobacco-brown net curtains of young singles, smeared with condensation. Little, crappy boxes of lives, filled with a wadding of degraded pop music and portable TV chatter. The culmination of five thousand years of human history. We had raised the pyramids and mapped the stars, we had made marble breathe and canvas glow, we had counted the hairs on the leg of the flea and conquered gravity; and now we sat slack-jawed in pasteboard capsules and consumed each other's shit.

He stopped. He was at the end of the block. Nick's flat. Two windows. One frosted — bathroom. The other — kitchen?

His breathing was shallow. He looked all around. Deserted. The flyover thundered.

Did she potter about in that kitchen, barefoot, feeling at home? Making cups of tea for the two of them?

The two of them.

All at once he didn't care what happened, didn't care if he was seen, as long as he did something, as long as he got some relief for his feelings . . .

Nick . . .

He raised the wrench, swung it in a great overarm swing, bashed in the window.

He was already moving swiftly away as the glass tinkled and dropped with small, icy sounds. Satisfaction ran with a nervous thrill up his arm and into his shoulder. He could surely be back in his car before any of the rabbits popped out of their burrows to see what was going on.

Put the bastard's windows in. It was a lot better than nothing.

He was in the car. He flung the wrench under the passenger seat. Start the engine, or not? Best to sit tight. A car hurtling away now would be very suspicious, if anyone was looking out.

Hand on the ignition key, he waited. Nothing moved in the block: no twitch of curtains, no one coming out into the lobby.

He watched.

The smash of glass had been loud, but not that loud. Not with the noise of the flyover. And not with the noise of all the little rabbits' moron music thumping away.

And besides, was this the sort of place where people looked out for each other? Wasn't this, rather, the sort of place where you locked your door and feigned deafness, avoiding trouble, afraid of a comeback? Wasn't this the sort of place where girls were raped in the dog-smeared grass amongst the Coke cans and the pizza boxes, and people said the next day that they hadn't heard a thing?

He froze as he caught the sound of running footsteps. They were coming nearer to the car, coming straight for the car . . .

His fingers twitched around the ignition key as a shadow fell across the bonnet —

And was gone again. A jogger, in pixie hood and gloves. He pounded across the car-park and disappeared down the alleyway that led to the shopping centre.

What was *she* doing now? he wondered, letting out a deep breath. Obviously not getting shafted

122

chez Nicholas. A quiet Saturday afternoon at home, drowsing in front of the TV dreaming dreams of the new lover-boy? Probably. There was no chance of his finding out, not with that black bitch Lisa who wouldn't let him through the door — plus of course that business about a harassment order if he didn't back off . . . But there was no *need* for her to talk in those terms — all he wanted to do was see her, just be close to her, to explain, to offer her *everything* . . .

His eyes were still fixed on the block of flats, looking for a sign. And as the minutes passed he knew that he was right. The smashing of the window had caused no comment, no display of conscientious citizenship. This wasn't Coronation Street. If anybody had heard it, they were lying low and hoping not to be involved. Welcome to the caring nineties. He allowed himself a small smile.

And he had a vision.

A vision of himself standing inside Nick's flat.

He let go the ignition key, absently ran his fingers along the burnt patch on his arm, experiencing the pain of it.

Standing inside Nick's flat . . . Right where he lived. Right where Mr Wonderful lived. Right where *she* visited him. Right where she had spent the night with him —

locked in his arms speaking his name GIVING herself to him GIVING herself to him how could she HOW COULD SHE?

— and the vision was not to be resisted, the vision was salvation, if he could just strike back like that it would stop him detonating, splitting, flying apart . . .

He was moving: purpose lifted him, sloughing off the heaviness of drink and lack of sleep. He seemed to float, to slice through the air. Within moments he was back outside the smashed kitchen window. One swift glance all around: nothing, no life, the world after the neutron bomb. Purpose lifted his arm, negotiated a careful way past the jagged glass, made his hand close around the handle of the window.

Hesitation . . . Then knowledge came to reinforce purpose. Knowledge that these shitholes were equipped with window-locks — meaning that when they were built back in nineteen-seventy-blank the cowboys who threw them up fitted them with the cheapest half-arsed little window-locks they could get away with and that years of locking them with a little piddling plastic key left the little piddling locks so abraded and loose that practically anything sufficiently small would turn them . . .

He ran his forefinger along the handle, felt the tiny keyhole. His other hand, driven by purpose and knowledge, was already in his pocket and pulling out his own set of keys.

Another glance around: post-apocalypse still reigned. He fanned out his keys, thumbed the smallest. Yes. It fitted some little padlock somewhere, he couldn't remember where . . .

Purpose and knowledge suddenly failed him as he stared at the key. The key was his — how could he not know where it came from? It must be part of his life, yet it was a blank, a migraine

124

hole in his field of vision. Terror possessed him. If he couldn't remember where one of his own keys came from, what grip did he have on his life? What other betrayals did it have in store for him? Was he walking on quicksand all the time?

Panic beat at him with leathery wings . . .

And then knowledge reached out a hand. *It was because of her.*

It was because of her that he was in such a state that he forgot simple little things like the origin of a spare key on his keyring. What was more natural? You gave someone *everything*; you *devoted* yourself to her, gave yourself to her completely, body and soul, for ever — for after all what other conception of love was worth while? — you tore your heart up by its roots and presented it *bleeding* to her, you did all this . . . And then she jilted you. She ditched you, and left you yearning and amputated; and practically before your tears were dry she was *FUCKING* somebody else . . . And you? Wasn't it natural that you were in a state, that you were lost and distracted and forgetful, the little things slipping your mind because the *one* thing, the great thing that held your life together, was gone?

Purpose flowed back into him in the wake of knowledge.

It was because of her.

And she had been in this flat last night . . .

Unknown key. But key to salvation. He took it in his right hand and, reaching up, bending his wrist at an acute angle, guided its diminutive tip into the window-lock.

Wiggled it gently . . .

Praise be to cowboy contractors and their development-corporation backhanders. The lock clicked with no resistance. He jammed his keyring back into his pocket and turned the window-handle.

One last manoeuvre: reach down, without slicing his arm off on glass shards, to lift the window-latch. Luckily he was tall, long-limbed.

It was done. He pushed at the frame from inside with his fingertips, and the window swung open.

A last glance round; but the mental dwarfs that were the late twentieth-century's version of humanity were all hooked up to their saline drip of technology, and were not to be disturbed by anything short of a meteorite making a direct hit on their Hitachi hovels. He grasped the sill, hauled himself up, clambered on to the sink, dropped.

He was in.

He swung the window to, carefully; just a couple of glass fragments fell outwards. He closed his eyes and took several deep breaths.

The smell of *his* kitchen swarmed into his head, the smell of another life — private, intimate, multi-layered. For a moment he felt giddy with the sheer pressure of it.

His kitchen. Nick — though it was an abomination to think of the name in that way, so casually and blandly, as if he knew this 'Nick', as if this 'Nick' were a part of his life, as if this 'Nick' were to be considered as a person instead of the blackest stroke of all the harsh black-slashed strokes that made up the ghastly monochrome of his life since the catastrophe.

'Nick' — the one who had been granted access to all the secret places of her being. The places that *he* had known — the places that he was the *right* one to know, of all the men in the world — and surely she must realize that, even now — in fact, wasn't that why she had run away from him, because it was just too perfect, the thing they had together was just so perfect that it was frightening?

Yes, that was surely it. Something so *right* was frightening. He could see that. But just let him have the chance, and he knew he could convince her that she needn't be afraid . . .

But of course there was 'Nick'. And it was 'Nick's' domestic air that he was breathing at this moment, the smell of 'Nick's' washing and 'Nick's' cooking and 'Nick's' aftershave and God knew what else . . .

He gulped, hawked, and spat on the kitchen floor. He opened his eyes and looked at his saliva pooled and bubbling on the tiles.

So it was Nick who had access to the secret places of her being . . . but *he* had access to *Nick's* secret places now.

He studied the kitchen, eyes flicking. A cornflakes box, oh, and tea-towels hung up to dry with pictures of stockpots and bowls of fruit on them: how very fucking bourgeois, Nick dear; last of the red-hot lovers. Mugs on the draining board. Two to be precise. And on one of them —

Was that a trace of lipstick? That was surely a trace of lipstick on the rim and that must be *her* lipstick . . .

He seized the mug and pressed the rim to his mouth. A vision, sharp as sixties technicolour, of her sipping from this mug —

He jerked, stopped. Perhaps it wasn't lipstick — perhaps it was just some discolouration in the glaze — perhaps this was *Nick's* mug that was pressed to his lips . . .

Grunting, he threw the mug away from him. It smashed against the edge of the worktop.

Which was good. Because what was being here all about? Being here was all about feeling better, getting even, letting off some of the steam that threatened to destroy him with its squealing pressure. Being here was about entering the place where she was apparently so deliriously happy with Mr Wonderful and *trashing* the place.

There was a spice-rack standing on the worktop. He removed each jar singly, dropped them on the floor. The spilled spices made rainbow colours like poster paint. He picked up a sharp piece of one of the jars and used it to slash through the calendar hanging on the door —

Stopped. A word written on the calendar attacked his eyes.

Amanda.

He threw the piece of glass down, held the torn pieces of the page together.

Underneath today's date, Saturday 17 October, were written the words 'Amanda away'. An arrow was drawn through to the next weekend.

He stared with passionate interest at the two felt-tipped words and the scrawled arrow, hearing his own rapid breathing.

Her name her name using her name how dare he how dare he . . . ?

He flipped through the slashed pages, looking for more.

Her name does he whisper her name does he cry out her name as he penetrates her as he comes inside her does he call out AMANDA AMANDA

does he?

DOES HE?

He ripped the calendar off the door, threw it down, kicked at it.

Amanda away, Amanda actually away from lover-boy for a whole week, Nick-the-fucking-stud-nurse actually having to go a whole week without her: well, poor old Nick, somebody give him a peanut . . .

He flung open the door from the kitchen.

And froze.

It was so like a physical blow that he flinched, feeling the tender nerves and muscles of his face tauten and twitch. It was as if the flat were hitting back at him for his breaking into it. It was horrible.

It was the sight of the bed.

An unmade sofa-bed, filling a good part of the floor-space of the studio flat's one room. A rumpled duvet hastily thrown across it. Two pillows, one each side.

This was it. This was where they . . .

He took trembling, weak, kittenish steps towards the bed. He could not have approached it more cautiously, with more wild terror and surmise in his brain, if it had been a sleeping lion.

He stopped, at last, by the bedside. He felt something crunch beneath his shoe.

He bent to pick the object up. He stared at it with the same molten concentration he had given the words on the calendar.

It was an earring.

A thundering cataract of memory engulfed him. He knew this earring. He knew everything she wore. He knew every single item; give him a pad of paper and he could have drawn every one right now right down to the smallest detail, right down to the last button, the last seam, the last earring . . .

The earring was warm: warm from his own fingers. But he could fancy it was warm from resting against her neck. He was so close to her at this moment, closer than he had been since the end

no not the end

and yet further away, further away even than in his worst nightmares because he was standing by the bed where she . . .

With a convulsive movement he flung the duvet back. Stared at the tortuous, writhing sheet.

Bile scorched his gullet. He crammed his knuckles against his lips to stop himself being sick.

The searing comets raced more frenetically

across his mind, blinding and mad.

He swung himself about, putting the hell-sight behind him. There was a chair, but he couldn't sit on that. He crossed the room unsteadily and sat down on the floor, his back to the bed.

He put his fingers to his temples and closed his eyes for several minutes.

When he opened them again he was calmer, but it was a dead calm, a lunar landscape. He studied the room without much interest: he had seen all that mattered now, he had seen the hideous black cancerous cells at its heart. His eye fell coldly on a cheap, chain-store desk. This, then, was an example of Nick-the-nurse's taste —

Letters.

He leapt to his feet and dragged open the desk drawers.

Letters, there might be letters, she might have written letters to lover-boy . . .

He raked through bills and bank statements, tossing them into the air.

Letters . . . letters signed with love and kisses . . .

Letters mentioning him, perhaps?

The thought that she might talk to Nick about him sent the comets whizzing faster.

What did she say about him? Did she mention that he had devoted his whole life to her, that he had offered her an intensity of love that gave meaning back to that debased word, that what they had had together redeemed this putrescent corpse of a world and was the only thing that made it worth preserving?

Or did she betray him, tattle his secrets, lay his memory out before her new lover to be laughed at and trampled upon?

He pulled the last drawer all the way out of the desk and hurled it across the room.

No letters. Perhaps Superstud Nick couldn't read. Perhaps Superstud Nick was just your regular late-twentieth-century guy, meaning a shit-for-brains swaggerer who talked about cars and thought he was having a cultural evening if he watched *Columbo* all the way through. Perhaps having a relationship with Superstud Nick didn't mean sharing your thoughts and your fears and your dreams and turning the dross of human life to gold by mingling your souls but just getting laid every night and perhaps that was where he had gone wrong perhaps that was why he had been ditched and thrown on the scrapheap —

His hands were reaching for the telephone to rip it out of its socket and smash it when he was abruptly stopped again. This time by the realization that there was an answering-machine, switched on.

No letters.

But she surely phoned Nick, sometimes.

He pressed the button to replay calls. Stood, amongst a litter of papers, one hand resting on the desktop.

And listened.

He was quite still. When her voice spoke he did not start, or react at all. This, like their love, was just one of those things that were meant to be.

Her voice. A good line, hardly distorted at all. He was so close to her . . . she might have been here in the room with him.

Her voice, speaking to him . . . and speaking to him none the less because she supposed she was speaking to Nick. It was him who was listening, and that was the way it should be. Always.

And if only he could speak to her in return . . . if only he could be alone with her, talk to her, explain to her . . .

"It's a bummer having to work Saturdays, isn't it? Well, I mean for you, I don't think this counts as work what I'm doing. I feel like I've walked on to a set for 'Dynasty' . . . And the food Alix and Ben left me . . . They got off OK this morning, by the way . . . Actually it's pretty lonely here — well, you know, it's lovely, but it's so remote and quiet . . . "

It was only when she laughed, at the noise of the cock crowing, that he reacted, closing his eyes and tightening his fists. He knew that laugh so well. That laugh belonged to *him*. How could she give it to this Nick, how could she *give* it to him . . . ?

"Anyway, here I am, better get used to it . . . No, it is lovely here, but I just wish — well, I wish you were here with me . . . "

He could hear her breaths, crackling slightly in the phone receiver. Like the breaths of lips against your ear, the tonguey, amplified breaths of lovemaking, clogged and heavy.

" . . . By the way, you can't think of a Gilbert and Sullivan opera that starts with P that isn't

133

Pirates of Penzance, HMS Pinafore *or* Patience, *can you? It's driving me mad . . . "*

"*Princess Ida,*" he said out loud, smiling. "It's *Princess Ida,* my darling."

"*Bye, duck . . . This tape will self-destruct in five seconds . . . "*

He switched the machine off. For some moments, motionless, he just let the echo of her voice fill his head.

Her voice. Hearing it again, he knew, with wonderful simplicity, that he could not live without that voice.

But he must let the echo die at last, because the words spoken by that voice had started a trail of memory that he must follow.

"*Alix and Ben . . . "*

The trail was fresh. He might be unable to remember where that little key came from, but where she was concerned there was no forgetting. There was the tragedy of it: other, commonplace lovers even forgot birthdays, anniversaries. He remembered everything. He remembered every word she had ever said to him. He remembered her mentioning an old schoolfriend called Alix, married to a man called Ben; he remembered her mentioning that Alix and Ben had some fabulous place on the Norfolk coast with holiday cottages attached.

Yes, the memory was perfect. And so *Amanda away* meant *Amanda at Alix and Ben's.* Looking after the place for them — that was plain from the phone call.

But there the trail went dead. He was close to her, yet not close at all. She was somewhere

134

in Norfolk. And he was still in hell.

And so that was where she was off to, so early this morning! And it was only afternoon, and already she had phoned Mr Wonderful Nick as if they had been apart for years!

Rage, against the man who possessed this flat — who possessed her — entered him again like a cold dagger.

The heavy glass ashtray went through the TV screen with a pleasing smash. The posters and prints — oh, Renoir, so original Nick dear, and Toulouse-Lautrec and good God, Waterhouse, why not go the whole tasteless hog and plaster your shithole with Atkinson Grimshaw moonlights? — ripped down from the walls with rich, snarling sounds. The dismal little Taiwanese squawk-box that pretended to be a hi-fi was soon reduced to its component parts. The collection of tapes — Jesus, cretinous pop music and bits of watery blues and jazz, did he make her listen to this trash, this just wasn't her style, how could they be compatible? — became a tangled mass of glistening brown ribbon. And the bookcase . . .

Well, he already had a pretty good idea of lover-boy's taste or lack of it, but it was still instructive to note his piddling collection of paperbacks as he tore at them. Doris Lessing, forsooth, and Fay Weldon, is this a New Man I see before me . . . ? Edmund White and David Leavitt, hallo-hallo, was this just a posey Gays-are-OK-by-me statement, or did it mean that Stud Nick wasn't averse to the odd fudge-nudger now and then . . . Oh, *Jewel in the Crown*, this

135

was more lover-boy's line, surely, anything that had been on TV and was nice and stodgy and middle-brow, yes, he got the picture . . . Oh, and of course, here were a few caring-sharing tomes about mental illness and nursing the handicapped, very fucking Mother Theresa, the self-righteous bastard probably thought he could walk on water, God he was going to be sick just from the *atmosphere* of this man, Casanova meets the Care Bears . . .

He stiffened, was still in an instant.

A noise in the corridor.

Ears cocked, mainlining adrenalin, he crouched and listened.

Footsteps coming towards the door —

(Hi you must be Nick)

— and stopping.

He felt the bones and tendons in his legs murmuring and grinding like overwound springs.

Sound of a key in a lock —

Not this one. Across the corridor, he would guess. Bang of a door closing, and a moment later the pulse of meathead music.

He breathed out. The interruption had halted the wild fugue in his brain, and he looked about him. Surveyed the chaos he had made here.

Enough?

But it wasn't enough. Nothing could be enough. Not as long as *she* was lost to him.

And here he had felt so close to her again . . . the signs of her presence, the sound of her voice . . . The thin, unending wail inside that was his loss of her, the tinnitus in his soul, had risen to screaming pitch.

136

Dully, he turned to the bookcase again, and his heart opened like a door.

Her writing. Her magical, never-to-be-forgotten writing met his eye. It was on a folded sheet of notepaper, propped up on top of the bookcase.

His hand trembled as he reached out to take it. Those funny tails she put on her *g*s and *y*s . . . he knew them so well, had kept every scrap of her writing, treasured them . . .

He must steel himself. This note would surely be addressed to Nick: there might be endearments, professions of love, even obscenities —

(I can't wait for you to fuck me again like you fucked me last night)

— and so he must be prepared for pain before he read it.

Even so, to think that she had touched this piece of paper just recently . . .

He slowly unfolded it, and read. At first he did not understand.

HOW TO GET TO UPPER BOCKHAM. *Take A47 as far as King's Lynn. At K. Lynn get on to A148 (Cromer road) at ring-road. Follow A148 through Fakenham and on to* HOLT. *On leaving Holt turn left at the first junction — there's a pub and sign saying* SHERINGHAM PARK *and* KELLING. *Follow this road (through woods) and then take the FIRST RIGHT TURN. This leads you to Lower Bockham (the village). Carry on through the village and turn at the road next to the church. This leads you down to* UPPER BOCKHAM, *hooray, and ME. Confused? you will be!*

137

Now he understood.

He read the note again, and smiled. She was always very good at giving directions and things like that — very clear-headed.

He folded the note and put it carefully in his breast pocket. He gave the trashed place a quick last glance before heading back to the kitchen window. It looked good, but really it didn't matter any more. His heart felt like a balloon.

He pushed open the kitchen window, hopped up on to the sink. Just to be sure, he patted his breast pocket. Felt the rustle. Yes, it was there.

"Darling," Ewan said quietly.

7

NICK was late getting away from work, and already the current of Saturday night was beginning to crackle through the streets. Cars were reckless throbbing sound-systems, adorned with dangling, tapping, ringed hands. Behind lighted windows, raucous mating-game TV programmes were setting the tone, and there was a mass squirting of hairspray in a thousand bedrooms. Older people obeyed an unheard curfew and hurried away from the city centre, where soon the tribes of the young would hold their corroboree — the Whitesocks, the Tealegs, the Patchoulis, the Political Monkeyboots, the People of the *Sun*. Bouncers stood sentry in pub doorways, shoulders brushing the jambs; bar staff slipped into the nightclubs by their uniquely seedy back-ways, which looked like the morning-after would feel. A great tuning-up was in the air, which would culminate in a night-town crescendo, a *tutti* of dance-floor pounding, the crash of tills, the tympani of fists, and the rattle of Durex machines.

Home, home, home: that was Nick's one thought. It had been a tiring day, the residents in lively form and one cherubic charmer named Leslie an especial handful when he discovered that pouring jugs of water down Nick's collar got an interesting reaction. Home, home, home: he wanted food and familiar things and he wanted to ring Amanda. Unfortunately he knew that he was nearly out of exasperating necessities like milk and bread and toilet paper, so there would be a further delay while he shopped.

He stopped at an Asian mini-supermarket on the fringe of the city centre. It stocked everything in the world and never closed. He added a four-pack of beer to his survival kit and headed for the till, pausing to glance at the video-racks. The covers said it all: men pointed guns, women pointed their breasts, and Macaulay Culkin pointed the case for infanticide. He moved on, but the pause cost him more time than he thought, because it meant that he bumped into Lisa Dickinson.

Lisa was Amanda's flatmate. She was an imposingly large and beautiful young woman from whom, at first sight, you automatically expected statuesque reserve. Instead you got a delightfully down-to-earth character with a Brummy burr and a bawdy laugh that rattled the light-fittings. Nick liked her a lot. But she was very talkative.

"Yeah, saw her off this morning, dead early it was, I was just getting stuck into the All-Bran myself. She looked pretty rough, actually, I don't know what the pair of you had been doing, but it looked like it takes it out of you, not that I can talk, I look like an elephant's backside in the mornings, well, I look like an elephant's backside at night as well, but at least an elephant's backside with a bit of lipstick slapped on it. I don't know, isn't it a pain shopping, I wish we could just take our food in on a drip, d'you know what I mean? Save all the bother. Then at night you could stick a bottle of gin on your drip and be well away. It seems funny in the flat without her, twanging away on her guitar, hearing that always makes me want to stick a rose in my teeth and stamp around, d'you know what I mean? Apparently it's dead posh this place she's looking after, but right in the middle of nowhere, I mean, shit, what can you do out there, they reckon everybody there lives till they're about a hundred or something but I reckon it just *feels* like that. That reminds me, did I tell you my dad's selling his house? Yeah, he wants to go back to Jamaica. I says to him, what are you going to do there, he says I'm going to sit on the porch and watch the sun go down, I says you can do that here, the sun goes down in Billingham just the same, and anyway how are you going to watch *Neighbours* every day there like you do here? There's him talking about flying back to Jamaica and he won't even go round the corner shop when the soaps are on because he doesn't trust the video, d'you know what I mean . . . ?"

Home, home, home: meeting Lisa sharpened the longing, because it reminded him of Amanda. And the first thing he was going to do when he finally got in was ring Amanda: dump the groceries on the floor and grab that phone. In the intervals of being doused by Leslie today, he had done a bit of thinking, and the conclusions that thinking had led him to could be expressed in the words *Go for it*. He was crazy

141

about her, and there was no point in behaving otherwise. If he was being clingy she would soon let him know. This business of watching everything he said and did in case it was too heavy was just plain ridiculous. It reminded him of a toy he had had as a child — an ingeniously jointed, spring-loaded plastic model of a mule. You took turns at hanging little plastic shovels and lanterns and coils of rope on the old mule's saddle, and when you put too many of them on, or did it too heavy-handedly, KICK! went the mule, bucking its hind legs in very convincing fashion and throwing the whole lot off with a clatter.

And if he was going to approach his relationship with Amanda as if it were a grown-up version of that toy, then he should never have got into it in the first place. He would regret it if he pushed it too far and she asked him to cool off, but he would regret it a hell of a lot more if he acted so inhumanly strong-and-silent that he lost her.

So that was that.

Phoning her, of course, was going to be as frustrating as satisfying. The sound of her voice would be like one of those itches that always occur in the one spot of your back that you cannot reach with either hand. The sound of her voice, in fact, was going to make him want to put his arms round her and hold her; but that didn't matter. Even the feeling of missing Amanda beat most feelings life had to offer. And OK, so he was hearkening to the rattle of the slop-bucket, but that didn't matter either.

He was in a corny state. He was so full of corn and slop just now that you could have extruded him and turned him into a million packs of salt'n'vinegar snacks.

Of course, people did end up like that toy mule sometimes, when they got very Involved. The whole thing got so heavy that they just flipped and sent everything flying. And you didn't have to go to Shakespeare to find instances of love and death bloodily mingled — just turn the pages of a Sunday newspaper. It was a state of mind he couldn't understand, perhaps because his instincts had always been to withdraw, to cut his losses and back off. The tumultuous house of his upbringing, vibrating with six children as well as two very full voiced and expansive parents, had been instrumental in that. Physically, there had been nowhere to go in that house when things got on top of you, no room to retreat to that wasn't already full of people and bicycles and dogs. So he had had to learn to make the space in his head. And once you had built and furnished that back room in your mind, you always had somewhere to go when things got rough.

Coward's way out, maybe. And in the past women had seemed to sense when he was retreating into that room, and got infuriated by it. One, who had begun by liking his calmness, had eventually called it downright inhuman. That had shaken him. Was he, in fact, the coldest of cold fishes? But even as he had wondered that, he had been settling down in the back room and closing the door on his accuser. So he supposed the habit was fixed. His emotional gearbox had three reverse gears, period.

But with Amanda he didn't need the back room at all: the place was thick with dust, he hadn't been in there for weeks. In fact he couldn't see himself wanting to go in there at all. It was a little scary, this new development in his life, but fine too. It was damned fine.

Home, home, home . . . He left the city centre behind, heading out for the townships along the bleach-lit parkways with their sad spreading of hedgehog pâté. Local radio, dimming and swelling as he passed beneath the flyovers, accompanied him. The squeaky DJ was conducting his Saturday evening romantic-requests programme, avowals across the airwaves. Siobhan says she loves Andy very much . . . Darren says he's sorry Lynne, can they try again . . . Natasha says are you listening, Paul, tonight's the night . . . Home, home, home . . .

Lurking teen-shapes infested the car-park outside the block of flats. Hanging Around, the one leisure activity for which the estate offered ample amenities. They left pockets of silence as he walked by, but he sensed their disinterest: he was glad to be twenty-eight, to them a nothing age. Older, and you carried a potential threat of authority: younger, and you were a rival to be clocked up, your every fashion detail a challenge.

He entered by the main security door, glanced in at the community room. George was there as usual, but in a condition that Nick recognized: the old man had remembered to take his medication at last, had probably taken two doses because he had missed the morning one, and was in a state of dreamy vacancy. He gave Nick a beatific smile and raised a hand.

"You OK, George?"

"M'all right." George smiled again, then frowned as if on the point of remembering something. "Eh, Nick . . . "

"Yes?"

"You . . . got a grey Cortina."

"That's me."

George gazed vaguely about him, shook his head at last and broke into the smile again. "Y'all right? I'm all right. I'm doing good. Yeah . . . "

Nick waited, but George was adrift again, peacefully.

"OK then, George. Take care. See you."

"All riiight . . . "

Nick passed down the corridor through a web of cooking smells. What should he eat tonight? He had those cheapo burgers in the freezer, but even he had to admit they looked and tasted like something a dog would choose to roll in. Oh, he'd eat later. Ring Amanda first.

He put the key in the lock of his door. Home, home, home . . .

He swung open the door, stepped into the little kiosk of a hall. Needing to pee, he opened the bathroom door, then halted.

He could feel a draught. Surely he hadn't been

so fuddled this morning as to leave a window open?

The door to the living-cum-bedroom was slightly ajar. Feeling cold, feeling horribly sure, he pushed it open.

His bag of groceries fell from his hand.

"Oh, Jesus . . . "

8

SHE had been turning lights on and had been surprised at how good it made her feel. It was like recapturing some of the exultation that must have thrilled through early man when he manipulated fire — the conquest of darkness, triumph over the oldest enemy.

Most of the farmhouse was lit up and the curtains drawn: the rooms looked like stacked boxes of warmth when she went out into the yard to lock the garage. She looked up at the sky. Autumn evening coming down with the physicality of a vast blanket; probably unnoticeable in town, but a great, peremptory fact out here. The encircling woods were seeping and melting into the elder darkness. Soon the rich dusk-colours would become blackness, and this would be the only island of light.

Amanda went back into the house and located the switches for the external lights in the hall. There was a line of them in a metal box on the wall: big, chunky switches that made a satisfying *thunk* when she snapped them on with the heel of her hand.

She opened the front door again. Lights blazed down from roof-mountings, all around the L-shape formed by the outhouses, making the courtyard a cube of bright daylight.

Take that, darkness.

But she wasn't finished yet. The cottages had

147

an external light in the courtyard that came on automatically, but there was still the leisure complex, a solider block of darkness up the service road. She hesitated. Couldn't she just lock it up for the night? But then it was only just gone half-past six. The Howards might arrive any moment now, and might not think it unreasonable to expect the facilities to be open. They might want just to fling their cases into Honeysuckle Cottage and leap into the pool or the jacuzzi. You could never tell.

So she ought to go up there and turn on the lights and make sure the place was OK. But what if Nick rang in the meantime? Of course, she could always ring him, but she supposed when he got in from work he would check the answering machine and then ring her, and . . .

"Tish poo," she said. "Pish tush." Get a grip of yourself girl. It wouldn't take a minute. It must have been all of fifty yards to the leisure complex.

And it wasn't as dark as she had thought, leaving the farmhouse behind and walking up the service road. Dark, but not that dark. She could make out the gently stirring shapes of the ornamental shrubs alongside the road. And the large plate-glass windows of the leisure complex reflected the light from the farmhouse below. As for the quiet out here . . . Well, it was quiet all right. Her footsteps on the asphalt rang out like the strokes of a swift hammer.

Here we are. She unhooked the great ring of keys from her belt, and swore. It would have made more sense to have singled out the right ones before leaving the light behind. Clever. She peered at the tags in the dimness. Did that say LC? Must be.

She separated the key, tried it in the lock of the main door of the leisure complex. It was a glazed door, and there was a figure standing on the other side of it looking out at her.

Amanda's entire digestive system seemed to squeeze flat. She sucked a coppery mouthful of air and stepped back. The figure stepped back too, pointing something at her.

It was the reflection of the bunch of keys, grasped in the figure's hand, that she recognized first.

Her own reflection.

Feeling as stupid as if she had been observed, she briskly turned the key in the lock and stepped inside. The hum of the pool plant was immediately audible, though something told her that it was one of those noises you only consciously heard at night, like the refrigerator, like the creaking of the stairs. She thought back to Alix's instructions on the pinboard. Switch box to the right of the lobby, that was it.

She found the box, switched on. The building filled with light. Ahead of her was a glazed door with matching side screens, opening into the swimming-pool area. To the left, timber steps led up to the upper level, where the gym and solarium were. She went through the glazed door to the pool area, compelled to admire. This was the place that always featured most prominently in the brochures for Upper Bockham, and gave it the edge over other cottage complexes along the coast. Not just the thirty-foot pool, irregularly shaped like a jigsaw piece with Greek tiles surrounding it; the design of the whole place was striking. The ceiling was open, vaulted, and clad in light pine, with broad skylights. At the far end the jacuzzi nestled in a stone surround, and more timber steps led up to the sauna and the changing rooms, pine again. Admittedly it did rather make Amanda think of the sort of place Scandinavian porn movies were filmed in, but it certainly did not have that dismal fishy atmosphere that clung to most indoor swimming pools, redolent of kids' wee and verrucas.

Well, here it was if the Howards wanted it. They would have it all to themselves, in fact, and could romp about just like in those movies if the fancy took them.

As she and Nick could have. Now there was a thought. Well, maybe not *exactly* like in those movies. She balked, for example, at wearing nothing but a pair of strappy slingbacks, styling her hair with curling-tongs, and cultivating a large red spot on her behind.

She left the leisure complex and made her way back to the farmhouse, wondering how it was that it had got so much darker in just those few moments. When, she wondered, did the owls clock on for the night? Was she going to be treated to her first blood-curdling screech while she was creeping about out here?

And the foxes. Don't forget the coughing foxes.

Yes, all right. Thanks for reminding me . . . In fact, as she came into the blessed light of the farmhouse courtyard, she thought she could hear something — a sound so faint it felt like a tickling on her eardrums.

Phone.

She pelted into the house. She almost knocked the phone off its table snatching up the receiver.

"Hello?"

"Hello, Amanda? Only me."

"Nick! How you doing? Have you been ringing long? — only I was outside, I came running in when I heard it . . . " She was glad she wasn't near a mirror, because she knew she must be wearing a big goofy grin.

"No, not long . . . How's things with you?"

"Oh, fine. It's seemed like a long day. Did you get my message?"

"Hm? Oh no, I haven't replayed the . . . Thing is, things are in a bit of a mess here. Would you believe I've had a break-in?"

"What? Oh, Nick, no . . . "

"I know. Got home from work a few minutes ago to find the place — well, it's one hell of a mess. They got in through the kitchen window."

"Christ, in daylight as well . . . "

"Amazing, isn't it? Well, it's not really, I mean it's always happening round here, the place is so dodgy. I've just been lucky so far. Looks like my luck ran out."

"Did they take anything?"

"Well, not as far as I can tell. Like I say, the place has been really turned over. I've found my building society passbook and stuff like that . . . It looks as if they just decided to trash the

151

place, basically. The stereo and the TV are all smashed up, and . . . things like that."

"Oh, Nick, you poor love . . . " Her heart ached for him. She could tell how upset he was from the gruff perplexed note in his voice: he was one of those men who got quieter and more correct the closer they were to tears. "Have you called the police? Not that it's much good now."

"Yes, they're on their way. Just thought I'd give you a ring in the meantime and . . . well, give you the good news. Sorry. Not much fun for you, having to listen to it."

"It doesn't matter about me . . . I just wish I could be there with you. Damn, why did I have to be in this damn place today of all days? You must be feeling terrible."

"Well, none of it was worth much. I'm not exactly Mr Hi-Tech. And there's none of — well, you know, when you hear about these things, often they spray stuff on the walls and piss on the carpet and all that, and it's not that bad. Just vandalism, I suppose. It's just . . . it's just the thought that somebody's been in here, do you know what I mean?"

"It's horrible. I'd hate that, I'd really hate it . . . Kids, do you think?"

"Probably. They're always lurking about round these places. I know you shouldn't pin it on them like that, but it's hardly likely to be the work of the local Women's Institute."

"No . . . " She laughed distressfully. "God, I wish I could — I wish Scotty could beam me up, so I could be with you right now."

"Same here . . . I don't know though. I've got the police coming, and you know what they're like. Talk to you as if it's you who committed the crime."

"I know what you mean." Most policemen made her want to scream and throw things: she sometimes felt that even the trigger-happy hands-against-the-wall-fellah paranoia of the American cop was preferable to the crooning, sneering, death's-head jocularity of the British bobby. "God, Nick, I wish you could be out of that place."

"So do I. Christ, so do I. But how can I? I mean how can I? They won't give you a transfer unless you pop out a few kids — as far as they're concerned you're housed and that's your lot. I can't afford anywhere else, I can't afford to buy . . . I'm just stuck."

"I know," she said unhappily. Again she perceived how upset he was, because he would never speak in that slightly snappy way otherwise. "Didn't anybody in the block hear anything or see anything?"

"Don't think so. Nobody's said, anyway. And the warden's nowhere to be found as usual. But you know what it's like here: keep your head down if you think you hear trouble. I've done it myself, I'm afraid." He sighed, and Amanda seemed to feel the expelled breath on her skin — wished she could, longed for him. "Sorry, love," he went on. "I've hardly asked about you. Are you OK there? Did you manage to get there on time?"

"Yes, I'm fine, really. I feel awful, because

153

there I was all ready to whine about how lonely it is here, and there's you coming home to something like that . . . "

"Well, it probably looks worse than it is. It won't be so bad once I've cleared up. I don't suppose there was anything on TV tonight anyway, was there?"

Her laugh was even more tremulous this time. "Don't think so. I did have a look in the paper a little while ago to see what was on, but there was only Cilla Black, and some Agatha Christie effort, and . . . oh, another showing of *Fatal Attraction* with the dirty bits cut out."

"I'm not missing anything then."

"Not really." A silence, which she wished to fill with a love she somehow felt disabled from expressing.

And you want to say 'Have my TV have my stereo' but not just that what you really want to say is let's get a place together and watch the same TV and listen to the same stereo and sod it if that makes us the dreaded Couple because that's what you want and it would be so good . . .

"Are you OK, Nick?" she said suddenly. Laughed again. "Sorry, I really blurted that, didn't I?"

She heard him laugh too. 'Blurt' was one of their words, as in one of those words that produced a foolish hilarity in both of them. It suggested hoary school stories. *'You're a horrid pig, Margot,' blurted Angela, seizing her lacrosse stick.*

"Yes," Nick said, "I'm OK. Like I say, it'll

soon be cleared up. I shouldn't have told you about it, really."

"Oh, you should, don't say that," she said. Reproachful, rather than hurt, but already they had fallen into a small hole of misunderstanding. "If you can't tell me . . . "

"No, but you know what I mean. I didn't want to worry you."

"You haven't. Well, you have, but . . . Oh, bugger, what a horrible situation."

"It is, isn't it? I wish you weren't there."

"I wish I wasn't here too . . . " She stopped. This was rapidly turning into one of those elliptical, incomprehensible lovers' conversations. "I just hope they catch the bastards who did it."

"So do I, but I can't see it. Oh, well, it's not the end of the world. I suppose I'll have to get that window boarded up for tonight. I think I've got some bits of hardboard somewhere . . . There's the intercom, that'll be the police. Amanda, I'll have to go — I'll ring you back when they've gone, shall I? Have to go . . . "

"OK . . . Love you," she said, but he had already put the phone down.

She wandered into the kitchen, wretched with the feeling of not being able to hold him. 'There's a space between my arms that's just your size' — she was sure there was a country-and-western song with that title.

What a rotten thing to happen. She hoped he wouldn't spend the evening on his own. When he rang back, she must urge him to call a friend or one of his brothers and have them over. He

155

shouldn't be alone, after that.

She wished she'd been a bit more help, too, instead of just going oh dear oh dear. In fact they hadn't communicated very well at all, they had been tuned off the beam somehow. But then, everything in their lives had been hunkydory so far: the great tester of relationships was misfortune. If you started tearing at each other the very first time God decided to piss on your chips, then you weren't going to be buying many anniversary cards.

She wandered the house, feeling sorry for Nick, wondering how his encounter with the Billingham constabulary was going, imagining how much supercilious offensiveness they would be managing to squeeze into the words, *And when was this, sir?* She realized she had forgotten to ask him whether he was insured. She doubted he would be, somehow. For such a compact, self-contained person, there were areas of his life that were curiously shambolic. He couldn't add up in his head; he had never learned to swim; he couldn't read a road map to save his life; he didn't possess a corkscrew or a pair of scissors or a wristwatch.

He did have extremely nice hands, though. They . . .

If there was no insurance, she could maybe dip into her savings and get him a portable TV. Once the grockles were settled, she could drive into Norwich on Monday and pick one out: if it was a chainstore she could order one from the Billingham branch, have it delivered . . .

Her ears pricked. Was that the sound of a

156

car? The Howards at last?

She listened. And to think that it was she who had been getting the creeps and lighting the place up like a Christmas tree, while it was Nick who had the break-in . . . Perhaps the country was the safe place to be after all . . .

There was the sound again. Not a car, but the discreet whoosh of the central heating firing itself up.

Her wanderings brought her to the bookcase in the lounge, and she stopped to look for something to take to bed with her tonight; she had forgotten to bring her own reading in the rush this morning. Something undemanding; sleep-inducing, preferably, because on top of the strangeness of her situation there was now worry about Nick, and she was going to be wide-eyed.

Some weighty stuff: so it was Ben who actually bought those hardback biogs that were reviewed in the Sunday heavies. Darwin, Benjamin Britten, Trollope. But those might turn out to be interesting, and what she really needed was something completely anodyne in its nullity, a book with which it was a matter of total indifference to you whether you turned the next page or not, a book like the ones written by machine in *1984*, a book devoid of mind and heart, the printed equivalent of thru-the-night TV . . .

Ah! the very thing. If all else failed, a few pages of Mary Wesley could always be relied on to summon the sandman at the double. She wouldn't need to anaesthetize herself with Ben's brandy after all . . .

She let the book fall as the phone rang again.

That was quick, if the police had gone already . . .

"Hello, Nick?"

"Sorry to disappoint you."

She had so expected it to be Nick that she did not recognize the voice for a moment.

"Who's . . . Oh, Sue, it's you, I'm sorry! I mean, I'm not sorry it's you, I just . . . "

"I reckon you'd better start all over again," said Sue. "How you diddling down there? Everything OK?"

"Yes, everything's fine. These Howards still haven't turned up yet, though."

"Probably the traffic getting out of London. Listen, duck, can I ask you a big favour?"

"Ask away."

"Well, we got a bit of trouble. John's mother's been taken ill."

"Oh, dear, not badly I hope?"

"It don't sound too good. Though she have had turns before. She's in a home over Dereham way — they just rung us. We're going to drive down there straight away, but the thing is there's Jamie. Thass not going to be any fun for him, taking him down there, especially if his grandma's really poorly, do you know what I mean? There's Tom and Gladys in the village who'd look after him, but they're getting on and they got these two bloody great Dobermanns and Jamie isn't keen — I can't blame him, I'm frit to death of 'em myself, So I wondered . . . "

"Sue, that's not a big favour, it'll be a

pleasure. Only thing is, I can't leave here till the Howards arrive, if you want me to come up to yours."

"Well, if it's all right with you, we could bring him over. That farmhouse is just about his favourite place in the world anyway, and he loves you. I can't swear he won't be any trouble, because he might make a liar of me — "

"I'm sure he won't be. Really, I'll be glad to have him. I'll be glad of the company. And I'm flattered — you know, that you trust me with him."

Memory took a vicious swipe at her: memory of her father, grief-stricken, losing control, yelling at her . . . *You should have taken proper care of Mark . . . but you didn't, did you . . . ?*

"I don't know how long we'll be," Sue was saying. "Depends how things are with poor old John's mum. I'll ring you when we get there and find out how the land lies."

"Don't worry — don't feel you have to hurry back. If it gets late, I can always tuck Jamie up on the settee or something. I know Alix and Ben wouldn't mind a bit."

"Thanks, Amanda. If you're sure it's no bother . . . We're just getting ready now, so we should be there soon. Sorry I wasn't Nick, by the way. You waiting to hear from him?"

"Oh — yes, just a quick call, you know." No point in airing more bad news.

"I'll get off the line then. We'll be round soon. And thanks again."

She had spoken nothing but the truth; she

159

would be glad as hell to have some company, especially now with her mind dwelling sadly on Nick and chafing at her inability to help him. It would be good having Jamie here; it would take her out of herself, stop her gnawing.

The Gibsons' van was drawing up in the courtyard within a few minutes. Jamie had the look of a boy who has recently had his hair forcibly combed.

"This is nice of you, duck. Sorry about the short notice," John Gibson said. That same preoccupied, polite note in his voice, stifling emotion, that there had been in Nick's: she felt piercingly sorry for him.

"I'm glad to help. Don't worry about anything here. We'll be all right, won't we, Jamie?"

"You make sure you behave yourself," Sue said, giving Jamie a kiss. She was wearing a very un-Sue like headscarf: Amanda guessed she must have been in the midst of doing her hair, a home tint or something, when the call came. Trivial domestic details suddenly blown apart by a crisis: she thought of Mark's Disney comic lying on the coffee table. No, she mustn't think of Mark. "Like I said, I don't know how long we'll be," Sue went on, getting back into the van. "I'll give you a ring."

"No problem. I hope everything'll be all right. Drive safely."

Two agitated faces in the lit windscreen of the van as it turned in the courtyard: mustered smiles, and waves to Jamie standing solemn beside Amanda in the porch. Then they were gone.

160

"Well! I didn't expect to be seeing you again so soon," Amanda said when the engine echoes had died away, and speaking with a breeziness that sounded phony even to her. "Let's go in, it's a bit nippy. What's in your bag?"

"My Game Boy," Jamie said.

"Oh, you'll have to let me have a go on it. Mind you, I shall be useless . . . I'm sure your nan'll be all right, you know."

"Yeah," he said uncomfortably, not looking at her. This, she could tell, was quite the opposite of indifference. A child in an American soap might look plaintively up into her face and say with a lump in his throat, "Grandmaw's going to be all right — isn't she?", but a real boy, who was really worried about what was going on, would throw up the shutters in just the way Jamie had done.

She would have to keep him entertained. It was a responsibility she was quite glad of — if she couldn't help Nick, she could at least compensate this way.

"Well, it's nice to have you here, anyway. I was a bit fed up on my own. Let's get some eats and make ourselves comfy."

Filling bowls with crisps and nuts and popcorn and carrying them through to the lounge gave him something to do and helped break the ice. She could tell that he was rather relieved to be here instead of going to see his sick nan, and that he felt guilty about it at the same time. She didn't blame him. Even if he had a fortunate life, it still wouldn't be so short of grim experiences that he had to

161

go looking for them when he was eight years old.

The TV schedule was uninspiring. They consulted Ben's video collection: Hollywood classics in the main. Jamie opted for Laurel and Hardy, reinforcing her good opinion of him.

It was only as the familiar cuckoo theme-music cranked up that she remembered that Laurel and Hardy had been favourites of Mark's.

Dear God.

Stop thinking about it. Stop thinking about it right now.

Jamie was licking his lips and getting the courage to ask something.

"You know *Fatal Attraction*'s on later?" he said tentatively.

She imitated Sue's Bugs Bunny. "Mmmm-yes?"

"Could we watch it?" Jamie asked, smiling and self-conscious.

"Were your mum and dad going to let you?"

From the way he nodded she guessed that the question had still been in the balance.

"I didn't get scared when I saw *Jurassic Park*," he said persuasively.

"Blimey, I did . . . Go on, then, you talked me into it." After all, she thought, the dirty bits had been cut out, and if he could stomach *Jurassic Park* he wouldn't be fazed by Glenn Close going apeshit with the cutlery. And besides, it was totally unreal; she didn't subscribe to this idea that kids couldn't distinguish between reality and fiction.

"Thanks." He settled back to Laurel and Hardy.

Amanda snacked, chuckled at the movie, thought about Nick. Would he be through with the police yet? Perhaps they had pulled someone in from the gangs of teens who roamed about the estate. Good, if so. Though even then, what had been done couldn't be undone. Someone had still thought it worth their while to break into an ordinary person's flat and wreck the place.

While Mr Hardy genteelly introduced his friend Mr Laurel, Amanda felt the squirming of a retroactive fear as she realized that the blank violence of modern life had reached out and touched them. You knew it was there, of course. Billingham, a Midland city of two hundred thousand people, had as much of it as anybody could want: just glance through the local papers. Two youths had pulled a paraplegic out of his wheelchair and thrown him into the river. Someone had set fire to a school's pet guinea-pigs. A father had swung his small son by the ankles and bashed him against the fridge door for spilling his Coke. It was there, a mad muttering beneath the chatter of normality. But it was remarkable how completely you could ignore it, until suddenly it decided not to ignore you.

Well, as Nick had said, it could have been worse, and it would soon be cleared up. But she couldn't help wondering: if someone could casually do a thing like that in broad daylight, what else might they do?

9

STUART and Fran Howard were tired of each other's company. As they were en route for a cottage holiday in which they would be exclusively in each other's company for a whole week, this was a bad sign.

They were driving north along the A11, and just approaching Norwich. The last time they had exchanged a word was some fifteen miles back, around Attleborough; and the words that they had exchanged then had turned the air blue.

This state of affairs was Stuart's fault, apparently. So he gathered. It usually was.

Fran Howard was looking steadily ahead of her at the unrolling road and giving him the profile shot. Giving him the profile shot was a term that he had mentally devised for those occasions in which she scrupulously avoided facing him whilst preserving a shining serenity. Someone who didn't know her as he did might have said she was merely sitting in the passenger seat and looking ahead at the road, and indeed the difference was subtle. It was also all the difference in the world. When she gave him the profile shot, he knew about it. When she gave him the profile shot, air-raid sirens howled and seismographs wobbled and thunderheads covered the sun.

He was going to have to say something. He

was going to have to put his head over the parapet and risk getting it shot off. By her standards this silence was quite modest in its dimensions, but you never knew: she might be going for a record.

He opened his mouth to speak; then hesitated, and passed it off as a cough. He had been about to ask whether she would like to stop off in Norwich for a drink, but a question like that was simply inviting a hail of machine-gun fire. For one thing, it was a Stupid Question, and he knew to beware of those. For another, it had the word drink in it, and Fran Howard, like Humpty Dumpty, could make words mean what she wanted them to mean. A 'drink', as taken by Fran with her friends with a lot of screaming and giggling, was a piece of harmless fun that just went to show how uptight men were; a 'drink', as taken or suggested or just mentioned as a mildly desirable thing by Stuart, was a symptom of incipient alcoholism, crass selfishness, intention to kill her with reckless driving, and hereditary delinquency. It was also an infallible reminder to her of someone called Richard, whom she had nearly married instead of him, and who besides being charming, fun, attractive and able to make love for hours on end, had never taken a 'drink' in his life.

So that, as an opening gambit, was somewhat comparable to putting his balls on the table and handing her a sledgehammer. He would have to think of something else.

The traffic? It was quite heavy, no doubt with yokels heading into Norwich for the Saturday

165

night hop with their best straw in their hair. But a reference to the heavy traffic might be construed as a reproach to her for their late start . . . and really, if he was just going to go on and on about that, she couldn't help it if she'd had an attack of cystitis just when they were ready to go . . . And *then* they would be on to the subject of women's plumbing and his utter insensitivity to its nuances . . .

Scrub the traffic. Unconsciously he sighed, and out of the corner of his eye he saw her stiffen, the bones in her wrist coming into prominence as her fingers clenched. Damn . . . the sigh was a bad move, the sigh could start anything, she could take the sigh in her elegant hands and turn it into a demonstration that he found her presence completely intolerable, and if that was the case then she might just as well be dead —

He snatched at the first thing that came to mind and said, "I wonder how Greg is."

She slowly turned her head.

Oh yes, well chosen, Stuart old boy. As acts of provocation went, that one made Pearl Harbor look like an innocent misunderstanding.

Fran, having completed the turn of her head, gave him a look. It was not her full-strength look — *that* was reserved for very special occasions, and it killed everything within a five-mile radius, poisoned the water-table, started firestorms, and mutated the livestock for the next three generations — but still it packed a wallop sufficient to make plants wither and goldfish float.

Having discharged the look she slowly turned her head back to its original position. Headlight beams roamed across the smooth planes of her face. Fine bone-structure, he thought randomly, good-looking woman still, if you didn't mind the black roots.

"Why?"

She came out with it so suddenly that he jumped.

"What do you mean, why?" he said.

She inhaled deeply, closing her eyes for several moments as she did so. He had christened this 'the Patient Grizelda Manoeuvre'.

"Why do you wonder?" she said at last, speaking as if to a very short-sighted lip-reader.

"I just wondered, that's all."

"You would."

If there was one thing he couldn't abide, it was that expression. It managed to be at once cryptic, insulting and unanswerable. And though it was a favourite of hers, it always took him by surprise. He would be expressing a perfectly uncontroversial admiration of a certain type of car or a house that was for sale, and out it would come: "You would." He would say in passing that he enjoyed such-and-such an article in the Sunday papers, and there it was again: "You would."

It infuriated him when she said that.

He said: "If I can't make a perfectly harmless remark — "

"It was not a perfectly harmless remark and you know it. Your exact words were 'I wonder how Greg is', when what you really meant was

167

'I wonder what he's up to'."

Stymied, he pretended to concentrate on the road for some moments. It amazed him, it never ceased to amaze him, how women could memorize everything you said. They could quote you verbatim from a conversation you couldn't even remember having. They had some sort of in-built stenography.

"Well, it's the same thing," he said, and then realized the magnitude of his error. He had been married for twenty-three years, and he ought to know by now that nothing is ever the same thing.

She had closed her eyes again, and was pinching the bridge of her nose between thumb and forefinger. This was a variation on the Patient Grizelda Manoeuvre, called 'the Blessed Martyr'.

She said: "It wouldn't be so bad if . . . "

"If what?"

She raised a graceful hand. "It doesn't matter. Forget it."

"No, come on. It wouldn't be so bad if what?"

She sighed, and he realized he had walked right into one of the oldest traps around. Leave remark unfinished, provoke a demand that it be finished, finish remark and then disclaim responsibility for it. *You did insist* . . . He cursed himself for falling for such a sucker punch.

Well, here it came. "It wouldn't be so bad," she said, "if you set any sort of example yourself."

168

"Oh, I'm sorry, I'm not a bloody codebreaker, I'm afraid you'll have to talk in language that makes some sort of bloody sense or we'll never get anywhere . . . " He was trying to sound brisk, but really he was bluffing, because here they were at the heart of the matter now and he knew it. The business of the waitress at the Little Chef, twenty miles back. He was a fool to think they wouldn't come back to it sooner or later. Quite incidentally he noticed that he had also shot himself in the foot with those 'bloodys'. Because, again, Fran could make words mean anything. A couple of 'bloodys' from him meant he was a man of violent temper and unforgivable coarseness, whereas letting fly with a torrent of 'fucks' when your nail varnish ran out at the third finger was, of course, Not The Same Thing.

"You know perfectly well what I mean." She lit a cigarette, with a parade of calm. "Why do you men have to be such skunks?"

He had to admire the sudden switch from the particular to the general. By nominating him as an apologist for the entire male sex, she forced him to fight on two fronts. But he wasn't going to be caught out like that this time.

"I really can't believe," he said, using one of her own weapons, the Voice of Exasperated Reason, "I really can't believe that you're still going on about that silly girl at the café. Surely not even you could be that obsessive."

"I love that. It's wonderful, it's priceless, it really is. 'Silly girl'. The way you put these women down even while you're trying to look

169

through their blouses. It just makes it even more obvious. That's what's so pathetic about it. Well, it's pathetic all round, really. She must have been, what, eighteen? Younger than Greg, for God's sake. Younger than your own son."

"At least she's working for her living." A diversionary move, that, because she had him sweating now.

"Oh, darling." Word-power again: Fran could invest that one word with a whole cosmos of contempt just by the faintest inflection. Mandarin Chinese was an unsubtle pidgin compared with Franspeak. "I think it's sad, really, that you resent your own son so much that you'd rather see him skivvying in a roadside café than going to university."

"Polytechnic. I know you tell your snob friends that he's at university, but you don't have to pretend to me, darling." But he was bitching on automatic: that crack about resenting his own son had got to him. Inhaling her smoke, wishing for a cigarette himself but refusing to put himself at the disadvantage of asking her to light him one, Stuart glowered. Resent Greg? Resent that monosyllabic changeling, with his odd herby smell and Artful Dodger clothes and gobbledygook textbooks, who periodically descended on them with a rucksack full of humming laundry only to spend the whole time on the phone to far-flung friends with incomprehensible nicknames? What was there to resent?

If the boy had been some sort of runaway success, then maybe . . . But Christ, look at him. Nearly twenty-one and he couldn't drive a car or put up a shelf or even change a plug. When Stuart was that age he was already digging for promotion and saving for the deposit on a house. Not footling about at an educational establishment where the chief component of the curriculum seemed to be the consumption of drugs. And constantly being defended by a mother who thought he could do no wrong . . .

Fran had returned to the attack. "It's the exhibitionism of it, that's what gets me."

"What?"

"I mean, I do realize," Fran said blandly, as if musing aloud, "that there's this strange compulsion to make a fool of yourself when anything in a skirt comes within ten feet of you. In a funny sort way I understand it. What I can't understand is why you have to do it so publicly. I suppose it's the same impulse that turns men into flashers."

NORWICH — A FINE CITY. He saw the phlegmatic welcome sign through a red haze of indignation. This was too much. Anybody would think she had caught him copping a feel of his secretary in an upstairs room at a party or something trite and sleazy like that. And all right, so she *had* caught him doing that once, but the point was that on this occasion there had really been nothing to it. In the Little Chef he had spilt some coffee on his trousers, and the waitress had brought him a cloth, and he had joked a bit with her while he was wiping himself down, and then joked a bit more with

171

her when they were leaving, and given her a hefty tip ... That was it. And yes, he had found her eminently fanciable, but it wasn't as if that showed ...

"Look, we're supposed to be going on holiday," was all he could find to say.

"Meaning?"

"Meaning we're supposed to be having a good time."

"You should have thought of that before you started ogling that girl."

You're losing this one, my old son, he thought. *You're losing this one by two falls and a submission.*

"I'm sorry," he said.

The trouble was, in the course of any fight there was an optimum moment for saying sorry. With careful judgement, and after a lot of experience, you could learn to pinpoint it. No matter how nasty the row, there was nearly always a window of opportunity, usually around the time when the silences got longer and the exchanges more fragmented. A pause, a gulp, a lowering of the voice as you played the apology card, and suddenly you had snatched victory from the jaws of defeat. And with luck you could even be reconciled in bed. Which almost made the rows worth having, as they were about the only occasions on which Fran allowed him near her nowadays.

Yes, there was an optimum moment for saying sorry, and as Stuart nudged the Rover on to the city ring-road, as a silence like an Arctic wind blew upon him from the passenger seat,

172

as her hand disposed of the cigarette in the ashtray with slow-motion emphasis, he knew that he had missed it by about the width of the North Sea.

"I can't believe you just said that," she said.

"What? Sorry? Is that a bad thing to say, then?" It would do as a reply, but already he was vanquished, corpses on the battlements and one box of ammo and the vultures circling.

"It's an incredibly stupid thing to say, if you really want to know. It's just about the most stupid thing I've ever heard you say and my God, that's saying something. And you know what makes me *so* angry? It's the fact that you must think *I'm* stupid. You must think I'm a complete cretin if you suppose that I'm going to say, oh well, Stuart's sorry so everything's all right. Good old Stuart's sorry for humiliating me at every possible fucking opportunity so everything's fucking hunkydory . . . "

He was glad that he had to keep his eyes on the road, because one sideways glance showed him that the most dreaded of all her manoeuvres was in progress: 'the Dance of the Teeth'. When Fran was really having a row, when she was really going into emotional meltdown, the bottom of her face underwent this extraordinary metamorphosis. Her upper lip peeled back to expose her neatly capped incisors and her lower teeth came shooting forward just like the alien in *Alien*, so that she suddenly had the jaw structure of a bulldog and she lowered her eyelids and filled her lungs and round and round, do-si-do went the Dance of the Teeth . . .

" . . . I mean, Christ, if this is what our holiday's going to be like, you behaving like this and then bleating about being sorry; I mean, if I've got to put up with this for a whole week, then I'd just as soon cancel the whole thing . . . "

Here at least was an opening to speak. "What do you mean, cancel the whole thing? You mean go home?"

"At least I'll have somebody there I can talk to," she said, executing a spectacular dental *entrechat* with a nostril-flourish thrown in.

"You're mad." He assaulted the car in front of him with a vicious blast on the horn for failing for several nanoseconds to leap forward at the green light. "If you think I'm turning this car round and driving all the way back to Bromley, after all the trouble of packing and getting ready and driving up here through . . . "

"I didn't say that. Did I say that?" His own loss of temper had put her on the defensive: score one for him. "All I'm saying is, if this is how it's going to be for the rest of the week, we might as well scrub the whole idea."

He was breathing hard through his nose, a habit that irritated her, as her glance showed; but for Christ's sake, did she have to notice every little thing he did . . . ? "Well, what do you suggest then?"

She shrugged. "I suppose we could stay here the night. Go home in the morning."

"Is that what you want?"

She shrugged again, adding that tremendously eloquent lifting of the eyebrows that meant,

174

What-Does-It-Matter-What-I-Want-That's-Never-Been-A-Consideration-With-You-Before.

"Bloody hell." He breathed harder, but his anger was wilting. Instead there was the regretful realization that the chances of a reconciliation were receding even faster than his hairline. "We've paid in advance, you know. We won't get a refund."

"Oh, well, if that's all that's important to you . . . "

"Look, are we going to Bockham or not?"

"You're asking me if I want to go? No. I don't want to go. Not any more."

"Right. We'll stay here the night then and go home in the morning. What was that place near the station we stayed in once?"

She lifted her chin. "Hotel Nelson," she said, ventriloquistically.

"Right."

They were silent while the car did battle with the city centre's hostile traffic and emerged at last in the Prince of Wales Road. The Hotel Nelson was by the river, which looked romantic in the early dark. Lights trailed in the water and there was laughter from a waterside pub across the bridge. Life was going on and people, damn it, were enjoying it.

In the hotel car-park the turning off of the car engine, after so many miles, was like the cessation of a headache. He lit a cigarette at last and they sat there side by side, eyes front, unmoving. It occurred to him, gloomily, that the front seats of a car were like a visual echo of the marital bed. God, you couldn't get away

175

from it. Wherever you were, you were supposed to sit together like two bloody lovebirds on a perch.

"What if they haven't got any vacancies?"

He let the blessed nicotine disperse the wild retorts that filled his brain. "Go somewhere else, I suppose."

"Where?"

"Seeing as we've come this far," he said carefully, "I don't see why we shouldn't just go on to Bockham."

She gave him a look like a blast from an oxyacetylene torch, but he managed not to flinch.

"Well, why not?" he said. "We can still go home tomorrow if you like. I'd rather get a good night's sleep there than stay in some hotel room."

"You would," she said, though with somewhat less acid than usual.

"And another thing — the Penningtons will be expecting us."

"The Penningtons aren't going to be there, they're on holiday, I would have thought even you could remember that."

"Well, the woman who's looking after the place will be expecting us, then."

"I suppose so."

This could go either way, he thought. It was very finely balanced. He put the row on pause for a minute and regarded the whirl of traffic that poured down Prince of Wales Road. The streaking lights made a strobe effect on his tired eyes: he had a dizzy feeling that the world was spinning round him. But then of course the world *was* spinning. Apparently it was love that made it do so.

"God, I've got a splitting headache," she said.

He made an appropriate murmur, idly wondering why it was that all her headaches, without exception, were splitters.

"I really don't fancy driving another twenty miles with this headache."

You won't be driving, I will. He managed not to say it.

She sighed. "But I suppose it will be quieter at Bockham."

"Sea air as well." Careful. Push it, and she might push the other way. One of the first rules of marriage was: never show too much enthusiasm for anything you wanted to do, because your partner would do her damndest to find reasons for not doing it.

"Of course, we could always ring through to Bockham and say we won't be coming."

"Yes," he said, "we could do that."

"It wouldn't exactly be a very nice thing to do, though, would it?" she said sharply, as if he had suggested it.

"No," he said, "rather short notice."

She sighed again and threw up her hands in a gesture that he had named 'the Queen of the Legitimate Stage'. "Well, there's no point in sitting here all night," she said. "Let's go to Bockham if we're going."

"Right." He started the engine again, and under its noise he managed to breathe unheard the words, "Happy bloody anniversary."

177

10

S HEILA MALBORNE opened her eyes to the sound of screaming and the sight of a woman's toothed and gaping mouth as a man gripped her around the neck and pulled her to him.

The man was grinning and the woman was screaming and there was a baying in the air and Sheila gasped and twitched, trying to pull herself out of the dream and finding it no dream but real, in front of her, deafening and blinding in bright flesh colours . . .

"Oh!"

She sat up, groped for the remote control and turned down the sound on the TV. The game-show screeching dwindled. The winning contestant being embraced by her husband mouthed her jubilation silently.

Sheila rubbed her eyes. Really, what rubbish they put on TV on Saturday evenings. And fancy her nodding off in front of it! She must be getting old.

Shivering with the chill of waking, she got up and closed the curtains, then turned to look at her living room. It appeared cosy beyond words, with the black and windy night outside banished by the heavy drapes. The books, the sewing-table, the pieces of china: all just as she liked it.

And hers. The place was as peculiarly her

own as her fingerprints. So different from the dreadful shared home of her marriage, where everything that met your eye was a lacklustre compromise. That, she thought, was one of the impossible things about connubiality as a way of living. You liked one sort of wallpaper, he liked another — and so what did you do? You put up wallpaper that neither of you particularly liked.

Without looking she reached out and switched on the table-lamp. The action reminded her of that lovely bit in *Silas Marner*: the old recluse's beloved earthenware pot, that seemed to lend its handle to him with an expression of willing helpfulness. Everything in the room was like that to her. Her home embraced her like a pair of loving, comfortable arms.

She shivered again.

It wasn't just the shock of waking to that cacophonous game-show: she was sure that she had been dreaming of something equally unpleasant. But she couldn't remember what. No images came to mind, yet the sensation of having had a dream clung to her; it was rather like when you were nibbling a biscuit as you worked in the kitchen, and you knew there was a piece of the biscuit left but you couldn't think where you'd put it down . . .

Her coffee cup was still by her chair. Sitting down again, she sipped, finding it nearly cold but not minding. Now there was another thing that being single freed you from — the necessity of constantly explaining yourself "Isn't that coffee cold, dear?" "Yes, it is a bit." "I should make a fresh one if I were you." "I don't mind

179

it." "No, I'll make one." "Are you having one?" "Yes, I think so." "Oh, well, in that case . . . "

She finished the coffee and picked up her embroidery. The wind was gusting outside, and cars and buses were growling and purring like beasts at large. But here she was, warm and sealed and safe.

And it was no good. After several minutes she found she had not worked a single stitch. Her eyes were fixed on the telephone across the room.

Ewan. That was what all this was about. Ever since he had left after lunch she had gone about her life as normal; washing up, finishing her crossword, popping out to post a letter, watching a sweet old British film on TV, chatting on the phone to an old and slightly tiresome friend who had rung her with some not very exciting news, cooking herself a light tea . . .

And all the time, like a pain that one refuses to acknowledge in the hope that it will go away, there had lurked at the back of her mind a nameless trouble and anxiety about Ewan.

And now it was as if she had reached that point where the pain becomes unignorable, and you have to confront the fact that something is wrong, and douse the pain with aspirin or take it to the doctor. And there the analogy ended. Because she did not know what to do to cure this nagging sensation that was not quite worry and not quite speculation but more like . . .

Well, it was more like fear.

The game-show had given way to commercials.

Montage shots of glamorous, lantern-jawed men advertised razors. They all looked like Superman but they were very caring and sharing too: they embraced elderly fathers and hoisted hygienic babies in between skiing and scuba-diving.

She had a flash of memory. It was prompted by that last image, of one of those smooth-shaven Adonises emerging in slow motion from the water with a grin so ruggedly ecstatic it might have been a rictus of agony. The memory was of Ewan's birth and the way that, as he was pulled from her in a shroud of blood and mucus, his creased, contorted little face had seemed to express a terrible reluctance. As if he had been done a dreadful wrong in being hauled into the world in that shocking, butcherly way.

Was that what her dream had been about? She couldn't tell. But the memory was swiftly followed by another, more recent and more conventionally unpleasant. One of the labourers at her ex-husband's farm had caught his hand in the baling machinery. The first joints of his third and fourth fingers had been sliced off like baby carrots and Sheila had glimpsed the horrible stumps when they brought him into the house to wait for the ambulance. The blood was expected, bearable: it was the *meatiness* of what remained that appalled her. Of course human beings were made of flesh; everyone knew that: yet somehow one both knew it and declined to acknowledge it. It had been shocking to be presented with such a graphic reminder that people were no more nor less than walking lumps of meat.

Memory, dream, memory of dream — it

181

didn't matter: whatever it was, it was all tied up with this feeling of trouble that was poisoning what should have been a perfect evening. And that was why her eyes kept dwelling on the phone. If she had a bad feeling about Ewan, then she ought to speak to him.

The problem was . . . well, she knew some people laughed at her intuitions, her attacks of the. creeps, her belief in horoscopes and clairvoyance. And if she were honest with herself she had to admit that sometimes there was a certain amount of wishful thinking in it. It was possible that she occasionally convinced herself she had had a bad feeling about something after it had happened. And what was it her youngest son Alan had said, when they had had that violent disagreement at Christmas? Something about her clinging to this Gypsy Rose Lee stuff because she was alone and frustrated and getting long in the tooth and she would swallow any mumbo-jumbo that seemed to give some point to life . . .

Her cheeks burned as she remembered. Unkind words, dreadfully unkind. And so terribly typical of Alan with his crudely efficient mind and student smugness. David, the middle son, was not much better. Only Ewan, though he was sometimes mildly teasing, seemed to treat these idiosyncrasies of hers with any indulgence. But then he had always been more attuned to the other side of human life, the side where emotion ruled instead of practicality and reason.

No, she still believed in her intuitive feelings, even if some of them were duds. After all, plenty of conclusions that were arrived at by sheer rational calculation turned out to be wrong too. So if she were going to exorcise this demon, lay these recurring memories of something strange and disquieting about her son's demeanour at lunchtime that had plagued her all day, then she ought to pick up the phone and ring him.

But there was another reason for her hesitation. She suspected that love problems were behind whatever was wrong, and if that was the case then she was very wary of interfering. It had always been her firm belief that this was an area of life not to be parentally tampered with. When her sons had girlfriends, she was always glad to meet them, and accept them as acquaintances and even friends — Ewan's in particular — but the mechanics of the relationship were their business and nobody else's.

They had not been many, anyhow, in Ewan's case. He was very attractive, she thought, but he was a serious man, not the sort to collect girlfriends like scalps. She was touched, though, that when he did go out with a girl he was always keen to introduce her to his mother. (Not his father . . . but it was mean to feel triumphant about that.) She remembered that very intense and striking girl he had met in his first months at university and brought home for the weekend. There had been the customary awkwardness about sleeping arrangements: Ewan's father had been very silly and old-fashioned over it, further strengthening Sheila's already formed decision to divorce him, but Sheila had simply felt it was up to them what they did and none of her business. More than that, however, she had felt sorry for Ewan at that time, knowing that he was entering that world that as a teenager you were so eager to get into, and that afterwards you could never get out of — the world in which sex existed.

She had pitied him because she knew he would be expecting so much of that world: not just dizzy heights of pleasure, but the *ne plus ultra* of romantic love, the ultimate mutuality, the complete and unsurpassable limit of togetherness, like those suggestive surges of sound in Wagner's *Tristan* mounting to the perfect union of two into one . . . And she knew that whatever he was expecting, he was not going to get it. She knew that he and the intense girl from university were far closer to each other when they sat on the sofa arguing about Nabokov than they ever would be while engaging in those overrated hydraulics in bed. She knew that sex divided instead of uniting. And in this Sheila could acquit herself of the bitter bias of an unhappy marriage. At the age of thirty she had had a brief affair, which anyone less blindly pig-headed than her husband would have detected; and the affair had been the complete opposite of her married life in all ways. But it had reinforced, rather than weakened, her growing conviction that sex was the place where the essentially irreconcilable difference between women and men showed most glaringly, like a worn patch in the carpet that simply couldn't be covered up or disguised.

Women couldn't understand how men could

dissociate sex and love: men couldn't understand how women could dissociate sex and physical attractiveness. Men readily went to bed with women for whom they felt no love, affection, or tenderness; women readily went to bed with men they found physically unappealing, and even to a degree repulsive. Sexual relations between men and women would always be either hypocritical or mutually destructive. In any act of heterosexual intercourse, Jack must know that Jill did not want it in the same way as he. She might want it less, or she might want it more, but she would never want it *in the same way*. The male and female experiences of desire were so widely different that insincerity and exploitativeness were inevitable in their relations. These were the unbridgeable gulfs of misunderstanding that Sheila had perceived: the best intentions would always be foiled by those ancient enemies, Willy and Fanny.

And that was why she pitied Ewan, seeing him embark on that doomed voyage; but she had never been tempted to say anything to him of it. Nobody's business but their own — that was her rule. And in turn, that was why she was now hesitating to pick up that phone.

Yet her bad feelings were so strong that even the rule of a lifetime seemed inconsiderable beside them. And another memory kept surfacing in her mind and nudging her towards action: the memory of that crisis he had suffered over leaving university, when his landlady had found him drunk and distracted in the small hours,

185

wandering her frosted garden with the skin of his hands cracked from the cold. What had he looked like and talked like when that crisis was brewing? Had he looked and talked as he had at lunchtime today — glassy, brittle, his fairness looking not so much a colouring as a disturbing absence of something?

She got up quickly, dropping her embroidery, and went over to the phone. Snatched up the receiver.

Again she hesitated, listening to the dial tone. What was she going to say? She could pretend she was just ringing for a little chat; but if she did that he could always outface her, talk away as if everything was all right even if it was not; he had always been good at covering up. And yet a bold, "Ewan, I'm worried about you, what's wrong?" might be no more productive.

An invitation to Sunday lunch. An invitation to him and Amanda. That would surely be the litmus test. She hated using such provocative expedients, but she could see no other way.

She pressed Ewan's number. She let it ring twenty times before she accepted that there would be no answer.

All right she told herself, *so he isn't in. You don't have to be Miss Marple to conclude from that that he's out.*

It was Saturday night, after all. And he had said at lunchtime that he would be meeting Amanda. And if, as she suspected, there were currently problems in that quarter, then no doubt they were sorting them out themselves, as was natural and right. So.

*So pick up your embroidery or your book and
stop being a wibbly-wobbly old fusspot. Cut the
Gypsy Rose Lee stuff, in other words.*

She looked at the stylized carving of a sleeping
cat on the coffee table. Nice thing. Ewan had
bought it for her last Christmas. Its smooth
curves made her wish to touch a real cat;
she loved them and missed having one, but it
wouldn't really be practical in the maisonette.

She felt that to run her fingers through a cat's
warm fur at this moment might just help to
soothe her mind. Help a little, anyway. There
was only one thing that would completely
soothe it, and that was knowing that Ewan
was all right.

He's out, that's all.

But she couldn't stop thinking of him
wandering round his landlady's frosted garden
in the middle of the night.

She picked up the phone and rang his number
again, and this time she let it ring thirty times
before slamming it down in disgust at herself.

What would Miss Marple say? That he was
out. And so would Hercule Poirot and Inspector
Maigret and all those awful bores.

The only alternative, that Ewan was not
answering the phone for some reason, was
simply too unlikely . . .

Sheila had a plunging feeling in her stomach.
She went to the window and parted the curtain
and peered out at the dark windy street and
her old Mini parked there, looking like a
brightly painted toy under the orange light
of the streetlamp. All the constituent parts of

her world in place, all the elements of the new life that she had laboriously built for herself and that she valued so much . . .

And tonight a ghost was walking amongst them, a ghost raised by her own busy brain, no doubt, but still blighting in its touch.

Would she be fretting like this over David or Alan? Difficult question . . . question that would not even arise, really. They were such different characters from Ewan. David's wife was a womb with a smile attached, and the couple seemed content to breed and bloat; Alan was a cool, satirical person who took what he wanted from life. But Ewan was somehow more vulnerable. As a child, that fair complexion of his had seemed to respond to stimuli with painful promptness: cold had chafed his skin, embarrassment had reddened it, illness had blanched it. He lacked, Sheila thought, that hard shell that you needed to get through life. Things got to him: he had bare wires somewhere. And perhaps because of that naked sensitivity he had cultivated a sort of protective colouration whereby he wouldn't let you see what was wrong. It was the same with drink: you could tell when Ewan was drunk because, instead of slurring and staggering, he became supernaturally precise and controlled, like a tightrope-walker . . .

Sheila had another flash of memory. Where these were coming from she didn't know, but this was the worst. It was of a piece of news film of a famous aerialist who had done a tightrope-walk between two high buildings without a net

188

and there, in front of the cameras, he had slipped, grasped the rope in his hands for a fleeting moment, and then plummeted . . .

Sheila clenched her lips tightly together. She picked up her purse, checked for her car keys.

Miss Marple and all the rest could go to hell. She was worried about Ewan and she didn't have to justify it to anybody. And the word worry originally meant to grab and gnaw with the teeth as in dogs worrying sheep and that was exactly how this felt. The worry had her in its jaws and she couldn't get out of it until she did something.

She turned off the TV, went out to the hall and put on her coat. Glanced at her hair in the mirror. A last hesitation, and then she was outside in the cool tangy October air and making for her car.

She stopped to glance up at her lit windows, softly glowing, a land of lost content; and to check in her purse again for her keys. But it was not only her car keys that she was making sure of. When Ewan had moved into his flat a couple of years ago he had given her his spare door key, in case he ever lost his and found himself locked out. That had never happened yet, and she had almost forgotten about that spare Yale tucked into the back of her purse. But there it still was. And if she felt she needed to when she got to Ewan's place, she would use it.

11

HE had been this way before, he thought as the country miles purred by beneath his wheels and Norfolk opened its secretive heart to him.

It was many years ago now, but he remembered it quite well. The Saxon place-names that loomed up out of the darkness on reflective signboards were familiar beneath their strangeness. When he was a child his family used to come this way on Bank Holiday weekends, to stay at genteel hotels in Cromer or Sheringham on the north coast. He could remember sharing the back seat with his two younger brothers, and how he had loathed their squabbling idiocy. He could remember the dining rooms of those hotels, with everyone whispering and giving each other glazed smiles over the brown windsor and the sodden cauliflower, and his little piggy brothers clearing their plates of everything that was put in front of them while he could hardly bear to eat, and the disdainful glances of the pretentious proprietors just because he wasn't a cheerful, cheeky little boy who pissed himself with pleasure every time they asked him whether he had been to the beach today.

Occasionally there had been forays into the brasher territory of Great Yarmouth, but he had hated that even more. Droves of Midland factory girls in grotesque warpaint, cramming into garish pubs and waiting to be picked up and taken to some gas-smelling caravan for a disposable shag. Even as a boy he had scented that rank smell of animals on heat and known it for what it was. And even as a boy he had known his outcast state as, shy and aloof, he had felt their mocking looks upon him like insolently licking tongues.

He had known then that that world was not for him: the world of the emotional quickie, the stunted attention-span, the editing down of passion to a series of soundbites. And he had been true to his creed. Hence his horror — he still could not think of it without a sensation of drowning, his outraged feelings closing over his head and stifling his breath — when Amanda had confessed to having once had a one-night stand.

He hadn't really sought the revelation. They had been talking round the subject in general one night, and she had volunteered the information. She had been young, she said; no more than nineteen. She had met this chap at a party where they had both drunk a lot, and ended up going back to his place and sleeping together. It was the only time she had done such a thing, she said, and she had felt pretty stupid and awful afterwards.

But what had stunned him and given him that feeling as if he were being punched repeatedly in the stomach was the way she related the story, with no shame or embarrassment, no consciousness that she was telling him something momentous. She had even mentioned the man's name. Matthew Hays: the name was lodged in his brain like a tumour. And she had mentioned, too, bumping into him by chance a couple of years later, and how awkward it had been.

His palms were sweating as he thought of these things, and his hands were sticky on the steering wheel.

How could she, how could she? He had been too numb to say much at the time, though his shock must have shown, because she had repeated, by way of explanation, that she had been very young. And she didn't seem to see that for him that was no explanation at all. He had been young once, but he hadn't done things like that, hadn't taken the most precious and exalted of human feelings and smeared them with shit. He just couldn't understand it: he hadn't changed over the years. He had always had precisely the same values and convictions. And he had thought hers were the same, because they were so perfect for one another.

He hadn't said much; but a keening of bewilderment had resounded down the corridors of his brain, and faintly echoed there still. And he still sometimes found himself compelled to undergo the torture that had kept him awake at nights at that time — the torture of trying to picture the scene.

What did Matthew Hays look like? Was he fair, dark, tall, short? What was it about him that was so attractive that, knowing next to nothing about him, she decided on the spot to go to bed with him and let him touch her naked body and probe his tongue into her mouth and thrust himself inside her? How could she make of that such a small matter? What had they said to each other? Did she come? Did she cling to him with her fingers in his hair (*fair? dark? short? long?*) and moan and come and come? In the morning did she look as he had known her, hair sleep-tangled, the faint marks of sheet-creases on her white back? Did Matthew Hays loll and watch her put on her bra with that quick fidgety motion that he knew so well he could see it now, reproduced on his mindscreen with photographic exactness?

Drowning. It was like drowning, even now, even now that he knew something far worse; the thought of it still stopped his breath and made the blood rush to his head in sick swoops . . .

He fumbled at the dashboard, managed to slot a tape into the cassette player. Fetched a deep, trembling breath as the rapturous flourishes of Strauss's *Death and Transfiguration* filled his moving box of light.

He could live with it. He had told himself at the time, shaken as he was, that he could live with it.

But it hadn't got any easier as time went by. The knowledge of that episode was not something he could lock away in a compartment of his mind labelled PAST, much as he wanted to. Because as his relationship with Amanda began to fray, that knowledge came seeping through like a poisonous damp. How could he pretend that that one-night stand from her past —

(years ago she said I was young and it was years ago — but she was the SAME PERSON

193

she was still the SAME PERSON)

— had no bearing on their situation? How could he ignore that knowledge, as things started going downhill and she pleaded tiredness as an excuse for going home early and alone, or for turning her back to him in bed, feigning sleep with her long T-shirt wrapped tightly and chastely around her? How could he ignore the knowledge, as she withdrew her body from him, that she had LET A MAN FUCK HER WHO SHE HARDLY KNEW? Here she was in a relationship of sincerity and intensity, a *real* and *committed* relationship; here she was with him, the one person in all the world who was meant to be with her, who would give himself to her one hundred per cent for the rest of his life, unquestioningly —

and yet SHE WOULDN'T MAKE LOVE WITH HIM, she had opened her legs to some nobody she had picked up at a party and let him TOUCH HER and TASTE HER and FUCK HER UP HER SOFT CUNT LIKE DOGS IN THE PARK SNIFFING AND RUTTING but she WOULDN'T DO IT WITH HIM . . .

He gripped the steering wheel, staring at the glowing vertebrae of cats'-eyes that studded the road ahead. He willed himself to keep control as the comets shot like flaming arrows across his howling mind.

He hadn't been able to keep those thoughts to himself, of course. As things fell apart between them, he had spoken out. Angry bewilderment had been her reaction, though he wondered how much of that was defensive. "But that's

194

the past," she had said. "You can't own my past."

Again, she didn't understand. He didn't want to own it: just share it. After all, he had had no secrets from her: he had delivered up his whole past to her, just as he had delivered every element of his being into her hands.

And, in the end, she had rejected it. Thrown it back in his face.

But no, not *in the end*. Because he had known, even as he admitted temporary defeat and backed off, that this was not the end. It simply couldn't be. He had known with mysterious and haunting certainty that their love was simply not meant to end this way. It was too large, too important. It was as well, really, to let her think it had ended in that pathetic, conventional manner, because the implications of it probably alarmed her. He could understand that: a love so perfect *was* alarming, and it was natural to shrink from its white fire. But she must have known, as he knew, that what they had together could not be finished so tritely and tamely; it was just a pause, a false cadence, an unresolved chord ready to modulate into harmonies more rich and thrilling than any that had come before.

It was only that knowledge, he felt, that had sustained him in these past few months. Without it he might have gone mad.

But as for the other knowledge, the knowledge that she had once had a one-night stand with a man called Matthew Hays —

(and he might have unknowingly walked past

195

that Matthew Hays in the street and that thought gave him a feeling as if something inside him some nerve-clustered part of him were being bent agonizingly back as a schoolboy bends back a ruler to the unbearable snapping point)
— well, that had seemed hideous enough. But, as she said, it was in the past, long before they had met. And he could live with it. Whereas what he now knew . . . about her and this Nick, and what was going on between them *right now* . . . It was beyond everything. He could only think of that worn phrase, 'More than flesh and blood can stand', as appropriate to it. Because his anguish seemed to make him vividly aware of his own physicality, of the flesh and blood that housed his yearning soul, the quivering tissue that must surely rend and tear and splatter if the intolerable pressure upon him were not soon relieved. He had once seen his father shoot a rabbit at close range, from a gun that happened to be loaded with heavy shot. The rabbit had become a miniature explosion of blood and fur and sinew, spinning. That was what he felt would happen to him before long, unless something changed.

He groped in the glove compartment, found half a packet of peanuts, tossed them into his mouth. They were dry and stale but he hardly noticed. When you felt the way he felt all the time, the so-called comforts of life became irrelevant.

What hypocrites women were, he thought, pierced with a sudden scorn like a scrawl of jagged lightning. They were always ticking men off for being obsessed with sex, yet they opened their cunts to any man who asked. That was it, in a nutshell: ask and it shall be given to you. Never mind romance, never mind truth and profundity and the slow magical fusing of two lives into one. Just lie on your back and spread them for any plausible con artist who asked.

They were all the same. It sickened him. He had resolved before to finish with the bitches, have done with them, just turn his back on the whole lying, lubricious crew. And he had meant it too. He still did, if it wasn't for . . .

Well, Amanda was the exception. She was different.

She *was* different . . . wasn't she? He *had* to believe that — even in spite of what he now knew about her and this Nick. He *had* to believe there was still the possibility of redemption. Because otherwise . . . otherwise there was nothing, and there might as well be nothing for ever more . . .

He was still on what passed for the main road in these parts, and every now and then a car came at him like a jouster with a hostile lance of headlights. He resented the presence of these other vehicles, could feel the glancing pressure of the trivial, mindless lives they contained as they passed him. He was glad of the taped music that held him and enveloped him and kept at bay the cretinous world outside his moving box of light.

Music: another thing he and Amanda had in common. (So *much*, they had so *much* in common!) Unlike that stupid cow Kerry

197

whose brain couldn't take in anything but those cheap jingles and jangles that stank to the ear like bubblegum-breath and who was always humming them and doing little wiggling dances to herself and telling him to cheer up and asking him what he was *thinking*, for Christ's sake . . .

A disaster, an unqualified disaster. He didn't know why he had ever got into it, unless it was simply that he was walking wounded from the break-up with Amanda and when you were walking wounded you leaned on any shoulder that offered itself.

(Temporary break-up temporary break-up with Amanda that's all it is . . .)

And perhaps too some naïve and optimistic part of himself had dared to think that it might be possible to get over Amanda and love someone else — some banal cheerleader in his psychology trying to prove a life-goes-on point. Whereas, of course, what that brief episode with Kerry had proved was quite the opposite. There was no question of loving anyone else, after Amanda.

With a shudder he remembered how swiftly Kerry had begun to disgust him — her cooing voice, her soft insistent hands, her feminine clutter with its little scents and appendages — how it made him want to explode like a bomb and blow it all apart . . .

A mistake. But at least it had proved beyond doubt what he already knew deep down inside. Amanda was the only one. Always.

He would be quite frank and honest about

that when he saw her; no need to hide from her the fact that he had tried to make a go of it with someone else, but it had been no good. And that would be an opening for her to confess that it was like that with her and this Nick really, and then . . .

When he saw her. It couldn't be long now: he had just passed a sign saying HOLT 5, and he had the rest of her lovely clear directions memorized from the piece of paper on the passenger seat. Inside him there was that feeling of haunting rightness that meant he was going to see Amanda soon. These dark Norfolk miles were bringing him closer to her every moment.

And he was bringing to her — himself. To be presented, yielded up, delivered over to her hands. Hers, for ever, as he was meant to be.

If she could only be made to see it.

Like the whine of a gnat close to his ear, he heard in his head what most people would say about him if they knew. *He was being unreasonable.* OK, so he was. He was being unreasonable by the standards of the canned hordes. He was doing what the vacuous Kevins and Debbies who met in some Ibizan meat-market and presently spread their brain-dead grins across the wedding columns would not do. But whoever said love was reasonable? Was it reason that throbbed through the soaring chromatics of *Tristan?* Was it reason that animated the visions of Dante or guided the pen of Sappho?

No, when he spoke of love he meant something far different from the dullard satisfaction of Shez

199

and Baz at having hooked each other out of a pool swarming with similar nonentities. What he meant was dark and rich and it had depths beyond fathoming. You only found it with one person and it was strong, strong as death.

And he simply couldn't *let* this happen. It was just wrong. With Amanda he had begun to get his life *right* at last. She had turned the tide that had always run against him. All through his life he had been crossed and thwarted. Time and again, whenever he had allowed himself to hope that he was breathing the clean air of a better future, he had come up against that tainted, dispiriting smell the world gave off, the smell of public toilets, piss on cold concrete, the stench of crass humanity. Time and again, he had put out the fine antennae of his nature only to feel the nipping and grinding of that vast mill of stupidity in which he was caught.

Misfortune had dogged him like a cunning, patient revenger. At every turn his potential had been frustrated. University, from which he had expected so much, had disappointed him. The teaching had been dull and hidebound and pedantic; he could still recall his disbelieving indignation at the criticisms scrawled across his essays, the way they had completely failed to understand what he was trying to say, completely failed to spot what made him special. He had tried to soldier on, but the atmosphere just stifled him, and at last he had come to the conclusion that there was nothing he could learn here. The tutors had given him some spiel about applying himself and adjusting to criticism, even leaned on him with some heavy stuff about university places being like gold-dust and not to be given up lightly. It was hopeless talking to them, really; they just didn't understand him.

He had tried to bounce back from that blow, too. The job at the Mid Anglia Press was fairly shitty, really, compared with what he was capable of and should have had by rights. But he had been prepared to make a go of it, if only to please his mother. And yet again, the obstruction and lack of understanding he met with was quite incredible. He didn't know what sort of kick these people got from such nit-picking and fault-finding; perhaps it was a sort of jealousy because they could tell he had gone beyond their crappy values. Whatever it was, he didn't see why he should have to put up with it. And once more, people's thick-headedness astonished him, as they actually asked him why he had given up such a job; even his mother had seemed not fully to understand. Well, if they had to ask, they would never know, it was as simple as that.

But of course, once the world had selected you as Number One Latrine, you had to accept the fact that the shit was going to be dumped on you in ever-increasing quantities. And so he had been forced into a succession of pissant jobs, where a certificate of imbecility was required along with the P45 and your brain was to be left in the cloakroom. Oh, and forget trying to pursue your interests outside work — forget the art classes, for instance, where the tutor had tried to crush your creativity with niggling about basic perspective and foreshortening. Just accept that your life was going to be one miserable and upsetting and defeating experience after the other.

But then he had always had an inkling of this — a submerged suspicion, like when you were a child and it occurred to you that the whole world might be a mysterious conspiracy. He remembered that feeling; remembered wondering whether after he had gone to bed everyone sat up talking about him; remembered fearing when he went in the car with his parents that they might be taking him to some nameless place to undergo some nameless and horrible experience for which he had been marked down since birth. Now that he was grown, he wondered if those feelings had been primitive, childish perceptions of what was now his settled conviction: that behind his life there was a shadowy presence, something that exerted a malevolent pull, a baleful moon to the tides of his existence.

Other lives, he saw, had reasonable chances. They had their sprinklings of bad luck, but seldom enough to blight them completely. But there was something marked about his life. The ground that he walked on had been mined. Sometimes when he dreamed, he seemed to come near the secret of this shadow, this negative equivalent of a guardian angel; but the insight was gone when he woke and he was merely left with the shadow's wretched consequences, which just went on and on . . .

Until he had met Amanda.

She had been his redeemer. At last he had

bucked the trend. Through his relationship with Amanda he had caught up with the other people, the ones who had a fair chance to start with. Finally he was playing with a full hand.

And that was why he must see her. There, if you liked, was the simple answer to any claim that he was being unreasonable in seeking her out like this. He needed her. He still loved her. Consumedly. And she . . .

She *must* love him. It was a simple imperative. This, this was all the world contained.

He had passed through Holt now, through a smug nest of lighted windows that inspected him like beady eyes, and there was the sign and the turning, just as Amanda had described it in her note. *Death and Transfiguration* had ended. He turned the cassette over and felt the hairs on his arms prickle as the orchestral whiplash of *Don Juan* sprang from the speakers. The music climbed like a young giant mounting titanic steps, became dizzy with its own energy, paused to unroll a shining carpet of melody with ecstatic love in its weave.

A memory of Nick-the-nurse's flat and its ghastly evidence returned to him. He had to clench his jaws together to stifle a moan.

But the moment quickly passed. He was too uplifted now for that pain to claim him for long. He was leaving all that behind, leaving it all far behind and heading towards a new beginning.

A new beginning for him and Amanda.

Really, it could hardly have worked out better. What he had been lacking these past months — and what had made him so wretched that his wretchedness, old and constant companion as it was, had taken on new and frightening forms — was the chance to talk to her. Just be alone, the two of them, so that he could put his case. But she had got it into her head that she didn't want to see him, and that bitch Lisa had done the faithful-friend bit and never let him in their flat, and he had done his best to respect her wishes . . .

(Or what she thought were her wishes. When the fact was she just didn't know her own mind.)

And so the opportunity had never presented itself. But now fate had reached out a hand to him. She was looking after this country place of her friends', alone, at leisure, far away from all the silly obstructions and trivial considerations that had kept them apart. It was the ideal situation in which to talk. It was the ideal situation in which their love — like a hardy plant flattened but not killed by the storm — could revive and flourish again.

And if it didn't . . .

At that thought he had a curious, detached sensation, as if a distorting lens had been abruptly placed over his mind. Everything outside it became unreal. It was a little like that no-man's-land just before you fall asleep, when the images of the waking world and the images of dream push down the barriers and mingle, and it no longer matters to you which is which. Because soon oblivion will come and stir them into a black broth and it simply won't matter . . .

He rubbed his eyes with one hand and fixed his attention on the road. It wouldn't do to lose his way now. The road was becoming narrower and rougher. Deep woods closed in on either side. From time to time a sharp bend was signalled by a repeated arrow sign like a giant chevron. Once a hare scuttered through his headlight beams with goblin steps.

He shivered. The evening had become chill, but the heater in his car was faulty and noisy and he did not want it to spoil *Don Juan*, which was just coming to its close. A shiver of a different kind traced his spine as that long-held discord on the trumpet sliced like a slow scalpel through the soft orchestral flesh, telling of the hero's death in bitterness and disenchantment; the rapture and glory evaporated and gave place to the lonely terror of silence.

His nerves jumped at the *clunk* of the tape player switching itself off.

The road was climbing now, and scurrying sand muffled the tyres. His headlights glanced on gorse bushes that seemed to freeze at his passing like stealthy creatures. On the right the woods thinned, and he glimpsed the fuzzy shape of a solitary house pinned on an expanse of meadow like a cut-out in felt.

No, that couldn't be it.

He slowed the car, peering for some landmark, wondering if he had gone hopelessly wrong and was miles from his destination, miles from Amanda, miles from salvation . . .

Lights. Bright little squares, like a half-opened advent calendar, appeared on the darkness

205

ahead. At the same moment something reflective at the side of the road caught his eye and he brought the car to a halt.

It was one of those twee village signs with ye-olde lettering and a piece of toytown artwork representing a jolly shepherd standing outside a windmill. Paid for, no doubt, by the tight-arsed, pinheaded, money-stuffed Jocastas and Guys in their flatties and corduroys who descended on these places like flies on fresh shit.

But it didn't matter. What mattered was that the sign said LOWER BOCKHAM and that meant he was absolutely on the right track.

Amanda had guided him here perfectly. She was wonderful.

And he was nearly there now, he thought with a beautiful, poignant tension at his heart.

He was so close to her.

He moved on through the village. It was scarcely even worth laughing at the old pebbled cottages that had been equipped with double garages and coachlamp porch-lights and burglar alarms and twirly wrought-iron gates and everything but a fucking moat and a drawbridge and they would have those if they could get them from Marks and Spencers. All this was nothing — merely Vanity Fair in the progress of the pilgrim towards his Celestial City.

The church was a shock. It was so large, and its presence was grimly dynamic compared with those tiled moneyboxes full of trend-eaters who wiped their arses with credit-card slips. Though faintly lit from within — some solicitor's bit in a long skirt and blue tights who thought she was getting close to the soil if she went round plumping the hassocks — it seemed to draw the darkness into its great bulk, and the tower was like a massive head, lifted, sniffing, alert.

It made him fearful for a moment. He watched it through the passenger window as he approached, slowing the car again, and felt that the tower was growing taller into the sky as he looked, rearing upwards with a cobra shrug of doom.

Then he wrenched his mind back to Amanda's directions: remembered how near to her he was. He swung the car round, followed the narrow turning that ran alongside the church.

This leads you to UPPER BOCKHAM, hooray, and ME.

The road was a switchback corridor of trees. It seemed to grow darker and narrower. And it didn't seem to be going anywhere.

Perhaps this was just some abandoned lane that would peter out in the middle of nowhere. Perhaps he had been set up. He felt a flush crawl up to the roots of his hair. Perhaps the bitch had set him up — perhaps, somehow, the bitch and that Florence Nightingale in trousers she was screwing had set him up for this and now they were laughing about him together . . .

No, it couldn't be. He recalled how straightforward Amanda had always been: no deviousness about her. That was one of the many reasons why he loved her. Because with most women you could never tell; they had this subtle air of always trying to put one over on you. They observed you out of the corner of

207

their eye. They gave you this doubletalk. You felt as if you were an experiment, and once you were out of the way they would write up their notes. They led you this dance whereby one minute you were to respect their two-fisted independence, and the next minute you were supposed to pander to their feminine fragility and there was something about all that business that just drove him *wild* . . .

Not Amanda, though. She was different. She *must* be different. He was basing his whole life on that assumption.

No, he could trust Amanda. His faith in her disarmed his rage, and he felt the hectic blood recede again from his face and neck. And at the same moment the road emerged from the greedy trees and he was in more open country, with the woods temporarily pushed back behind a steep meadow; and up ahead of him he could see lights, numerous lights, and a well-marked turning and a gateway . . .

She had done it. This was surely the place. She had brought him here swiftly and safely. He glanced at the dashboard clock: seven-forty. It had been a two-hour drive, and he was tired, stiff, aching.

But the tiredness was sloughing off him as he drew near to the turning, and the modest signboard set at an angle on the neat grass verge slowly revealed its magical characters to his puckered eyes. The tiredness was lifting, and soon the burden of his misery would be lifted too, the burden that he realized now could scarcely have been borne by anyone else so patiently and uncomplainingly. Indeed, it seemed to him that he must have had some sixth sense that this strange and wonderful reconciliation lay ahead, and that it was that subconscious knowledge that had sustained him through his ordeal these past months.

He slowed the car to a halt and studied the signboard.

UPPER BOCKHAM

The tiredness was all gone. His heart pounded. His blood surged. He was all pulse, all vigour.

He waited a moment, turning off the engine, studying what lay ahead. To the right he could see a block of cottages, blank and unoccupied. Further down the road, a barn-like building blazed with light; beyond that the road seemed to turn. It was all cloaked with trees down there, but he could see more lights, and a gabled rooftop.

A deep, fleecy quietness and peace lay over the place. He smiled. It was a good place. It was a place for lovers.

And it contained Amanda.

It was going to be a surprise for her, his turning up like this. But then during one of their quarrels — how silly and unnecessary they seemed in retrospect! — she had said he lacked spontaneity. Well, you couldn't get much more spontaneous than this.

He thought of the Sunday morning request programme they used to listen to on Classic FM. Along with requests for their favourite piece of music, lovers sent in their stories, of how they had met or how they had parted only to find each other again. This could well be one of those stories. *Though we had split up, I knew deep down that I still loved Ewan as I could never love anyone else. But I suppose I refused to acknowledge it. Then one weekend in October I was looking after a place in the country for some friends who were away. Ewan turned up on the doorstep having driven all the way from Billingham because he just had to tell me that he loved me and when I saw him standing there I knew . . .*

And the music would be *Tristan*. He could hear those dizzily ascending sequences now, could feel them in his veins.

With great care he started the engine again and turned into the narrow service road that led to his prize.

12

THE one disadvantage of Ewan's flat, otherwise quite an enviable little home, was the difficulty of parking near it. The made-over street of Victorian houses was close enough to the mainly pedestrianized city centre to make it an attractive car-park, especially on Saturday nights when no one was much inclined to take notice of 'Residents Only' signs. So Sheila had to park her car a couple of streets away, and for all she knew, Ewan had had to do the same. There was no telling from that whether he was in or out.

Nor was there any telling from the exterior of the building. The ground-floor bay-window was in darkness, but then that was his bedroom; he might be in the living room or kitchen at the back.

Yes he might be. But if he is in, why isn't he answering the phone?

Sheila stood before the gate, gnawing her lower lip, looking at the house.

It would seem, my dear, spoke up the infuriating voice of Miss Marple, *that if he is in, and is not answering the phone, then he simply doesn't want to talk to anyone.*

But not even his mother? Not even his mother, who was closer to him than anyone?

Sheila thought again of Ewan in his landlady's garden, and the unfathomable panic that had brought her here fluttered again in her chest.

Surely, whatever it was, he could talk to her about it?

She rested her hand on the cold iron of the gate.

What was she doing here? Her cosy, blessedly solitary, blessedly uncomplicated home beckoned her. All she had to do was tell herself to stop being silly and go back to her car.

Her mouth trembled. She had never known that hesitation could be like bodily pain.

A sound somewhere to her left alerted her. A few doors down a young couple occupied a darkened porch, entwined. The female half was responding to the mouth pressed against her ear with whispers of, "Piss off! Piss off will you?" that rose higher in scandalized hilarity. She saw Sheila turn her head, and fell silent, nudging. Her partner withdrew his tongue from wherever it had been and joined her in staring.

The scrutiny of those two untouched, unfriendly young faces pushed Sheila into a decision. With a smart, "Good evening", she opened the gate and walked up to the front door.

Her knocking sounded loud and agitated in the night-time street. There was something arresting about any knock at the door, even if it was at your neighbour's, overheard: you could never be neutral about it. As she repeated her knock, Sheila was tinglingly aware that the lovers were still balefully watching her and wishing her gone. Well, really, if they decided to have a knee-trembler in an open doorway, what did they expect . . . ?

But she felt dreadfully conspicuous. And more unnerved than ever by the dull, hollow sound of her knocking at Ewan's door. He was not answering, just as he had not answered the telephone.

And that meant one of two things . . .

Nonsense! It means only one thing, and that is that Ewan is out, and you should go home at once!

And if she went home? Would she be able to relax and put it out of her mind? Did this ominous feeling, that was swelling within her and making her sweat in the crisp evening air, seem like the sort of feeling that would just go away?

All at once she knew what the sound of her knocking reminded her of. It was somehow like the knocking of policemen just before they broke down the door . . .

Fumbling in her purse, she found the spare key that Ewan had given her. Her shaking fingers dropped it before she could get it to the key-hole. She heard the metallic clink as it hit the doorstep, but when she bent to pick it up it seemed to have disappeared.

The lovers preserved their watchful silence as she crouched and groped about with her hands. The path was overgrown with grass and moss and several times she touched something moist and unpleasant. If only Ewan would leave his hall light on, at least there would be some illumination from the glass in the door . . .

Ewan . . .

She found the key just as her back was beginning to moan in earnest: it scarcely seemed possible that it could have skittered away so far. She gripped it as if it were a live thing that might escape, and inserted it in the key-hole.

It wouldn't turn. The door refused to open.

Had Ewan double-locked it? If so he must be inside. But why would he have done that? Could he have gone to bed? At a quarter to eight in the evening?

She was still wriggling the key in the lock out of reflex, and she jumped when it suddenly turned. The door came ajar at her push.

Of course, the key hadn't been used: it was stiff. She withdrew it and pushed the door open.

"Hello?" She stepped into the dark hall. "Ewan — it's only me."

There was a crackling sound beneath her foot and she nearly slipped. A letter on the doormat: she picked it up. Even in the darkness she could tell by the feel that it was one of those that are never any fun, the ones with the little cellophane windows. Probably he hadn't bothered to pick it up for that reason . . .

"Ewan!" she called again. "Don't jump, it's only me, Mum. I'm sorry to burst in on you like this . . . "

For a moment she thought she heard a dull pounding, like music behind a closed door. Then she realized it was her own heartbeat vibrating in her ears, and hammering faster, as if to tell her that he was not going to answer.

214

She reached up and turned on the hall light and pushed the door closed behind her.

"Ewan — anybody home . . . ?"

She was still holding the letter. She was about to put it down on the hall table when she saw that there would be no room for it.

The entire surface of the table was covered by a dusty drift of unopened letters. Some were plainly circulars: many were not. She could see red bills there.

Carefully she slid one of the letters out of the bottom of the heap. It was postmarked 5 July. Three months old, and still unopened.

But this doesn't make sense. I saw him just this lunchtime, and he seemed all right . . .

Ah, but he didn't, did he — isn't that why you're here? Isn't that true? And isn't it also true that you haven't been round here to see him for a long time — you with your nice, settled, hermetically sealed little life, always expecting him to come to you just when it suits you?

She tried to replace the old letter and put the new one on top, and the whole pile slid with a ghostly pattering sound to the floor.

"Ewan!"

Sheila flung open the doors of the bedroom, the living room, the kitchen, the bathroom, turning on the lights and calling his name.

She didn't know what she felt when it quickly became clear that he was not here.

Breathing fast, as if she had been running, she stood in the living-room doorway, thinking. There was a curious musty smell in the air;

215

unconsciously she was grinning up her nose like a cat.

He's not here. So what are you doing? What are you doing creeping about in your son's flat?

The answer came swift and fully formed: following my fear. She didn't know if it even made any sense to her, but there was utter conviction in it.

She went forward into the living room as if she had been propelled by a hand in the small of her back.

Like most unmarried men, Ewan was quite a tidy person — in sharp contrast to his father, who had always behaved as if there were a platoon of Edwardian housemaids to pick up after him. And so Sheila could not at first quite connect the state of this room with the son she knew.

It wasn't just the dust that lay on every surface like the fuzz on the skin of a peach, or the yellowing newspapers, or the strewn cassettes and books, or the withered sticks that used to be potted plants, or even the empty beer cans crowded on the coffee table and the mantelpiece. It was the signs of something that went beyond mere slobbishness. The ashtray was not only heaped with cigarette butts, but beside it on the carpet was a much larger heap — as if, once the ashtray became so full that he couldn't stub a cigarette out in it, he had simply emptied the whole lot on to the floor with a turn of the wrist. Everywhere there were plates covered with crumbs and dried-on food, as if each time he ate he used a new one and then let it lie. And worst of all — worst because it reminded Sheila of something a caveman would do rather than her clever, civilized, fastidious son — the corner of the room on the right of the window was taken up by a pile of debris, flung there as you would fling the most unpleasant rubbish in the dustbin.

She approached it. She found she was walking on tiptoe. She found, too, that her nostrils were twitching again. The smell was bad, very bad, a smell that called for disinfectant and sluicings of hot water. Again she had to remind herself that this was Ewan's flat she was in — Ewan who had always been so careful about bathing and whom she had often seen frown in disgust when his father was making an especial pig of himself at the table.

Somehow, that Ewan that she knew had become this Ewan — someone who could live in this mess and smell and not mind it.

Shrivelled apple-cores, hamburger cartons, pizza boxes, crisp bags, cigarette packets, used tissues — anything disposable had been tossed on to the heap in the corner. He would get mice, Sheila thought, gingerly picking a tin can from the pile. The thought that a mouse might be hiding inside the can gave her a shudder, but it was not that that made her drop it with a gasp of disgust.

It was a half-empty can of baked beans, or had been. The residue inside it had turned to a rotten blue paste that gave a puff of powdery spores when the can hit the floor.

Sheila retreated as if she had uncovered a snake. There was something about that mouldy can that brought a terrible dizziness rushing to her head. In her haste she bumped against Ewan's hi-fi. The CD drawer was protruding like a rude tongue. Absently she noticed that the gleaming hi-fi was the one unsullied element in the room.

He can't have been living like this. Her mind was still in denial mode, and kept blinking up the same uncomprehending message. *He can't have been living like this. Not Ewan. I know him. He can't . . .*

She should have been prepared for the kitchen, but still it shocked her. Nothing seemed to have been cleaned or put away for months. Used teabags had simply been dropped on the floor, and some had been trodden underfoot. On the worktop lay some potatoes and onions that had sprouted until they looked like a grotesque arrangement of cactus. A bottle of milk had become a bottle of solid cheese. The glass door of the washing machine was fogged; when she opened it she flinched back at the fusty smell of the wet clothes that had been left to mildew there.

He can't have been living like this.

The bathroom was too dirty to linger in. When she came to the bedroom she felt a momentary relief, because to the eye it presented nothing worse than a jumble of soiled clothes and an unmade bed. But that was quickly followed by the worst feeling of all, a feeling that seemed to touch some hidden nerve of mistrust and

218

abhorrence; and that feeling came from the smell. It was not a strong smell. It was an emanation, peculiarly male, from those stale sheets and tossed frowsy underthings; a salty, close atmosphere that put her in mind of the man she had once had an affair with and the way that, even as she had willingly entered his bedroom, she had sensed something beneath the after-shave and the neat pillows and thought, *Lair. That's what this is. You can smell it in the air. Leave them alone, and they make lairs for themselves.*

But not Ewan. This just wasn't like Ewan, not any Ewan she knew: still that thought kept dully repeating itself in her brain. But as she turned in haste to get out of that bedroom, her bafflement at last brought another thought shunting along in its train.

Amanda. Surely Amanda can't know he's living like this.

Impossible. She wasn't one of these squeaky-clean girls who looked as if they were wearing cast-iron knickers, but certainly squat squalor was not her style. If she had seen Ewan's place looking like this . . .

Perhaps she hasn't.

Suddenly a hopeful interpretation of this whole business occurred to Sheila, and she snatched eagerly at its filmy substance. Perhaps Ewan wasn't living here at all. Perhaps he had impulsively left the place and moved in with Amanda. And perhaps that accounted too for his odd, preoccupied mood and his reluctance to bring Amanda to lunch any more; he was

219

hesitant about telling his mother that they had taken this undeniably big step. Perhaps . . .

The idea was disintegrating even as she clutched at it. She knew Amanda's flat; they had bumped into each other in town once, and Amanda had invited Sheila back there for a cup of tea. The flat was rather a curious place, at the back of a chiropractor's surgery, with two floors — Amanda's room was up a flight of stairs, which gave her a nice feeling of privacy. But it was still a shared flat. Lisa, the other tenant, had seemed very nice on that one occasion when Sheila had met her, but the fact remained that a third person — especially a boyfriend — would surely have made the place very awkward and overcrowded. She couldn't imagine any of the parties being very happy with such an arrangement.

But then, that was thinking rationally. And somewhere today — perhaps when she had woken to game-show cacophony with a feeling of unfocused dread, perhaps when she had picked up that tin can half full of reeking mould — somewhere today the reliable engine of rationality had switched off. The battery was dead and the lights were out and she was groping in the dark with the fingertips of intuition.

Lair.

Sheila had another bitter flash of memory. Lying in bed with her lover one afternoon she had said, idly (or had it really been idly?), "What would you do if you were married and you found out your wife was having an affair?" And her lover had brushed a little

220

cigarette ash from the hair on his chest that was like wire wool and answered, "I suppose I'd kill her."

What a fool she had been, she thought now — and thought for the first time. What a pointless business. She hadn't loved the man. She couldn't honestly say that she had found him particularly attractive. It was resentment against her husband and the no-life she had with him that had driven her on. When she took that grotesque, lolling thing inside her, she wasn't fucking her lover: she was unfucking her husband.

Power games. No wonder men called it names like 'tool' and 'weapon'. No wonder the sewer-mouthed brats she was called upon to teach said, 'It's fucked' and, 'Fuck you' and, 'He's totally fucked up'. With their guttersnipe instinct they knew the word meant destruction.

Her eye lit on a drawing pinned to the bedroom wall by the door. Amanda: she recognized her at once. An excellent likeness. She was in profile, looking pensive. The drawing was unfinished, as most of Ewan's tended to be. Such a pity he wouldn't fully apply himself, because he had definite talent. It was unusual for him to preserve one of his pictures like this. He had done several nice sketches of Sheila that she had wanted to keep, but he always threw them impatiently away.

So much potential, Sheila thought, admiring the drawing. If only people would understand him better . . .

221

Understand him? Do you understand him? Do you understand what's been going on in this . . .

(lair)

. . . flat that used to be such a nice, stylish little place? Do you understand what can have been going on in Ewan's mind to make his home look like this?

Do you . . . ?

There had to be an explanation. For the sake of her own sanity, there had to be. She had built so much of her new life on the foundations of her easy mutual understanding with her son. It was a solidarity scarcely expressed but powerfully felt.

The thought that there could be another side to Ewan's life, like the dark side of the moon, was beyond bearing.

She seemed to catch another whiff of that sour, intimate smell from the airless bedroom. She hurried out with what she tried to convince herself was not a shudder.

Back in the hall she noticed the telephone on the wall. *Had* he been living here? She tried to examine the receiver for dust or fingerprints or — oh, but it was impossible to tell, and ridiculous. Miss Marple and co., for all their hard-headedness, didn't live in the real world.

She preferred to think that he had not been living here, for whatever reason. Because the alternative gave her that feeling that, if it was not a shudder, was as near as damnit.

Worse than a shudder, maybe. Because it was a shudder inside her mind.

Sheila gripped her keys. Keys to her car, keys

to her home; keys to a safe, sensible world. Except that now it had a hairline crack running through it.

Where to now?

That the question should raise itself at all showed that using those keys was not an option. To go back home would only be to take this chill and this smell and this unease with her and lock herself in with them.

Luckily an answer to the question had already formed in the back of her mind. Amanda. Amanda must know something about this — and if she did not, she would surely be as concerned as Sheila was. Alternatively, and most likely, Ewan was with her now. Either way, it was Amanda she must seek out.

Yes. The decision freshened her, and she left the flat briskly, closing the door behind her with a bang that startled the couple still soldered together in the nearby porch.

"Nice evening for it, isn't it?" she said as she headed past them down the street, and the look of shocked affront on their faces — the young simply couldn't bear the thought of older people knowing about sex — made her want to chuckle aloud.

Yet she couldn't deny that the lifting of her spirits was really down to one thing, and that was getting out of that flat.

That lair.

13

"THERE'S a car," Jamie said casually, his eyes still fixed on the TV screen. "Is it?"

Amanda looked up in surprise from the hearth; she had been laying logs for a fire, not so much for warmth — the farmhouse boasted several miles of radiators — as for the feeling of security it would provide: the primitive coming out in her again, she supposed. She hadn't heard the car or seen the headlights, but she had to admit she had been miles away; thinking of Nick, wondering when he would ring back, wondering if this time she could overcome the fundamental recalcitrance of the telephone as an instrument of communication and actually convey to him what she wanted to convey.

"Must be the Howards at last," she said, getting up from the hearthrug. "Those grockles we've been expecting." She noticed Jamie turn down the TV on the remote with a blind, automatic action. His mother must have told him so many times to turn it down when there were visitors that it had become a Pavlovian reflex.

She went through to the hall. She could hear the engine of the car now, and the slither of its tyres on the gravel of the courtyard. Catching sight of her reflection in the polished milkpan hanging on the wall, she saw that that little groove had appeared between her eyebrows. That groove meant she had been worrying about something. She had never managed to catch herself in the act of puckering up in the frown that caused that groove, but the visual evidence was conclusive.

Worrying over Nick, of course, Nick entertaining Mr Plod in his trashed flat. She thought of the times they had had together in that flat — not wild and glamorous times, OK, nothing that would uncurl a metropolitan journo's lip; but good, warm, happy times nonetheless — and she felt something that, if it wasn't quite a lump in the throat, certainly wasn't a thrill on the G-spot either.

She would help him get the place straight once this week was over. Maybe they could completely redecorate it, scourge it of this horrible thing that had happened. She would suggest it when he rang back.

Knocking at the front door. She went to open it, wondering what the Howards were like. *Really nice people*, Alix had said. *If you like cheese*, Ben had added.

She opened the door.

"Oh, my God," she said.

It just came out. The sight of Ewan Malborne standing there was simply so impossible, so unbelievable; she found herself gaping and gasping the way people did in films, the way that never looked quite convincing . . .

"Hi," Ewan said.

Unbelievable . . .

But worse than that, it wasn't unbelievable,

225

not deep down where her instincts lived. Down there some grim sceptic, some Grumpy amongst the dwarfs of her subconscious, had always refused to be convinced that Ewan had finally got the message, that he wouldn't give it one last try.

But all the same, it was a dreadful shock — as if everything that had happened in the past few months had been a sweet dream and now she was waking up to the intractable reality . . .

She struggled to speak. "What the hell . . . ?"

Ewan held up his hands. "I know," he said. "I know. I shouldn't have sprung on you like this. I haven't got any excuses. I'm sorry, I'm really sorry. But I just had to come. I just had to see you."

Amanda found herself glancing behind him, as if she half-expected to see some 'Candid Camera' crew lurking in the drive and ready to jump out and tell her it was all a joke. But there was only a car — his presumably, though it was a different model from the one he had driven when they had been together. Still gaping, she transferred her gaze to him. He stood quite still in the porch, his hands in his pockets, looking at her with a sort of rueful appeal. He looked weary and rumpled. Those faint smudgy shadows under his eyes — they gave him that touch of wistfulness which, God help her, she had once fallen for — were darkened by fatigue, and that in turn threw into relief the intense blueness of the irises. He put up a hand to push back the tangled blond fringe, and the horrible familiarity of the gesture made her heart sink.

226

Yes, it was Ewan all right. No ghost, no hallucination, no trick. God alone knew how, but Ewan was here, here in Upper Bockham where she had been feeling practically as cut off from everything as if she were in a lighthouse.

Oh shit.

"Look," Amanda said, "I — I really can't believe this is happening, I mean, how come . . . where did you spring from?"

"I've just driven down from Billingham." Ewan rubbed his eyes with the heel of his hand. She remembered that gesture too, though she wished she didn't. "Fair old drive, isn't it . . . ? Amanda, I'm sorry, I shouldn't have done it, I know. I'll clear off again as soon as you like. I didn't mean to startle you or disturb you or anything — well, no, that's a stupid thing to say, of course that's what I've done."

"You can say that again." The shock, like a blow to the funny-bone, had worn off only to be replaced by sharp anger. "What on earth do you think you're playing at? After all this time . . . after what we said last time — "

"What *you* said." The quick retort gave way to a sorrowful smile. "No, I know. Like I say, I've got no excuses. I just . . . " He looked away from her, blinking, his gaze becoming unfocused. "I just had to see you face to face one last time, and ask you one thing . . . That's all."

"What could you possibly have to ask me?" Amanda snapped; and thought, oh God, this is just what was so awful about being with him, the way you were forced into adopting this tart, stiff-necked tone, the hard old dolly with hands on hips, and then you felt guilty for being like that . . . "Look — Ewan, we've said it all, we've said it over and over again and I really don't see the point in this at all."

"I know," he said again, quietly, resignedly. He dug his hands deeper in his pockets, hunching his shoulders and staring across the courtyard. "I know that. I mean, I haven't come here to — to flog that dead horse any more. I realize I made a king-sized prat of myself a while ago — you know, when I wouldn't face facts. And I'm sorry for that. I suppose in a way that's partly why I had to come. So I could see you, face to face like I said, and just say sorry for being such a prize pain in the arse all that time."

This was unexpected; though she was still wary. She remembered the way he could always rustle up some humble pie if he thought that was what would go down best.

"Well, it's OK," she said uncomfortably. "It's history now."

The TV had been turned up again, and the sound reached them. "Sorry," Ewan said glancing behind her, "have you got company?"

"Yes — well, I'm sort of babysitting . . . Look, Ewan, wouldn't it be best if we just forgot this ever happened. Like I say, it's all history now, and you've said sorry and that's fine but it really doesn't matter — we've both got our own lives to lead, so — so let's just leave it at that."

"I can't."

Ewan was shaking his lowered head and scuffing the gravel with the toe of his shoe.

"I can't," he repeated in a low voice; and there seemed to be real pain in his tone.

But you remember that tone, too, don't you? Yes indeed. Ewan employed that tremor of pain as expertly as a good violinist employed vibrato.

"I really don't see why," she said, dismayed to hear herself forced into the Hard Bitch role again.

"All right." He took a deep breath. His eyes were as blue as a humid June sky. "I'll come clean. The question I wanted to ask you, the question I just had to ask you . . . I mean, that's really why I drove all this way, no good pretending otherwise . . . " He swallowed. "It's just that I've heard a rumour that you're going out with somebody else, and I just had to find out the truth of it." He spread his hands, looking pale, tired, hopeless "That's all."

She studied him. "What do you mean, *somebody else?*" she said carefully.

His eyes met hers, nakedly.

"Somebody *else*," she said. "You mean somebody other than you?"

He shrugged, then said huskily, "Yes."

"But I'm not going out with you, Ewan," she said. Sod it if she was having to be the Hard Bitch; she was going to nail this one. "I stopped going out with you a long time ago. That's finished. So I can't be going out with *somebody else*. I might or might not be going out with somebody, but either way it just isn't any of your business. It's none of your business, Ewan."

229

Ewan rubbed a hand across his face, nodding vigorously but abstractedly as if he were listening to a radio debate and agreeing with some strong views.

"You're right," he said. "You're absolutely right. What can I say? That's exactly what I've been telling myself all the way here. It's none of my business . . . But it doesn't make any difference, Amanda. Look, it didn't work out between us, OK, but that doesn't mean we don't understand each other. The way we think, and everything. So you'll understand that I could drive all the way here telling myself it's none of my business and that I'm being stupid and that I ought to turn round and go home — but that I still couldn't stop myself. You know? Yes, we should be reasonable about these things, but it just doesn't work out that way, not when your feelings are involved. I'm not going to insult your intelligence by pretending otherwise. You see?"

Amanda was silent, not because she didn't know what to say, but because her mind was being peppered with memories like a hail of arrows. Memories of her life with Ewan — you thought you had its measure, but you didn't really until something like this happened, just as you couldn't truly remember what a migraine was like, how excruciating it really was, until you had another one. His words, his little strategies — the *You're right, what can I say?* strategy, the *I won't insult your intelligence* strategy — it was like hearing old tunes that you'd forgotten you knew. A golden oldies programme in which

230

the oldies weren't particularly golden and you were embarrassed that you ever hummed along to them.

She remembered them all now. But there was one thing she had forgotten. She had forgotten how nice it was not to have to listen to them any more.

"Ewan . . . " She resented having to say that name. She really resented being put in the position of having to say that name, as if there were still something between them, as if she hadn't wiped that name off the blackboard long ago. "Look, this is stupid, this is pointless — I mean, I really think you should go now and just forget the whole thing . . . "

Ewan raised one eyebrow, very wry and *c'est la vie*. That, God help her again, was another thing she had once found cute, until she noticed that he turned it on and off like a tap.

"Ah." He ruffled the crown of his hair with the flat of his hand. "Hm. I think I'm on a loser here. I rather think I'm up shit creek without a paddle, as Lady Bracknell said to Lord Windermere." He coughed and fixed her with the look that she remembered from the Ewan Malborne Fab Forty as the last-ditch look, the look that said, Damnit-I-can't-have-any-secrets-from-you, the little-boy-caught-in-the-act look, the sad-but-impish-to-the-last look. "OK. But just to be a complete pain in the arse one more time — I don't suppose you could just give me a one-word answer before I go?"

"One word answer to what?"

"Well, the question."

231

She knew, of course, the question. And it was, as she had said, none of his damn business. Her relationship with Nick was hers, hers alone, and she wouldn't have it fed into the liquidizer of Ewan's obsessiveness, where everything came out Ewan-flavoured.

"I don't like this, Ewan," she said. "I don't like you coming here like this and I don't like you confronting me with these questions when it's nothing to do with you. I don't like it one bit." She recalled the last time he was hassling her, and that stupid cow at work — the one with the hobble skirts and the laminated make-up — getting wind of what was going on and braying, "Aren't you *flattered?*" And her icily immediate answer, *No I am not. I am not flattered and anybody who would be has got big problems.*

"I'm not exactly having the time of my life myself," he said.

"Well, why do it then?" For the moment she spoke out of genuine bafflement. "What's the point . . . ?"

The phone was ringing. *Nick*, she thought, and felt that that thought must be written all over her face, betraying her like a deep blush. Against her discomfort rose a voice of protest: *What's all this about betraying? It's none of his business, remember? You're not going to let him make you feel guilty again?*

Ewan said nothing, his eyes luminously regarding her. The phone kept on ringing.

"Phone," called out Jamie helpfully from the sitting room.

"Can you answer it, Jamie?" she called back. "Look, I'm sorry you've come all this way for nothing — "

You're apologizing to him! What are you apologizing to him for?

" — but really, I don't see the point. I've said everything I've got to say to you — I said it months ago. So . . . "

"Amanda, it's Mrs Pennington!" Jamie called. "She says can you come quick."

"Oh, look, just give me a minute," Amanda said to Ewan in confusion. She hurried through to the sitting room, where Jamie importantly held out the receiver to her.

"Hallo, Alix?"

"Amanda . . . " Alix's voice was lost in a gargle of interference.

"What? Sorry, I couldn't hear."

"I said it's a terrible line!" Alix's voice suddenly emerged through the crackling with such a doppler effect that Amanda flinched. "I'm afraid it's going to go kaput on us any minute, so I'd better be quick. Just ringing to say we're here, and Florence is wonderful except for the phone lines . . . " Alix's laugh turned into a feedback wow that had Amanda wincing again. "Is everything OK there?"

"Yes, everything's fine." Except for Ewan . . . But she wasn't going to mention that. No way. Because he was going to get his marching orders in a minute and then she was going to try — *try* to forget that it ever happened. "Jamie's with me — well, of course, you spoke to him. I'm looking after him for the evening — hope

233

that's OK. John's mother's been taken ill and they've had to go over and see her."

"Oh, no, how awful! I remember Sue saying she was quite poorly before. Oh, how rotten, I do hope everything will be all right. Listen, give Sue and John my best wishes, won't you? And hey, of course it's all right about Jamie! I'm glad you've got some company there. Have you — "

Another static burst, ear-splitting.

"I'm sorry, Alix, couldn't hear . . . "

"I was just asking if you'd heard from Nick, but I think we'd better call a halt to this one and I'll ring you tomorrow. Just as long as you're OK."

"Yes, I'm fine, don't worry about a thing. Thanks for ringing, Alix . . . "

Their goodbyes were inaudible. Amanda put down the phone and looked at Jamie. He was plainly full of curiosity about who was at the door but was too shy to ask. *Believe me,* she thought, *you don't want to know.*

"Right," she said. "You OK, Jamie? I shan't be a minute."

It was too much to hope that Ewan would have taken the hint and left. Take the hint? She had spent weeks dropping him a hint the size of a reinforced steel joist . . .

And oh God, she had thought he had finally taken it. And yet now here he was again. This really couldn't be happening . . .

She found him in the hall, just inside the open front door, leaning against the wall.

"Sorry," he said. "Just that it's a bit nippy out there." He squinted at his reflection in the milkpan. "God, I look the pits."

Amanda gave voice to the question that had been unpleasantly with her all this time like a hair in the mouth. "How did you know I was here?"

He coloured slightly. "Well, it's no good pretending. I'm afraid I pestered Lisa until she told me where you were. I said I'd found a bank card of yours at my place and I wanted to send it on. She wasn't keen, as you can imagine. But you know what a persistent bastard I am."

He gave an abashed little smile, a smile that had ceased to work on her half a year ago. She was about to say 'Never mind the *persistent*, just *bastard*'; but she let it go. What was the point? They had nothing to argue about, because there was nothing between them.

"Well, I don't like you bothering Lisa like that either," she said. "But I suppose it's done now. I don't see what the point of it was, but it's done now. You've found me, nothing's changed, your car's out there, and I suggest you get back in it and go home and get on with your own life and let me get on with mine."

She had begun speaking coolly, but then emotion had shown through — because this *was* upsetting, she couldn't deny it to herself — and from the look of quickened interest on Ewan's face she knew he had picked up on it. He had some sort of affective equivalent of infra-red that could zero in on the merest pinpoint of hurt.

"All right," he said softly; he had a deep voice that could go right down to a velvet whisper.

"I suppose it's no good me saying this, but I honestly didn't come here to upset you."

"You haven't," she said, a little too quickly.

"Well . . . if you say so." He gave her the gentle look that said *I know you better but I won't press the point.* Christ, she thought, hadn't he even come up with a new repertoire after all this time? Had he really come all this way just to offer her a suitcase of the same old samples? "And I *am* going," he went on, "though I can't expect you to believe that either. I mean, I don't blame you for the way you're feeling, after the way I acted. I was a brat, basically."

Was?

"And I know I've got no right to ask this question — "

"That's right, you haven't," she said.

She saw a little giveaway twitch then; he couldn't keep up this humility indefinitely. The look of pique appeared not in his eyes but in his mouth. Amanda watched mouths, and had learned a lot from them; they were the real windows of the soul. Ewan's was a thin, indrawn mouth, the feature that stopped his good looks short of outright glamour-puss. A spoilt mouth.

"It isn't what you think," he said, all patience again. "It's not like before. I mean, the reason why I've got to know whether it's true about you and this — this other guy. I've got to know so that I can start again. Yeah, sounds corny and stupid, doesn't it? But it's true. I've got to know for certain, not just through rumours, so that I

236

can say OK, fair enough, and draw a line under the whole thing and start a new page. That's what I want to do. That's what I need to do, just to get my life finally straight again. So you see, the reason why I'm asking is just a plain selfish reason really."

She watched him, her arms folded. "But that line's already been drawn," she said distinctly. "It was drawn when we finished, ages ago. My seeing someone else or not seeing someone else doesn't enter into it. That line's been drawn, Ewan. Or it should have been. So draw it now, and then go and leave me alone."

He was silent for some moments, staring at the floor. Finally he stirred, levering himself off the wall and jingling his car keys in his pocket.

"I've got to admit that's pretty definite," he said with a sigh. "Even to me. Mr Thick Skin." The self-mocking smile that followed this got no response from her. "I don't suppose there's any chance of a quick cup of tea before I go? My mouth's like the bottom of a parrot's cage."

Perhaps because he did look haggard and defeated, some weakling part of her piped up: *Well, you can't refuse him a hot drink after he's driven all this way. Surely.*

But though she let the weakling have its say, it was outnumbered. She just knew Ewan too well. She knew his stalling tactics of old. Cup of tea, use the phone, use the loo — it didn't matter so long as he stayed in the game, so long as he didn't have to leave the field. He always had this blind hope that he might be awarded a penalty in the last minute of injury time.

237

"I'll just drink it quickly here," he said. "I mean, I won't come in."

You are in, she thought. *Nobody asked you, but you got in.*

"Just a second," she said.

She turned and walked down to the kitchen. Took a can of Seven-Up from the fridge. Brought it back and handed it to him.

"Here you go," she said.

The protest was merely a flicker, quickly covered over again by the sad humility. "Thanks," he said. He popped the tab and drank.

"I don't see as it would hurt," he said after she had watched him through several mouthfuls. "You know — seeing as we *are* finished, and it's all history — I don't see as it would hurt in that case, for you to tell me. Whether the rumour's true. I mean, where's the difference? I'm just someone you know, so there can't be any big deal about telling me."

"You aren't just someone I know," she said; and thought, *Uh-oh, bad move.* Because immediately Ewan was looking at her all soulful and significant.

"No," he said huskily, "I'm not just someone you know — am I?"

"That's right," she snapped, trying to drag the exchange back to where she wanted it, "you're not just someone I know, you're someone I used to go out with once upon a time. And that's all you are. No more, no less. You don't have any hold over me, you don't have any right to know anything about me, you don't have any stake in

238

my life whatsoever. So now we've established that, please just drink your drink and go."

Ewan gazed at her a moment. Then he turned his head and took another sip of soda. From his sudden grimace as he did so she thought he must have hurt his lip on the can or something. Then she saw he was crying.

Oh shit.

It still cut you to see that. Nobody could witness tears unmoved. But in this case you had to balance the smart of compassion with the memory of other occasions when the waterworks had been turned on with suspiciously neat timing.

"I'm sorry," he said, drawing in a great shuddering breath, pinching his eyes shut. "I'm so sorry . . . I'm a lousy liar, Amanda . . . I can't pretend . . . I just can't bear the thought of you with someone else, because I — I still love you . . . " He held up a hand. "I know, I know I shouldn't say that, I know you don't want to hear it . . . I never *meant* to say it, believe me. I've tried, I've tried so hard to — to smother it, to kill it. I thought I was getting there. But just — just seeing you again, it — it brought it all back." He scrubbed a hand across his face. "I'm really sorry. I didn't mean this to happen. I'll go now. Just — just give me a second . . . "

She was breathing fast, her lips clenched. He was certainly playing hell with her. And what stopped her from feeling even the tiniest tug of tears herself was the perception that he damn well knew what he was doing.

"It's just — it's just the not knowing for sure,

239

you see. That's what makes it worse. When all you've got to go on is rumour. You know, I — well, heard it through the grapevine. Cue for a song." A watery smile. "So then you can't stop thinking about it — wondering if it's true . . . And yes, I know it's nothing to do with me, I've told myself that a million times, but still I can't stop torturing myself . . . "

"Well, what good is knowing for sure going to do? I mean, will it make it better or worse if you know?"

"It'll make it better." He drew himself up. "It will make it better if I know. Don't ask me why. It just will."

She frowned. Damn him, he was getting it out of her. Well, what the hell, there was always the chance that he might see her and Nick together in Billingham some day anyway. And if it would get rid of him . . .

But what was so bloody awful, and what was not going to go away, was the fact that she had been living in a dream. All this time blissfully thinking he had cooled off and yet here it was *again* . . .

"Yes, I'm seeing somebody. I don't know why I'm telling you this. When we broke up I don't remember signing anything that said I had to take the veil for the rest of my life . . . "

She stopped, because he was giving her a look that she didn't understand. There was almost a smile there, something covert and knowing. It made her so uncomfortable that she went on irritably, "Anyway, what's the big issue? I mean,

240

I thought you were going out with someone new yourself . . . "

Bad move again. She saw her mistake instantly, saw it in the way his eyes kindled: ah, so she was interested in what he was doing; she wasn't indifferent to news of him: very revealing . . . !

Well, think what you like, sunshine. I certainly was very interested indeed to learn that you'd found some other sucker to go out with. Mainly because I'm interested in anything that gets you off my back.

No point in saying it, though. There was no point in saying anything to him at all: everything was a handle. She just felt miserably tired all at once, exactly as she used to during those exhausting quarrels that had punctuated their relationship. She just wanted him gone.

"Yes, I . . . " He looked at the can of soda he still held, frowned, put it down on the French provincial cabinet that stood in the hall. "Yes. You've been straight with me, so I should be straight with you."

She wanted to scream. *There's no question of being straight with each other. Lovers would talk like that when they were working something out. And we are not lovers.*

No point, no point. Don't give him any handles.

"I have been seeing someone else just lately," he said. "But it didn't work out. In fact, it was a fairly complete disaster. Don't get me wrong, she was nice, she was really nice. But the trouble was, she wasn't . . . "

241

Amanda knew what he was saying, but she wouldn't acknowledge it even so far as to meet his probing eyes.

"Well, like I say, it didn't work out. But I did really give it a go. I wanted to make it work. But it was no good because — "

"Well, that's a pity." She cut him off. "Sometimes these things work out and sometimes they don't. Fact of life really. You just have to face it." A few dead leaves came scurrying in through the open door behind him. If wishing could make you telekinetic *à la Carrie*, then Ewan would have been hurtling through that door and across the courtyard like a paper sack in a gale. "Now, was there anything else?"

Hard and hurtful . . . yes, all right. But in the end it was the only weapon you had left. Through weeks and weeks of wretchedness, when their relationship was on the skids and she was looking for the exit, Amanda had been disabled from finishing it by that one thought: *I don't want to hurt him.* It had become a mantra, hypnotizing her. It had put her into such a trance of paralysis that she only slowly became aware of her own pain; only slowly posed herself the question, *So what do you do instead? Stay with him for the rest of your life — sign up for fifty years of depression and despair, and reflect on your deathbed that, oh well, at least you didn't hurt him?*

No. You had to hurt, some time. And with a normal person you only had to do it once. Amputation; done, over. But Ewan — here he was back for more, giving her the long

242

reproachful look that said, *You've hurt me . . .*

"Well?" she said.

Ewan turned his face from her. "It's killing me, seeing you like this. Knowing . . . " His voice was stormy with tears. "I should never have come. It was crazy, I know. I just — I just had to see you . . . I don't understand, I'll never understand it . . . " He made a helpless gesture. "Where did we go wrong?"

"Oh, *God.*"

It was a cry of weary disgust, impossible to contain: perhaps an element of relief in it too, because that was it, that was the snapping point, she was going to have him out of that door right now . . .

He was looking at her, differently. Very still.

"Why 'Oh, God'?" he said.

She shook her head. "I'd like you to leave now."

"Why 'Oh, God'?"

"Forget it, just go."

"Why 'Oh, God'?" Unmoving, tone unchanged. "Ewan — "

"No, come on. Why 'Oh, God'? You can answer me that, can't you? I don't think that's asking much, is it? Why did you say 'Oh, God'?"

"This is ridiculous — "

"Come on." Hectoring now, unbearably hectoring; he had even taken up that stance that she remembered from when he was spoiling for an argument, weight shifted to left foot, head on one side, right palm outward. "Come on, let's have it. Why did you say, 'Oh, God'?"

"Because it's such a bloody cliché, that's why! This where-did-we-go-wrong bit! A bloody cliché!" Goaded to it: drawn in.

"Oh, well, I'm sorry. I'm very sorry, I should have realized." Here was another golden oldie she had forgotten, the lightly acidic loftiness. "I should have realized I've got to watch every word I say. But, you know, I wasn't aware that you were giving marks out of ten for originality of thought. You don't tend to bother about that sort of thing when your fucking heart's breaking, you know, when you're hurting inside like I am you tend to speak from the gut and if it's a cliché then it's a cliché, I would have thought that's fairly understandable really but perhaps I'm wrong . . . "

She had walked past him, opened the door as wide as it would go. Stood holding it like that.

"When you're ready," she said.

He studied her, trying to see how the land lay. Like a golfer deciding which club to use.

"It's no fun, you know," he said at last. "It's no fun feeling like this. Like you've got nothing, nothing to live for . . . "

"Tell it to the Ethiopians, I'm sure their hearts bleed for you."

He gave a short, disdainful laugh. "I sometimes think you like it, you know. I sometimes think you really like seeing me suffer."

Well, I can think of worse sights . . . She made herself draw a deep breath. "No, I don't, Ewan. I don't want you to suffer. I want you to get on with your own life. That's what I want. I want

244

you to just get on with your own life, away from me. I'm saying that for the thousandth time; and I'm saying it for the last time. And if it ever needs to be said again, it won't be me saying it, it will be a solicitor." Some people got off on this sort of thing, relished the drama. It made her feel sick.

But at least it had got through. He had turned pale, and he was floundering. "But how can . . . you can't do this to me; I mean, it's killing me inside . . . "

She said nothing, kept her station by the door.

"All right then." His face turned set, almost prim. He took out his car keys and looked at them with martyred distaste, as if they were just another example of the shitty end of the stick that life continually offered him. "If that's all you've got to say to me after I've driven half the night to see you . . . "

Didn't ask you to. But she knew now that any reply was a mistake: it kept him in the game. Schtum, that was the only way.

"Right." He took a step towards the door; then paused, eyebrows raised, very casual, as if some chance thought had occurred to him. "Where did you meet this new guy you're shagging by the way? Pick him up one night at a party?"

All she could do was bite her lip and stare him out; remembering in the meantime that making you out to be a man-trapping tart had been one of his specialities, though of course that hadn't stopped him dropping sidelong remarks about

245

frigidity towards the end when she couldn't bear to have him near her.

"You've really fucked me up, you know that?" he went on in the same conversational tone. "My life is completely fucked, and all because of you. How does that make you feel? Well, silly question — quite obviously it doesn't particularly bother you. That's obviously your style, fucking people's lives up and then ditching them. Well, don't worry. You won't be hearing from me again. I'm not a complete masochist. I just hope you can live with yourself, that's all. Especially when you finally come to realize what you threw away."

Amanda's hand tightened on the door-handle. Well, he had pretty well run through his repertoire now: the lip-curling nastiness was usually the last trick in the bag. Just keep silent, and it would soon be over . . .

And after he's gone, you're still going to feel like shit. You always did, after these encounters.

Didn't matter. As long as she got rid. And now, thank God, he was actually stepping across the threshold, he was actually going . . .

Wait. There was more; he was turning to her. One more throw. And incredible as it seemed, he was inclining towards her as if to touch her, as if to embrace her . . .

"Amanda," he said. Yearningly. "I'm sorry. Please . . . "

She couldn't speak; but fortunately her expression did the job. What she was feeling must have been expressed with perfect clarity by the look on her face, and that sent him flinching back as firmly as a slap.

There was one last look, a look that seemed to have a curious upward shadow about it, as if he had held a torch under his chin. Then he was moving, swiftly, striding out of the door and across the courtyard, a muttered "Goodbye" thrown over his shoulder by the wind. His head was down as he flung open the door of his car, got in, keyed the ignition. He stayed that way for a few moments, revving the engine —

go go just go

— and then the tyres spun out gravel and the car growled round the courtyard in a wide arc and pulled away.

Going.

Sharp right at the leisure complex. Accelerating up the service road.

Going.

She stirred and ran through into the kitchen, where the window gave a view of the gates and the main road. She parted the curtains. There were the brake-lights of Ewan's car, just visible through the trees, as he paused at the gates. Left indicator-light winking —

going

— and then the car turned out of the gates on to the main road, change of engine note, accelerator roar, and sped away.

She opened the window, heard the car-sound dwindle into the distance, fade, disappear.

Gone.

Amanda let out a breath, leaned her forehead against the cold glass, closed her eyes.

247

After a moment she closed the window and rearranged the curtains. She went through to the hall and closed the front door. The Seven-Up can was still where he had left it on the cabinet. She hoped it wouldn't leave a ring. She picked it up between finger and thumb, carried it through to the kitchen and binned it.

It didn't happen. Just pretend it didn't happen.

No, no good. She could throw away the can, she could send Ewan packing, but she couldn't deny that old wounds which she had thought permanently healed had been set aching again. All the sheer claustrophobic awfulness of that time in the early summer had been revived. It was a farewell performance, a special appearance for one night only, but it certainly packed the old wallop.

And just to show that nothing was missing, the weakling inside her was making one of its tremulous suggestions. *I hope he doesn't do anything silly*, it said.

That was a laugh, cried the rest of her. That was one big laugh. Do something silly — as if driving all the way down here to say, *Where did we go wrong?* wasn't silly. As if the whole scenery-chewing business he had put her through at the time of the break-up wasn't silly. As if a blind, egotistical refusal to stop flogging a dead horse wasn't silly.

And flogging a dead horse was putting it mildly. Ewan was not so much flogging a dead horse as hitching his wagon to a crate of cat food and saying 'Gee up'.

248

And besides, she had long ago had a bellyful of worrying whether he would do something silly. Throughout their time together he had used that possibility as a weapon. She had lost count of the times he had thrown a wobbly that included dark hints about not wanting to live any more; lost count of the times she had found herself fearfully phoning him after he had done a big storming-out number, just in case he had done something silly, and waiting in sick suspense while he let the phone ring a satisfactorily frightening number of times before picking it up with a moody "Hello" . . .

Yes, she had finally had enough of that. Especially as she had begun to suspect that doing something silly was not really on Ewan's agenda. Because as far as Ewan Malborne was concerned, anything that removed Ewan Malborne from centre stage was bad news.

She ought to go back to Jamie; it was daft, but she had a grubby, guilty feeling about being plagued by her ex when she was meant to be looking after the little boy — like some grotesque babysitting Americanette in a spook movie, parking her charge in front of the TV while she called up to invite her boyfriend over for a spot of necking before they both got creamed by Freddie.

He's not my boyfriend. Nearly twenty years on, and she was in much the same position as when she had cried indignantly over the graffito on her duffel-bag: SIMONS YOUR BOYFIEND.

BOYFIEND. Well, that was closer to the truth,

249

anyway, when it came to Ewan.

Aren't you flattered?

In a word, no. (And by the way, dear, I think you'll find you could get your typing speed above three words a minute if you cut your nails back a few inches or so.) Flattered was not what she felt. Angry was what she felt, depressed also. And in the end, just now, she had even begun to feel a little bit alarmed as well. That was partly why she had brought up the subject of a solicitor again. Shaking that stick at him seemed to be the only thing that worked.

Well, at least she had got rid of him. But not, she realized, without first telling him about Nick — or at least that she was seeing someone.

She had had no intention of doing that because, as she had said, it was none of his business; but out it had come. She was annoyed with herself for allowing him to manipulate her even that far.

Nick. God, she hoped he would ring soon.

Tell him what had happened? No, not now. Eventually, maybe, if she had to. But letting the separate worlds of Ewan and Nick touch was the one thing she had always resisted, and she still did. To talk to Nick about Ewan would be like admitting that the asshole still had some claim on her, that he was part of the present instead of the dead past. And besides, Nick had enough on his plate at the moment.

She went back to the sitting room. Laurel and Hardy had ended and Jamie was occupying himself with his Game Boy while he waited for the main, fatal attraction. But he couldn't keep the curiosity out of his gaze.

Amanda shrugged and smiled. "Just someone I knew," she said.

14

SOMEONE was in, but they were a long time answering the door, and Sheila was growing nervous. The door of the flat was right at the back of the rambling old house, and to get to it she had had to negotiate a passage which looked innocent enough in the daytime but at night was all cobwebs and ivy and things that reached out to touch her. At the rear was one of those old, overgrown, rank-smelling town gardens, swallowed up in darkness. And the wind was getting up, the sort of wind that made scuffling, purposeful noises and set your ears tingling till you could almost feel them cocking like a sleeping dog's . . .

Sheila kept knocking. She didn't know what else to do.

An exterior light suddenly came on directly above the door, half-blinding her. She was still blinking and seeing bright smears when there was a rattle of locks and the door came open as far as the chain would allow.

"Amanda?" Sheila said, squinting. "It's only me — Sheila. I'm sorry to bother you . . . "

The blobs cleared from her vision, and she saw that it was not Amanda but her flatmate. She was in a dressing-gown and her hair was up in a towel.

"Oh, hello, it's Lisa, isn't it? Sheila Malborne — d'you remember, we met . . . ?"

"Oh, sure, right, hello. Amanda's not here, I'm afraid." Lisa unfastened the chain and opened the door wide. "Would you like to come in? I mean, can I give her a message or anything?"

"Well . . . thank you, I don't want to disturb you, I'm afraid I've fetched you out of the bath . . . " The door gave straight into the kitchen; stepping inside, Sheila began, "I'm so sorry to turn up like this, but I just wondered — "

"No, no problem, glad of a bit of company, not a very nice night, is it, I was just going to have a cup of tea, do you fancy one?" Lisa bustled about the kitchen, her height and the piled-up towel giving her the look of a domestic Cleopatra. "Innit marvellous, Saturday night and I'm staying in to wash my hair, that's what you're supposed to say when you're trying to give some fellah the brush-off, chance'd be a fine thing; I mean, there's no reason really why Saturday night should be any different from any other night, but it just feels different, you know what I mean?"

"Yes, I know." Saturdays were her favourite days, and they did have a different feel about them — until this one. This one had a feel like no other day in her life. She thought of those putrefying beans again and said quickly, "You don't happen to have any idea when Amanda will be back? Because the thing is, I've been trying to get in touch with Ewan, I suppose it's rather urgent. He's not home, so I assumed he was with Amanda . . . "

253

She stopped. Had she said something wrong? Lisa was giving her the oddest look. Thinks I'm being a fussy, possessive mother, maybe. Perhaps I am . . .

"Why should he be with Amanda?" Lisa spoke with pure puzzlement.

"Well . . . " Sheila smiled, but behind the smile, sky-rockets of alarm and suspicion were going up. "Well, like you said, Saturday night . . . "

Lisa put down the teacups and switched off the kettle. "Wait a minute, I think we must be talking at cross purposes here. You're looking for Ewan, right? And you thought he might be with Amanda?"

"Well, yes, dear, he said they'd be meeting today, and after all . . . after all, they do spend a lot of time together as couples tend to, and so . . . "

Most extraordinary look Lisa was giving her. How beautiful she is, Sheila thought randomly. And oh God, I think I know what she's going to say . . .

"Mrs Malborne, Amanda's away. She went this morning, she'll be away for a week. But anyway — didn't you know? Didn't you know they'd finished?"

She seemed to await an answer: Sheila managed to shake her head.

"Yeah, they finished. Amanda isn't seeing Ewan. Well, unless thing have changed drastically since this morning, and I doubt that *very* much. Yeah, they split up — must be, what, months ago now — "

254

"*How* long?"

"Well, let's see, Amanda took that holiday back in June, and it was well before then . . . " Embarrassment was struggling with curiosity in Lisa's face as she said, "You didn't know?"

Sheila put an unsteady hand to her forehead, tried to collect herself. "I — er, no, he didn't tell me . . . I mean, he didn't mention it, you know what men are . . . "

"Mm-hm." Lisa was observing her closely.

"Oh, well, never mind, I've obviously got hold of the wrong end of the stick somewhere . . . Why did you say you doubted it very much?"

"Eh?"

"When you said — you doubted very much that things had changed. How did you mean?"

"Oh, well . . . " Embarrassment was winning now. "Well, Ewan didn't take it very well. The break-up, I mean. There was a lot of hassle, things turned a bit nasty — "

"Nasty?"

"Well, like I say, he couldn't handle it, and for a long time he wouldn't leave her alone and — look, Mrs Malborne, I don't think it should be me telling you this . . . "

"No, no." Sheila gave her a little smile, but she wasn't seeing her. She didn't know what she was seeing.

Yes she did. She was seeing the dark side of the moon.

"Like I say, I thought you knew — "

"Not to worry, dear. Doesn't matter." Sheila didn't know whether this bright smile was

255

convincing: it felt like a tight sticking-plaster on her face. "It's remarkable, isn't it, what men forget to mention? I've noticed that before."

"Yeah, they're funny buggers . . . " Lisa hesitated. "You're sure he said it was Amanda he was meeting today? You haven't got it mixed up? What I mean is, I know he's been going out with this girl who works at our place. Kerry her name is, Kerry Walden. Maybe he meant — "

"You know this girl?"

"Yes, I know her. Not all that well, she works in accounts and I'm in packing, but I went to a party at her place once and I know her to speak to, you know. It was a while ago now — dunno, six or seven weeks maybe — when I heard she was going out with Ewan, and I've seen them together once or twice."

"Kerry Walden."

"Yes, nice girl, petite, really pretty. You see what I mean, I just wondered whether you'd perhaps got it mixed up, whether it was her Ewan mentioned and you sort of misheard or something . . . "

"Very likely. Very likely. Yes, that must be it." The smile was hurting now, really hurting. "Yes, of course — silly of me. Well, I won't disturb you any more. Thanks for the offer of the tea, but I really must be going. The thing is, I . . . " Was the appeal in her face too naked? She couldn't help it, if so. "I do really need to see Ewan quite urgently, and I wonder if — if he is with this Kerry, whether you could perhaps tell me how to get in touch with her."

"Sure, no problem. I don't think she's on the phone, but I know where she lives. It's over in the new town, Sheepwalk it's called. I remember because they crack me up the names they give these places, I mean it's just miles of little concrete boxes and the nearest a sheep ever gets to it is the freezer cabinet at Sainsbury's, you know what I mean? It's number twenty-two, I'm pretty sure it's number twenty-two, but anyway you go through this arch and there's this sad little kids' playground with a couple of tree stumps, you know, and it's the one right in front of you."

"Sheepwalk. Right. Yes, they do give them funny names, don't they . . . ? Well, it's been very kind of you. I am sorry for all this mix-up."

"That's OK." Lisa's eyes were smiling, but they missed nothing.

Sheila opened the door. "Silly, isn't it," she said, and she could hear a flutter in her voice and she hated it when that happened but she couldn't help it, "all this time . . . all this time he must have been talking about Kerry and I sort of assumed he was talking about Amanda . . . "

She got out of there, fudging a goodbye, knowing that Lisa did not believe her. Got out of there, sweating, hardly knowing which way she was going, stumbling along the passage, feeling panicky and lost, feeling that she must track Ewan down and soon.

All this time . . . all this time . . . Lisa must have known; must have known there was no mix-up, must have seen the truth in her face.

Ewan had been living a lie to her, all this time. Living a lie to his own mother. He had talked of Amanda and the things she was doing and the places they went to together . . . and it was all fantasy.

Why didn't I know? How was it I didn't see it? And what else don't I know about him?

The poor love, she thought. There was something terribly unhappy seeping through all this, something wretched and heartbreaking. And yet the state of his flat, added to what she now knew, suggested something more than unhappiness. Sheila was glimpsing dizzy depths, tunnel perspectives. She was frightened, the more so because she did not know what it was that was frightening her.

Ewan, where are you?

She unlocked the door of her car. It was dirty — washing the car was one of those jobs she felt life was too short for — and while she had been with Lisa, someone had written CLEAN ME in the grime on the side of the bonnet. And they had added, or someone had added, a sketch that was familiar to her from classroom blackboards: a schematic penis and testicles, as crude and clear as the rounded *M*s you drew as a child to represent birds in the sky.

A pud, they called it. She had seen it a hundred times. And yet the sight of it now, boldly defacing her car as if she had been picked out and targeted, appalled her. She scrubbed it away with her glove.

Where are you, Ewan?

With this Kerry Walden, perhaps. She didn't know whether she hoped so or not. But she was going to find out.

15

THE Game Boy was a revelation. It was impossible. "It's just too *fast!*" Amanda said, laughing helplessly. Jamie laughed along with her, but with a certain constraint; he was clearly rather disappointed in her capabilities.

It cheered her up at any rate; diverted her at a crucial moment from putting her head down and getting tearful and upset. And she didn't want that: Ewan had given her too many nights of grief, and she was damned if she'd let him slip her another one.

She was damned, too, if she was going to accept any post-dated cheque of pain from tonight's proceedings. The knowledge that Ewan was still carrying some sort of demented torch after all, the knowledge that he wasn't safely ensconced in a new relationship — well, she had these, but that didn't mean she had to do anything with them but stash them away in a mental file marked OF NO INTEREST.

VJ Day, indeed. The only analogy she could think of for this last spectacular effort of Ewan's was those Japanese soldiers who occasionally turned up in Philippine jungles, waving the emperor's flag and thinking the war was still on. In fact, what startled her most about the whole sorry business was that Ewan was making a fool of himself; and she knew that that was the one thing in the world he hated. Behind the soft voice and self-deprecating smile that had initially attracted her she had soon found one uptight dude standing so stubbornly on his dignity you couldn't shift him off it with an earthmover. There had been several grim spats that had originated in her 'showing him up' by such outrages as having half a drink too many or getting the giggles in a public place.

And the loo in the Wheatsheaf. Don't forget that.

Ah yes. An episode that ought to have been comic, and that Ewan had turned into a horror-show. On their way to a party one night — quite early on in their rough island story — they had stopped off for a drink in a pub called the Wheatsheaf. Ewan had gone to the toilet. Five minutes had passed, then ten minutes, then fifteen. Finally a friendly old codger had come up to her after a visit to the loo and said her boyfriend was stuck in one of the cubicles. Something had gone wrong with the lock. The barman was trying to get him out . . .

Well, it was funny. Maybe it wasn't Oscar Wilde material but it was funny, especially as Ewan's first urgent whisper to the old codger taking a leak in the next partition had been something along the lines of, 'Call the fire brigade'. And Amanda, doubled up, had honestly believed it was the sort of laughter that the two of you shared when you were lovers. Or that at least the other party would inevitably crack up and see the funny side. But when the barman at last jemmied the lock and released

261

him, Ewan's face was like thunder. There were no thanks to the barman, no acknowledgement of the offer of a drink on the house. Without even looking at Amanda he had steered her out of the pub and then launched into a white-lipped tirade, the substance of which was that there was no point in their going to the party now and the evening was pretty well ruined and they might as well just go home . . .

They did go to the party, eventually, after a lot of cajoling on her part; they were still at the early stage where she would spend a lot of bewildered, anxious effort coaxing him down from his high horse instead of leaving him up there to get saddlesores. They had gone to the party, and there Ewan had subjected her to his own special Death of a Thousand Cuts — a succession of subtly sarcastic putdowns that left her feeling like something peeled off the sole of a shoe.

A salutary reminder, really — just in case the weakling inside should start whining about him not being such a bad sort and she shouldn't have been quite so hard on him. However, even the weakling seemed to be acquiescing in the general opinion, and admitting that he really *was* a twenty-four-carat bastard.

Amanda had just relinquished the Game Boy when the phone rang, which was just as well as she might have dropped it in her eagerness to answer.

But it wasn't Nick. After a moment's payphone rattle, Sue came on.

"Hello. Amanda? Only me. Everything OK?"

"Yes, fine," Amanda said, knowing immediately from Sue's tone that everything was not OK at her end. "How's John's mum?"

"Not too good," Sue said flatly. "It's got to be hospital, quick. They're moving her to the Norfolk and Norwich. We're going with her. Any minute now. Thought I'd better let you know . . . Duck, I don't know how long we'll be, it look like we're going to be ever so late getting back to Bockham in any case . . . I'm so sorry, would you mind hanging on to Jims . . . ?"

"Of course not, don't worry. We'll be fine. I'm enjoying his company. Alix rang, by the way. She said to give you and John her best wishes, and she hopes everything'll be all right. Is John OK . . . ?"

"Quiet. Very quiet . . . Is Jamie behaving himself, any road? He's not been pestering you about that creepy film that's on tonight, has he?"

"No, no," Amanda said, tipping Jamie a wink, "we're just about to watch a Disney video. Shall I put him on?"

Jamie's end of the conversation that followed was mostly made up of phlegmatic yeses: kids weren't afraid of the throbbing telephonic silence that adults felt compelled to fill with Poohlike hums and sighs and Sos . . . That the admonitions to be good had also included some careful words about his nan's condition was plain, though, when Jamie came off the phone and excused himself to go to the toilet. It wasn't that he was going to bawl his head off Amanda saw — more that he was afraid

263

he might if he had to hang around for some sympathetic remarks.

While he was gone, Amanda tidied round and then parted the curtains at the french windows to look out. That wind was rising again, and there were shadowy agitations in the garden, tossing tree-shapes and furtive flittings of dead leaves; even the stars seemed to be in motion. A feeling of oppression came over her; at some point the evening had crossed over into night, a bad night with bad things at large in it: Nick's burgled flat, Ewan's visit, and now Jamie's nan being taken to hospital, with all the direful associations that that word carried for her. Not that she had ever been in hospital; none of her family had, in fact. They were the sort of blessed lucky people who never had to have anything to do with hospitals. Except for that one occasion — and here was the ghastly irony of it — when Mark's irreparably smashed body had been taken into Billingham District and suddenly hospitals couldn't be ignored any more, suddenly the hospital was a great, godlike fact in their lives and would never cease to be so, the word would leap out at them from town plans and street signs and news reports . . .

And then there were children's paintings, Amanda thought. You could never look at them in the same way again, after walking down a long, seemingly endless, antiseptic-smelling corridor papered with children's paintings.

With such thoughts haunting her, there was no resisting the impulse to give Jamie a quick hug around the shoulders when he reappeared.

He took it well, though he looked relieved when the shrilling of the phone rescued him.

And this time it just *had* to be Nick . . .

No. Incredible, but no. It was Lisa. This time Amanda had a job to keep the disappointment out of her voice, though Lisa was so bubbling over with the story she had to tell, high on a buzz of scandal, that she didn't seem to notice.

" . . . Yeah, Ewan's mum — poor woman, I don't think she knew where to look . . . Anyway, when she heard about Kerry, she wanted to go and suss her out, I suppose, so I told her where she lived . . . So it turns out Ewan's been cracking on that you and him are still an item, all this time, can you believe that?"

"I can believe it," Amanda said dully. "It doesn't surprise me." Though as the news sank in, she found that she was surprised, even after tonight's shenanigans. All this time . . . could Ewan really be *that* flaky? "The thing is — well, as you can imagine, he's been here. He found me here, and I've just had the big where-did-we-go-wrong number all over again."

"He's been *there*? You're kidding!"

"Uh-huh." Even given Lisa's habitually emphatic way of talking, Amanda thought the astonishment was a bit rich, considering . . . "He left not long ago. So it looks like he hadn't cooled off after all." The disappointment that had been lurking within her burst out. "Oh, Lisa, why did you have to do it? Giving those directions . . . "

Lisa sounded puzzled. "Well, I didn't see what else I could do, it didn't seem like any big deal . . . "

"No. Never mind." Amanda regretted her outburst immediately; she recalled how staunch an ally Lisa had been all through the bad time. She had manned the drawbridge against Ewan so often, it was no wonder she had weakened in the end. And as he had said, he could be a very persistent bastard. "Anyway, he's gone now. And I really don't think we're in for an encore, not after what I had to say to him."

"God, how awful . . . Amanda, are you OK?"

"Yes, I am, honestly. Sorry for what I said just now, Lisa."

A pause of more puzzlement, and then Lisa went on, "Well, anyway, that's not the only person I saw today. I bumped into Nick when I was doing a bit of shopping — "

"When was that?"

"Oh, I don't know, six, half-six, why?"

"Oh — it would have been after that. He's had a break-in. He rang me tonight to tell me about it."

"Shit, no! Was it bad?"

"Pretty bad, I think. He was going to ring me back when the police had been . . . "

"And I'm taking up the line, bummer, sorry, Amanda! Listen, I'll get off now. I just thought I'd better let you know about Ma Malborne. Talk to you later, yeah?"

"Thanks, Lisa. Bye."

She put down the phone. Contemplated it.

And contemplated ringing Lisa back straight away, because something just wasn't right. Lisa Dickinson was the least disingenuous person she had ever known. If she had let slip Amanda's whereabouts to Ewan, as he had claimed, she would surely have made a clean breast of it to Amanda instead of glossing it over. Unless she was just too embarrassed by her lapse and its consequences.

It didn't feel right . . . But she did want to leave the line clear for Nick. Maybe she could call Lisa later, once Nick had been in touch again, and get it sorted out.

Yes. That was the best plan. She turned back to Jamie.

"Well, it looks like you're going to have to put up with me for quite a while," she said. "I don't think your mum and dad will be all that late . . . but if you feel tired any time, let me know and we'll make up a bed so you can have a snooze."

"All right," Jamie said, with polite scepticism. When you were eight you didn't entertain the possibility of getting tired: it just hit you.

Amanda went back to the task of laying a fire. There were highly polished brass fire-irons — shovel and poker and brush — hanging beside the logburner, and she caught a glimpse of her face reflected in the shovel. That groove between her brows had gone deeper; she didn't look good.

But at least it was the real Amanda. And as the implications of what Lisa had told her crept closer to her, she felt the need to hold on to that identity tightly. Because all this time there had apparently been another Amanda around, the Amanda that Ewan had been pretending was still his lover, a ghost-Amanda in whose existence Mrs Malborne — and God knew who else as well — had implicitly believed. The ghost-Amanda had never broken it off with Ewan, wishing she had never set eyes on him; the ghost-Amanda was as happy as a sandboy with Ewan in a fairytale romance that never ended.

It wasn't a nice thought. Even worse was the suspicion that Ewan might have begun to believe in the ghost himself.

16

HE was driving blind, red-misted, the car just careering along the surface of the road like a pool-ball at the break, and if another vehicle had come along the dark country road in those couple of minutes while his head was a mad balloon he would have been so much kebab-meat instantly.

That wasn't a thing that scared him. He thought about death a lot; whilst some people ignored its very existence, the possibility of death was for him a constant companion. The notion of reaching out and grabbing it instead of tamely waiting for it to come to him had always been part of his mental furniture too. This life that had been palmed off on him was no great shakes, and it would be good to sign off from the whole shitty business and watch the shapes of failure and persecution that haunted him howl their anguish as he drifted out of their reach into oblivion.

But there was no other traffic, and as the red mist lifted he began to slow his speed and to get a grip of the wheel and, slowly, of himself too.

The bitch had sent him away. His rage was only partly at that; it was also at himself for allowing it to happen. He had lost control of the situation somehow, back at that overgrown rich-kid's wendy-house; somehow the things he had meant to say hadn't come out right, somehow

269

the magic that was just waiting to happen between them had failed to jell, somehow the sheer *rightness* of their reunion had failed to communicate itself to her . . .

But most of all, she *hadn't listened*. That was what frustrated him, and made him a little impatient with her. She was playing a silly and rather dangerous game, continually denying what she must feel, refusing to acknowledge what was staring her in the face. You couldn't go on with that sort of bad faith, that sort of repression, without coming near to breaking-point. He knew that from his own experience these past months.

No doubt about it, she was stubborn. Only a love as strong as his could have held out against such stubbornness. Luckily his love had no end, its resources never ran out, because he was going to have to be strong for both of them.

Bitch.

The word kept rising into his mind like acid in the throat. The bare-faced way she had *admitted* she was being shafted by that drongo who worked in the funny farm, casually admitted it with her one real true lover standing there putting himself at her mercy . . . It was a wonder she didn't start telling him what Nurse-fucking-Dugdale was like in bed and how big his prick was and what it felt like when he stuck it up her . . .

And even after he had humbly swallowed that, she wasn't finished with him, but just had to go on to give him a thorough dressing-down in that fucking patronizing *female* way, and then when she was through with that, showed him the door as if he was *nothing* to her instead of *everything* . . .

Bitch.

And he had gone, too. Other men, feeling what he was feeling and knowing what he knew, might not have done that. Instead they might have . . .

Well, never mind, the fact was that he *had* gone when she had told him to, in spite of the provocation he was under. Because that was the sort of love he bore her. A love of perfect understanding, a love that did not question, that did not set conditions; a love that was completely adaptable, protean, that yielded to everything yet was damaged by nothing. A love that did not know the word *impossible.*

And she was just going to have to be brought to see it. That was all there was to it. She couldn't go on hiding from the truth for ever; she would destroy herself. The problem was breaking down those mental barriers she had erected so as to bring the beautiful message home to her. And even before that, there was the renewed question of sheer physical access to her, because she had sent him away and as a parting shot repeated those threats, those *intolerable* threats that just made him want to *shake* her because it was such sacrilege, such vandalism, to taint love with that legalistic crap because love made its own laws, it stood above all that, fierce and proud . . . And it made him out to be some sort of *criminal* for loving her . . .

Bitch.

271

He spotted a turning, a rutted farm-track that led to a field-gate. He turned the car into it, parked, shut off the engine. Stared at the rich nothingness of the field, listened to the hooting of the wind, felt it shake the car slightly, no more than a tremble through the bodywork, as if a great beast were rubbing slow flanks against it.

Sent away with his tail between his legs. Door closed against him. Mocking bitchwords of hate and belittlement the only reward for his great enterprise.

And now it was at an end and she was sitting there smug in Goldcard Farm thinking he had slung his hook for good.

Oh, no. Not yet, my lady.

An opportunity such as this was not likely to present itself again. And devotion that had survived through months of agony when every other part of his life had just fallen rotten and disregarded away from him like diseased flesh — well, devotion like that wasn't about to throw in the towel at the first setback.

He had a tape of Wagner that included the *Liebestod* in the car: Haitink and the Concertgebouw, it didn't have the white-knuckled drive of Solti but it was still a performance with the right glow. He slipped the tape in his pocket.

Mood music.

He started the engine, reversed carefully out, and turned back on to the road.

Going back the way he had come. Back to Upper Bockham. Back to Amanda.

It wasn't really a choice. You could give it

272

names that had been debased through overuse, names like destiny and fate. But they weren't necessary. No words were. The compulsion that took him back to her was a force like gravity, a fact of existence that there was no possibility of resisting.

And no reason to resist it, either. After all, who in their right mind would say that gravity was a *bad thing*, and that submitting to it was some sort of moral delinquency? The question just didn't apply.

And oh God she had looked so beautiful and heartbreaking, the memories of their time together had just gone leaping forth between them like a bridge of rainbow . . .

Well, one thing had come out of that first unsatisfactory meeting, anyhow. Seeing her again, talking to her, being so close to her . . . well, he had just *known*, there and then, that this was simply not a love that ended. The last stone in a great edifice of certainty had been laid as he had looked into her eyes, and nothing now could ever throw it down but the final cataclysm.

He was driving very slowly, the gates of Upper Bockham still a couple of hundred yards down the road. He was looking for a strip of verge flat enough and broad enough to park his car. A mistake, just rolling up like that in front of the house. He would have to be more subtle, use subterfuge if necessary.

This would have to do. He swung the car on to the verge, scraping the sills against a thorny hedge. He got out. It still projected a little on to

273

the narrow road, but it didn't matter. So little mattered, once you had refined life down to its burning, passionate essence.

Yes, his approach had perhaps been mistaken. What he had to bear in mind, and had forgotten in the first fury of rejection —

(Bitch)

— was that it had been a tremendous surprise for her, and surprise would naturally make her defensive, even hostile. He could understand that. He could forgive that. Well, now the surprise would be wearing off, and she would have had time to reconsider.

He started walking along the edge of the road, towards the gates.

And the other thing, the crucial thing that he must remember, was that she didn't know her own mind. So even if her attitude hadn't changed by now, he must keep that realization before him. Even if she was still offish and dismissive and contemptuous and pretended that she didn't love him and made out that she loved this Nick or at least was letting him fuck her letting him fuck the arse off her letting him fuck her till his balls were blue just as she had let that Hays guy fuck her just as she let anybody fuck her except him —

(bitch bitch bitch)

— even then, even if she still wouldn't face facts, he must remember that she didn't know her own mind.

Because the alternative was too awful to contemplate. The alternative gave him that unreal feeling of dissociation, looking through glass at a world that didn't have anything to do with him.

He turned in at the gates of Upper Bockham, moving carefully, soft-footed.

The enchanted castle. The prison of her own stubbornness, from which he must free her so that their life could begin again. It might not be a question of climbing up Rapunzel's hair or chopping his way through a forest of thorns, but that blind, self-deceiving stubbornness of hers presented just as formidable a challenge in its way.

He paused, studying the block of cottages off to his right. A standard lamp in the central courtyard lit them cleanly but softly; with their pebbled walls and tiled roofs they looked like gingerbread houses. Precisely, of course, what attracted the *haut-bourgeois* shitforbrains who came here — the same sort of human slurry who had dumped on him at the Mid Anglia Press — thinking they were getting a slice of real country life. Let them try being brought up on a farm, then they'd know that country life wasn't walking your fat-arsed pooch round some rural Disneyland but being up to your knees in blood and shit most of the time.

Was there anyone else here? Or was Amanda alone apart from this kid she was minding? The parking area in front of the cottages was empty, and there didn't seem to be any lights on, but it was worth checking out.

Softly he trod the gravel path that ran round the inside of the horseshoe-shaped block, glancing in at windows. Each cottage

275

had its name spelt out in phoney ironwork by the door: Dairy Cottage, Seashell Cottage, Orchard Cottage, for Christ's sake, as if there were any orchards on this stretch of North Sea coast, Honeysuckle Cottage . . .

No signs of occupation. Only his own face rode like the moon through the rows of windows. He was startled at how pale it was.

Having made the circuit of the cottages, he paused again, pressed close to the end wall of the last one, looking down the service road to the clump of trees that screened the farmhouse, and then away to his right at that big new building all lit up. What was that place? He had passed it directly in the car first time round, but now he saw that there was another way to it. A flight of rough stone steps set into the turf led down from the cottages, past a couple of ponds, to the rear of the building.

He picked his way down the steps, his trainers slipping a little on growths of moss. As he drew near the building he saw that the rear of it was a paved area with a rockery and a couple of metal tables. Light was pouring out from two patio windows.

Anyone? His steps grew more cautious as he approached the windows, ready to slip away if there were any signs of life. But the view that the broad patio windows gave him of the interior was so clear and unequivocal that he relaxed. An indoor swimming-pool, all fitted out with the sort of stripped pine that made the rich bastard over-achievers think they were being terribly modern as they dipped their cellulite in the chlorine. He circled round the building; another smaller window gave a view of a games room with tables for pool and ping-pong, empty again. The bright light, taken together with the utter silence and vacancy, made a strange effect. As if everyone had been snatched away, vaporized — something like what various Yank jesus-freaks called the Rapture. God's final great pick'n'mix, when he whisked the corporeal bodies of the chosen up to heaven for an eternal members-only night. While the rest of us, presumably, hung around waiting to get fried.

It was all bullshit. Death was just a blank screen and a faint hum, no more transmissions ever. The only true rapture was here on earth, if one had the sensibility to apprehend it, and the courage to seize it.

He came round to the front of the leisure complex. The short stretch of service road that curved round to the farmhouse was in front of him.

He did not take the road but cut across it towards the belt of trees that clothed the rear of the farmhouse. Scrambling up the sandy slope and slipping in amongst the trees, he kept his eyes fixed on the glowing lights of the farmhouse.

There had to be a back door. Given this strange fixation of Amanda's about not letting him get near her — just to *talk* to her, for pity's sake, just to be with her and talk things out — there was little point in him trying the frontal approach again. He was just going to have to be a bit clever, and also a bit less deferential. When the stakes were this high, any means were justified. And what sort of love was it that wilted before a few petty pseudo-moral conventions? All's fair . . .

He emerged from the trees, and gave a gasp as someone punched him in the gut.

Lover-boy what if Lover-boy joined her here from work or something was in the house all the time maybe . . .

Doubled up, he glared all round him, face aflame, ready to hit back, ready to do more than hit back, ready to . . .

No one.

What the . . . ?

Still doubled up, he saw a faint horizontal gleam directly level with his eyes.

A wire fence. He had walked right into it. Lucky he'd been moving slowly and cautiously.

So what was this all about? A little further ahead there was a low stone wall that marked off the garden proper. Why the fence — to keep out anyone on less than fifty thousand a year, anyone who didn't have their path smoothed for them every fucking step of the way, anyone who wasn't prepared to brown-nose their way through life even though it meant they got slapped down time and time again . . . ?

Wait, though. When he'd parked in the courtyard he'd seen what looked like a henhouse. A little Gucci henhouse, so that the snotnoses could play at farming. The poor suckers probably thought a wire fence would keep the nasty foxes away.

Must be. And if they were that naïve they

278

probably wouldn't bother with sensor security lighting — they would assume that rural life was like an everlasting episode of *Postman Pat*. Serve them right if they did get broken into, really. Show them what a cesspool the world really was.

He climbed the fence and moved off down the garden, cautiously still, but more confidently.

No, Lover-boy couldn't be there. She had made that long slobbering I-miss-you phone call to him, and that had suggested that they would be apart for a good while.

That phone call . . .

He remembered it, and he thought of Amanda as he had seen her just a few minutes ago, and now he was really penetrated by the knowledge that she was letting that other man touch her. Yes she was. The knowledge tore into him, split him, a brutal fistfuck of an idea that left him standing paralysed in the middle of the garden, grunting.

The comets whirled. His brain was a spinning-top. Letting him touch her letting him touch her

(bitch bitch bitch bitch bitch bitch)

she was letting him —

He took an unsteady step backwards, and felt something crunch beneath the heel of his shoe.

He cocked his foot up, examined the sole. A snail. It was still just alive, a writhing mash pierced by the fragments of its own shell. The thing that was meant to protect it had killed it. He studied it with interest for several moments and then picked it off and threw it into the grass.

He looked up, and as he came to himself he realized that he was practically in full view from the rear upper windows of the house. He hurried forward into the cover of some tall shrubs that formed a windbreak round the kitchen garden. Stood there collecting his thoughts, calming himself down, scanning the building. He couldn't see any back door . . . but the house was an L-shape and this was only one wing. Round the corner, the other wing joined on to the outhouses, and if there was going to be a back door anywhere . . .

His nerves jangled like a railful of coathangers as a screech ripped through the air. Both lulled and tensed by silence, he seemed to feel the sudden harsh noise scraping on his eardrums like fingernails on a chalkboard. His muscles were flexed for flight even as his brain decoded the sound and identified it as harmless.

A cockerel. One of those off-the-beam ones that were always crowing no matter what the hour. He had been right about the hens, then.

He breathed out, a prickly circlet of sweat on his brow.

Well, that should have alerted any fox within five miles. And it would take more than that pissant fence to keep it out.

It would take more than that to keep *him* out, too. More than hollow threats about law and solicitors. More than parrot phrases about there being nothing between them and they should lead their own lives. He had to smile: those excuses she had trotted out must have seemed so transparent, even to her. You couldn't keep the truth out with such feeble defences: it just came battering its way in.

But then she always would argue black was white if she got it into her head. It was sweet, really. She was wonderful.

He moved quietly forward and turned the corner of the house.

17

THE departure of the police had left Nick feeling worse than before. The long if sympathetic lecture on crime prevention seemed to him a prime example of closing the stable door after the horse had bolted; and the canvassing of his neighbours, with their ain't-nobody-here-but-us-chickens refusal to be involved, had given him the chill suspicion that if someone had been performing impromptu surgery on him with a chainsaw they would still have put their hands where their hearts should be and sworn that they hadn't heard a thing.

Then there was the footprint. The police had got quite excited about that for a moment. A perfectly delineated footprint, right in the middle of the spilled spices. You could see the whole pattern of the tread on the sole that had made it, so clearly that you could match it exactly with the make of shoe . . .

So clearly that Nick had recognized it, and ruefully lifted his own foot. His own shoe.

That was when he had got a bit ratty with the police. They had suggested that he should have left things just as they were rather than trampling all over the place, and he had said something like, That was all very well but this was his flat, didn't they see that, this was his home that had been broken into and it wasn't easy to be that calm and collected about it.

Yes, well done mate, he told himself. Nice to see you can keep your head under pressure. Why not lie face down on the floor beating your fists on the carpet and have done with it?

The PCs didn't seem offended; they must have been used to it. And after they had finished shining a torch on the grass outside the broken window and shaking their heads and establishing for the umpteenth time that nothing traceable had been stolen, and had finally left, Nick sat down on the bed with his chin in his hand and reluctantly asked himself what he had expected them to do. Drive round the estate and collar the first juve in a reversed baseball cap they saw? Set up a nationwide manhunt? Get on to Interpol?

No, there wasn't much they could do. And there wasn't much he could do either. Track down the warden maybe — the bar of the Silver Jubilee round the corner was probably his best bet there — and see if the old soak had some wood or hardboard or something so that he could nail up the window. That was the job of the housing association really — these flats had been taken over by housing associations when the development corporation wound up in the eighties — but Nick knew better than to expect any joy from that quarter. The association that called itself his landlord was staffed by clueless power-dressers who placed vulnerable people like George in lonely blocks miles from anywhere and then wondered why so many of their tenants vacated their premises feet first under a blanket.

And, of course, there was the clearing-up to do. But as Nick sat on the bed cupping his chin and sniffing the acrid scent of after-shave left behind by the Billingham Constabulary, he hadn't the heart for any of that. All he wanted to do was ring Amanda back, as he had promised.

And damn it all, he couldn't do it. He tried it twice, and twice he got an engaged tone.

He felt piqued at first. She knew he was supposed to be ringing back, so why was she making calls? Then he felt ashamed of himself; it was after all quite within the bounds of possibility that people might ring her. Bad: he had caught himself in the act of thinking that he was the only person who existed in Amanda's world. Caught himself, in fact, in the act of being clingy.

He made himself put the phone down. Looked round at his wreck of a flat.

A ripple of quite uncharacteristic violence ran across the surface of his mind. From the first moment of discovery he had been dismayed, resigned, and generally no more than very pissed off — whereas his brothers would have been tooling themselves up under their car-coats and swearing vengeance with a variety of colourful expletives. And he, usually, would have been the one who talked them out of it. But now he knew a moment of wild anger, and in that moment he didn't want the police to catch whoever did this, he wanted that satisfaction himself, he wanted to grab and hit out and punish —

And get yourself beaten to a pulp in the process, said a laconic voice inside him, and he was himself again.

He needed a drink. If he was starting to get fantasies of being Clint Eastwood, then he definitely needed a drink. Booze, which left some men picking fights with lampposts, turned him into a teddy-bear. He remembered the four-pack he had bought on the way home; it was in the bag he had dumped by the door. He pulled out a can and took a long drink.

Ah, well. He would try ringing Amanda again in a minute. And if he still couldn't get through he'd go and unearth the warden and get that window fixed. Even Clint Eastwood wouldn't fancy sleeping in a draught like that.

All of a sudden he wished he could draw, as an idea for a cartoon popped up fully-formed in his head: Clint in the middle of a field pointing his gun at a Mohican-cropped youth with a pitchfork. Caption: GO AHEAD, PUNK. MAKE MY HAY.

Alas, he couldn't draw to save his life. Maybe he could try to explain it over the phone to Amanda. Though it was probably the sort of thing that struck you as funny but went down like a burning Spitfire when you tried to tell it.

Didn't matter. When he did get through to her, he wanted to establish some sort of normality between them, including the telling of bad jokes, because he had the uneasy feeling that he had said something wrong when he had talked to her last: that

285

retrospective unease that grows as you try to replay the conversation in your head. The last thing he needed was a misunderstanding with her now. Physical distance, and the malignancy of the telephone, had a way of magnifying those misunderstandings until they were monsters, dangerous and intractable.

He looked at his watch. Two more minutes or the end of his beer, whichever came first, and he would try ringing her again.

18

S TUART HOWARD couldn't believe it. They were nearly there. They were just entering Lower Bockham, and were no more than a couple of minutes from their destination. All the way from Norwich they had managed to be at least civil with each other, and they had even found something to agree on. The local station was playing hits from the sixties, and they had both said they didn't make them like that any more. And had further agreed that that was the trouble with being their age — mid to late forties: it wasn't that the music the young listened to nowadays shocked them because it was different, it shocked them because it was such a crappy imitation of what *they* used to listen to.

And in this conciliatory vein they had got within a mile or so of Upper Bockham and Stuart had even begun to dare to wonder whether the evening might not end in the best of all possible ways after all . . .

And here they were *arguing* again.

How did it happen? — that was what he wanted to know. All he had done was make a remark about that really tacky bungalow at the end of the village, the one with the painted cartwheels outside the gates, and jokingly compared it with her friend Janine's taste for barnyard relics. Which were all very

287

well in some historic Grade I cottage, but sticking those mouldy wooden ploughs and milkchurns all over a semi in Twickenham just looked bloody ridiculous . . .

And the next thing he knew Fran was going for his throat.

"I'm well aware you don't like Janine and never have done but I really don't give a shit. I could mention a few friends of yours I'm not exactly crazy about either, but I won't, because unlike you I don't get any particular buzz out of quarrelling, thanks all the same."

What was that supposed to mean? *He* never picked a quarrel. All he said was . . .

"Wait a minute, what friends of mine?"

"What?"

"These friends of mine that you're not crazy about. This is the first I've heard of it. So who exactly did you have in mind?"

Sighing, she reached up her hands to gather up her hair at the back and flick it over her collar. He didn't have a name for that gesture. All he knew was that it made him want to gnash his teeth and tear trees up by the roots.

"Well?" he said.

"Just leave it, Stuart."

And as for that expression, it made him want to go into vertical take-off. *Leave it* — just what you would say to a dog snuffling at something nasty.

"No, I don't think I will leave it." Blood rose to his head. Quarrelling, when did he ever quarrel? "I think I'm quite justified in asking, I really do. I mean, this is quite a thing to find out,

288

you know, that you actually hate all my friends, this is quite a revelation after twenty-four years of marriage — ”

“I didn't say *all* your friends.”

“Oh, well, that's something, I suppose. Have to be grateful for small mercies . . . ”

“And I didn't say I *hated* them.”

“Near enough.” He swung the car past the church. On the radio, Dusty Springfield sang 'I Only Want to be with You'. Stuart thought about his friends. What on earth was there about them that she could object to? “What on earth — ”

“All I said was that I'm not exactly crazy about some of them. I'm not exactly crazy about a lot of boring golf talk all mixed in with smutty jokes and schoolboy innuendoes while they slosh back pints of beer as if they were teenagers instead of grown men, if you must know. I'm sorry, that's just me. It's just the way I am.”

He tried to speak calmly. “I've never noticed any of my friends making smutty jokes.”

“You wouldn't.”

The top of his head was going to come off, he was sure of it, the top of his head was going to come blasting off like the cork from a champagne bottle.

“Am I to take it you mean *I* make smutty jokes?”

“When you're with them. They all do it, they're all the same, that crew. They're a smutty joke in themselves. They're past doing it so they talk about it. It's like an obsession.

289

And that's why I think it's a bit rich of you to make fun of Janine. At least she's married to a man who respects her and respects *himself* and has decided to grow old gracefully instead of sucking in his belly and wiggling his eyebrows every time a woman under thirty passes within a hundred yards of him."

Janine's husband. Oh, boy, once she got on to the subject of Janine's husband you were in for it. Janine's husband treated her like a little rose. Janine's husband could cook cordon bleu, build a split-level extension, choose exquisite presents, fascinate with Shavian wit, make love like a tiger, and have a caring conversation about PMT all at the same time. Janine's husband had done everything except be born in a fucking stable in Bethlehem.

"Well, I'm quite used to your habit of wild exaggeration, darling, but this time you've really gone over the top," he said with what he felt was admirable coolness. "As far as I can recall, neither I nor any of my friends have ever wiggled our eyebrows at a woman. And what your idea of a smutty joke is I can't imagine, but seeing as your general attitude to sex would make Mother Theresa look raunchy, I dare say it's anything with the word bum in it." He realized that he had blown his chances of a duvet-tango not only tonight but probably for a month to come, and went on bitterly, "What gets me is you're so prudish about a bit of harmless fun, and yet there's Greg doing a lot more than wiggling his eyebrows at that glorified tech college and catching God knows what and you won't hear a word said against him."

The silence that met him from the passenger seat was ominous. He was glad he had to keep his eyes on the narrow country road ahead. On the radio the Rolling Stones had crunched into 'Let's Spend the Night Together'.

"Well," she said at last, "you couldn't have given yourself away more clearly."

"What?" It was infuriating not being able to turn and look at her face, even though he knew her expression would only infuriate him further.

"The reason why you're so jealous of Greg," she said in a serenely reasonable tone. "What you can't bear is the thought that Greg is actually very attractive to women."

Greg? His brain did a loop. Greg, who dressed like a refugee and could barely keep himself in Rizlas?

And *jealous* . . . ?

She went on: "And what you can't bear above all is that Greg's doing what you wish you could do."

"*What* . . . ?"

He flung his head round to glare at her, taking his eyes off the road.

"Look out!"

The car parked on the narrow verge and sticking out into the road loomed into the headlights as if it were hurtling towards them. Stuart wrenched the wheel, skimmed past it with an inch to spare —

Not even that. He heard the scraping.

291

He was swearing in a long incoherent stream as he pulled the car into the side of the road a few yards further along and got out. Fran stayed put but wound down the window.

"What are you doing?" she demanded.

"What do you think I'm doing?" He crouched to examine the scratched paintwork along the rear passenger door, touching his car tenderly.

"God, Stuart, it was hardly anything. A tiny scrape. I bet you can't even see it."

"I damn well can," he said. He was having to strain his eyes to make the scratch out.

"Anyway, you can't do anything. Come on, we're practically there."

"I can do something. I can take the number of whatever idiot decided to leave his car here." He found a stub of pencil in his pocket and an old till receipt, scribbled down the registration number. "Make a complaint — "

"You're always threatening to make complaints about things and you never do," she said, as if to remind him that they were in the middle of an argument.

He didn't need reminding, however, as, still grumbling, he got back in the car and started the engine; because what she had said just before this interruption had really got to him.

It showed, he supposed, that their marriage hadn't become stale, if after twenty-four years of bickering she could still get to him like that.

So his son with the hedgerow haircut was the great ladykiller, was he? While he couldn't cut the mustard any more, couldn't he?

The headlights illuminated the sign, UPPER BOCKHAM.

"Thank God we're here," Fran said, clutching her brow. "My head's killing me."

The radio played, 'I've Got You, Babe', as they turned in at the gates.

19

AMANDA had just got the fire going when the cock-crow rang out. She must have jumped a foot in the air.

"Oh — flaming hell!" she said, just managing to cut off a more earthy exclamation in consideration of Jamie's presence. "He's doing it again — I'll wring that daft bird's neck!"

Jamie chortled, knowing quite well what she had been about to say. "He'll probably keep crowing like that, do you shut him up," he said.

It took Amanda a moment to work out that that multi-purpose Norfolk 'do' meant, in this case, 'until'. "How do I shut him up? He's . . . Oh! damn, I see what you mean; I haven't shut the hens in the coop, have I? They're still in the pen . . . Damn, damn, how did I forget that? I thought I was all organized . . . "

Well, so she had been. But then everything had started to go haywire. First Nick's trouble, and then Jamie's arrival, and then everybody ringing her one after the other — not to mention Ewan . . .

"I'd better go and do them now. Do you want to come with me? We've got another quarter of an hour till the film comes on."

She was glad when Jamie acquiesced. It was no good pretending she fancied swanning about out there alone, with the wind moaning and the owls queuing up to shriek at her. And she had to confess that she didn't feel entirely at home with the hens themselves, especially when they started that fluttery darting-about on their scaly legs.

They went out by the back door, between the kitchen and laundry room, Amanda taking a bowl of feed as bait. In spite of the kindly light that swathed the house and outbuildings, Amanda could not help but be aware of the murmurous darkness beyond its perimeter, a darkness that just stretched on and on. In fact, if you faced in the direction of the sea, the next light was probably in Norway.

"Bit spooky out here, isn't it?" she said, her voice seeming to come out with unnatural distinction in the night air.

"It is a bit," said Jamie, and she couldn't tell whether that was nervous agreement or country unconcern. How could Alix and Ben bear to live in such remoteness? Though of course, there were the cottages — the place was full of people for at least half the year, and that would surely give it a different atmosphere.

And on that subject, where were these Howards who were supposed to be coming tonight? Surely they would have rung if they couldn't make it. Though perhaps they had been trying to — she had been on the phone half the evening.

"OK, chooks," she said, carefully opening the gate of the pen. "No trouble now, we've got a film to watch . . . "

The hens didn't seem to care about that, nor about the food she rattled in their bowls.

Whether they were upset by someone different coming in, or whether there was a fox about as Ben had said, she didn't know; but certainly they showed no inclination to settle down for the night. They ran frantically around the pen like . . . well, like headless chickens was the only simile she could think of, and that was not wholly appropriate.

"Come on . . . come on, chooks, bedtime . . . What *is* the matter with them?"

"Got the wind up their tails, I reckon," Jamie said.

"They'll get sage and onion stuffing up their tails if they're not careful . . . "

They had just succeeded in shooing one of the birds into the henhouse when the sound of an engine pierced the flapping of the wind. Headlight beams sliced through the trees that surrounded the garden. You could see a short stretch of the service road from here, and through it passed a car with a roof-rack full of luggage, heading down towards the house.

"Is that them grockles?" Jamie said.

"Hallelujah, I do believe it is!" Her own feeling of delighted relief took her by surprise; she hadn't realized just how creepy she had begun to find the solitude of this place, and how much she had been longing for people to be around. "Come on, Jims. We'll finish up here in a minute."

She swung the gate of the pen shut behind them, in her haste not noticing that it bounced ajar again, and they hurried through the house to the front door. The car was just pulling up in the courtyard as Amanda opened it.

"Hello, Mr and Mrs Howard?" Her smile of welcome was quite unforced: people, people!

"We're late, I'm terribly sorry. Got stuck in some traffic coming out of London." The man getting out of the car reminded Amanda a little of Ben Pennington — or perhaps a cousin of Ben Pennington, older and gone to seed. The toothpaste smile and baby-blue eyes were having a hard time holding their own against the dramatically thinning hair and the thickening waistline which, in the way of such men, he seemed to think he disguised by squeezing himself into the tightest trousers possible.

"That's all right," Amanda said, "just glad you got here. I should think you must be tired out."

"You said it. Absolutely bushed."

Somehow she had known from the first moment of seeing him that he was one of those men who used words like 'bushed'. She rather fancied he would say, 'take a raincheck' and, 'catch you later' as well. Mrs Howard, meanwhile, had stayed in the car, merely winding down the window. A bird-boned woman with a bleach-blonde pageboy who looked as if she had won the pools and forgot to post the coupon.

Amanda said, "Well, everything's ready for you. I'm sorry, did Mrs Pennington say — ?"

"That you'd be here holding the fort: yes." Mr Howard's smile went into overdrive. "I'm terrible with names . . . "

"Amanda." She shook the proffered hand,

which was fleshy and embedded with gold rings. She saw what Ben had meant when he'd said "If you like cheese."

"Stuart."

"Nice to meet you." It seemed the only natural and polite thing to do to look expectantly at Mrs Howard next, but the only response was a smile like a paper-cut followed by an aloof lowering of the eyelids. "This is Jamie," Amanda went on quickly, remembering how horrible it was to be introduced when you were a kid. "Well, like I say, Honeysuckle Cottage is all ready for you, I should think you'd like to get settled in. I'll get you the key. Would you like me to come up with you . . . ?"

"Thanks," Mrs Howard said, "but you needn't trouble, we know our way around."

"Home from home," said Stuart Howard, reaching up to redistribute his hair and revealing a batik pattern of sweat under his armpit. "We've been coming here for years. Absolutely love it, don't we, Fran?" As Mrs Howard inexplicably did not appear to hear he went on, "Of course, we take our main holidays overseas — popped over to Tunis this year, tremendous, we've got some photos actually, you must see them — but for a quiet break, this place is unbeatable."

"It's certainly quiet," Amanda said.

"The people are so friendly as well. I mean, you hear about country people being offish with outsiders, but we've never had anything like that, have we, darling? And the Penningtons tell us they had a terrific welcome right from the word

298

go. Love the different pace of life as well, I mean working in the smoke nowadays is just hell, isn't it? Are you from London?"

"No, no," Amanda said, thinking, *'the smoke'* — *he actually said 'the smoke'.* "Billingham."

"Oh, right. Hey, that's a really up-and-coming place, isn't it? Read about it in the *FT*. Big expansion."

"Yes, it's changed a lot." She didn't like to tell him that thrusting Billingham had suffered a bad case of brewer's droop when the recession hit, and that now there were twelve thousand unemployed chasing two part-time jobs in an ice-cream parlour. He probably wouldn't listen anyway: he couldn't have more plainly proclaimed himself an eighties man if he'd been wearing a striped shirt. In fact, now that she noticed, he *was* wearing a striped shirt.

"We've been thinking of upping stakes and moving out for a while now," Stuart Howard said, leaning on the bonnet and keeping the smile going. "You know, ease out of the rat race, get a better quality of life. Thing is, London's so handy for us where we are now — you know, you've got the galleries, the theatres, it's all there, you name it."

"Yes, that must be nice," Amanda said, trying to hide her amusement. As soon as metropolitan people started waxing lyrical about the proximity of the theatres, you knew they hadn't actually been to the theatre in the last twenty years; and a certain tightening of Mrs Howard's already tight jaws suggested that she was aware of it too. "Well, I hope everything's in order in the cottage. If there're any problems, you know where I am, just give me a knock. I'll get you the key."

"Shall I fetch it?" said Jamie, ants in his pants, afraid they'd miss the start of the movie.

"Oh, thanks, Jamie, would you? You know where the key board is."

"Nice little boy," Stuart Howard said. "Brother?"

"No . . . " The stab of pain the word gave her obliterated for the moment the intended cheesy-compliment. "No, I'm babysitting for him. His mum works here."

Stuart Howard snapped his fingers. "Hey, the cleaner's little lad, I thought his face was familiar. He's grown a hell of a lot, hasn't he, Fran?"

"They do," said his wife in a bored voice, not looking at him.

"Have you got children?" Amanda asked.

"One son. He's at university," said Fran Howard, showing animation for the first time. Opportunity for swank, of course, but it also seemed to be a putdown of her husband, whose smile dimmed a few watts. In the brief silence that ensued, Amanda found that her mind was singing, *Love and marriage, love and marriage . . .*

Stop it. "What's he studying?"

"Chemistry," Mrs Howard said.

"Stinks, as we called it at school," Stuart Howard said, turning up his smile again and making with the crinkles at the sides of his eyes. All Amanda could do was smile in reply, thinking, *What a berk.* People just didn't call chemistry 'stinks' at school, except in Billy Bunter stories.

Jamie was back with the key. Mrs Howard pointedly took it and said, "I don't think there's anything else, is there, Stuart? We've got a lot of unpacking to do."

"Right." He jerked his hand off the bonnet as if it had been electrified. "Everything but the kitchen sink," he said to Amanda, looking as if he would wink if he dared. "Anyway, sorry about the delay. Nice meeting you. You'll be here all week, right?"

"That's right."

"Great. Well, thanks again." He opened the driver's door. "Catch you later."

He said it, thought Amanda with a sort of queasy joyfulness, as the car made a circle of the courtyard and turned back up the service road to the cottages with a Road Runner 'beep-beep', on the horn. She waved a hand, wondering whether the row had already started or whether they would wait till they were in Honeysuckle Cottage before hurling the verbal crockery.

Oh, well. At least there was life at Upper Bockham now, and she and Jamie were no longer alone.

20

HE watched them coming out of the back door, Amanda and the boy, summoned by the cock-crow that had startled him.

He was beyond the light, amongst the shrubs, and the wind was causing such a commotion of thrashing boughs and rustling leaves that he could even risk movement, confident he wouldn't be seen. He crept round the shrubbery in a wide arc, keeping them in view as well as the back door.

He watched them go into the chicken pen, and he had to smile at Amanda's blundering efforts to get the birds in. She was such a townie. She disliked the country as much as he, though they had both been forced to put up with it — she when her parents moved, he from birth. It was another thing they had in common.

When the headlights stroked across him, his heart seemed to stop for several moments: his jacket was open, and his white shirt seemed to him to stand out like a flag. But though she raised her head, it was the car she was interested in.

He watched her run into the house with the boy. He watched the back door swing to behind them, but not fully shut. A vertical strip of warm indoor light remained between door and jamb, beckoning him.

He hurried across the garden. Stood with his hand resting on the back door, peering into the crack, listening. His heartbeat syncopated again as the door suddenly pushed against his hand, but then he felt the draught on his skin and realized the pressure had been caused by the front door opening. She must have gone through to greet whoever was in the car.

Gently he pushed the door open another six inches or so, guessing from the slight resistance and from the snatches of sound that the front door was still open. He listened intently. Clunk of car door, voices . . .

Lover-boy? The thought made his veins feel as if they were filled with mercury. But OK, if so, if it had to be that way . . . they could have it out right now.

"Amanda . . . to meet you . . . "

No, not Lover-boy. Visitors, surely: there was a woman's voice too. And now he heard Amanda say something about a key.

Visitors. That was fine. Once they had gone and snuggled down in Sickbag Cottage, he and Amanda would be alone.

He pushed open the door a little further and slipped inside.

A huge kitchen, rustic meets hi-tech, just what he'd expect from these flash cunts. Bags of crisps on the table — she was a great snacker, bless her, she hadn't changed. No, she hadn't changed . . .

Voices still outside. Chit-chat.

His eyes flicked, taking in everything. Door to the left: must open on to that brick passage he

303

had glimpsed from the garden. Separate utility room or something. This door, walk-in pantry. Other door, open, giving a glimpse of a long hall, the rest of the house . . .

Footsteps coming down that hall. Kid's. This way.

He stepped into the pantry, pulled the door almost closed. His eye to the gap.

The kid came trotting into the kitchen, looking around self-importantly.

Made straight for the pantry.

He held his breath.

They wouldn't understand . . . he just needed to see her . . .

The kid stopped. Reached up on tiptoe to the wall beside the pantry. Small hand a few inches from his face . . .

The hand came away clutching a key with a wooden tag attached.

Key board. He hadn't spotted that.

The kid turned and trotted back out of the kitchen. Down the hall, out of sight.

Ewan slipped out of the pantry. He studied the key board a moment. The hook with the Dymo-taped label 'Honeysuckle' was empty.

For a few moments more he stood motionless, listening. More chit-chat, but it sounded as if they would be moving any minute.

Noiselessly he went into the hall. The front door at the end was open, but he wasn't visible to them out in the courtyard. A long-cased clock ticked gutturally. Above it he could faintly hear the sound of a TV turned very low. It was coming from a room to his left.

He went in, pushing the door to behind him.

A sitting room, stinking of comfort and money. Huge stone fireplace with logburner, recesses with vases of dried flowers, beams, thick velvet curtains, Corot prints, bits of stoneware. Better Homes and fucking Gardens.

But there was one touch that was out of place. A guitar, a deep blue Ibanez Classic, propped against the wall.

Amanda's guitar. He recognized it at once, and a cloud of unendurably sweet and poignant memory enveloped him.

Her deft fingers moving on the fretboard. Plangent chords like soft kisses after tears. He had envied her. He had tried learning the piano once, knew he had it in him, but the piano tutor was a pedant, her endless criticisms had spoiled it and he had stopped.

Amanda's guitar. Her fingers . . .

(Her fingers that wouldn't touch him touched Nick though oh yes touched Superstud Nick oh yes scrabbling in his flies for his prick every night probably bitch bitch bitch)

No.

No, he kept forgetting, it wasn't going to be like that any more. Not after tonight.

He touched the guitar fondly.

He would ask her to play for him later, when they had got things sorted out at last.

Something close by his elbow let out a shriek.

Phone.

He swallowed the coppery taste that had

305

leapt into his throat. The phone was on a small circular table. Was its ringing penetrating enough to reach them outside?

And who might it be?

He extended his hand towards the receiver. Hesitated. Then snatched it up and put it to his ear.

The voice was immediate and eager. "Hello, Amanda?"

Ewan closed his eyes.

"Amanda? It's Nick. Sorry I was so long getting back to you — I've been trying to ring . . . Hello?"

Behind his closed lids, lights danced like campfires across a vast, dark plain. Temptation, oh so great a temptation to speak . . .

Hi Nick how'd you like the new decor in your flat?

Temptation to be resisted at all costs.

"Hello?" The voice scratched like a little fly in his ear. The voice of Lover-boy. Miles and miles away, where he belonged. "Amanda, you there . . . ?"

Ewan slowly, gently, replaced the receiver. Squashing the little fly.

He bent to examine the telephone wire, ran it through his fingers until he came to the main connection point, low down on the exterior wall. Extension lead there too.

He pulled out the whole connection, tucking the terminals out of sight under the rug.

They wouldn't want to be disturbed.

21

NICK stared in bewilderment at the telephone receiver in his hand. He was sure he hadn't dialled the wrong number.

Had they been cut off?

Ringing this Bockham place was getting to be like phoning through to a war zone. He dialled again.

This time there was nothing. No ringing, no engaged tone, nothing. He gave the receiver another glare, and had to resist an untechnological impulse to shake it.

They must have been cut off somehow — a fault on the line or something . . .

His glance strayed to the four-pack, now three-pack, of beer. He had finished the first in double-quick time.

No, forget the beer. There was only one intoxicant he wanted at the moment and that was Amanda's voice.

Had they been cut off? A growing maggot of unease suggested otherwise.

To be honest, it sounded more as if she had put the phone down on him.

He frowned, considering. In his past relationships, this would normally have been the moment when he started thinking about retreating to that back room in his mind. But with Amanda it was different.

He rang the operator, explained that he was trying to get through to his girlfriend, said he wondered if there was something wrong at his end, asked him if he would try calling the Bockham number. The operator, a man with an amused Indian lilt in his voice, soon got back to him.

"No, there's nothing wrong at your end, sir. It sounds as if she's pulled the plug on you. Sorry."

Pulled the plug on him?

The operator sounded as if he suspected a lovers' tiff. But they hadn't had a tiff.

Had they?

He tried ringing again. Still nothing.

Cloud-shadows of disquiet drifted across his mind. He paced unseeingly round the debris of his home. It seemed to him more than ever imperative that he should remember what he had said to her when he had rung her that first time.

But how could he remember, exactly? He hadn't really been thinking at the time . . .

Which was a bad sign in itself. Often it was precisely during those moments when your brain was in neutral that your mouth went disastrously off the road.

He stopped and looked around him. He was going to have to do something with this place, the broken window at least. He ought to go and find the warden.

But what if Amanda rang him in the meantime?

He set the answering machine: that took care

of that problem. But in truth it was the opposite problem that was bothering him: what if she *didn't* ring? — and he still couldn't get through to her?

Think. Think what it was you said.

He left the flat, locking the door behind him (now *there* was a laugh). Walked down the fuggy corridor, past the ranks of blue doors that masked mysterious other lives. The very ordinariness of the cooking smells and the hi-fi tremors only increased his frustration. Surely somebody must have heard or seen something . . .

Looking in at the community room he remarked the absence of George, who had probably ambled upstairs at last to eat. When the police had been there he hadn't thought it worthwhile to mention him as a possible witness: George had been in a haze of medication when he had come in, and besides he knew the old man wasn't keen on the police, who on a past occasion had chosen to mistake the symptoms of his mental illness as narcotic bolshiness and used him as a human boot-scraper in the back of a Black Maria.

But the initial dreaminess might have worn off by now; and he usually knew most things that were going on in the block. Nick hesitated a moment at the stairwell, then sprinted up to George's flat.

The old man was slow to answer, but all smiles when he did; then all sadness when Nick told him what had happened.

"That's a terrible thing. Come in, come in. That's terrible . . . "

"Sorry, George, I've interrupted your tea," Nick said, his olfactory nerves going critical at the smell of the ultra-spiced stewpot standing on the worktop.

"No, no. I gotta let it cool anyhow. Man, this a terrible thing you telling me. What did they take?"

"Nothing, as far as I can tell. The place is just turned upside down."

"You know what makes me angry? You know what really makes me mad? Not just they don't respect you and your home. They don't respect themselves. Plenty of people gonna call them shit all through their lives. So what they doing acting like shit in the first place? They don't want to be no better than shit, is that it? I don't know." There was no anger in George's eyes, nor the vague euphoria of his medication, only a slow, tired thoughtfulness. "What the police say? Say you done it yourself for insurance?" He gave a sudden, raunchy yelp of laughter.

"They might have been thinking it. I don't know, they asked around, but nobody seemed to know anything about it . . . I just wondered if you'd heard or seen anything unusual."

George stirred his stew with a bread-knife, setting off fresh firecrackers of scent. "I never heard no glass," he said, shaking his head. "Nothing like that. Only, like I told you, there was a guy looking for you this afternoon."

"Was there? What guy?"

George put on his glasses to taste the stew.

Well, why not . . . "Didn't I tell you? When you come in?" He looked at Nick, and then gave another laugh. "Maybe not. Maybe I was riding my little pills. God bless my little pills. Yeah, this guy, he come knocking and asking for you. Say you want to sell your car, he's interested, stuff like that. I was going to take a message for him, yeah, but he said no, said he'd come back later."

His car? Nick had no intention of selling his car. Nobody in their right mind would buy it, for one thing. "Did he give his name?"

"No name." George shrugged. "He talked like he knew you. That's all that happened today, my man." He looked at Nick over his glasses. "You think he had something to do with it? I don't reckon he looked like no burglar, but you can never tell."

"No . . . What sort of guy was he?"

"Youngish. Short fair hair, fall like this over one eye. Thin kind of guy, nervy, all like he was made out of wire, you know? How tall are you?"

"Five nine."

George studied him. "OK, I'd say he was six foot, six foot one. You get a picture? You know him?"

"I don't think so." In fact, he was sure so. He couldn't think of anyone he knew who fitted that description, certainly no one who knew where he lived.

It didn't make sense. But one thing it did make. It made the random act of vandalism by opportunistic kids that he had assumed

311

to be behind the break-in look reassuring in comparison.

"You want to tell the police?" George looked wary. "Tell them I said . . . ?"

Nick shook his head. "But thanks, anyway, George. I wish everybody else had been as helpful."

"Everybody's frightened nowadays," George said unconcernedly. "Take it from me, man, when you come to die, don't do it on the street, 'cause the last thing you going to see is people stepping over you and looking in the shop windows . . . Your place must be shit to be in, man, you want to share my stew?"

Nick's taste buds were all in favour, but there were certain other parts of his anatomy that vetoed the idea. "That's really kind of you, I wish I could. But I've got to go and fetch the warden and get my window boarded up. Thanks again, though."

"No problem. You tell that warden he's not doing his job, as if he don't know it."

Nick turned to leave, negotiating with care the stalagmites of lumber that filled the tiny flat. George's interior decor wouldn't have made sense to anyone who wasn't George; it was one great salvage operation, a memory-hoard. Edging past the crowded coffee table, Nick's eye fell on something among the cocoa-tins and lucky pixies and souvenir matchbooks that he had never noticed before.

"That's my wife," George said, picking up the mounted photograph. "You never knew I had one, huh? Yeah, I loved her quite a lot,

312

but we didn't get on together, don't know why, so we decided we better split. I still like to keep her picture around, because we had some good times, you know."

"She's really pretty."

"Well, she was *then*, but I don't know what she looks like now. Maybe all gone to shit like me." George laughed and replaced the photograph along some careful alignment known only to him. "Eh, when you going to hitch yourself up with that nice girl I see you around with, anyway?"

Nick was sure his face wasn't blushing, but it felt as if his insides were. "Don't know if she'll have me. I mean, it's early days yet."

"Nah, man. You want to go for it. You don't want to let her slip through your fingers, you know? It can happen, man, happen before you know it.

"Well, I'll try my best." Nick wondered if he looked as troubled as he felt; perhaps so, because at the door George said, "You take care of yourself, you hear? You already had one terrible thing happen, we don't want no more. So you take care."

22

"THAT'S them sorted," Amanda said when the Howards had driven up to the cottages. "Come on — must be nearly time for the film."

They raced back into the house. Jamie darted straight for the sitting room while Amanda paused to lock the front door. She felt so much better now that she knew there were people around — even a man who looked as if he always put his hand on his secretary's shoulder when he leaned over her desk and a woman who looked as if she wore a barbed-wire bra.

She followed Jamie into the sitting room, and found him standing rigid just inside the doorway. Looking over at the armchair by the fireplace.

Ewan was sitting there.

Amanda heard her own sharp intake of breath before she burst out: "How the hell did you get in here?"

"Back door. It was open," said Ewan, leaning forward with his elbows on his knees. And actually smiling, in a mildly apologetic way. "Well, you were busy, you know, with the visitors, so I thought I'd just let myself in."

"Well, you can just let yourself out again." She felt like a seething pot, about to spit and spark: her voice was a hiss. Seeing Jamie's troubled look, she touched his arm. "Sit down,

Jamie, and put the film on. He's going." She glared at Ewan. "Aren't you?"

He gave her a suffering look, then hung his head and ran his hand through his hair. "I can't ... Amanda, please, I can't go ... "

"Don't start. Just don't start that again, Ewan — "

"I'm not. I'm not, just listen a minute. I had to come back because my car's broken down. It just died on me and it won't budge."

"Where?"

"About halfway up the road to the village. I had to leave it there. I mean, it's the middle of nowhere, what else could I do?"

"Well, you're in the AA, aren't you? Ring them and get help. And then sling your hook."

"I've rung them." He pointed to the phone, gave the apologetic smile again. "Sorry, that was a bit of a cheek, I know. But I thought you wouldn't mind me doing that, at least. Gets them here quicker. Gets me out of your hair, I know that's what you want ... " His voice and lip trembled a little; then, with a sudden transition that reminded her horribly of the rapid changes of expression that flit across a baby's face, he beamed and said, "Do you remember when I joined the AA? There was that stall in town where they were touting for new members — we were looking for a birthday present for my mum, and the guy at the stall buttonholed me and just wouldn't give up till I'd joined. He looked just like that old boy in *Coronation Street*, what's his name ... " He flicked his fingers, seeming not to notice Amanda's frozen

315

stare. "Well, anyway, he was the spitting image, mannerisms and everything, and you couldn't stop laughing, and neither could I in the end — I could have been signing my life away for all I knew. I don't think we ever did get that present . . . "

She waited for him to stop chuckling, and to get her voice under some sort of control.

"How long will they be?" she said.

"Oh, I don't know, they said it would be a good while, it's so remote here . . .

"Well, you'd better go to your car and wait there for them. You wouldn't want to miss them."

"Oh, it won't be yet — "

"I don't care. Go and sit in your car and wait for them."

"Come on, I'll freeze — "

"I don't care about that either. I don't want you here." She went to the sitting-room door and held it wide open, trying to ignore the voice that reminded her she had done this before. "Walk."

"Look, Amanda — " he stood up, making a shrugging, oh-so-reasonable gesture — "there really isn't any point in my going to the car. I mean, the only location I could give the AA when I rang was Upper Bockham, you know? I could hardly say I'm on a country road in the middle of nowhere. So when they come, they'll come here."

"OK, when they come here I'll give them the message that you're with the car, halfway up the road to the village." She fastened her eyes on his, registering nothing at their melting appeal but a profound disgust. He could give her that Gainsborough's-Blue-Boy look till hell froze over, and all it would make her do was toss her cookies.

"Let me stay, Amanda." His shoulders dropped and his hands went out beseechingly and she suddenly remembered a toy she had once had, a little jointed giraffe on a plinth — you pressed the bottom of the plinth and all the joints shifted to a different position with just that sort of prompt *writhe* that Ewan had just shown. "Please let me stay. Just for a while. The breakdown people won't be here yet. I'll sit and watch the film with you, that's all. It's so long since we did that. Remember those times? When we'd watch a late-night film together, just you and me, and maybe it would be a crappy film but it didn't matter because we were together and that was all that mattered . . . Or sometimes you'd just be reading a book and I'd look up and see you sitting there and the happiness, it just filled me, and I'd want to reach out and touch your hair, but even that wasn't necessary when my happiness was so complete — and it might spoil it anyway, the moment, the closeness . . . "

That wasn't closeness, she thought lucidly. *I'd have to read a book, to take my mind away from you — and even then I felt as if you wanted to dig your fingers into it.*

The faint, lyrical smile was on his face, but he was watching her closely.

Reading her thoughts?

317

Other memories swarmed, nipping her, reminding her. Memories of his deviousness. The spinning of tales . . .

He seemed to think her silence a good sign, and softened his voice a little more. "Please . . . let me stay . . . "

"There's no point."

The crispness of her tone brought two spots of red to his cheekbones.

"There's no point, Ewan, I've just remembered — Mr Howard, up at the cottages. He's a motor mechanic, so Alix told me. He won't mind having a look at your car, I'm sure. It's probably quite a simple thing. You didn't say exactly what was wrong with it, did you? We'll go and ask Mr Howard now, shall we? And if he can't get it going, there's a towbar on his car, he can give you a tow to the village or somewhere — "

"*No!*" The flush was enough to give him away, even without that sharp negative, though he tried to recover himself "No, look, like I told you, I've got the AA coming, so — "

"Well, you can call them back and say you've got the problem sorted out — you said yourself, they won't be here for ages."

"No . . . " Frowning, groping. "You don't understand . . . "

"There's nothing wrong with your car at all, is there?" She couldn't feel any triumph, only a disdain that went down to her guts.

"Stop it." There was the jointed toy again, the abrupt switch in the set of the body, this time to a hangdog pathos, Pierrot centre stage and spotlit. And there were tears again, beading on his lashes. "Stop it, Amanda, stop it . . . Why do you have to keep on hurting me? You've hurt me so much, so much . . . "

Amanda glanced at Jamie, sitting still and pale, and thought angrily: *He shouldn't have to see this. He's got years to go before he has to get involved in this crap; hopefully he never will.*

"Your car's perfectly all right," she said levelly. "I don't know where you've left it, but I think you'd better go and get in it right now and just drive — back to Billingham, into the sea, I don't care where you go as long as it's nowhere near me."

His voice was full of the clicks and moistness of tears as he said, "I'm not asking much. I really don't think I'm asking much. Just to talk to you, be with you for a while. I don't see that that's such a big deal. Just for us to spend some time together . . . as friends."

She nearly let out a whoop of disbelief. *Friends? What sort of a friend would do what you've done to me? With friends like that, who needs enemies . . . ?*

But no. *No. Remember, don't give him any handles.*

"OK, we're friends," she said briskly. "And friends respect each other's wishes. And my wish is that you go, right now."

Something came into his eyes then, something leaping and shadowy that had nothing of tears in it; but then he set his jaw in a familiar pettish expression and said, shaking his head, "I'm not leaving, Amanda. Not until — not until you tell me something."

She groaned inside. Surely not the answer-me-one-question business again. "What?"

"Tell me . . . " He struggled for breath like an asthmatic. "Tell me that you won't see — see this other guy you're going out with any more. Tell me you'll stop seeing him, and — "

"OK, that's it. Out." She wouldn't even look at him: just held the door and pointed through it.

"Oh, Amanda, just listen . . . My darling, don't you see what a mistake you're making with him? I've just got to make you see, make you realize that it's doomed. If *we* couldn't work it out, what chance have you got with him, whoever he is? Because we were perfect together. We *are* perfect together. You know it. That's why I've got to make you see — stop you going ahead with something that just isn't going to work, something that's going to destroy you if you don't come to your senses, see what your *real* feelings are — "

"I know what my real feelings are!" A mistake: she knew it at once; she had entered a dialogue, the one thing not to do, but her anger was ungovernable now. "And I damn well know what my real feelings are about you!"

"You don't, darling. No, darling, I'm afraid you don't."

He was smiling calmly, and shaking his head in that superior way that she remembered from a score of wretched arguments, and it was that, even more than the *darlings*, that blew away her

320

self-control. "I know exactly what I feel about you, Ewan," she gritted. "Nothing. Just nothing. I'm not going to say hate, because that implies some sort of strong feeling about you and I know that in your bloody cracked, obsessive way you'd seize on that and turn it around, so let's just say nothing. Or let's put it another way, the best way I can think of: you don't mean shit to me, Ewan. Understand? Finally, at long last, understand? You don't mean *shit*!"

Ewan just stood there. He didn't even blink.

Then he started laughing.

It was a low, throaty, world-weary laugh, full of scepticism and tolerance. The laugh of fond parents at the prettily naïve remarks of their children.

It stopped Amanda in her tracks for a moment; she thought she knew all his moves, but this . . . *This is tough on Jamie*, she reproached herself. *Shouldn't have lost my temper like that. What must the poor kid think? He'll grow up full of complexes. OK, no more blowing your top, just get rid of him any way you can so Jamie doesn't have to go through any more of this . . .*

"That was good." Ewan was coming out of his laughing fit. He spoke with patient cheerfulness. "I've got to admit it, darling, that was good. You nearly had me convinced there for a minute."

"Ewan — "

"No, let me finish, please, if you wouldn't mind." A professorial joviality now. "Let's . . . " He steepled his fingers. "Let's just go back to first propositions, shall we? Can you do that

321

for me? Then we'll get somewhere. Now: in the first place, *why* do you suppose I cooked up that story about my car?"

She shook her head, more out of weary despair than anything else.

"Because — " brightly he lifted one finger — "I had to see you. Because I had to be with you. Note that: had to. Not wanted to, or wished to. Had to. Why . . . ? Because I love you. Because I love you. Shall I keep saying it, so you'll get the message? Because I love you."

And now there was nothing else to say, never mind what would be best or worst, never mind what would be kind or cruel; only one possible reply and no other. "Well," she said, "I don't love you."

Another long moment of stillness, and then he tipped his head back and regarded her as if she had asked him to believe some transparent and not very clever fairy-story. "Oh, please," he said disdainfully, "let's not reduce this to some silly tit-for-tat word-game . . . "

"I'm not. I'm telling you, straight out, because it seems like I have to if either of our lives are going to go on, not for any other reason. I don't love you."

She wasn't storming at him any more: just setting it out.

And as she did so a voice within — maybe the weakling, she didn't know — whispered, *You could be making a mistake here. Whether you're bawling him out or speaking in words of one syllable, you're still treating him as if he's sane and reasonable. And you know what?*

322

I don't think he is at all.

Ridiculous. He was acting stupidly and obsessively, had been for months, but —

And remember Lisa's phone call? He's been telling Ma Malborne that you're still together.

She became aware of something too that she had resisted acknowledging: Ewan smelt. A thing he had never done; he had always been scrupulous about hygiene. It was an unwashed smell; not the settled mustiness of the habitually grubby, but the sharp, foxy odour of someone who had let himself go.

Ewan's eyes were half-closed; he was clucking his tongue and murmuring, "Amanda, darling . . . really, Amanda . . . "

The little voice inside wouldn't shut up, and as she listened to it a cool syringe of numbing certainty entered her. *He's flipped*, the voice said. *He's really flipped.*

"Darling . . . " He cupped his fingers in a Gallic way, as if trying to put something complex in a nutshell. "You and I . . . we're one. Do you see? One. So we just can't be separated. It just can't be done, not without destroying both of us." He was sweating, she saw, and saliva was collecting at the comer of his lip. *Flipped.* "It's time to wake up and smell the coffee, sweetheart. Fooling around with this Nick is just — "

"How did you know his name?" She cut him off sharp. "I didn't tell you his name. I didn't tell you anything about him." She started to tremble. "Just what have you been up to?"

"Hm? You what say? How did I know his name? Oh, I know a lot more than that about him, darling," he said pleasantly. "Please don't think I'm that fucking stupid. I know all about your precious *Nick*. I got a good whiff of that festering pile of shit some time ago, don't you worry. What is it about him, hm? Big dick? Fill you up well, does he? There must be something. Can't be money, not by the look of that hole he lives in . . . "

"It was you." Certainty, and horror. "It was you who broke into his flat. You bastard, it was you, wasn't it?"

Ewan's lips went tight, and his eyes bulged. "It doesn't matter," he said convulsively. "Amanda, it doesn't matter . . . Just tell me you're not sleeping with him. I don't care if you go out with him, just say you're not sleeping with him! Just say it!"

His voice went up like a train whistle and Jamie looked frightened and Amanda thought again, *Flipped* and told herself urgently, *Don't antagonize him now this is dodgy this is seriously dodgy . . .*

"No, I'm not," she said. "No, Ewan, I'm not, we just go out, we just . . . "

She couldn't say any more. Ewan's eyes were hooded, his neck scarlet.

"Liar." A little snarling spray escaped his lips. "On top of everything you lie to me. I *know*, Amanda, I *know* you've stayed the night at his place, I *know* you stayed there last night, I've seen the very same *bed* where he *fucked* you and the *spunk* all over the fucking *sheets*, I mean what did you do for Christ's sake did you do it so many *times* that it just ran out

324

or did you bring him off all over your *tits* and all over your *face* or what, I mean come on, darling, let's hear it, I want to know — "

"Get out." She left the door and walked over to the phone. "Get out now or I'll call the police."

"Phone's not working, darling," he said with a quick, bare smile. "Must be this wind, a line down somewhere or something."

Keeping her eyes on him she lifted the receiver. Dead. He must have tampered with it.

Flipped . . .

She put the receiver down. "All right then." She reached out for Jamie's hand. "If you won't go, we will. Come on, Jamie. We'll go and get in the car and fetch the police . . . "

She got hold of Jamie's hand just for a moment before he was jerked out of her grasp, screaming.

23

SHEEPWALK proved more difficult to find than Sheila had expected. Here in the new townships they didn't have streets, just hugger-mugger collections of dwellings, and when you came to a sign saying 'Fairacre' or 'Ryesdale' you were none the wiser, for exactly where did Fairacre begin, where did Ryesdale begin, where did either of them end?

It was particularly difficult when your brain was spinning with frightening conjectures, and you didn't know what you were going to find when you did hunt the place down.

But at last she came to the arch and the dismal little playground just as Lisa had described it, and there was number twenty-two right across the way. The place was deserted, and the resounding tap of Sheila's footsteps sent a little shape scurrying out of the shrubs. *Rat*, she thought with dread, but then she saw the way the creature moved, as if with a dainty lifting up of skirts. A hedgehog.

"It's late for you, Mrs Tiggy-Winkle," she said. "You should be at home, hibernating." And she thought: *I wish I was too. I wish I could pull the covers over my head and not have to think about any of this, ever.*

She took a deep breath and rang the doorbell.

The girl who answered did not really fit Lisa's description of Kerry Walden. She was

326

plump and acned and regarded Sheila with cowlike eyes.

"Hello . . . I'm sorry to bother you, I'm looking for Kerry Walden."

"That's my sister," the girl said.

"Is she in?"

"Yeah." For a moment the girl seemed to have taken root on the doorstep, but then she stirred. "Kerry!"

Sheila was left staring at a poster in the hall of someone uninvitingly named Iggy Pop for several minutes.

"Yes?"

The other girl had appeared noiselessly, and was looking at Sheila with doubtful politeness This must be the one, Sheila thought: petite and pretty, just as Lisa had said.

And very reminiscent of Amanda in her colouring.

"Hello, is it Kerry? I'm so sorry to bother you at this time. I'm Sheila Malborne."

The girl's dark, serious gaze did not waver, and she said nothing.

"I'm Ewan's mother. I'm afraid we haven't yet met, which is a pity . . . Er, the thing is, I'm looking for Ewan. It's quite urgent and I wondered if he was here or if you knew — "

Kerry was starting to close the door, with a small, tight shake of the head.

"Wait, please . . . I'm sorry, this must seem odd, but I really do need to see him . . . "

"He's not here." The door was almost closed. Sheila saw how pale Kerry was. "He's not here,

327

you won't find him here."

"Do you have any idea where I can find him? Please — I wouldn't press you, but the point is I — I'm rather worried about him."

"So you bloody should be."

Kerry's expression was grim and hard. Sheila's heart turned over. "I'm sorry, I don't understand."

"Look, I don't know where he is, all right? And to be honest, I couldn't give a sod. He could be six foot under for all I care."

"Wait — Kerry . . . You do know who I mean, don't you? Ewan Malborne. Perhaps I've got it wrong, I was given to understand that you and Ewan were, well, seeing something of each other . . . "

"I know who you mean." She was curt. And so very pale. "You haven't got it wrong. Well, no, you have. We're not seeing anything of each other any more, thank God."

Another break-up. Sheila sighed. "Ah. I see . . . What do you mean, I should be worried about him?"

Kerry's lips quivered. "Forget it."

"Well, I can't very well forget it — he's my son and — "

"You should be bloody well ashamed, then, if he's your son!"

The girl was near tears, but she had touched Sheila on the quick, and brought out the schoolmarm sharpness. "I'm sorry, my dear, I don't know what sort of tiff you had with Ewan, but I do not like you talking about him in that tone of voice . . . "

"Oh, don't you? Well, you can't know him very well, that's all I can say, or else you're just bloody stupid."

Sheila could tell from the awkward *bloodys* that this was a girl who hardly ever swore, and somehow that perception alarmed her even more than the dead whiteness of her face. And it was out of that alarm that she began blustering: "Well, really, I don't see that there's any need for this, I only wanted to ask a simple question, I really don't see . . . "

The words died on her lips as Kerry Walden rolled the sleeve of her pullover up to the shoulder and held out her bare arm a few inches from Sheila's face.

Such nice white skin. Except for the upper arm, where there were four ugly, greenish discolourations. Bruises. They were fading now; God knew what they must have looked like when they were fresh.

"That's your son for you," Kerry said. She held Sheila's eyes for a moment, then clawed her pullover up to show her bare midriff. White again, except for . . . Sheila winced at what she saw. She could almost make out the marks of the individual knuckles.

"So, no, I'm not seeing your son any more. And I think that's just as well, because if I was I would be in hospital." The girl's face was fierce with unshed tears as she jerked her pullover down. "Get the picture?"

"How . . . why . . . ?"

"Oh, I annoyed him apparently. That's the

329

only reason I could make out. I can't think of any other reason . . . " The door began to close in Sheila's face. "I can't think of any other reason, except that your son is a fucking maniac."

24

THE block warden, when Nick found him, was very eager to help. Having a tenant report a break-in while he was in the pub was bad enough, but when he learned that the police would want to see him as well he didn't know whether to shit or go blind. He even left half an inch of bitter in his glass.

"They have it too easy, you see," he grumbled as he helped Nick nail up the window with a few lengths of hardboard from his store. "It's all handed to them on a plate. What's the point in working, when the state keeps them in luxury? What's the point in keeping on the right side of the law, when all the courts are going to do is pat them on the head and tell them to be good boys in future? No, this country's going to the dogs, if you ask me. There's no respect any more. Everybody expecting something for nothing. Nation of hooligans and immigrants, that's what we're turning into. Mind you, I blame the parents. They don't get the discipline at home, that's the trouble." Nick responded with a few noncommittal murmurs, lost in a strange illusion that he was listening to a conference speech by the Home Secretary.

Lost, too, in troubling memories and more troubling speculations, which advanced to the forefront of his mind once the warden had shambled off. Hammering the nails in more

331

securely, he tried again to think of anyone he knew who fitted George's description of the fair-haired stranger. No: there just wasn't anyone. So was that some sort of thief's ruse? Had he been under observation for some time, his movements watched, his work patterns noted?

That was a frightening thought. But why go to all that trouble just for a spot of small-time vandalism?

It didn't make sense.

But what was beginning to make sense, and pretty unpleasant sense, was his inability to get through to Amanda.

The things he had said to her on the phone were coming back to him now — just fragments at first, but fragments that swiftly coalesced into a damning whole.

He had been snappy with her when she had said she wished he could get out of this place. *So do I, Christ so do I . . . what can I do? I can't afford to buy . . . I'm stuck . . .* There had been a lot more of it. His cheeks burned as he recalled his peevish, ranting tone.

And then, when she had done nothing more than express her sympathy and say how bad she was feeling for him, he had come out with that priceless remark, *I shouldn't have told you about it.*

Very sensitive, that. The Silver-Tongued Cavalier strikes again. It sounded awful to him, now, just on mental playback; what must it have sounded like to Amanda?

Well, old son, it must have sounded uncannily like, 'Get lost, you're no big deal in my life

332

anyway.' Or perhaps, 'There's no point in talking to you, you only overreact, just leave me alone.' Or maybe, 'I wish I'd never called you, you've only made things worse.'

The more he thought of that phone call, the more he felt he had been a snotty, offish, self-pitying bastard.

Come on . . . One phone call? One phone call, making you feel this bad, this worried?

OK, maybe not the phone call all by itself. But the phone call dovetailed with those thoughts that had occupied him just this morning — thoughts about whether he was holding back too much, whether he shouldn't have gone to Bockham to spend the week with her, whether the message she was getting from his habitual caution was one of disinterest, whether she'd got hold of the idea that he wasn't serious about her and in the solitude of Bockham was turning the idea over in her hands . . .

And maybe this wasn't quite enough to make him fear that he had been so blind and crass as to seriously endanger his relationship with Amanda. But taken together with the fact that she had pulled the plug on him, it was more than enough.

He darted to the phone again, dialled Upper Bockham.

Dead.

He sat down in a heap on the floor, hugging his knees.

OK, so she had the arseholes with him, and had pulled the plug on him. What could he do about that? Surely she would have to speak to him again at some point. And then, when they were talking again, he could make sure this little misunderstanding was cleared up. Hell, lovers' tiffs, they happened all the time.

Nick shook his head.

He wasn't convinced.

He wasn't convinced, because he knew Amanda. Amanda always played it straight down the middle. She didn't go pale and enigmatic and suddenly do the washing-up with a lot of banging and crashing and mutter, 'Nothing', when you asked what was wrong. She didn't hide a grievance under a ton of silence and expect you to spend hours digging around to find it. She never let the sun go down on her wrath. If she was going to throw a wobbly, it wouldn't be over some little misunderstanding. It would be over something big.

And what was more, she wasn't the type of person who rather enjoyed the falling-out and then all the psychological fencing that finally got the two of you back to where you started. In fact, if there was one thing she really hated, it was mind-games; Nick suspected that a past relationship was responsible for that. So there was no question of saying, *OK, if you want to play it that way,* unplugging his own phone, and rolling into bed. That would be piling mistake upon mistake.

No, he felt he had good reason to worry, simply because she never worried him without good reason.

So where did that leave him?

It left him hugging his knees in the middle of a wrecked flat and entertaining the strong suspicion that, through his own obtuseness, he was at least close to losing the girl he loved like crazy.

And she was miles away, on the Norfolk coast. She was miles away, and he couldn't phone her.

He could only wonder what she was doing now.

25

FRAN hadn't quite left the unpacking entirely to him. She had emptied the contents of one suitcase on to the floor so as to extract from it her favourite, floor-length, aluminium-lined, don't-even-think-about-it passion-killer nightie, plus the little bag that contained the evil-smelling oils and unguents with which she anointed herself before bed. Oh, and not forgetting the sleeping tablets, and the eye-mask and the earplugs as well. When Fran hit the sack, she didn't just switch off, she took an axe to the fusebox. Lying in bed with the whole kit on from bedsocks to face-pack, she was invulnerable to anything short of a direct hit from a Sidewinder missile.

And so when Stuart saw her pile all this gear into her arms and start up the stairs, he knew it wasn't even worth protesting. But he did it anyway.

"You're surely not going to bed yet?"

She turned her head and looked icicles at him. "Why not?"

He shrugged. "It's only just nine. I thought we could — oh, I don't know, go down to the pub in the village or something."

"No, thank you, Stuart." She floated up the stairs, her feet hardly seeming to touch them. "The barmaid might be under seventy, and I really don't think I could stand you making a fool of yourself again today."

He tried to convince himself that his mind was full of stinging replies, but actually he couldn't think of a single thing to say.

He returned his attention to the suitcases, but once he had found the bottle of Scotch and the bottle of dry ginger he found he had lost interest in the unpacking. He shoved the cases under the stairs, flung off his jacket, poured himself a drink, and prowled moodily about Honeysuckle Cottage, ignoring the sounds of Fran buckling on her armour upstairs.

And to think that twenty-four years ago tonight they'd been on their way to Paris, laughing at the silliest things, and barely able to keep their hands off each other . . . Of course, they could barely keep their hands off each other now, but in a different sense. He remembered a dinner-party when they were young, and Fran tipsy and mischievous, catching him alone in the kitchen and unzipping his fly and getting him out there and then with people in the next room . . . Ah, well. If Fran were ever to do such a thing nowadays, she would make sure she had a garlic-crusher in the other hand.

At least the cottage hadn't changed: same beams and whitewashed walls, horsey prints, chintzy chairs, kitchen a cunning integration of stone and pine. The familiarity reassured him a little; he had a gloomy consciousness of time passing, leaves turning. What was it about time nowadays? He never used to be aware of it passing. Now he always seemed to be watching it flash by him like an InterCity 125.

337

He supposed it was because he had less of it — as in less of it left. He had read an article somewhere which pointed out that, given a life expectancy of seventy, you had more of your life left to live than you had already lived up until the age of thirty-five. After that, the ratio went the other way. Morbid crap, he had thought at the time. Now he saw that it had an undeniable truth in it, and that the box of cornflakes was more than half empty and there was only dust in the bottom.

On the coffee table there were the handbook of regulations for visitors and the usual leaflets, local tourist board bumph. He flicked through them: the Broads, Cromer Fisherman's Cottage Museum, Historic Norwich, Blakeney Bird Sanctuary . . . All very nice in a soporific way. All very nice if you had someone to share them with, someone loving, someone who understood you . . .

He swigged whisky, feeling sorry for himself, and turned on the little TV in the fireplace alcove. A film was just starting that he remembered from the cinema to have contained some pretty horny scenes, but it would have been neutered for TV. He watched for two minutes, then wandered again.

He remembered that parked car that he had nearly run into on the road down to Bockham. The whisky fuelled his indignation. That was bloody irresponsible, the way that car had been left. He would complain. He really would put in a complaint about that. The police would surely want to know: it might be stolen.

You're always threatening to make complaints about things and you never do.

What a bitchy thing to say. And not true, not true at all. He had written that letter to the local paper about the new bypass plans, and a damn good letter it had been too, they had all been impressed with it at the office. All right, the paper hadn't printed it, but he had definitely sent it, she couldn't deny that. And come to that, *she* was always saying she was going to take evening classes, in Spanish and painting and origami and God knew what, but she never did . . .

He stopped himself; he was always doing this lately — carrying on an argument with her in his head.

Anyway, he ought to report that car. But then there was always the chance that it belonged to some local yokel, and that parking your vehicle in the most stupid and dangerous way possible was some sort of untouchable rustic tradition going back to the year dot. And if you dared to make a fuss the miserable hayseeds who lived around these parts were liable to shut you in a wicker effigy and set light to it or come relentlessly after you like in *Deliverance*, all shotguns and bad teeth.

He nosed about the kitchen, flicking switches, with a morose hope of finding something not working and thus giving him a reason to gripe. No such luck; there was never anything shoddy at Upper Bockham.

But damn it, he had a reason to gripe, he had a damned good reason to feel very miffed indeed. When you were having a row, you traded the verbal punches with a certain degree of freedom — but that crack she had made had not only been below the belt, it had been swung with a loaded glove. Comparing him with Greg . . . saying he was jealous of the little oik . . . making out he was some sort of frustrated old letch who couldn't cut the mustard any more . . .

Well, he could have disabused her of that notion if he'd wanted; he could have told her, for example, about the well-stacked divorceé in the wages office who'd been coming on strong to him for weeks. He thought it reflected rather well on his power of self-restraint that he hadn't. Though a less flattering interpretation of his silence was that he was simply gobsmacked.

They're past doing it so they talk about it. Her portrayal of his friends as a bunch of sad, middle-aged bores beseeching every passing female with a hopeless glad-eye was so stinging because it was so plainly meant, in Fran's elliptical way, to include him as well.

He glanced out at the courtyard before drawing the curtains. Dead as a doornail; they were the only people in residence, and it would be no surprise if it stayed that way all week, at this time of year. Half the fun of coming to Upper Bockham was meeting the other visitors: there was that Mrs Franklin, for instance, who sunbathed on the patio in a bikini made out of less material than a pair of shoelaces . . .

Dead as a doornail. So this was the thrilling

prospect in store for him for the next seven days.

Why, then, was he not completely downhearted, with Fran upstairs modelling a line of nightwear designed to withstand the atmospheric pressure of the planet Jupiter, and no doubt planning a thousand and one ways to make his life hell for the coming week? And with a ragged wind moaning around the eaves, and no sign of anyone in the other cottages to relieve the monotony?

There was a reason, a reason that was like a low flame under his mind, beginning to communicate its heat at last. And a reason that furnished the best possible riposte to Fran's contemptuous estimate of the amount of lead left in his pencil.

The reason was the young woman called Amanda who was looking after the place for the Penningtons, and who had seemed quite exceptionally pleased to see him.

Actually pleased to see him . . . Fran might find that rather strange, as she had apparently stopped being pleased to see him round about the time of the introduction of decimal coinage, but as far as he was concerned the evidence was incontrovertible. That chattiness, those smiles — and this Amanda was a little cracker when she smiled, she really was — and those hints about knowing where to find her if there were any problems . . . Well, the more he thought about it, the more he was convinced that the girl he had briefly met up at the farmhouse couldn't have sent out a stronger signal with

341

a radar dish the size of Jodrell Bank.

Not that that would have been of any interest to him at all, if Fran hadn't topped her generally mulish mood with those insinuations about him. He was no dirty old man: he could take it or leave it. But he couldn't see that any man could have been totally impervious to such an invitation as that, let alone a man who had just been informed by his wife that he was a pathetic toe-rag with all the pulling power of a pork butcher's in downtown Tel Aviv.

Now if only there was something amiss in the cottage that he could go up to the farmhouse and report . . . His absence certainly wouldn't be noticed; once she was earplugged and dosed Fran would sleep through a sonic boom. If he could just find a halfway reasonable excuse, he could slip out and go and knock on the door and then just follow his nose, see what happened . . .

He started hunting about the kitchen for flaws with renewed energy — and then something stopped him. Something that had never happened to him before. Stuart Howard experienced a moment of bleak self-knowledge. Compressed into that moment were the realization that Fran was right about him, that the girl up at the farmhouse had shown him nothing more than friendly politeness, and that what he really wanted was someone to talk to because when he was alone he was conscious of rushing down the hill to fifty and when he was with company, preferably young female company, he could persuade himself he was still twenty-five.

The moment was quickly gone: the mists of ego rose up again and blotted the terrible knowledge from sight. Stuart hardly knew that it had happened. But he knew that something had pulled him back from the brink of decision.

He mixed himself another drink and drifted back to the armchair in front of the TV. He let the Scotch take over with its smooth line in comforting patter. Perhaps if he listened to it long enough, it would lead him back to some sort of decision. If not, it could always sing him a lullaby.

26

AMANDA recognized the knife immediately. It was the smallest and most wincingly sharp of a set of three that hung on the wall above the stone bread-bin in the kitchen. Now it was in Ewan's right hand, and its bright blade was pressed under Jamie's chin. Ewan was holding the boy tight against his legs with his left arm, and Jamie's eyes were staring into Amanda's.

Shards of thought. *Flipped.* And, *Phone dead.* And, *No-one here to help.*

And also, cruellest shard of all: memory of Mark. As Ewan had seized Jamie and pulled him to him and brought the knife out of his jacket, Amanda had seen double. She had not only seen Jamie's awful terror as he was plucked from her, she had seen Mark lying in the road with blood in his hair. And like a howling down a long tube came her father's voice: *That's typical of you! You should have taken proper care of Mark as well, but you didn't, did you . . . ?*

"All right, all right." Her voice came out as a sob, though this was like no weeping she had ever known. Jamie hadn't made a sound; his eyes were enough. They tore her heart by its roots. "Ewan, I'm sorry, truly, I'm sorry, I've been awful . . . Yes, let's talk. Just let Jamie go, and we'll talk . . . "

"Well, *talking's* all very well, darling," Ewan

344

said. Was he smiling, or just gritting his teeth as he gripped Jamie? She couldn't tell, couldn't read him any more. Something had gone out of his face. It was as pale and strange as the moon that lingers into a winter morning. "We've done quite a lot of *talking* already, and it hasn't exactly been edifying material. Mostly Amanda Blake, the village bicycle slagging Ewan off. Mostly Amanda Blake, the original good-time-had-by-all, telling Ewan that he's a piece of shit which is a bit rich really considering he's given up his whole life for her — "

"I'm sorry, Ewan, I'm so sorry," she babbled. *Grovel — grovel to him — do anything, just get Jamie away from him.* "I didn't mean those things I said, none of them, I don't know what came over me . . . "

"'I don't know what came over me'," Ewan echoed in a mocking falsetto. "Well, I've got a fair idea, Amanda. I imagine Mr Superstud Nicholarse came all over you just last night, didn't he? Isn't that the way you like it? I bet you do. You could hardly *stand* to have me *near* you, apparently, but oh with Nick of course it's different, I'll bet you practically *bathe* in the fucking stuff, don't you?" He licked his lips, regarding her with an alert, almost perky look. "Well, don't you? Come on, darling. You can answer a simple question, I hope."

"No. It's — it's not like that, Ewan. It's not what you think, it's . . . Please just let go of Jamie and then we can talk properly and I can tell you about it. It's not a proper relationship at all, it's a bit like you said with that girl you

were seeing, you know, just not working . . . "
Forgive me, Nick. I have to say it. "Really, it's
no good at all, just — "

"Ooh, you little fibber!" he said, and the joky,
campy tone frightened her more than anything
that had happened, and for a moment she was
afraid she was losing it and that she simply
wasn't going to be able to handle this —

No. Think of Jamie. Concentrate on Jamie.

"It's true, Ewan. It's one of those things
I — I didn't want to acknowledge even to
myself — that I'd made a terrible mistake, just
like you said. I've been trying to think of a way
to get out of it, but it's so hard . . . "

"Have you, sweetheart? Oh, my goodness,
that's not like you, you don't normally have any
trouble *dumping* men when you've had enough
of them. I thought it came easy to you, I thought
ditching a man who'd given you everything and
then waltzing off to get your pussy filled by the
next sucker was right up your alley, eh, darling,
I thought it was just like falling off a log for you,
that was my impression anyway, do correct me
if I'm wrong — "

"No, Ewan, don't, please — I feel guilty enough
as it is." That word *guilty* was a good choice: she
saw his eyes kindle. Guilt was meat and drink
to Ewan. She pressed the point. "Please don't
make me feel worse . . . it's been bad enough,
trying to handle this guilt . . . "

She kept her eyes on him, even as she made a
pretence of wiping them. Mind-games. The thing
she loathed most of all. Mind-games with her ex
(BOYFIEND)

346

but she was going to have to play them. It was her only chance. Put a lid on the fear, put a lid on the despairing memories of Mark that Jamie's white face called up, put a lid on her love for Nick and her hatred of this man who had her cornered. Stifle them all, and play the game until she could seize the advantage.

"Well." Ewan shifted, and for a moment she thought he was going to let Jamie go. But instead he edged backward, keeping tight hold of Jamie, and lowered himself until he was sitting on the sofa, the boy clasped between his knees. The knife still glinted under Jamie's chin, catching firelight. "I must say it's a little bit late in the day for you to be feeling guilty, darling. I presume you mean guilty about the way you've treated me — unless I've got the wrong end of the stick completely. Perhaps I have. Perhaps it's Nicky-poo you're talking about. Perhaps you mean you feel guilty about continuing to let Nicky-poo screw the arse off you when you feel that your relationship with him is — now what were your words? — a terrible mistake. Perhaps that's what you mean, but really I shouldn't let that worry you if so, darling, because it never has in the past, has it? I mean, take that Matthew Hays effort, on your own admission you hardly *knew* him and didn't really feel anything for him but that didn't stop you, did it, that didn't stop you letting him hump you, did it, didn't stop you letting him inside you right up to the balls, did it now, hm? So you see what I'm getting at when I say it's a *teeny* bit late in the day to be feeling guilty, don't you, poppet? But still, better late than never, that's what they say."

"I know it sounds bad," she said, hanging her head. *Keep the hate down, even when he's talking like this. Keep the hate and fury down for now, because they're no use to you.* "I know I haven't got any excuses. All I can do is hope you'll understand. I wouldn't blame you if not. A lot of people wouldn't understand . . . " A gambit worth trying: Ewan's self-image had always been based on having finer feelings than the common herd.

"I think I might understand a bit better, my darling, if you hadn't threatened me," he said. "You shouldn't have threatened me, Amanda. First it was all that business about getting a harassment injunction against me or some such nonsense, as if I was one of these sickos who go pestering women who don't want to know them. And then you had to go and threaten me with that again, when I drove all the way down here with my heart breaking in two just on the off-chance of seeing you. And *then*, when I'm not trying to do anything but talk our problems through, you have to go and threaten me with the *police*, as if I were a criminal, as if it were a *crime* to love you and want you, as if it were a *crime*, that's what makes me so *wild*, darling, and I think I'm entitled to feel wild, Amanda, I really think you've brought this on yourself and you've got no one else to blame — "

"You're right," she stammered, seeing the fierce bloom breaking out on his cheeks, seeing his hand tremble, "you're right, I know it, I don't know what I was thinking of, it was

348

stupid — I mean, I don't know what I would have said to the police anyway, they would probably have laughed at me — you know, like you said, you drove all this way just to talk to me and there's certainly nothing bad about that . . . " *Overdoing it,* a voice warned her. *He'll spot that. Hold back.* "Anyhow . . . I'm sorry."

Ewan's face was blank for several seconds. Then he broke into a broad smile. "That's all right, darling," he said. "It's sweet to hear you say sorry. Oh, look darling, I do wish you'd sit down, I don't know why you're standing about there like a spare part . . . Yes, you always did have a really sweet way of saying sorry. I mean, with some people you can tell immediately it's not real, but you always said it as if you meant it." His eyes glittered, and for an instant they seemed to be made of exactly the same material as the knife. "So. We're going to talk, are we?"

Gingerly she sat on the edge of the armchair. "I — I'd like to."

"Hmm. Well, let me tell you something first, darling, and I suggest you listen. It's this: I don't care any more. I've been to hell, Amanda. You sent me there. So the things that would bother most people don't mean a shit to me. I wouldn't give a toss if the two-minute warning sounded and we were all going to get burnt to a crisp in a nuclear war. I don't give a toss about Jamie here. But I don't particularly like doing this to him. If it was just up to me, I wouldn't be doing it. Do you see what I'm saying? If anything happens

349

to Jamie, it'll be your fault." He paused, and it was as if he dangled the memory of Mark before her like a broken marionette. "It'll be your fault again, Amanda."

Oh, you bastard, she thought with a white-hot stab of pain, and for a moment she feared that the words must be written on her face. But she managed a nod of humility, and he seemed satisfied.

"Good," he said, and her heart pounded as he lowered the knife away from Jamie's throat. "Now we're getting somewhere. Uh-uh, no you don't", as Jamie made a move to run to her. "You can sit here right by me. We don't want you wandering off, thank you very much." Keeping a tight grip on Jamie's belt at the back with his left hand, Ewan hoisted the boy on to the settee beside him. His right hand still cradled the knife, and its shining blade cast weird dapples around the walls and ceiling as he wagged it. Amanda, rigid, tried to flash Jamie a glance of reassurance, but it was dangerous; Ewan might interpret anything as a signal.

"By the way, darling, you're looking lovely," Ewan said. "You've grown your hair a bit. I always did like it long. Do you remember — " he chuckled — "that time when you had a go at cutting my hair, and it ended up all sticking out in clumps at the back like I had some sort of awful disease? And then that really trendy guy at work came up to me and asked where I'd had it done because he thought it was dead smart? That was so funny . . . "

He laughed reminiscently, and Amanda thought, could not stop herself from thinking, *I wish I'd stuck the scissors right between your shoulder-blades.*

"Well, come on then." Abruptly the laughter was gone, like something wiped off a slate. "You're the one who wanted to talk, darling. Don't just sit there like a stuffed dummy. Don't just sit there as if butter wouldn't melt in your mouth. Or anything else for that matter."

The snarl that crept into his voice made her tremble again. "Please, I — it's difficult . . . "

The smile was back. A coaxing smile. "Oh, darling. I was only joking. So come on. Let's hear it. Apparently this thing with Nick isn't working out. Not what I'd gathered at all, but I'll take your word for it. So tell me what's wrong." Smiling, but watching her, oh so closely. "Tell your uncle Ewan all about it. In what way is Lover-boy a letdown, precisely? No good in bed? Hm? Or perhaps he has unspeakable tastes in that direction. Perhaps he likes giving you one up the shitter. Is that it? I wouldn't have thought that would bother you, sweetheart, not with your record, I wouldn't have thought giving head to a donkey would faze you particularly, knowing your habit of dropping your knickers for anybody who asks you — oh, except for someone who really loves you and values you, of course, that seems to be a real turn-off where you're concerned; I mean, that seems to be about the only thing that stops you dripping at the gash like a fucking leaky tap. I speak from bitter experience, of course. Oh, well, perhaps

351

it's something else. Perhaps he has a penchant for dressing up in women's clothes. Is that it? I must say I didn't see any sign of it in that pukey bedsit of his, no frilly lingerie festooning that charming breezeblock — "

"I can't tell you." She cut him off because she couldn't bear to hear him bragging about what he had done to Nick's flat, but she snatched at a half-chance at the same time. "Ewan, I can't tell you about it — not with Jamie here. It's too . . . "

"You must think I'm *stupid*." Ewan's voice rose to a roar, and Jamie flinched. Then, instantly, he switched to falsetto again. "'Oh, oh, Ewan, I can't tell you about it, not with Jamie here. I can't tell you about my non-existent problems with Nick while Jamie's here, so let go of him, and then when he's safe I'll turn into a complete bitch again and tell you what a stud Nick is and how he's hung like a bull and how I'm deliriously happy with him and then when I've done that and really rubbed your nose in it I'll turn you over to the police'. That's it, isn't it? That's what's going through your mind, isn't it?" He pulled Jamie over on to his lap with a savage jerk and pressed the blade of the knife against the boy's soft cheek. "*Isn't it?*"

"No — no — I don't know . . . " She was sobbing, gasping; part of her mind moaned, *Failed, no good, you can't do it, you're going to fail Jamie just as you failed Mark*, but another part urged her, *Keep thinking, keep thinking, keep in the game* . . . And it was in obedience to that part that she cried, "Don't

352

hurt him — please, Ewan — I can't hide anything from you, you know I can't, I never could — just don't hurt him . . . "

She hid her face in her hands, and couldn't risk looking up to gauge his expression for some seconds. When she did at last look up, she found him watching her just as intently as before, the knife still denting the skin of Jamie's cheek. But she saw too a little smirk of satisfaction playing about Ewan's lips.

"No," he said. "No, you can't hide anything from me, Amanda. It's about time you found that out."

He relaxed his grip on the knife slightly, allowing the blade to break contact with the skin. A red mark showed up. Jamie's eyelashes beat twice with soft terror. Amanda let out a slow silent breath.

"Well, we're getting somewhere, at any rate," Ewan resumed urbanely. "So, seeing as you can't hide anything from me, let's go back a bit. Let's test the truth or otherwise of something you said to me earlier, shall we? I wonder if you can guess what it is."

He paused. Amanda shook her head.

"No? It was something very important to both of us . . . Still no ideas? Your memory must be going, darling. Nicholarse must be shafting your brains out. OK, I'll remind you. You said to me, and I quote, 'I don't love you.' There. Ring any bells?"

"Ewan, please, don't do this — "

"Shut up a minute, darling, if you wouldn't mind, and let me finish. Now I don't want there

353

to be any misunderstandings. I must establish that this is what you said before we go any further. I need to have verbal assent, as the police say. So. Is that or is that not what you said to me?"

"Yes. Yes, I did . . . but Ewan, I don't know what I really think or feel; I mean, I'm all so mixed up inside . . . "

"Oh!" He raised a sardonic eyebrow. "So there is hope after all, is there? Well, bugger me backwards and put the flags out, there is actually a gleam of hope in this fucking pit that I call my life." Then his tone completely altered, suddenly turned feverish and urgent. "Oh, my darling, if I thought that was really true, if I thought there was a chance for us, do you think I'd be doing this? I'd let Jamie go, and we could get in the car and just drive off somewhere and put this all behind us. A new start! What do you think?"

His voice had dropped almost to a whisper. Amanda nodded her head, reminding herself, *Don't overdo it.* "Maybe," she said, hesitant, "I don't know . . . maybe we could . . . "

A long look at her, and then he shifted in his seat jauntily, like someone about to take part in a parlour game. "OK. OK, like I said, we'll test out that thing you said. We'll find out what the truth is." He moved his right hand so that he was holding the knife loosely at Jamie's throat, and with his left he pushed back his tangled fringe. He winked at her.

"Come here and give me a kiss," he said.

354

27

NICK was making the bed. It was the one piece of tidying-up he could face. He was making the bed with great care, as if it were the most important thing he had ever had to do; folding the clean sheet around the corners with geometric precision and smoothing and smoothing them across the mattress, plumping the pillows into a perfect lozenge shape, shaking the duvet repeatedly so that it fitted inside its cover without a wrinkle.

He didn't know why he was doing this, and yet at the same time it seemed absolutely unquestionable that he do it. His slow, deliberate, almost machine-like movements reflected the suspension of his mental processes. His brain, which had been thrumming and resounding with a million questions and conjectures, had turned into a blank screen. Waiting for a message. And meanwhile his body had taken over the whole business of living.

His body, having at last finished the making of the bed to its satisfaction, took him over to the phone again. It picked up the receiver, dialled the number of Upper Bockham, listened once more to the dead tone, put the receiver down. It stood for a minute, motionless. Then it took him over to the bookcase. It began rooting through the heap of torn and scattered books and papers.

355

It was looking for one particular piece of paper, the piece of paper on which Amanda had written the directions for driving to Upper Bockham. There was presumably a reason for its hunting for this, but it had yet to appear on the screen.

After a while his body gave up the search; it was hopeless trying to find one slip of paper in a flat that had been turned upside down. Instead it took him over to the chair, sat him down, and began putting on his shoes, which he had slipped off in the expectation of not going out again tonight. His hands tied the laces with the same precision they had shown in making the bed, but they moved more quickly now, as if his body had stepped up a gear or two. Then it lifted him to his feet and took him over to the cupboard and got out his coat and put it on. He was surprised to find that he was apparently not staying in, that he was not going to get into that bed later, that he was going to do something else entirely; but he acquiesced. His body knew what it was doing.

And his body had stepped up another gear. It was hurrying him to the door of his flat, hurrying him to lock it behind him, hurrying him down the corridor. And by the time he reached the security door it was running. Legs pumping, breath quickening, heart accelerating — every part of it working for maximum speed.

And by the time he felt the cold air surging into his lungs and the hardness of the car-park tarmac stinging the soles of his pounding feet, Nick knew what he was doing. The screen was

356

flashing up the message that his body had already received through its own mysterious subtle circuits and acted upon.

Drive.

Go to Amanda. Nothing else matters. Go to Amanda.

The elation of decision hit him as he got into the car and started the engine, and he experienced an adrenalin high that left him light-headed for several moments. But a glance at the somewhat basic road-atlas that he kept in the back seat was enough to bring him down. He recognized the general route, but once he was past Holt he would be flying blind. Upper Bockham didn't even seem to be on there.

He looked at his watch. Nearly nine. He could get there by eleven, if he drove fast, and if he didn't get lost. Amanda was a night-owl; and anyhow, it didn't matter if he had to wake her up; nothing mattered as long as he got to her and sorted out whatever in hell all this was about.

His euphoria dimmed again as he acknowledged that sense of direction was not his strong point. In fact, it was something of a joke among his work colleagues, who told the home residents to tie a string to him when they went on outings.

Well, his instincts had done good work for him so far tonight; he would just have to trust to them again.

He pulled out of the car-park, and his headlights measured out the first few yards of his journey — cut the first short slice out of a darkness seventy-six miles long.

28

SHEILA stood on the pavement outside the police station, watching her condensing breath being whirled away on the windy night air.

This was the old police station, in Billingham city centre, close to the river in a dingy district of ancient wharves and peeling grain warehouses. There was a spanking new main headquarters nowadays, a suave, hi-tech building out in the leafy townships, but to Sheila that place had something bogus about it. A real police station, a place that you had to go to when all was not well, a place that most of the time you did not want to think about, should look like this — gloomy brown brick and barred frosted windows and a forbidding door with a pediment over it.

Sheila dug her hands in her pockets and tapped her heels. For the first time she wished she had not given up smoking. Cigarettes might kill you, but they were just made for moments like this, moments when you hesitated before having to do something awful.

There was, of course, still an alternative. She could go home or go to a callbox and phone the police instead. But the trouble with the phone was it was just too easy to put down if your nerve failed.

A trio of teenage girls approached her along

358

the pavement, arms linked, shoes clopping horselike, their heartless young faces full of happiness and malice. They were singing or chanting something Sheila didn't understand. She withdrew to the wall to let them pass, but they swerved so as to brush insolently against her, and they were laughing as they carried on their way; hoarse sensual laughter of the sort that was once heard at bear-baitings and public executions.

Horrible girls: normally she would have been sharp with them. But she wasn't up to it now. Not the way she was feeling. All she could do was sadly and fearfully think of the many pleasant girls there were around. Girls like Amanda. Girls like Kerry Walden.

Sheila bit hard on her lip. She remembered coming into town with her parents when she was a very small girl, and sometimes fearfully wondering what would happen if she got lost. Peering through the high back window of the old Wolseley at the kaleidoscope of alien streets, she would think, *What if I lost Mummy and Daddy and I was left standing on that corner there . . . what would I do? What would I do?* The sheer vastness and strangeness of the world had appalled her.

And now, forty-five years later, she stood on the pavement in the centre of a city that was utterly familiar to her and felt something of the same dread. The world was no longer a place in which you found a cosy niche, but something naked and blank and taut as the skin of a drum and you were a speck set down in the terrible midst of it.

What about his friends? Maybe he's with friends.

This idea had occurred to her on the way here, but it was such a weak and tottering idea that she hadn't bothered with it. Now, faced with the alternative of walking into the police station and speaking her son's name, she put her hand under the idea's arm and listened to what it had to say.

She was willing to be convinced. But the idea soon collapsed and died. Ewan had so few real friends. It wasn't that he had trouble making friends, but that they so often let him down and turned against him. There was that very nice and remarkably clever young man called Martin with whom he had been good friends for some time. Then Martin had gone to Leicester to do postgrad work and, though Leicester wasn't far from Billingham and they had seen something of each other at first, the friendship had fallen away. Martin had turned superior and was always trying to put Ewan down —

That was Ewan's version, anyway.

The bitter rush of scepticism with which she thought these words was in some ways worse than anything that had happened today. Because it was as if some harsh fluorescent light had been turned on and now everything about Ewan had to be seen and examined in the glare of it. He had lied to her about Amanda, pretending they were still together. He had lied by omission about Kerry Walden

(and she had seen the most terrible omission

of all with her own eyes and that was why she was standing here summoning up the nerve to enter the police station)

and so how could she know what else he had lied about, how could she take at face value anything about her son? When he had complained of the friends who had turned against him, the trust broken and the confidences betrayed, she had taken it for granted that it was so — had indeed felt indignantly sympathetic on behalf of the son who was so unguarded and vulnerable that people immediately spotted it and abused him. Even as it had kept on happening to the point where he really had no friends to speak of she had chosen to believe his version.

Chosen to believe. The pitiless light now bathed her own motives too. She had chosen to believe because it suited her. For years she and Ewan had been allies: *you and me against the world*, as the drunks said. They had both seen through the bullshit; they both declined to acclaim the emperors new clothes. When Ewan had said, as he so often did, *They don't understand me*, her own ego had got a shot in the arm too.

If he was the sort of man that she now feared he was, thought Sheila, then she had connived at making him so.

No no I won't believe it.

Kerry, haunted eyes never leaving her face, clawing up her pullover . . .

You've got to believe your own eyes.

Sheila turned and pushed open the door of

the police station, forcing herself into movement with such a lurch that she must have looked like a drunk, like the old man in the capacious drunk's-overcoat who was arguing desultorily with the desk sergeant.

Sheila waited while the old man, red-faced and white-bearded like Santa Claus on the skids, had his incoherent say before shambling out. The desk sergeant raised his eyebrows at her like a shop assistant who has just served an awkward customer.

"He'll be back in ten minutes, when he's thought of something else to say. Not a very nice night out, is it? That wind goes right through you."

Somehow this chattiness — as if being in a police station were perfectly normal — was more than Sheila could bear, and she burst out, "Please help me, I'm worried about my son."

"Yes?" The desk sergeant offered a smile and casually opened a large, black-bound book. "How can we help? Can I have your name, by the way?"

"Malborne, Sheila Malborne." Distractedly she tried to think of one nice experience in your life which required you to give your name. No: there weren't any. They were all nasty.

The desk sergeant was looking at her expectantly.

"My son," she said again. "His — his name's Ewan, Ewan Malborne. E-W-A-N. I . . . " Her mind tangled like a snarl of knitting. Somewhere down the corridor to the left of the desk a heavy door banged, and someone started shouting. The place smelt like school, she thought: hot pipes painted with three layers of beige gloss, diluted disinfectant, old varnish.

"And your son's age?"

"Twenty-eight."

Her cheeks were burning. Though the desk sergeant tried to disguise it, she knew he had been expecting her to speak of someone younger, a child or a teenager. *Should be flattered.*

Not flattered though. Just wretched, anguished, wanting to be anywhere but here. And feeling, in spite of the frightful new knowledge, that she was betraying Ewan.

"And what exactly's the problem, Mrs Malborne?"

"He's — he's missing."

The sergeant made a note. Sheila's eyes wandered desperately, seeing hideous brown, PVC-covered benches with rips in them like wounds exposing the foam flesh beneath, a noticeboard full of chirpy crime prevention posters, a low table with a large glass ashtray on it. The last public place in the western world in which you were allowed to smoke.

"And how long has he been missing?"

Sheila looked at the floor. "Well . . . I saw him this lunchtime."

"Your son lives with you?"

"No, no . . . He has his own place. I've been there, he's not there. He's not — he's not with his girlfriend either." She knew as she spoke — she had probably known even as she had set out for the police station — that she was not going to report what really frightened her.

Amanda. Kerry. "I've been trying to find him, you see . . . "

"There was somewhere he was supposed to be, is that what you're saying? And he hasn't turned up?"

"Not — not really." A headache announced itself behind her eyes. "It's just that . . . I'm worried about the way he's been behaving lately. I think he might be depressed."

I think he might be dangerous. That was what she wanted to say, and that was what she could not say. It would have been buying peace at the expense of a treachery which even now she could not contemplate. *My son. He means so much to me. My own son.* And she remembered again Ewan being dragged screaming and bloodied from her womb, the memory brutally mixed up with the bruises on Kerry's white flesh, and she thought with wild horror, *Perhaps whatever's in him came out of me as well.*

"I'm sorry, Mrs Malborne," the sergeant said. "Can you give me a clearer idea of why you think your son's missing. You saw him this lunchtime, you say?"

Sheila nodded miserably.

"What does your son do?"

"He works at the Edith Cavell hospital. In catering. But no, he's not at work today." As the sergeant seemed to look doubtful she said, "Look, I know he isn't, he — I know his shifts, we're very close, that's why I can't imagine where he is." The headache had moved round and become a skullcap of bright pain: she felt the nerves of her face twitch as another heavy,

364

institutional door banged close at hand.

"He's not with his girlfriend, you say? And she has no ideas about where he is?"

Which girlfriend? she thought hysterically. *The one he pretended he was still with, or the one he beat up?*

"No. They — I think they've fallen out anyway."

The sergeant nodded as if he had expected that. "Friends?"

"They don't know either." Lie after lie. *Admit it, dear Ewan doesn't have friends any more.* Down the corridor the shouting was still implacably going on, as if someone were delivering a mad sermon. All at once Sheila just wanted to get out of here. Anything was preferable to this.

"He's been acting strangely, you say — "

"I didn't say that!"

The sergeant looked his surprise at her tone. She saw that he wasn't writing anything down. "Has he been drinking a lot, that sort of thing?"

"Something like that." Sheila's lips quivered. "Not happy. Something wrong. Not happy. Oh, look, I know you can't do anything — "

"Well, yes, we can. When it's a question of a missing person, we can. But I'm afraid from what you've told me we can't classify your son as a missing person. It's only, what, a quarter-past nine. Does your son like to go out on the town: pubs, clubs, that sort of thing?"

"He . . . he does go out."

"You see what I'm saying, Mrs Malborne.

365

Your son is his own individual. I'm sure you're right to be a little bit concerned about him if he's seemed depressed lately, of course you are . . . "

He thought she was a silly interfering possessive mother: it was written all over him. She didn't care any more. Just let her get out of here.

"The time to be concerned is if he doesn't come home all night. I mean — is that a thing he would generally do?"

You mean does he pick up bimbos in clubs and spend the night with them. I don't know: I don't know what he does any more.

"Not as a rule."

"Well, my advice to you is to leave it a while. See if he comes home at a reasonable time tonight, which I'm sure he will. But if not, or if you think of anything else that will, you know, give us a firmer idea of what the problem is, then don't hesitate to contact us. All right?"

Sheila nodded, unable to speak. She felt like a child about to get out of the headmaster's office.

"I do know what it's like," the sergeant said, his local accent suddenly coming out. "I'm got two teenage girls myself. They seem to like worrying you to death, don't they? Tell you not to fuss, but they'd hate it if you didn't."

"Yes." She was already backing to the door. "I dare say you're right. I'm sorry to have bothered you — "

"Not at all. You did quite right. But like I

366

say, give it a while, and if there's still no sign of him — "

"I will. Thank you . . . " As she got to the door it swung open: three young people in Saturday-night gear crashed in, one with blood pouring from his nose all over his white shirt. The other two were boy and girl, and all three were arguing at the tops of their charmless voices. The eternal triangle, Sheila wondered? Whatever, she was glad of the diversion to cover her exit.

Glad she could get out to the fresh air and burst into tears without the kindly cynical eyes of the sergeant on her. Glad she could hurry down the street to her car in weeping silence and not have to feel her abdication of responsibility hammering into her like a nail with every evasive word. Glad she had escaped without letting her real fears about Ewan out into the unforgiving world.

No. She was going to keep them inside her, as she had kept him inside her for nine months. But she had no illusions about how easy they were going to be to keep. They were already biting at her insides like a greedy worm. She could only bear them because she could not bear the alternative.

And how long she would have to bear them she did not know. The desk sergeant had said he would come home sooner or later: *leave them alone, and they'll come home, dragging their tails behind them.* The desk sergeant, of course, had not seen the tin can full of mould, or Lisa's expression of bewilderment, or the bruises on Kerry's skin. Yet Sheila now clung to those words of his as if he were an infallible oracle — simply because she had nothing else left to cling to.

At least she knew where she had to go.

She waited for her eyes to clear before starting the engine and pulling out. As she came to the bridge over the river, a car full of youth hurtled past her, boombox beat and streamlined obscenities trailing from the open windows. Along the riverbank, close at hand, a few ancient willow trees swayed in the wind with the mournful dignity of chained elephants in a garish circus.

She knew where she had to go, and she was soon there. The porch that had contained the libidinous couple was empty now. Someone had been colourfully sick on the pavement. There were still no lights in Ewan's place, but she knocked, just to be sure, before using the spare key again and going in.

The sour smell, the lair-smell, seemed stronger than ever; but she didn't much care. Even the idea of tidying the place up was quickly dismissed. She turned on all the lights, then went into the living room. She did not bother taking off her coat. For a moment she considered switching on the TV — but no. There would be screaming and lovemaking. Instead she picked up the first CD that came to hand and slotted it into the machine and then, having flicked away the rubbish with the heel of her hand, sat back in the armchair.

Wagner, of course. The *Tannhäuser* overture.

She moved through a dark and solemn forest of brass until the gleams of the Venusberg music shone through the massy chords and orchestral riot took over, restless and scintillating, neurotic with desire.

Sheila listened and waited, unknowing how long she must wait or what the end of the waiting would be.

29

EWAN was waiting.

Amanda became aware of a clock ticking. It was the carriage clock on the corner cabinet. She hadn't noticed it ticking before.

Jamie was still pulled over on to Ewan's lap. Very much like a child who has stayed up too long and leans over and nods off on his dad. Until you saw the knife.

The touch of that knife-blade on Jamie's skin was intolerable to see. It was like seeing fingernails digging into a balloon — your nerves screeched and you had to move, to shout stop it, to forestall the awful result —

Except that, in this case, that sort of reaction was the one thing she must not do. She mustn't become hysterical at that knife-edge denting Jamie's throat, because the man holding it was on a knife-edge of his own.

And Ewan was waiting. He chirruped and puckered up his lips, jocularly.

"Just one kiss, darling," he said. "Just one's all I need."

I'd rather kiss an open sore.

She must suppress these thoughts. He might read them. He might wiggle the shoe-horn of his obsession under her conscious mind and find something he didn't like. And then . . .

She got to her feet. Her legs wobbled under

370

her as if she had the flu. She stepped forward. Jamie's eyes turned painfully in their sockets, seeking her out.

If I could only get that knife . . .

No. Of all thoughts, that was the most dangerous. Squash it. Start thinking you were Cynthia Rothrock, able to rectify the situation with a few smart martial-arts moves, and you would kill Jamie as surely as . . .

As surely as you killed Mark.

Mind-games. Mind-games were her only hope. Though she hated them, surely they weren't beyond her. She had had a good teacher.

Amanda took another step. Then another. She was close to Ewan now: could see the fair stubble on his narrow jaw, the roots of his hair, the labyrinthine shape of his inner ear, the long-fingered hand grasping the knife . . .

And even as she slowly bent down and inclined her face towards him, the sight of that hand and that knife sparked an explosive thought in her mind that she just couldn't extinguish: *My God! I used to go out with this man! I've been to bed with this man! I voluntarily mixed up my life with this man's once upon a time!*

But that was the trouble. You never knew. You had to let them in first, before you could know what they were really like. And once you'd let them in . . .

AIDS wasn't so inexplicable. It was an externalising of the danger you were in, the risk you took every time you ceased to be self-sufficient and bent your lips towards the lips of another person . . .

371

As she was bending her lips towards Ewan's. The distance between them was narrowing, narrowing . . .

And his eyes were burning into hers like two naked bulbs and she couldn't meet them and as she felt his breath on her face she was afraid she was going to be sick, not from physical disgust but from a disgust at everything he represented in her life . . .

His hand came up to touch her cheek and at the first light contact of the fingertips she couldn't help it, she had to jerk her head back and his eyes took on that hooded appearance and she knew that he had seen the repugnance on her face —

(you can't hide anything from me)

— and then the hand was coming towards her again but faster this time and he slapped her across the face.

"You *bitch*!"

She recoiled, clutching her cheek. Such a thing had never happened to her before and she was astonished at the pain. It was as if a hot flat-iron had been pressed to her face.

"You couldn't even do that, could you? You couldn't even bear to give me one kiss! And yet you were quite prepared to *pretend*, to try and fool me again!" Little drops of spittle were falling from Ewan's lips; she saw them land on Jamie's flinching face. "You must think I'm *stupid*, Amanda! You must think I'm really *stupid*!"

"I'm sorry . . . " The pain was so intense that she couldn't think. She struggled to find the right things to say, the things that would keep her in the game. "It isn't easy . . . after all this time . . . I'm so confused . . . "

"Oh, I don't think so, darling. I don't think you're confused at all. Not when it comes to me, anyway. When it comes to me you're quite clear in your mind as you've always been: treat Ewan like shit, keep him dangling on a string, make his life a complete misery, destroy him bit by bit and *laugh* at him as you do it. No, no confusion there, darling. Everything's plain as a fucking pikestaff, thank you very much." She saw Jamie wriggle, but Ewan merely tightened his grip without taking his eyes off her. "I think you'd better go and sit down again, darling, it's obviously such a horrible experience for you having to be within three feet of me, we wouldn't want you throwing your guts up all over me . . . well, it wouldn't bother me particularly because that's precisely the sort of treatment I've come to expect from you, but we wouldn't want *you* to be made uncomfortable, dear me no."

Still clutching her face, she retreated to the armchair, trying to rake together her scattered thoughts, trying to shout down the wail of panic and despair inside her. *No. I haven't failed. It isn't over. I lost that move, that's all.*

She saw Jamie wriggle again. She didn't dare meet his eyes. She could only silently beg him, *Don't struggle, Jamie. As long as you don't move, he's liable to forget you're there because he's so crazily wrapped up in himself. But if you move . . .*

373

"I think I'm on the wrong track here, you know," Ewan said conversationally. "I think I've been on the wrong track all the time. Don't you?"

Not understanding, she could only shake her head.

"Oh, shake not thy gory locks at me, sweetheart: you know perfectly well what I mean. . That's what pisses me off about you women. I mean, you expect us to be fucking mindreaders and know exactly what's wrong when you get the hump and yet you come out with this innocent-Miss-Pears-oh-what's-the-matter-I-don't-understand crap." He gave a sigh that was like the rasp of sandpaper. "I'll have to spell it out then. Where I've been on the wrong track, it seems, is in my whole attitude to love. I've been very naïve, I'm afraid. You see, I've always thought it was one of the important things of life. The holiness of the heart's affections, as Keats said. I had this foolish idea that love should transcend and redeem all the petty crap we have to put up with on this turd of a planet. And because I thought that, I also thought that you should give it everything. D'you see what I'm saying, darling? That's where I went wrong. I thought you searched for the one person on earth who could make you whole, and devoted yourself to them, undyingly, come hell or high water. And I found that person, and I was true to what I believed. And look where it's got me." He snorted with laughter. "It's funny, really, when you think about it. I needn't have bothered at all. I could have just chatted you up in a pub

374

or at a party or something and then gone home with you for a quick one. Because that's the way you do things, isn't it, darling? Oh, don't look at me like that. I remember you telling me of just such an incident in your murky past. Unless that was a lie too. No telling with you. But perhaps it wasn't an isolated incident. Perhaps it was such a habit that washing a different bloke's spunk out of you became just a normal morning routine like brushing your teeth. Who knows, perhaps you were at it when we were together. Those nights when you'd ring me and say you were tired or you didn't feel too good or your parents were coming over — perhaps you had some bloke's whang jammed up your fanny even as you *spoke* — "

"You hit me."

She had to speak, to dam this stream of filth; but she also needed to take the initiative again, and something had suggested itself.

"What, darling?"

Trying to put hurt and bewilderment in her voice, holding her face, she repeated it. "You hit me."

"Ah, diddums." He was curt, but his expression had changed, he was faintly uncertain. "Don't you think you deserved it, darling?"

"I don't know . . . maybe . . . It isn't that. It's just . . . it's just that that was the way it always was."

"Liar." His voice fluted, and he cleared his throat to get it back under control. "No, darling, lying again. I never once laid a finger on you, as you well know."

"I know you didn't . . . but it was just the same. You said you loved me but you never really showed it. It's like I was always getting a sort of slap in the face, even if it wasn't a physical one. I always wanted to believe . . . I suppose I still do, if only you could *show* me this love that you keep talking about . . . then things might be different . . . "

"I don't believe this. I really don't believe this." That telltale colour was in his cheeks; she had rocked him back a bit. "I mean, what else can I do? Tell me that. My whole *life*, my whole life belongs to you. What more could you want? You tell me."

Let Jamie go. But no, it was too soon for that. "Well," she said tremulously, "you could — you could say sorry for hitting me."

He studied her. His eyes were as narrow as a cat's in sunlight. "And what would that achieve?"

She shrugged. "Probably nothing much. But don't you see, Ewan, we've got to make a start. I'm not stupid, I know now that we've got to try and sort this thing out between us. I can't just say OK, let's get back together and give it another try, just like that, because you're not stupid either and you'd know that that wouldn't be real. If we're going to get anywhere we've got to really work out where we went wrong . . . " Her mind was feverishly working. Keep him talking, that was what she had to do — and preferably that heavy pseudo-psychological twaddle that he loved, because once he was into that there was no stopping

376

him and he surely wouldn't want the distraction of Jamie around . . .

And that was all that mattered, get Jamie away from him, get Jamie safe. Then it would be just the two of them and then . . . And then what? How was she going to get out of this? Because if there was one thing she could not rely on, it was that Ewan was suddenly going to see reason. No sir. Amongst all the self-pitying, self-justifying bullshit he had given her she had spotted one grim nugget of truth — when he had said, *I don't care any more.* There was no doubting that: he had flipped too far. And so even the brightest scenarios she could conjure up turned vague and dark when it came to the question of getting away from him.

Someone will come . . . Yes, someone would come eventually: Jamie's parents would be back at some point tonight, and would come to collect him. But it might be very late. And what would Ewan's mental state be when Sue and John's van rolled up in the courtyard . . . ?

That depended on her. On how well she played the game.

"You're priceless, you really are." Ewan was shaking his head. "Working out where we went wrong. I love the way you manage to shuffle some of the blame on to me so casually. Let me refresh your memory, darling. *You* ended our relationship. Not me. I was happy — I was so, so happy, I felt as if I was living in a dream . . . and then you shattered it by turning round and saying we were finished. You gave me the push, sweetheart, let's be clear about that. You

377

threw me over. Packed me in. Dumped me. Dropped me. Ditched me. Jilted me. Isn't that the way it was?"

"Only because I felt — "

"Answer a fucking straight question for once in your life, you dumb slag. Isn't that the way it was?"

"Yes — I — yes, it was," she said, trying not to wince at the snarl that came into his voice again. "It was me who finished it — "

"Hallelujah, praise the Lord, the bitch admits it."

"But I'm just trying to explain why. I felt — trapped. Afraid of what was happening. Afraid of something so deep. Afraid of such a commitment . . . " *God forgive me — if lies do blacken your soul mine is never going to be clean again.* "It was a way of chickening out, I suppose . . . running away from the truth . . . "

Ewan held up a warning hand. "Just one moment, darling. Am I to assume, from this talk of chickening out, that you are considering the possibility of chickening in again? Of you and me making a new start?"

"Maybe — in time, if we — "

"Oh, well, I hate to be a killjoy, darling, but I feel I ought to remind you that this person proposing a new start is the very same person who a moment ago had to stop herself spewing up at the prospect of kissing me. Remember? I mean, correct me if I'm wrong, but it's not a very good lookout if you find me physically repulsive, is it?"

"Oh, Ewan, that — that isn't the main

378

point, the sex thing really doesn't matter that much — "

Oh no.

Bad mistake, big bad mistake . . .

Ewan's whole body had gone taut, like the flexing of one great muscle. His nostrils were pinched.

"What I mean is . . . "

"Jesus Christ." The soft guttural tone with which he spoke these words terrified her into silence. "Oh, my Lord in heaven, darling, that puts the lid on it, that does." The sudden laugh he gave was like a gasp of suppressed agony. " 'The sex thing really doesn't matter that much.' My oh my, where have I heard that before? I've got to admire you, darling. the way you came out with that, bold as brass. It ought to be written down, really. Put among the great quotes of the century, right next to Hitler saying he had no further territorial ambitions in Europe and Nixon saying he wasn't a crook. Blake, Amanda: 'The sex thing really doesn't matter that much.' " Ewan gave a squirm. "Well, my darling. for someone who doesn't think sex is important you seem to have a pretty healthy appetite for it. Except with me, of course. Anybody else and you're frothing at the gash. And this isn't just the jaundiced speculation of the jilted lover, sweetheart. I've had it from your own lips just what you got up to in the past. And I *know* for a fact that you're sleeping with Master Nicholarse, that you slept with him last very night as was, in fact. So don't give me this pure-as-the-driven-snow crap,

379

darling, if you expect this little talk of ours to get us anywhere. Do you hear me?"

A vein like a tortured worm was standing out on his temple. Amanda averted her eyes from it. Gone wrong, she had gone badly wrong there, God knew how much ground she had lost. "Yes," she said, "I'm sorry . . . that was a silly thing to say."

"Wasn't it just." Ewan's right leg was twitching, juddering; she couldn't tell whether it was that that was causing the visible shivers that were running through Jamie's prone body. "That's what pisses me off about you women. The stinking hypocrisy. The way you make out that access to your bed is such a great privilege that we're supposed to go down on our knees in slobbering gratitude for it. The way you make out that you're magnanimously demeaning yourselves by consenting to perform this nasty act. And all the time your cuntlips are sticking out so far you can hardly get your knickers over them. All the time you've had so many cocks up there you have to stop and remind yourself who this one belongs to. 'Let's see, if it's Tuesday this must be Nick.'"

He was trying to get a rise out of her, testing her out. Just like he used to in the bad old days, when he was spoiling for a quarrel. It was just the same.

Except it wasn't the same, because this time he had

(flipped)

a knife at a little boy's throat and the more she saw him and the more she heard him the more convinced she became that he would use it if the vagaries of his obsession wandered just a little further off the map of sanity.

"I can see why you feel like that," she said. "But what I'm trying to say is well, with us it wasn't just sex, was it? The relationship was more than that, deeper than that." An obvious ploy, maybe, but maybe not; she couldn't after all overestimate the size of Ewan's ego, a spoilt pet always lifting its overgrown head to be stroked.

"So deep, in fact," he said with a sardonic cock of his head, "that you had to end it."

"Yes," she said quickly, "it was something like that, yes."

He tossed his head. "Amanda Blake, High Priestess of Bullshit."

But she could see the covert interest in his face, and she felt she had gained a little ground. Or time.

Ewan said abruptly, surprising her: "Is that a drinks cabinet I see over there?"

"Yes . . . Would you like a drink?"

"No, darling, I'm auditioning for the fucking *Antiques Roadshow*." The sudden change from scowl to smile that followed this reminded her of the game you played with small children: pass your hand across your face while your expression changed behind it, happy, sad, happy, sad. "Only joking, darling. You do take things so seriously. Yes, I'd love a drink. What's in that mahogany monstrosity, then?"

"There's gin, vodka, Scotch . . . "

She waited. He was staring at her.

381

"Don't tell me," he said with precision, "that you've already forgotten what I drink."

"Scotch, of course . . . " She almost stumbled as she got to her feet and went over to the drinks cabinet. Her hands shook; the mad clinking and crashing with which she got a drink poured out would have been comic in a TV sketch. Comic. Funny. She wondered if anything in her world would ever be funny again.

His eyes on her were as palpable as fingertips. She reeled in a few wild ideas only to toss them overboard at once. Hurl the whisky bottle at his head? Run for the door? Throw the contents of the glass into his eyes? Smash the glass and lunge with the jagged edge?

Nothing was quick enough, not with that blade at Jamie's throat. Nothing was even to be considered while that was there. A vision of Mark's blood standing bright and metallic on the road assaulted her.

Not one drop. She was not going to see one drop of Jamie's blood. Her whole being must be concentrated on that one universal aim.

She turned and walked carefully over to Ewan with the glass of Scotch.

"Thanks, darling," he said. His fingers touched hers lightly as he took the glass, and he smiled up into her face. "Cheers. This is like old times, isn't it?" He sipped as she retreated to the armchair. "My God, Glenfiddich, would you believe. Well, of course, it would be, wouldn't it? The smell of money is pretty overpowering here, if not the smell of taste. Done well for herself, your old schoolchum, hasn't she? Amazing what you can get if you've got a cunt and a pair of tits and you use them in the right way. Wish I'd been born with them myself, in a way. Could have ended up with half-a-million-quid's-worth of real-estate just through opening my legs, instead of struggling through life every miserable step of the way and still ending up with nothing." He raised his glass. "Oh — aren't you having one, darling?"

She shook her head.

"No? Not keen? Strange. You go drinking with Nick, I know, because I've seen you."

It should have been no surprise to learn that he had been spying on them; but still the thought of it was like the creeping of nausea a little further up the throat.

"Well, I suppose it's different with Nick. *Everything*'s different with good old *Nick*, of course. Next time I enjoy the sunshine I shall have to remember that those glorious beams are coming straight from Nick's *arse* and give thanks accordingly, shan't I? Hm? I must say you're not very good company tonight, darling, I'm having to make all the conversation. And you were the one who wanted to talk. I wonder what subject will get you going, as it were? Well, I know, of course. St Nicholas himself, I'm sure he's never far from your *lips*. So come on. Let's hear it. Not all about Eve but all about Nick. Come on. Tell me about him."

She wasn't prepared for this; even now, her heart protested that Nick and Ewan must be kept as far apart as the poles, further, not part of the same world . . . "Oh — oh, Ewan, really, you don't want to know about him . . . "

Ewan smiled. "Don't tell me what I want and what I don't want," he said, with something in his voice that was like the crawling of insects and that made her begin hurriedly: "Nick, he's — he's twenty-nine, he works as an auxiliary nurse."

With nothing for it but to tell, she told, laying out the bones of Nick's life before Ewan with a revolted feeling that actual desecration could hardly have made worse. Born in Billingham, though his parents were Londoners who had moved up to the city ahead of the overspill flood of the seventies. His father was a butcher who ran a stall at the market; his mother worked in the cigarette kiosk at Tesco's, the only time of her life when she was not smoking. His three brothers seemed to be involved in various things involving second-hand cars and warehouses; his two sisters were married, one of them to an actor who had the vaguely familiar face of a sitcom neighbour. As a child he had had asthma but it didn't bother him much now . . .

She tried to keep her recital as dispassionate and factual as a CV. But it was hard not to let the warmth show through as she spoke of him, and she was afraid that Ewan saw it. She faltered to a close. "That's about it really . . . there's not much to say . . . "

Ewan regarded her for some seconds with tight, pursed lips. "Well," he said at last, swallowing the remainder of his whisky, "isn't he the dreamboat . . . And what about that mole just under your left breast?"

Amanda stared back, numbly.

"The little mole, just under your left breast, darling. He's seen that, I suppose? Does he kiss it? Or isn't that his style? Is he just a wham-bam-thank-you-ma'am sort of chap when the pair of you get your kit off? And what about the way your pubic hair goes up just a little higher on the right side, has he noticed that? You see, I remember it exactly. I remember every bit of you, every single thing. I've sat in my room these past months and thought of you so hard I've been able to picture you inch by detailed inch . . . until it seemed, you were *there* and I could just reach out and touch you . . .

He slowly extended the hand that was holding the empty tumbler as he spoke, as if he saw his vision captured in the crystal.

Then with a flick of the wrist he threw it at her.

Amanda dodged aside in time: it was really a toss rather than a throw, and the heavy glass hit the bookcase behind her and fell to the carpet without breaking. But the sheer random casualness of the action hit her with more terrifying force than any missile could have. For the first time she felt herself near to screaming.

"Fuck you, Amanda," Ewan said with the same brittle unconcern. "You needn't look at me like that. You've brought this on yourself, you know, really. You see, you should have told me. That's where you fell down. It might have been different if you'd told me that you were going out with this Nick, from the start . . . I love that abbreviated name, by the way. Just 'Nick'. Like he doesn't want to use the *Nicholas* in case it makes him out to be a bit poufy. 'Nick' — that's got just the right sort of abrupt manliness about it, but with a touch of friendly man-of-the-nineties approachability too. Like, he's no Giles or Guy, but he's not a Gary either. I mean it suggests an essential *niceness*, doesn't it; I mean I'll bet he doesn't scratch his balls when he gets out of bed in the morning, does he? Though perhaps you scratch them for him, hm?"

Amanda had never noticed before how closely a smiling face could resemble a bare skull. She wrestled with her stifled breathing. That smell coming off him was not just physical. This was a soul gone rotten.

"No, like I say, darling," Ewan went on, "it would have been different if you'd told me, instead of going behind my back. That's significant in itself, that *shows* your guilt, that you had to be underhand about it, and leave me to find out by chance." Suddenly he was bellowing. "I mean, how do you think that *feels*, Amanda? Finding something out like that. I mean, how do you think that *feels*? Have you any idea of the pain, the suffering, knowing something like that . . . ? Oh, of course you haven't. You're one of these people who just drifts through life, blissfully smiling, never getting hurt. And fucking up other people's lives as you go. I mean, you really seem to get off on that, don't you? You really like fucking up other people's lives? Ruining. Destroying.

386

You've certainly destroyed mine, sweetheart. And then there was Mark, of course."

The way he just came out with Mark's name like that — *using it* — brought Amanda close to the edge. She tensed all over, her limbs wanting to move, to lash out, to fight him with fists and teeth . . .

And he knew it, as he studied her face and gripped Jamie a little tighter. With a feeling as if she had been hit over the heart with a cosh, she saw that Jamie was crying, crying as quietly as he could, crying as much as he dared.

"Yes, you certainly fucked up Mark's life good and proper, didn't you, darling? Killing your own little brother must rank as one of the most thorough-going fuck-ups of all time. And of course one would imagine you fucked up your parents' lives in the process. But did that bother our Amanda? Oh, no, she just sailed gaily on, shagging her way round half the male population of Billingham, and in the meantime just taking time out to fuck up Ewan Malborne's life on the way, just for a bit of fun . . . "

She couldn't hold it: the tears dripped from her lashes. Tears for Jamie, tears of terror . . . and tears for Mark and that small kernel of truth she saw amongst the rant. He had got to her, the bastard had got to her . . .

No tears for him, though. Not for him. If she could get Jamie safe, it wouldn't be tears she would give this bastard.

If she got Jamie safe . . .

Use the tears. Bring them into the game.

"I'm sorry, Ewan," she sobbed. "I never

387

meant to hurt you . . . and I know you've been hurt before, that's the awful thing . . . " *Remember the quarrels . . . remember the way the aggression could be the tip of an iceberg of self-pity.* "The thing is, I've been lucky . . . and so I tended to forget you haven't had it so easy . . . "

"God! Tell me about it." His ready assent was only partly covered by the sneer. "I don't know what you're crying for, darling. I'm the one who should be crying, if anybody. God knows I've had to put up with so much shit in my life that it's a wonder I'm not crying every waking minute. And I feel like it. I feel like it right now. You don't suppose this gives me any pleasure, do you?"

"No," she said, "I don't suppose it's very nice for you."

"What ever has been?" he questioned violently. "I ask you, what ever has been, in my life? You know what I've been through, you know all the crap I've had to put up with. I never hid anything from you, never kept anything back. I told you it all. Now, I ask you, would you have wanted my life?"

I wouldn't have wanted your mind . . . "No," she said, "no, I wouldn't."

"Nice of you to say so." He stared at her a moment, then went on, his mouth falling into a little *moue* of sullenness. "The crazy thing is that I was ever surprised at the way you've treated me. I ought to know by now not to expect anything better. I ought to know by now that expecting a fair deal from this shitheap

388

of a world is simply not on, not where I'm concerned, but like a fool I let myself dare to hope, I dared to think that maybe this time I was on to a good thing and that it wouldn't be taken from me . . . "

And here it came, the iceberg below the surface. It was true, as he said, that he had told her all this before — *ad nauseam*, in fact; but for once that was to the good because she could partly tune out, nodding and agreeing at the familiar places, and fix her attention on what her next move would be. And as his gaze turned inward in maudlin self-absorption, she was even able to telegraph what she hoped was an encouraging smile at Jamie, and also to flick her eyes over to the carriage clock. Nine-forty; further on than she thought, but still not late, still nowhere near the time when she could start to expect Sue and John back, the time when she could expect the outside world to take a hand in the proceedings. The responsibility was hers alone for the foreseeable future; and she realized that in this situation the foreseeable future extended no further than Ewan's next hair-trigger change of mood . . .

" . . . Those dickheads at the Mid Anglia Press . . . talk about two-ulcer men doing a four-ulcer job . . . basically it was a case of inferiority complexes all round because, while they were putting on this hold-the-front-page shit they knew deep down that they were failures, pathetic nomarks who'd never been able to rise above the level of the provincial press, and what really narked them was that

I'd seen through that and I didn't care if they knew it . . . "

He was in full flow now, his face puckered in the brooding frown that she knew from the nights when uncorking a bottle of wine had meant uncorking the genie of Ewan's self-regarding gloom. He didn't even look up at her murmured replies; he seemed to forget the fact that he was holding her and Jamie captive at knifepoint, as if it were the merest indifferent circumstance like the weather or the day of the month, while he meandered down long tunnels of embittered reminiscence.

" . . . and Dad never even asked me why I wasn't working there any more. Crazy, isn't it, the way I go on being hurt every time when people are bastards to me. I suppose I expect too much of them; it's like, every time I'm prepared to give them the benefit of the doubt, and that's how I end up being used time and time again . . . "

Amanda nodded and nodded, trusting to the redness of her eyes to testify how heartrending she found the story of his life, while her mind ticked over like a dynamo and the minute hand of the clock moved like a flower growing.

What if she were simply to stand up and walk out of the room? Would he be so surprised and puzzled that he would just run after her, relinquishing Jamie . . . ?

Wishful thinking. The knife, the knife, always remember the knife . . .

What if she were to say she needed to use the toilet? He might let her do that — and at

390

the first sign of her trying to make an escape he would . . . Maybe she could climb out of the bathroom window — oh, ridiculous, she'd break her neck even if she could squeeze through it, and besides, he would still have Jamie and always there was the knife, the knife . . .

OK, there was the knife. But would he really use that on a little boy? Wasn't he bluffing? After all, this was *Ewan*, for God's sake, not the Night Stalker or Son of Sam or one of those other sickos from the true-crime books; this was a man she *knew* . . .

Well, yes it was. Indeed it was. And what she knew by now was enough to convince anyone but the most cockeyed optimist that expecting normal standards of behaviour from him was simply asking for trouble. And what was more, all those true-crime monsters started out as men that people knew. Ted Bundy didn't pop out from a toadstool: he was a man that people knew.

And even leaving aside all this, the fact remained that, even if it were a million to one that he was bluffing, those odds were too short. Because it would be Jamie who would have to pay. And once she accepted that sort of Russian roulette, then she was back on the sunbaked pavement after school, letting Mark run on ahead because the chances were that he wouldn't come to any harm . . .

" . . . that girl I went out with when I was at Sackvilles Insurance . . . I mean she had had a bad time, you know, men had really treated her like dirt and I really don't think she'd ever met anyone who was into committed relationships only and would treat things properly and seriously from the start . . . and Christ, you'd think that would count for something instead of making her decide to use me to get her revenge on the whole fucking male sex . . . "

Frontal assault . . . ? Again the knife, the knife . . . It would have to be something so devastating and instantaneous that he wouldn't even have a chance to move his hand . . . There was Ben's shotgun in the glass case on the kitchen wall . . . but Christ, she'd have to find the key on the keyring and unlock the case and the gun surely wouldn't be loaded and she had no idea how to load a shotgun, shit, that was the dumbest non-starter of an idea yet . . .

Dive at him, wrest the knife from his hand, now while he was taking a trip down that twisted memory lane? Try it . . . ? Her breathing quickened painfully as she thought of it. It would have to be so quick. If he saw her coming for a split second, that would be all he would need to jerk the knife and . . .

If anything happens to Jamie, it'll be your fault . . .

" . . . I was finished with women before I met you, darling. Oh, I know men always hand you that line, but in this case it happens to be true; not that I expect you to believe it, seeing as you seem to have this urge to spit on anything that smacks of sincerity. I was finished with them, I'd been hurt just one time too many . . . "

The minute hand was approaching ten o'clock

as slowly and ceremonially as if it were some momentous event. Which it had indeed become to Amanda's frantically beating mind, she didn't know why. Unless it was because her nerves were stretched out like spun glass and were shrilly demanding a decision and ten o'clock would provide the spur, the signal . . .

And the shape that that decision would take was hovering before her and she was ready to say yes, that one will do, that one will have to do because Ewan's monologue was running down and that belligerent consciousness was coming into his eyes again . . .

And the plan wasn't bad if she could execute it properly. The plan required her to be a superlative actress — to break down, and go weeping and crawling over to him —

slowly: he mustn't suspect her moves, mustn't be startled —

and confronting him with counterfeit love, begging him for forgiveness, maybe putting her hand on his knee as she sobbed out her heartfelt wish that they should make a new start together, wipe these past months from the calendar and really try to make a go of it, they surely could . . . And this time she would be prepared, she would conquer the revulsion that had made her flinch from his lips. Actresses had to make up to men they wouldn't touch with a bargepole, and if they could do it for a pay-cheque then so could she, with so much more at stake . . .

And remember that ego, that slavering glutton of an ego that couldn't resist a single titbit . . . Pander to it, use his name a lot, invoke

393

his sufferings on her behalf . . . *Oh, God damn him to perpetual hell that I should have to do this, but stroke his thigh and caress him and just get him so involved that he's not thinking about anything else . . .*

Especially Jamie. Play the big lovers' reconciliation scene so hard that he just has to join in and then Jamie is a distraction, yes, a nuisance to be pushed out of the way, let go of, sent away, sent out of the room, and *then . . .*

The hands of the clock did not so much reach the position of ten o'clock as stiffen into it. The rigor mortis of time.

Ewan had fallen silent. His eyes dwelt on her, saturnine, searching.

"I don't know why I'm telling you this," he said. "You don't care."

She didn't answer; just gave him the most melting look she could summon up.

"What big eyes you've got, grandma," he said. He grimaced and shifted in his seat with a hollow chuckle: was that a puzzlement auspicious for her plan, or a danger sign that said she had fatally miscalculated?

She never knew, because at that moment there was a loud knocking at the front door.

30

THE Scotch Stuart Howard had been drinking was Teacher's, his favourite, and it had slipped down so nicely that nearly half the bottle was gone.

He couldn't believe it when he looked at the bottle, nor when he consulted his watch; what had he been doing? But he knew, of course, what he had been doing. He had been lolling in front of the disregarded TV and looking through one of Fran's magazines — one of those *Cosmo*-type magazines with a name and a logo like a trendy hairdresser's, as thick as a telephone directory and curiously fragrant from the various scent samples stuck to the glossy pages.

He would rather have died than admit it, but he thoroughly enjoyed reading through these magazines of hers, and he always felt a faint flicker of excitement when he saw a new one sticking out of her shopping bag. There was just something fascinating about them — the glimpse into an inexplicable feminine world, the frank talk of clitorises and underarm shaving, the relentless and comprehensive assessment of men. The scale of priorities of this world appealed to him; its streamlined sassiness excluded the unsatisfactory elements of life that seemed always to be dragging him down nowadays. Here there were no incipient paunches, no washing-machines that needed replacing, no grown-up children with a smothered contempt in their eyes, no relationships that were merely an eternal, jaded stalemate without drama or real pain. Nothing tired, nothing workaday, nothing compromised.

And nothing *old*. Nothing that sparked in him those terrifying images of the years flying off the calendar like autumn leaves, of the day when his body would be nothing more than an uncomfortable and troublesome shell, of himself sitting in an overstuffed chair opposite Fran wondering whether or not to wash the car again.

And OK, he also found these magazines quite a turn-on, and he was willing to bet that plenty of other men did too. Even the ads for facial scrub carried a sexual charge — those swan-necked women bending their haughty profiles towards the water and scooping up the gunk with fingers a mile long. So different from those so-called 'glamour' magazines, where it was so obvious that the poor exploited chumps dislocating their hips to give the camera a gynaecologist's-eye-view against a background of flock wallpaper were really thinking of what to cook for tea tonight or how they were going to pay the gas bill. That stuff was about as glamorous as a warmed-over hamburger, and he prided himself on never having felt anything more than a faint disgusted tumescence on being confronted with it. But this — this was what he called glamour. The artful black-and-white photography might show no more than the contours of white shoulders above a black bra, a pair of crossed legs in stockings impossibly sheer, a couple embracing with shadowy abandon behind venetian blinds . . . well, it was what he called erotic. No sleaze about it. It made you horny but romantic too; it seemed to remind you of dreams you had had but had forgotten, dreams in which some glittering opportunity that had eluded you through life was yours at last . . .

It also brought back with technicolour vividness the face of the girl up at the farmhouse, and — perhaps with the aid of the whisky — reinterpreted her behaviour towards him in the most significant light. Surely he had been over-cautious in even allowing himself to doubt what those looks and smiles had meant. After all, as this article in the magazine said, body language was the one language in the world you couldn't lie in. That glittering opportunity that flickered through his dreams and wafted its promise from these pages with their stylishly backlit liaisons: what if he were to miss it through timidly refusing to read the signals?

He flicked off the TV, which had been muttering away at low volume while he drank and read, and sat for a minute looking at his reflection in the darkened screen. It was reassuringly short of detail; a half-tone sketch of a surely not at all bad-looking, reasonably fit-looking man in his forties (no need to be more specific than that). And if this was what the girl up at the farmhouse had seen when they arrived, well . . . Of course in a stronger light the slight thinning of the hair and the odd line on the face might be visible, but then they were the marks of maturity and it was no myth about *those* being attractive, the magazines were always saying so, always pouring scorn on those baby-faced pretty boys who looked as if they needed burping before they could get down to business . . .

No, he didn't see what he had to be afraid of, he really didn't. The girl up at the house might even be wondering why he hadn't come knocking . . .

"You are a bit pissed, though."

He had said it out loud, to his own surprise. The voice didn't sound like his own, but it was familiar for all that. It was a voice that was more often an internal one, liberated perhaps by the drink; it was the voice that sometimes, just occasionally, suggested to him that he ought to buy Fran some flowers, or that he was nagging at Greg for no reason at all, or that the down-and-out he passed by in the street with a fastidious grimace might conceivably have been him. The voice was, in fact, a fairly complete pain in the arse, and he didn't see why he had to listen to its priggish Jiminy-Cricket tones tonight of all nights, when he considered that he had a perfectly legitimate grievance.

So he'd had a few drinks, he told it — so what? Who wouldn't, after what Fran had said earlier?

When you're pissed, your judgement goes, whispered Jiminy. *And before you know it, you've made a prat of yourself.*

Well, maybe, he thought, irritably throwing

down the magazine. But was feeling a prat any worse than feeling completely miserable and lonely and rejected and insecure in a sanitized holiday cottage with wind grumbling down the chimney and miles of darkness pressing itself against the windows?

Yes, probably, said Jiminy, infuriatingly. *Yes, if she laughs in your face.*

Stuart studied his reflection a little more. Was that the distortion of the glass, or did he look flabby?

He sighed and picked up the magazine again. Bugger you, Jiminy, he thought. You needn't think you've won. Just give me a minute, and then you'll see.

He didn't need a minute; he needed only ten seconds, because it was then that the light-bulb above his head fizzed and went out.

For a moment he was actually annoyed at the inconvenience of this — before the tremendous implications hit him. Then he leapt out of his chair.

His decision had been made for him. No need for an excuse now, there *was* something genuinely wrong in the cottage, and it was entirely natural that he go up to the proprietor's farmhouse and report it. It would be downright strange if he didn't. No main light in the living room? Outrageous.

He flicked Jiminy Cricket away and squashed him.

On his way to the door be paused and listened for any sound from upstairs. Nothing; only the vast silence of Fran's resentful hibernation. Then he darted back to the TV for a last look at himself and a hasty re-thatching operation. No, he didn't look flabby. It was just the curvature of the screen — the TV was a pretty old model. He tutted. You'd think the Penningtons would run to an FST, the prices they charged for these places. The sight of the whisky bottle in the bulbous background was another useful reminder; he dug in his pocket for peppermints and popped one in his mouth.

Ready. He went to the front door and opened it to a gust of boisterous night air. At the last moment Jiminy Cricket twitched and with his last gasp pointed out to Stuart that he had almost certainly seen some spare bulbs in one of the kitchen cupboards during his discontented roamings earlier on.

True . . . Stuart hesitated.

But the girl wasn't to know that he'd seen them, was she? If he *had* seen them — which he wasn't a hundred per cent sure of. After all, who in their right mind went nosing through every cupboard in the place the minute they arrived?

Jiminy gave up the ghost with a whistle of despair, and Stuart stepped outside. He winced as the wind swiftly rearranged his hair to disadvantage. Oh, well. After a moment's debate he locked the cottage door behind him. Unlikely in the extreme that Fran would wake up and chisel her way out of her nightdress, but if she did he didn't fancy the possibility of her sallying out in search of him, not if things looked hopeful up at the house: now that *would* be just his luck. Besides, even if nothing did come of it, she would go spare at the idea of being left asleep in an unlocked house even for a minute. She was crazy about home security, always imagining noises and suspecting prowlers. Not that a prowler could possibly get anywhere near her unless he happened to be carrying a pneumatic drill and a case of dynamite; but then there was no reasoning with some people: once they got an idea fixed in their head they would lie to themselves rather than give it up.

He crossed the small parking area that adjoined the cottages and started up the service road. He noticed that the leisure complex up to his right was still open. He wouldn't mind a swim — though the light in that place was a bit unforgiving, and the Tunis tan had faded now. It certainly would be something if he could persuade the girl — Amanda, he must think of her by name to join him for a dip. Of course, there was that little kid of the cleaner's that she was looking after, but it would surely be near his bedtime . . .

The lighted windows of the farmhouse seemed to wink like saucy eyes as the wind-tossed trees wagged back and forth in front of them. Stuart was breathing harder than he cared to admit as he came to the courtyard. He rehearsed his line in his head: a simple enough line, but he wanted it to sound authentic — which, of course, it was. *Sorry to bother you, but there's a light-bulb not working in the cottage* . . . No, use her name, it built a bridge immediately. *Sorry to bother you, Amanda, but there's a light-bulb not working in the cottage* . . .

401

A few paces short of the front door of the farmhouse he stopped, aware of a faint sound behind him like the skittering of furtive feet.

They hadn't got a guard dog here, had they . . . ?

He turned, and the large red hen that had been tentatively approaching him turned too with a squawk of panic and went fluttering and scurrying away, only to stop after a few yards and look back at him in a long-necked, dithery way.

Good job it hadn't been around when they had driven into the courtyard earlier, Stuart thought; he didn't fancy getting stuck with a bill for a flattened chicken. And there was another one over by the garage, a grey, with the same scatty lost look. The place was alive with vagrant poultry. Shouldn't they be shut up? Weren't there foxes and stoats and weasels and all that *Wind-in-the-Willows* crew out here in the sticks at night?

Well, it was a handy development anyway. It would give him an extra excuse for knocking on the door. *Oh, and I couldn't help noticing these hens are out, did you know . . . ?*

Yes, things were working out rather well. She might even need a hand getting the hens in to the coop or the pen or whatever they lived in. Stuart checked his breath by cupping his hand in front of his mouth, then stepped up to the front door and knocked.

31

E WAN glared at Amanda in fury as the knock was repeated, louder this time. "Who the *hell's* that?" he hissed. He had gone sensationally white, as if all the blood had simply leached out of him.

Blood . . .

Jamie . . .

"I don't know, I don't know," she said, heartbeat booming in her ears, the whole situation suddenly transformed, as if a continuous note had been turned up to shrill, unbearable pitch.

"There was no car — I didn't hear a car," he said. "Did you hear a car?"

"No . . . "

"Who is it then?"

The knock sounded again: Ewan's leg juddered violently.

"It must be the Howards," Amanda said, "it must be, there's no one else here . . . "

"Ignore it then."

Another knock: Ewan jumped visibly, glared again.

"They know I'm here," Amanda said helplessly, "they — "

"All right, all right!" Ewan jerked himself upright, dragging Jamie to his feet. "See what they want. And just get rid of them. *Fucking* people, why don't they leave us alone!" The knocking again. "Go on, go on!"

403

Gripping Jamie by the back of his pullover, pushing the stumbling boy ahead of him, Ewan followed her out to the hall. The door to the dining room was further along, diagonally opposite the front door; Ewan reached in and turned out the light and then slid inside, holding Jamie close against his legs. He pulled the dining-room door half-closed.

"All right. Now answer it. Just get rid of him. And remember, I can see you, darling. I can see everything you do."

Amanda nodded. The hammering of her heart was so loud she was sure everyone must hear it. It almost drowned out her hurtling thoughts: *someone here, Howards surely, what to do? Take chance, take some sort of chance? What though? Ewan watching her. Some mute signal — how? The knife, remember the knife . . .*

"Open it, you stupid cunt," Ewan gritted.

She pulled out her bunch of keys, unlocked the front door. Prayed that Jamie wouldn't try to scream out . . .

Chill wind sprang with a whoop into the hall as she swung the door open, bringing with it a faint brassy odour of liquor. Stuart Howard stood there, hastily trying to smooth his disarranged strands of hair.

"Ah, hi." He presented her with his smile. "Sorry to bother you, but there's — er, sorry to bother you, Amanda, I mean, but there's a light-bulb not working in the cottage . . . "

She was going to have to say something. Ewan was watching her and Ewan had Jamie and she was going to have to say something

404

but she felt paralysed, limbs, tongue, mind, everything paralysed except some disembodied will beseeching him, *See that something's wrong guess that something's wrong help me help me . . .*

"Which light-bulb?" It came out as a croak, it didn't make any sense, but at least her voice had unlocked itself.

"Er . . . the overhead light . . . in the sitting room." Stuart Howard was making with the smile still, but he was frowning slightly too.

"There should be spare light-bulbs in the kitchen cupboard under the sink," she said. Was she talking normally? Her mouth felt as if she were speaking Chinese.

"Ah, right." The remains of his smile were still in place, but he was looking at her very quizzically "Sorry, have I come at a bad time?"

"No!" she said quickly. "No, well, not really, it's just . . . Was there anything else?"

"Hm?" He glanced her over, as if he noticed her rigid stance, but she couldn't move. "Oh! yes, there was one other thing. I've noticed there are some hens still outside, well, two at least, out in the courtyard . . . " He gestured over his shoulder. "I don't know whether there are more . . . I just wondered if you knew . . . ?"

"Oh, damn, I forgot, I — I was just shutting them up for the night when you arrived . . . " Just before the world had caved in on her: the moments when she and Jamie, laughing, had chased the hens round the pen seemed now like the last moments of content she would ever know. "I must have left the gate of the

405

pen open . . . I'll get them in straight away. Thanks for letting me know."

"No problem. Just thought it was a bit dangerous, you know. Foxes and so on. Wouldn't want to lose them."

"Yes," she said woodenly. Was that a noise she had heard from the dining room? Had Jamie . . . ?

"Horrible night, isn't it?" Stuart Howard said, turning up the smile again. "Sort of night that gives you the creeps. I — "

"Yes," she said again. "Well, thank you for telling me. About the hens. You'll find the light-bulbs in the cupboard. Good night."

She closed the door; her muscles were so stiff that she almost slammed it. When she turned round she found that Ewan had stepped out of the dining room into the hall.

Holding Jamie. Who was tear-stained and blanched with fear at the knife still hovering by his face — but unhurt. She let out a pent breath.

Then she saw Ewan's expression.

"What the hell do you think you're playing at?" he said slowly, his jaws working. "Just — what — the — hell — "

"I didn't do anything!"

"Oh, no? You told him you'd get the hens in. What did you have to say that for? Why couldn't you have just left it? What are you trying to pull?"

"Nothing! Nothing, I — I didn't know what to say, I wasn't expecting him to say anything like that, I didn't even know the hens were loose . . . "

Ewan stared into her face, breathing shallowly and fast. Down the hall the long-cased clock clucked like an old drowsy hen itself. Amanda did not shift her gaze from his.

"Well . . . " he said at last. "I dare say you didn't. But you needn't think you're going out there. You just leave them be. Your rich bastard friends won't miss a few chickens."

A possibility, a glimmer of possibility . . . "Ewan, I can't," she said, heart thundering again as the idea took shape. "Mr Howard's expecting me to get them in, he'll notice if I don't . . . " Gamble: Ewan had only heard Stuart Howard say 'the courtyard', hadn't seen the gesture over his shoulder: Ewan wasn't familiar with Upper Bockham as they were, didn't know you only said 'courtyard' for the area outside the farmhouse, not the square between the cottages. "He's got the bloody things scratching around outside his door up there. I mean, he's going to notice, Ewan, he's going to think it's pretty strange if I don't go and get them in. He's one of these pernickety types, you heard him going on about that lightbulb — "

"Shut up."

He gazed past her at the door, lips moving slightly. She had rattled him: good, but don't rattle him too much, just let that work on him, just look confused and anxious but not the true anxiety, the anxiety about whether this was going to work . . .

It must work, it must work . . . Get them outside, out of the house; and then it was a different ball game because she and Jamie knew

407

Upper Bockham and he didn't and there must, there must be a chance . . .

"All right, we'll get these fucking hens in," Ewan snapped. "But don't think you're going wandering off on your own, darling. We'll do this together. And don't think you're finished with me tonight, either. We haven't finished our business, you and me, Amanda, not by a long chalk. Understand?"

She nodded: she had no need to fake her expression of fateful seriousness.

32

STUART HOWARD stood for some moments looking at the closed front door.

He wasn't entirely sure how he had expected this to go, mainly because the fresh air had revealed to him just how squiffy he was and he had been a bit fuddled when it came down to it. But what he had most definitely *not* expected was such a weird and contradictory mixture of signals. He thought he was a pretty good reader of women, but what *that* was all about . . .

He returned slowly across the courtyard, glancing back once or twice. The red hen made a little neurotic dash towards him and then darted away again, crooning fretfully.

"Yes, chuckie," he murmured, "I know just how you feel."

He retraced his steps up the service road, thinking. Once he heard a pattering behind him, but when he turned it was only a few crisp leaves doing the twist in an eddy of wind. By the time he got to Honeysuckle Cottage and unlocked the door, the fumes of whisky had cleared from his brain somewhat, and he was thinking to more purpose.

Well, Jiminy Cricket had been right about the light-bulb, anyway. Stuart set about changing it, whistling softly to himself. He took the dead one through to the kitchen, dumped it into the pedal-bin. The sight of cooking utensils reminded him that he was hungry; he hadn't eaten since they had stopped at the Little Chef on the way here, and there digestion hadn't exactly been encouraged by Fran going into her emotional spin cycle when he dared actually to look at the waitress instead of giving his order with his hand over his eyes . . .

He peered in the fridge, and was for a moment outraged by its complete emptiness, until he remembered that they hadn't unpacked yet. They had brought enough food with them to see them through until Norwich awoke from its stern Sabbath on Monday morning and let its famished citizens into the shops, but the food was still stowed away somewhere amongst the luggage. Including, he recalled, a lot of chilled stuff that would spoil if it were left there overnight. Fran had obviously assumed that he would deal with it. Thanks a bunch, Fran. His resentment against her reawoke like a muscle strain.

He briefly weighed the inconvenience of having a load of uneatable food tomorrow against the satisfaction of being able to say Well, you went to bed without even thinking about it; you can't expect me to remember everything . . . No, not worth it. He went through to the hall, and began unzipping bags and rooting about amongst what seemed to be the entire transplanted belongings of their household. Sandwich toaster, what the hell did they want that for, they never even used it . . . and a box of flowery stationery, for Christ's sake, what were they going to do, sit around writing copperplate letters home like something out of Jane Austen . . . ?

He was only griping on the back burner, however. Bubbling away at the front of his mind was the thought of the girl up at the farmhouse. She had given him a sort of brush-off, all right; in fact at the end she had practically slammed the door in his face. But if that was what a brush-off was like out here in the boondocks, then it wasn't such a bad experience. Because he had never had a woman gaze into his eyes quite like that. It was as if she was trying to see down into the depths of his soul. Even as she gave him that hasty, almost curt spiel about the light-bulbs and the hens, her eyes had been searching his face as if she were committing it to memory.

Killer eyes, too. Rich, warm eyes, like the darkest of dark rum. And now that he came to think about it, a little shadowed underneath, as if she might have been crying . . . Now that made the whole thing even more of an enigma. One thing was for sure, he had stood in the force-field of a strongly charged emotion when he had stood before that front door, even if he couldn't tell what kind.

Stuart found the eatables and carted them through to the kitchen. There were a couple of party pies there, and after he had stowed the rest, he ate them, standing up, without a plate, without mustard, greedily, washing them down with milk from the carton. Fran would go up the wall if she saw him doing this. One thing

411

marriage did for you — it gave you back the enjoyment of stolen pleasures that you thought you had lost as a kid.

A kid . . . Of course, she had the kid with her. Maybe that was why she had stood there blocking the doorway and telling him one thing with her mouth and another with her eyes. The kid was probably rubbernecking behind her. Little jugs have big ears. She hadn't got the kid into his jammies and up the wooden hill to Bedfordshire yet. She couldn't talk with the kid around. Couldn't invite him in with the kid around. At least not if what she had in mind was . . .

Stuart's ears burned. The ghost of Jiminy Cricket wailed that he was jumping to conclusions, but he ignored it. After all, she had meant *something* by that odd behaviour, that was for sure. And when he had asked if he had come at a bad time, she had practically fallen over herself to say *No!*

All of which suggested that, far from being a write-off, the evening still held distinct possibilities.

Poor girl had those wandering hens to deal with as well. She was probably finding looking after this place more of a strain than she had thought.

Stuart swallowed the last morsel of piecrust and then, prompted by a flash of visual memory, went back to the heap of luggage in the hall.

Digging around for the food, he had come across the toolbox he always brought with him when they braved the wilds of Norfolk; for some reason Fran always snorted with derision at it, but she would laugh on the other side of her face when the need arose. Here it was. And inside, just as he thought, his flashlight. A good solid rubber-cased flashlight with a powerful beam; he had put in new batteries just yesterday. He flicked the switch to test it, and a disc of brilliant light big enough to dance in hit the wall under the stairs.

Perfect. Perfect for helping to track down errant chickens on a dark night. He flicked it off, did another quick repair job on his hair, and went to the door, rehearsing his line. *I thought this might help . . .* Not that he felt he would need it. He had a strong feeling that she was going to be pretty glad to see him again anyway.

33

"GO on," Ewan muttered. "You first."
Amanda opened the front door and
stepped outside. She didn't need to
look back: she knew that Ewan was right behind
her, one hand tightly gripping Jamie's collar.
And in the other hand, though he was keeping
it out of sight, was the knife.

The knife, the knife . . . That sliver of steel
was like a black hole at the centre of her
world — unignorable, inescapable, everything
converging on it, everything swallowed up in
it . . .

The wind made her shiver, brought her back
to herself.

Take one thing at a time. You've got him
outside, you're not trapped in the house any
more, good, good, now keep your head . . .

Casting about for any sign of the hens, her
eyes also made a frenetic survey of the terrain.
To the right, the entrance to the service road;
to the left, the south wing of the farmhouse and
then the double garage, the little path leading
to the henhouse and the garden behind it, then
the woodstore, then at right angles to that and
directly in front of her the stone-built outhouses
that had once been a cow-byre. All drenched in
sodium light —

"Get a move on." Ewan's voice was like a
cold iron bar laid across the back of her neck.

"Where are these fucking birds . . . ?"

As if in answer, the large red hen — Alix's favourite, Clara, the one she had been warned liked to go walkabout — came bustling over to Amanda making a noise like a rusty gate.

"Clara . . . come on, girl . . . "

The bird, with typical obtuseness, stopped and looked doubtful as Amanda bent and extended a hand in encouragement. Behind her Ewan sighed dangerously. Amanda saw that, though it wasn't her cup of tea at all, she was going to have to grab the hens in her arms and deal with them that way.

A handicap she hadn't foreseen. But it was the only way, she had no help, and Ewan was waiting and watching —

No one to help . . .

An idea. *Mind-games, remember mind-games.* A pale shimmering spectre of an idea, beckoning her.

She jerked forward and made a grab at the hen, putting a little extra clumsiness into the movement. Clara, predictably, squawked and scrambled out of her reach before stopping a few feet away and looking back at her with imbecile apprehension.

Ewan sucked in breath sharply. As Amanda crept towards the hen again, she risked a glance over her shoulder at him. He was as tense as a cornered cat, the knife in his right hand held upward like a cudgel. His mouth was slightly open, tongue quivering and flicking at his exposed teeth, and his eyes swung from side to side so swiftly you could almost feel the straining

415

of the muscles inside the skull. Tightly pressed against his legs, his cheek creased by the side studs of Ewan's jeans, Jamie stared hollowly. She couldn't tell whether he was seeing her, or whether his overloaded responses had mercifully shut down.

Mind-games.

Get Ewan away from Jamie.

She made another grab, and this time she felt feathers and brittle bones, but then the hen was darting away from her, shrieking and gobbling. Though it looked as if it was changing its mind about its direction at every step, Amanda saw it was heading for the shelter of the woodstore, an old flint construction open at one end rather like the stable in a Christmas crib display.

Ewan's voice rose unsteadily, a boy's voice half-broken: "For Christ's *sake*, what are you doing . . . ?"

"Look, it's not easy," she said, risking a note of protest. The hen was hesitating on the threshold of the woodstore, cocking her head first at Amanda and then at the neat stacks of firewood inside with their hen-shaped hiding-places.

Amanda glided stealthily forward. "Come on, Clara," she crooned, "come on . . . " *Don't come on, though. Do the opposite. Don't make it easy for me . . .*

The hen stood stock still until Amanda was within a foot of her, and then obeyed her mental command and disappeared with a flutter into the dark spaces of the woodstore.

"Jesus! You stupid bitch, get it, get it for

fuck's sake!" Ewan hissed.

She threw him a look over her shoulder; a look to measure him, gauge his nerves — but also a black look, a look he was meant to see, a look of aloof contempt that she would not have dared to give him unless she had decided it was the one move in the game she must make. She felt the look connect, then turned her head and made as if to peer into the woodstore and, speaking low and deliberately, said: "I wish Nick was here."

The gamble, must be taken must be taken, just get him away from Jamie don't fail Jamie the way you failed Mar . . .

"What did you say?"

Edge in Ewan's voice, unmistakable when it went clipped and posh like that, *good good press it press it —*

"I said I wish Nick was here," she said, larding the contempt with impatience, face still averted from him as she peered into the woodstore. "He'd be able to help me. He'd be some use."

She heard Ewan draw in a breath like a sick man's snore. "Oh?" he said. "Oh, I suppose *Nick* is the great Mister fucking handyman, is he? *Nick* is Saint Francis of Assisi when it comes to animals, I suppose? I suppose Mister Wonderful Nick is *better* than me in a situation like this?"

She took the peevish, taunting tone into her like an invigorating drug. *Go for it.*

"Yes," she said casually, turning her face to him. "In fact, Ewan, he's better than you at *everything*." Second's pause, *tense yourself.*

417

"One thing in particular."

A quiver went through him, almost a ripple, as if she saw him through hot rising air.

Then he went for her.

He was five or six feet away and she just had time to whip herself round and face him before he cannoned into her, his hands gripping her sweater just above her breasts, slamming her backwards against the corner wall of the woodstore so that pain sprang up her spine and her breath left her —

"*You bitch you fucking bitch* — "

and his yelling, split face was an inch from hers and the knife was still gripped in the curled fingers of his right hand so that the blade stuck up so close, so close to her cheek —

"*say that again you fucking slag* — "

but he had let go of *Jamie*, in his madness he had let go of Jamie and the little boy was standing there alone five or six feet away staring and bewildered and free . . .

She fought for breath, dredged breath up from her guts and screamed "*Run Jamie run Jamie run now* — "

and in the same moment brought her knee up and drove it into Ewan's groin . . .

He doubled up, grunting, and his face bumped against her stomach and now was the moment for a swinging kick that would drive his nose up into his brain but the moment was taken up by glancing up to see Jamie turn on his heel and run —

yes done it

— see Jamie running off into the darkness

behind the outhouses and now it was just her and Ewan . . .

He came up from his crouch gasping and spitting fury, and before she could hit out again his hands came up and gripped her wrists, pushing her backwards into the woodstore. They grappled for a moment and then she felt the weakness of his right-hand grip, just thumb and clenched knuckles clamping her forearm because he was still holding on to that knife, loosely, clumsily, and if she could just —

Bite.

She ducked her head and bit his right hand, not the little nip that ladies gave in bodice-rippers but snapping and tearing at him like a dog so that skin ripped and blood like warm and bitter tea was on her tongue . . .

Ewan screeched. His hand flew back and the knife left it, glittering once as it spun away into darkness, over the stacks of wood, landing somewhere behind them with a muffled clatter, gone.

He was still mulishly holding on to her with his left hand, right hand crammed into his mouth, eyes above it full of pain and a weirdly prim outrage — *how dare she . . . !* — and though she struggled and tugged she somehow could not break that grip on her sweater . . . And then, as he tightened it by twisting and bunching his fist, his knuckles grazed her breast and it was the loathsomeness of that contact that gave her the last extra ounce of strength and with a plunge and a cry she broke away from him.

419

She broke away from him, turned, started to run. She would have got clean away from him if Clara the hen had not chosen that moment to flee the woodstore too. Amanda had made five yards across the courtyard when the panicked bird zigzagged in front of her and then collided with her feet like a feathery football. She lurched, stumbled and staggered like a tired hurdler, and went down.

The asphalt surface of the courtyard flayed her elbows and knees, but worse than that she was winded for a second time, and when Ewan loomed over her she could only bat out at him with her hands, squirming round on her behind and trying to hoist herself to an upright position.

"You bitch." Ewan slapped her hands away, and his blood spattered on her. "Oh, you bitch, you bitch, you bitch . . . "

He drew back his foot and kicked her in the side.

The pain dazed her beyond screaming. She could only writhe and hit out blindly, grasping at his jeans, her nostrils filled with the sour unwashed smell of them.

" . . . you bitch, you bitch, you bitch . . . "

His hand got hold of her hair, and he drew back his foot a second time, and it was then that a bright beam, sharper than the sodium lights of the courtyard, fell across them and pinned them in its glare like players on a bloody stage.

"I was wondering if . . . "

It was Stuart Howard's voice, and it was Stuart Howard who had come round the corner of the farmhouse bearing the flashlight in his hand. And it was Stuart Howard who had now stopped dead, twenty feet away, and was staring at them in such bewilderment and shock that a tiny bead of saliva fell from his open mouth.

"Oh my Christ . . . " The flashlight wavered in his hand. "Oh my Christ . . . "

Amanda's voice ripped her throat like glasspaper as she screamed at him: "*Help me help me get help please . . .* "

Probably Stuart Howard did not fancy the look in Ewan's eyes: probably he thought that going for the police was safer than trying to be a hero. Whatever, he stared for two more seconds, stammered something about the police, and then turned tail and ran.

What happened next Amanda did not understand for a moment: Ewan grunted and disappeared into the woodstore. Hiding . . . ? But then he was out of there again, and holding something in his hand that she did not want to recognize; no, she did not want to recognize that thing that Ewan was swinging in his hand as he ran after Stuart Howard . . .

but you do recognize it it's the wood-axe the axe they use to chop the wood the axe that hangs on the wall just inside the woodstore . . .

Stuart Howard did not run well. It was not a thing he ever had to do. He was overweight and out of condition. He had not even reached the turning of the service road yet. Just as he heard Ewan's footsteps pounding up behind him he seemed to put on a spurt, as if his body had suddenly tapped some reserve of vital instinct,

421

but by then it was too late. Ewan swung the axe left-handed, in a looping, out-of-control arc like an amateurish bowler at cricket. The head of the axe went in between Stuart Howard's shoulder blades and did not come out. It made a heavy thick sound like a split bag of sand. Stuart Howard gave a loud piggish snort, his shirt turning bright red from collar to tail. His legs buckled under him in a rubbery way like a drunkard's and he wet himself as he toppled forward. He hit the ground like a dropped puppet, body all wrong, the axe still sticking out of him. One of his slip-on shoes had come off and the socked foot kept jerking and twitching for a while.

Amanda lost it. She snapped. Kneeling on the ground she began to scream and scream and she could not stop. And by the time her brain jolted into life again and made her stop the screaming and get to her feet Ewan had come back to her, and his fist was heading for her face with blackness in its wake.

34

EWAN wept a little as Amanda sagged back unconscious on the asphalt, and he dug his arm under her head so that she wouldn't bump it. The whites of her eyes were showing between fluttering lids, like a sleeping cat's, and her nose was bleeding. Her head too . . . ? No — that was his own blood, seeping from his bitten hand into her hair.

Their blood was mingling. That was as it should be, at least.

Ewan bent to kiss her lips, lightly.

"I love you, darling," he whispered.

He glanced up at the body of the man with the axe in it. It had stopped moving. Ewan sighed. He detested violence. But he simply could not let anything come between them; that was all there was to be said.

He stole another kiss, then sighed again and lifted Amanda up gently in his arms. It was a pity it had to be this way . . . Yet there was also a sort of rightness about it, a fitness. Maybe this was one of those things that was meant to be. He was shaken yet not truly surprised. A love such as theirs could not be expected to end tamely, he saw now. Such intensity could only come to a grand resolution.

All that remained was to see it through properly.

He carried Amanda into the house. She felt as

light as a feather to him; he would have carried her across forests and deserts and ice-caps, content only to be close to her and to serve her . . . In the hall he hesitated. He had to see about that kid; he had to get things right for the final apotheosis. His darling might wake, and not understand, and try to get away in her confusion or even misguidedly plug in the phone and call the police . . .

He carried her through to the kitchen and then into the brick passage where he had noticed a door with a lock on it. He set her down on the floor and propped her tenderly against his upraised knee, taking the bunch of keys from her belt. She moaned and stirred a little. His heart ached at the sight of the blood on her lip.

"It won't be long, darling," he whispered, hunting through the keys. Cottages, garage, several marked LC, what would they be . . . ? "Just a little while." Laundry, that looked a likely one. He tried the key in the door: it opened. He switched on the light and glanced inside: washing-machines, boiler, stone sink. One tiny window. He stooped and picked her up again, carried her inside. There was a black bag of laundry in the corner and he laid her on the tiled floor with her head pillowed against it. Her lips were moving faintly; the poor darling would be in pain when she woke up. But it wouldn't be for ever.

"It won't be long, my lovely," he said. "Then we'll be together again."

He went out and locked the door of the

laundry room behind him. Impulsively, he kissed the door.

His hand hurt; it needed bandaging. He found the first-aid box in the kitchen, hastily strapped his hand with webbing and stuck it down as best he could with tape. It would do. There was something far more important in here, something he had noticed first time round. He had not expected to need it then; but once again he wondered if this was one of those things that are just meant to be.

The shotgun was in a case on the wall. Of course, these Hooray Henrys went the whole hog when they played at Farmer Giles. Ewan had been brought up with shotguns and had never liked them — much to his father's disgust — but this was a matter of necessity.

He found the key on the keyring, opened the case, took the shotgun out. Oily smell. Ewan broke the gun, examined it. Clean as a whistle; Hooray Henry probably had a servant just to clean it. Cartridges too, in a compartment at the bottom of the case. Slip one in, another in the pocket.

He was all set.

"Come out, come out, wherever you are," he crooned to himself, leaving the house with the gun over his arm.

Shit: something he had forgotten. The body of the man still lay on the far side of the courtyard. There was a wife, wasn't there? Supposing she came looking? He made a detour into the woodshed, found a length of tarpaulin. It would have to do, he was in a hurry. He covered the body, weighting the tarpaulin down with stones. It was distasteful, but you couldn't worry about these small discomforts, once you had stripped life down to its passionate, naked essence as he had done.

There. Could be just a load of gravel or sand or something. He wouldn't be missed yet, and if the wife finally did come knocking, he just wouldn't answer the door. Nothing must disturb them, now that they were finally together.

He cupped his hand around his mouth and called: "Jamie! Jamie, where are you?"

The echo travelled round the courtyard like a ball round a roulette wheel.

"Jamie! You can come out now. Everything's all right. Amanda wants you . . . "

you you you . . .

The boy must be hiding out somewhere; he surely wouldn't have got the nerve up to run all the way down the long lonely road to the village, the state he was in — the little brat was half-catatonic. Ewan sighed in exasperation. This was just typical, typical of that negative influence that was always being exerted on his life, dragging him down and spoiling things. He wanted to be with his lovely Amanda; the most important moment of their lives was coming up. And here he was having to chase round after a wretched child who had nothing to do with the tremendous event, the beautiful consummation of destiny that was unfolding like a flower that blooms once in a thousand years.

Just leave him? Even if he had taken off for the village, he would be a long time getting there.

426

Traffic on that road? Highly unlikely . . .

But there was the wife; shit, there was the wife up at the cottages and if Jamie had gone to find her . . .

Ewan broke into a run, up the service road, past the leisure complex — a glance in at the windows, he could check in there afterwards if it was no go — and up towards the block of cottages.

He didn't want to kill anyone, but if it had to be . . . He felt free and light-headed, seeing the world as it really was, a bright sphere of deceptive glitter, nothing worth unless it were tossed away for love.

35

JAMIE didn't know where he was running to. He was aware that there was grass under his feet and trees up ahead, and something told him he was in the big garden behind the farmhouse. But he wasn't sure about it because something was also telling him that this was a dream. His legs seemed to be moving with that heavy slowness that he knew from bad dreams where he was running away from a creature that had no face and that wanted him. It was dark and silent like in a dream. And horrible things had happened like in a dream, things with a knife, things with a strange man . . .

But he was crying, the sort of long, open-mouthed crying you did when you were little and that you were too old for now; and in dreams, somehow, you never cried.

So it was real.

He was amongst the trees now, and he dimly remembered from playing here before that there was a wire fence somewhere and you had to be careful —

He remembered just in time, because here was the wire fence right in front of him. He had nearly run into it.

He stopped, panting and holding his side. He felt dirty, like he wanted a proper bath, and again he couldn't think why for a moment.

Then he remembered it was because of the

man. The man had held him tightly against his body and the man smelt, not the BO smell that Mrs Murgatroyd had at school but a funny vinegary smell that had something to do with the knife and the way the man looked at Amanda and the things he said to her . . .

And now Jamie knew why he was running. It was because Amanda had told him to. And Amanda was with the man now and fighting him . . .

Jamie gave a last loud sob and made himself stop crying. He started to climb over the fence because he knew he had to do something, knew he had to find someone to help. But he felt funny inside his head. He kept thinking of the smell of the man and those things he had said — things he half-understood, things that the boys at school whispered and giggled about, things that he had whispered and giggled about himself but which now made him feel frightened and sick and wanting to cry again. And he kept thinking of other silly things, like missing the film he had wanted to see, like whether the ducks would be down at the ponds or whether they went over to the river at night. And he wanted to go and see the ducks, he wanted to so badly, and he wanted to hold somebody's hand and he wanted to cry . . .

The hem of his pullover snagged on the top of the fence as he climbed over, and it was that that seemed to give him a jolt and stopped his head going funny. His thoughts all came together like a scattered pack of cards swept up and patted into a neat deck. He tugged at the pullover

429

till it tore, knowing in a swift, grown-up way that things like that didn't matter now and he wouldn't get into any trouble. All the little things that usually mattered so much, the things about how to behave that made so much of his life into a puzzling maze, weren't important any more. There was only one thing that was important and that was helping Amanda. And though he had said he didn't want a girlfriend ever he had lied a bit because if he ever did she would be Amanda, or someone just like her.

He ran down the slope and climbed over another fence, on to the service road. He knew what to do. There were the Howards up at one of the cottages — Honeysuckle Cottage; he remembered because he had fetched the key from the board when they arrived. He could see their car, parked in front of the block. Mr Howard had come knocking to ask about a light-bulb and Jamie had almost cried out for help then, even with the man holding the knife next to his face, and he had only stopped because he had sensed that Amanda didn't want him to . . . Mr and Mrs Howard would help, all he had to do was bang on their door — and that was another thing that didn't matter now, he could bang as hard as he liked and shout at the top of his voice — and they would answer and they would help, and it would be all right . . .

He was out of breath and there was a stitch in his side when he reached the door of Honeysuckle Cottage. There was no knocker or letterbox, because these weren't proper houses, and so he had to hammer on the door with his knuckles. It didn't sound very loud, so after a moment's hesitation — doesn't matter, remember — he started kicking at the door.

There was a light on downstairs, but the curtains were drawn and he couldn't see in. He stepped back to look at the upstairs window. Something made him think about the things the man had talked about and he wondered if that was what they were doing, up there, in the bedroom. Then he felt sick and ashamed at himself and knew he would never whisper and giggle at school again.

He started shouting, shouting for help, kicking at the door . . . No one came. And then the sound of his own voice scared him. It echoed back from the other cottages and when he looked round their blank, empty windows, surrounding him like great glassy eyes, scared him even more. And then he thought of the man and how the man might hear him shouting and come after him . . .

He gave another sob, he couldn't help it, and before he knew it he was running again. The darkness of the empty cottages and the loneliness and the wind and the thought of the man coming after him were too much. Perhaps Amanda had got rid of the man . . . perhaps he could get into the house and hide somewhere, or hide in the garden or . . .

He didn't know where he was running to; he was afraid his head was going funny again. All he knew was that he couldn't bear any more to be alone . . .

431

36

CLEVER, sunshine, very clever, thought Nick as he parked the car on a soft verge and admitted himself lost.

The stupid thing, the really stupid thing that made him feel more pathetic than anything since he had been in the school play at the age of thirteen and had had one line in the whole piece and had forgotten it, was that he hadn't yet got to the difficult part of the journey, the part that had required detailed instructions. In theory he should still be coasting along the main road, with the tricky turns only popping up once he passed Holt. But not only was there no apparent sign of Holt, he was pretty sure that this narrow wooded ribbon of tarmac that he had somehow got himself on to could hardly be called a main road even in rural Norfolk.

He groaned and switched on the interior light and dragged out the road-atlas again. How his workmates, and the home residents come to that, would hoot if they heard about this latest exhibition of Nick Foster's celebrated navigational skills. Normally he would have seen the funny side too. But not tonight: tonight he was angry with himself, livid, as he seldom was with any other person. This just wasn't cute any more, he told himself. This was the behaviour of a prize dickhead.

Despairingly he stared again at the blandly

schematic map, which made the road system of the eastern counties look as direct and uncomplicated as a chessboard, and again he was reminded of school: gazing at quadratic equations on the blackboard and knowing with a horrible certainty that never, even if he lived to be a hundred and spent every waking minute of his life on them, would he ever begin to have even the faintest notion of what the hell they were all about.

He flung the atlas into the back seat and hit the steering-wheel with the flat of his hand, immediately regretting the theatricality of the action. Outside the windows, slabs of pure, ploughed Norfolk mocked at him between the trees. *Miles and miles of us, bor. All looken the bloody same.*

And this was the end of his grand design. For this he had set out so urgently from Billingham, expecting the rustbucket Cortina to waft him to Amanda's arms, like a magic carpet. (To her arms? Well, so he ardently hoped, but it was fear that it was not so, that something was badly wrong between them that had driven him on.) And instead he had ended up lost in a landscape which did not appear to have seen a wheeled vehicle since Boadicea's chariot.

OK, so you're lost. So what are you going to do? Sit here picking lint out of your navel until the sun comes up?

Retreat to that back room in your mind? Say cheerio to Amanda, if so. Once you close that door, you know it doesn't open again.

Amanda . . .

433

His hand went to the ignition key, and just at that moment the inside of the car filled with light.

Headlights, right behind him. A car coming up slowly . . .

He couldn't believe it. A police car.

He was about to open the door and hail it, but there was no need for that. The cruiser moved in and halted in front of him. The police constable got out slowly and slowly walked along the verge to Nick's car, moving as if he were wading through knee-deep water.

"Hello," Nick said, opening his door and leaning out, "I wonder if you could tell me — "

"Evening sir, how are we?" The policeman cut him off with a blunt blade of singsong Norfolk. "Can I ask why you're parked here?"

Parked hair, thought Nick, slow to disentangle the accent, what's hair got to do with it . . . ? "Oh," he said, "oh, I see . . . well, I'm lost."

"Lost are we, dear oh lor," said the policeman, beginning a leisurely circuit of Nick's car. He was a stooped man with a beaky nose, like a placid eagle. "Is this your car, sir?"

"Yes . . . " Nick fumbled for his driving licence, handing it over the roof. He glanced at his watch as he did so: ten twenty-five, Christ . . .

The policeman looked at the licence as if it were a pleasant family snapshot that Nick had offered to show him, then handed it back. "Cor, dear, you want to see about them sills, my ole booty," he said, running a tender hand along the Cortina's scrofulous bodywork.

434

"Yes, it's a bit of a state," Nick said. "Look, is everything OK? Only — "

"Yi-is, everything's OK by me, sir," the policeman said, finishing the tour of Nick's car at last. "Can't help wondering what you're dewing parked here, though."

"Well, like I say, I'm lost."

"Where you supposed to be, then?"

"Well . . . I was on the A47."

"A47, dear oh lor," said the policeman, easily, as if he would like to carry on chatting about this all night. "Where you coming from, sir?"

"Billingham. And I — "

"Billingham, thass a fair way. I went on a course there not so long ago. Nice place. So where you heading to?"

"Well, it's a place called Upper Bockham, it's — "

"Bockham, wait a minute, I know it — well, I know a Lower Bockham, up on the coast Cromer way, thass the place you mean, is it, sir?"

Nick nodded, and looked his desperation. "Can you tell me how to get there?"

The policeman sucked in a whistling breath through his teeth. "I can, sir. But that'll take you a while to get there. Not in a hurry, are you?"

435

37

THE smell was the first thing to imprint itself on Amanda's reviving consciousness.

The smell was a warmish, stringent, starchy one, overlaid with a tinge of pleasant disinfectant. For some moments she simply lay still, her eyes closed, analysing the smell and trying to place it.

Other signals gradually reached her from other parts of her body: pain, and a hardness beneath her, and a softness supporting her head.

Hospital.

She found herself lightly smiling, as if she had solved some amusing puzzle. *I'm in hospital. I've had some sort of terrible experience, but it's over and they've taken me to hospital to make me better . . .*

She opened her eyes, and could not believe what they showed her.

Quarry-tiled floor, stretching away in vorticist perspective. Whitewashed walls. Big smooth white shapes of a central heating boiler, a washing-machine, a tumble-drier. A stack of cleaned and ironed pillowslips.

She stirred. This wasn't right, this wasn't what she had expected at all. And yet she knew this place, knew it quite well . . .

Pain blazed out from her nose and cheek as she raised her head, and in the same instant memory hit her like a speeding car.

Memory. All of it.

She flung her arm across her eyes as if by that means she might blot out the mental vision of the axe swooping down and the white shirt that became a red one. No good, no good. She saw it. She saw it all.

She jerked, snatched at breath like a crying baby, let out a hoarse scream.

It was the scream that mercifully cut the memory off for the pain that resulted from opening her jaw wide was so shatteringly brutal that for almost a minute her mind had room for nothing else.

When at last the shock waves had subsided she lay still, not so much gathering her strength as dully wondering whether there was any left in her aching body. The memory was still there, and always would be, a brief newsreel endlessly revolving, but her mind had temporarily curtained the screen for her own sanity. It showed her other memories instead. Ewan, swinging his fist towards her. Jamie, running.

Jamie. He had got away, she had done it . . . But *had* he got away? Where was Ewan?

She started to struggle to her feet, but just for a moment the curtains parted to give her a peek of the horror again, the axe and the blood —

There — you see? You've killed another one. They die like flies around you . . . "*If anything happens to Jamie it'll be your fault . . .*"

Your fault your fault your fault . . .

"No." She moaned a desperate denial, and

the moan changed to one of pain as she got to her feet and felt a vile stabbing in her side. Ewan had kicked her there, of course . . . She lifted her pullover, glimpsed a bruise the size of a purple cabbage, hastily covered it again. She felt sick. Lifting a hand gingerly to her face, she found blood from her nose, but it had dried. Even now some dozy, homebody impulse said, *Wash it at that sink, get it nice and clean,* as if none of this had really happened and there were nothing of more importance than personal hygiene to consider. Perhaps this was how it was when your world collapsed around you; you clung to the trivial tokens of normality, they found you sitting among the smoking ruins clutching your favourite coffee-mug . . .

She shook herself, fighting off the numb apathy that threatened to overcome her again. Get moving. Get out.

She rattled the door handle: locked. If Ewan had locked her in, then where was he? Was it too much to hope that what he had done —

(don't think of it!)

— had finally got to him and he had left, picking up his car from wherever he had left it and burning rubber?

Oh please God yes. But remembering what was in his eyes — or rather what was absent from them — Amanda was not hopeful.

The window, at the other end of the room. It was high up and very small, like an old-fashioned lavatory window. Too small to get through . . . ?

The big stone sink was directly beneath it.

She climbed up and balanced awkwardly on the sink's edge, knees trembling. The metal-framed window had a simple handle and no lock; all she had to do was turn it . . .

After twenty seconds of pushing, the palm of her hand felt lacerated and the handle had not budged by a fraction of an inch. Shit, didn't it ever get steamy in here, didn't they ever have to open the window?

No: there was an extractor fan a few feet to her right. This was a window that just wasn't used. It was either rusted or painted shut.

Anyway, look at the size of it. You'll never get through there. Just give it up, just lie down and close your eyes and perhaps things will sort themselves out . . .

No. It was amazing how small a space human beings could squeeze through if they had to. Giving up was no answer — even if Ewan had gone, there was still Jamie, she had to find out what had become of Jamie . . .

She jumped down from the sink, her bruises yelping, and began rifling through the storage cupboards that stood opposite the washing-machines. There had to be something, something that she could force the window open with . . .

Or smash it?

She thought for a moment. All very well if you could clear the frame of every last jagged piece, but anyone who had ever seen a broken window would know it wasn't as simple as that. All very well if you had a bit of clearance when you climbed through, but in that little window she would have no more clearance than a squirt of toothpaste coming through the nozzle of the toothpaste tube. It would be like squeezing through a mouthful of razor-sharp teeth.

But if she couldn't get it open, then . . .

Find something. She hurled the contents of the cupboards on to the floor: cleaning materials, dusters, washing powder, steam-iron, rags, sink plunger, more rags —

Something clanked. She scrabbled for it.

A spanner. Just a small spanner such as you might use to tighten a washer, but it would do.

She clambered up on the sink again and used the spanner as a lever, jamming it between the casement wall and the handle and pushing down with both hands. For some seconds nothing happened, and her battered face sang a keening song of protest as she gritted her teeth together; her bruised side joined in as she pushed harder, throwing her whole body behind it . . .

The handle shifted, with such a jerk that the spanner fell from her hands and dropped with an almighty clangour into the sink. She didn't bother to retrieve it. She gripped the handle again and pushed. The window unfastened with a sort of sucking sigh of old, flaky paint. She pushed it open.

Cold starry air funnelled in, so fresh it gave her a high for a moment. She thrust her head out as far as she could, peering round the vague, inky spaces of the garden, alive with cryptic movement as the wind passed among the trees and shrubs whispering secrets . . .

"Amanda!"

440

Her heart seemed to hit her breastbone as the voice spoke directly beneath the window. She looked down.

"Amanda, it's me . . . "

Jamie's tear-stained face gazed up at her. He was standing on the gravel path below the window, reaching up his hands, whether to help her or in terrified appeal she couldn't tell.

"Jamie, what's happened . . . ?"

"I saw you from the garden," he said. "I'm scared . . . "

"Where's Ewan?"

Jamie shook his head miserably. "I don't know."

"Jamie, go and knock at the door of Honeysuckle Cottage. Mrs Howard's there. Tell her — " *That her husband's dead?* " — tell her what's happened. They've got a car, they can — "

"I tried, I tried, I kept knocking and shouting and nobody came . . . Amanda, I'm so scared, it's so dark, I don't want to be on my own . . . "

Amanda heard the choked, hysterical note creeping into his voice: he was dancing on the spot and reaching up to her just like a toddler wanting to be picked up. He had been so brave and calm throughout his ordeal, Amanda thought; now it was catching up with him, he was cracking and no wonder . . .

And oh God I thought I'd saved him I thought I'd got him safe but what if Ewan's still around? I've got to get him safe . . .

"Jamie." She tried to speak gently, soothingly. "Jamie, it's all right. I'm going to try to get out

441

of here, but I might not quite be able to manage it. So I want you to run away now, get clear from Upper Bockham. Run up to the village — or if you see a car on the road, wave at it and make it stop."

"I can't," Jamie sobbed, and she saw that shame at himself was doubling his distress, "Amanda, please, I can't . . . I don't want to leave you, I'm scared . . . don't make me leave you . . . "

It was no good. "All right," she said. "Just stay there. I'm going to try and squeeze through here. You be ready to catch me when I come down."

She spoke briskly, partly to reassure herself; because while she had been craning her neck out of the window the horrible conviction had grown on her that she was not going to be able to get out this way. Her shoulders against the sides of the window felt as wide as a linebacker's, her breasts were jammed painfully against the sill, there was just no way . . .

"All right, here I come . . . "

She put her arms through the window, groped at the outer stonework. Heaving, she tried to pull her shoulders right into her body, to transmute herself into a creature without bones, without form, a snake, a worm . . .

The unbearable pressure on her squashed breasts would have made her gasp if she had been able to breathe at all: her collarbone and ribcage felt ready to splinter like matchsticks at any moment. Her pounding pulse sent fresh waves of pain through her throbbing face. The

442

muscles of her legs, straining with the effort of balancing on the edge of the sink, thrummed like piano wires.

And all of this was for nothing, because she could not get through the window.

She squirmed her way back inside, massaging her shoulders. Jamie was still gazing up at her with terrible expectancy.

Don't give up don't fail him . . .

She glanced down at the sink. There was a bar of yellow soap there.

"Jamie," she said. "I'm going to take my sweater off and try again. I want you to grab my hands and really pull. It doesn't matter if it seems to hurt me, just keep pulling. All right?"

She started to draw her sweater over her head. Stopped.

No answer from Jamie.

Had he run after all?

She poked her head out of the window again.

No, Jamie was still there, standing on the gravel path. Except that he wasn't alone. Ewan was standing right behind him, one arm around his neck. Over the other arm was a shotgun.

"There you are, you little monkey! I've been looking everywhere for you!" Ewan was smiling. He looked up at the window. "Hello, darling. Don't try to get through there, you'll hurt yourself. Now then, you little devil, come along with me, you've given us enough trouble for one night."

Jamie had gone rigid and white. His mouth

was open but no sound came out. Only his eyes retained expression, fixed on Amanda, begging her.

"Don't hurt him!" she screamed. "Ewan, please, don't hurt him!"

Ewan looked up at her as if she had said something rather silly and tasteless "Honestly, darling, what a fuss. Of course I'm not going to hurt him. I'm just going to take him for a game of pool. That's all." He gave Jamie a little push. "Come on sunshine. Chop chop."

"Ewan, please . . . " She was pleading now, abject. "Please don't hurt him . . . "

The smile remained, but a frown came down over it like a blind. "For Christ's sake, darling, how many more times? We're just popping over to the leisure complex, which is a much more fun place to be for a little boy, you must admit." He prodded Jamie again. "Off we go, Jamie. Quick sticks. I'll be back in a few minutes, darling. Now, you won't do anything silly, will you? You'll get down from that window, won't you?" he said pleasantly.

Numbly, Amanda nodded.

"Well, do it then, fuckface," he said, his tone unaltered.

She dropped down to the floor. Through the open window she heard Ewan's voice cheerily call out: "Good girl! See you soon."

Then two sets of footsteps, dying away.

38

E WAN pushed and hurried Jamie along the service road, keeping the muzzle of the gun cocked at the stumbling boy's shoulder.

He was rather proud of his patience, because he really could have done without this distraction at such a momentous juncture, and he had wasted time snooping round the cottages and then the leisure complex looking for the brat. Though one compensation was that there had been no signs of life at Honeysuckle Cottage; with any luck the woman had gone to bed and wouldn't bother him.

That was what mattered: that they should not be disturbed. He didn't give a toss about the boy; as he abhorred violence he preferred not to have to hurt him, though that was an option if he was forced into it, as he had been forced with the man from the cottage. The main thing was to get the brat out of the way quickly so that they would have the house to themselves. It was simply a matter between him and Amanda, and the boy didn't come into it, he was an irrelevance. He didn't really expect Amanda to believe that, since she was stubbornly determined always to think the worst of him, had probably told Superstud Nick all sorts of lies about him as they lay in bed together with his spunk trickling out of her

445

and down her thighs . . . But it didn't matter, love didn't set conditions, love didn't ask for anything but to give and serve. He would be true to his word. The boy could have his life in this putrescent world, if he wanted it.

He opened the main door of the leisure complex and thrust Jamie inside.

"In you go."

The boy staggered and nearly fell with the force of Ewan's push. When he had recovered himself he turned and stared at him with that frozen vacancy that was so irritating.

"Go on. Go and play pool. Go and have a swim." Ewan thumbed through the keys marked LC, found the one that fitted the main door. He closed and locked it. "Drown your fucking self for all I care." Jamie was still standing there in the vestibule, blankly regarding him through the glass door. Ewan tapped once on the glass, waved, and left him.

And now at last they were alone! He took deep breaths of the crisp air as he made his way back down to the farmhouse. Autumn air, unbearably poignant. Seasons: they were like differently shaped glasses that held the liquor of your experience — whether it was so much piss and dregs like most of his life had been, or the choice vintage of a perfect love such as he had found with Amanda. It was in a bitter January that they had met: a narrow, crystal flute had first held that rare wine . . .

It occurred to him that they had never had a Christmas together, which was a pity. He was sentimental about Christmas. Not religious, just

446

sentimental. It was a good time for lovers, a time when the world stood still and quiet for a moment and they could savour their togetherness, thinking of the year that had passed and the year that would come . . . He felt sorry for people who weren't in love at times like Christmas, because it was only when you were in love that you could fully appreciate that sense of a special occasion. Yes, it was a pity they hadn't had Christmas together.

But tonight they would have their own special occasion. Tonight was not unlike Christmas, because their own special redemption was coming into being. You didn't have to be a believer in mumbo-jumbo to sense that fate had been at work today, fate arrowing towards its resolution like a ray of white light to a prism that would reveal its glory as it destroyed it.

He quickened his steps as he crossed the courtyard. He didn't want to keep her waiting.

39

NOW she knew the truth of the phrase 'paralysed by indecision'.

She stood beneath the laundry-room window, straining her ears long after the footsteps had faded out of hearing. Though she was physically motionless, her mind was in an uproar that seemed to spill over the fringes of madness. What was he doing to Jamie? She hadn't saved him, she'd killed him, just like Mark . . . Suppose he was simply going to keep Jamie as a hostage like before? But a hostage against what? He'd killed a man, he'd killed a man, he was over the edge, there was no knowing . . . Supposing she heard a shot? If she heard a shot she knew, she knew in her bones that that would be it, the props would fall away from her mind and she would sink gladly into everlasting twilight . . . But could she still save Jamie? Should she try the window again? But Ewan's look as he told her not to . . . supposing an escape attempt was the very thing that would doom Jamie — was that what he had meant? And how was she to tackle Ewan? Ewan had a gun and Ewan just didn't care any more . . .

And the minutes were ticking by. *I don't know what to do, I don't know what to do . . .*

She had played the mind-games, and thought she had won. She should have known that when it came to mind-games, Ewan was

448

unbeatable . . . And now she couldn't come up with any more strategies, any more psychological feints and dummies and trick-shots. It had all gone far beyond that — even though a blindfold disbelief still kept surfacing and protesting that this was only a last spat with an ex-boyfriend.

No, she wasn't just dealing with an obsessive lover any more. She was dealing with a killer, a

(BOYFIEND)

man who was way out on a mental limb, swaying in a wild, unearthly wind.

And she wasn't dealing with him, didn't know how any more. The cupboard was bare. No: one thing remained. Quite a new thing, but fully formed, no question of that. Hate. A virulent, everlasting hate. But she didn't know how that could help her . . .

Her heart stopped beating, seemed in fact to disappear, her whole chest becoming a vacuum: she had heard a noise. A bang —

(shotgun the noise must have been a shot)

No, she knew the noise. It was the bang of the front door.

He was back.

. . . Alone?

Her heart juddered like a decrepit engine: her blood sang in her ears.

Jamie what had he done with Jamie . . . ?

She pressed her ear against the laundry-room door. She could hear him moving about, faintly. Minutes passed, each an eternity.

What was he doing?

A foolish squib of hope that he was lifting a

449

few valuables before taking off sputtered within her and died. No, not Ewan. The only thing he was interested in was — oh, God help her, the only thing he was interested in was her.

The noises had stopped. What the hell was he —

There was a rattling, so close to her that she jumped.

The lock. The door was being unlocked. She stepped back, suddenly aware of her complete vulnerability — that spanner, where was that spanner?

The door opened and Ewan stood there with a faint, tired smile.

"Darling," he said. "I'm so sorry about that. Are you OK?"

He still carried the shotgun. Not broken over his arm. Ready.

"What . . . " Her lips felt as if they had been frozen with novocaine. She was shivering. "What — have you done with Jamie?"

"Like I said. He's in the leisure complex. He'll be all right in there. It was a bit of a nuisance having him around, wasn't it?"

"You — " Her voice cracked: it was unrecognizable, a high, frantic cawing. "What have you *done* to him what have you *done* to him . . . ?"

Ewan sighed, though patiently. "Darling, I haven't done anything to him. He's in the leisure complex where he can amuse himself and be out of our way. Now you'll just have to take my word for it."

She stared at him, not knowing what to

450

believe, not knowing anything for the moment but that pure, overwhelming hate.

"Anyway, sorry I've been so long," he said. "I had to get things ready. Come on, darling. Let's calm down a bit, shall we? We've had a bit of a grim time all in all. Come on into the sitting room." He stood aside from the door, with a courtly gesture. "Come on."

She didn't move. She stared into his face, trying to read it, unable to read it.

"Come on, darling." He spoke softly, but he lifted the muzzle of the gun, very slightly. "I'm waiting."

Somehow she got her legs moving. Her very skin seemed to bristle as she walked past him, close enough to feel his breath on her.

"That's it. That's the way." He was behind her as she slowly walked down the brick passage and into the kitchen. "Come on and get warm by the fire."

The muzzle of the shotgun was there, just visible out of the corner of her eye all the time, like the nose of a devoted dog. There was nothing she could do. She entered the sitting room, moving like a sleepwalker.

And for a moment she did think she was asleep and dreaming. The room looked sickly beautiful. The lights had been dimmed right down and the antique candelabras that usually stood on the dining-room table had been brought in and lit and placed in appropriate corners about the room. The fire had been banked up and its light made red magic of the bottle of wine and the two glasses, already poured out, that

451

stood on a little table by the hearth. Beside it, taken from the dining room too, was a vase of hothouse flowers.

"Bit like a tart's boudoir," Ewan said with an apologetic laugh, as she paused just inside the door. "Best I could do at such short notice, I'm afraid." Amanda felt, very lightly, the muzzle of the shotgun touch her shoulder-blade. "In you go, darling."

She twitched and moved forward into the room. The warm heavy air seemed to cling round her like some sweet, viscous fluid.

"One or two of those candles are scented," Ewan commented. following her. "Nice smell, isn't it? Sandalwood, I think. Over there, darling. That's your seat. By the fire. You look done in."

He had set a windsor chair by the fireplace. Feeling the nudge again in the small of her back, she went to it, turned herself about. Ewan nodded encouragingly.

She sat.

"There." He stood smiling down on her for a moment. "That's nice. This is quite like old times, isn't it? Have some wine, darling. It's good stuff, I think."

This, she thought, this must be what hypnotism must feel like, this slow, unreal feeling . . . and this feeling that your voice isn't part of you, that it will come out like a robot's . . .

She curled her fingers around the ends of the chair-arms. They felt like claws.

She said: "What have you done with Jamie?"

452

"Dear oh dear, Amanda, change the record. I've told you twice." Ewan had set another chair facing her, six feet away, and now he sat down in it. He held the gun loosely and comfortably across his lap, its black eye pointing at her. "Jamie's all right. This is nothing to do with him, anyway. It's just us, darling. You and me. This is all I've ever wanted, you see. To be close to you. You and me, as one . . . It's too late now, I know. You made me kill that man, and I don't expect people to understand why I had to do that. But anyway, it was just one of those things that had to be, I suppose. I don't regret it. I don't regret anything, now that we're together, Amanda." His voice was tender, syrupy, like a distillation of all the elements of the room, the firelight and the scent of the perfumed candles and the wine and the flowers. Madness filled the air like lazy motes, like a slow shriek infinitely prolonged.

"In a way, you know, this is just as it should be, though it's perhaps hard for you to see it just now. Even a love like ours, you see, is vulnerable to time and chance. The world would eat into it like a maggot sooner or later. Better this way than decay. Better to burn out than rust out, as they say. And I'm happy, darling. I want you to know that. Yes, you hurt me, you hurt me very badly, but that's all forgotten. Right now I'm so happy . . . "

His eyes glittered like coins in the dancing light. She could not look away from them. The heat of the fire and the sandalwood scent wrapped sick loving arms around her and she

453

sat like a caught animal, transfixed, blank, every perception and response displaced by perfect terror.

"Aren't you going to drink your wine, darling?" he said. "No? Well, we don't need wine really, do we? I think there's only one thing we need for this moment. Music." He smiled brightly. "I've got it all ready for us."

There was a small black object on the floor by the chair, and as he bent to pick it up she recognized it as the remote control for Ben's hi-fi.

"It looks like an impressive system," Ewan said, pointing the remote control at the hi-fi and pressing a button. A red light winked on and cassette spools began to turn. "We should hear it just as Wagner meant it to sound, full and enveloping. And of course, we can have it as loud as we like. There's no one to hear. You know the music I mean, of course." As he spoke a familiar, cloying, unresolved chord sighed out from the speakers, followed by slow uncurlings of woodwind. Ewan breathed in deeply. "*Tristan and Isolde*. The Prelude first, of course. And then the greatest piece of all, the Everest of music — the *Liebestod*." His eyes roamed her face, and his voice was like a soft stench in the overheated air. "The Love-Death."

40

JAMIE knew what it was to feel guilty; he had felt guilty just the other week, when he had accidentally knocked down and broken his mum's flower-vase and she had thought their playful new kitten had done it and he had kept quiet instead of owning up. But that sort of guilt was nothing like this. This hurt him, hurt him with a pain he had never known before, and for some time he could only press his hands and face against the cold glass door and let the guilt bear down on him like a crushing weight.

He had failed Amanda. He should have faced the dark and the fear and the funny babyish feeling in his head: he should have faced them down like a bully and run to the village to get help. And instead he had stayed, crying and being silly, and the man had come back with a gun . . .

Jamie knew about guns. His dad's family worked on farms, and he knew what guns could do, and it wasn't like in films.

The man had a gun, and he had gone back to the house. Back to Amanda. And meanwhile Jamie was locked in here, where he couldn't do anything to help, where he could only wait.

It was all his fault.

All his fault . . . the knowledge of that was something so bad inside him that he didn't even want to cry. Crying made you feel a bit better, but he didn't want to feel better.

Out there was all darkness. He had no idea what the time was. He supposed his mum and dad would be back eventually, but somehow his mind couldn't grasp at that thought, it seemed far-off and unreal like the idea of being grown up. For now, for ever, there was only this night: there was only him, and Amanda, and the man.

Jamie remembered the man's smell, and the things he had talked about, and he felt hot and sick.

What was the man doing now?

And what if the man came back to get him?

Jamie jerked back from the glass door: the darkness beyond it might contain the man, might yield him up at any moment. Vaguely he thought of that darkness as what the man lived in, as a fish lives in water. He might suddenly appear out of it as he had done before, and this time . . .

Jamie turned and hurried through the lobby into the swimming-pool area. That panicky babyish feeling was back and he couldn't control it. His footsteps made loud, slapping, echoing noises in the huge space, and that scared him even more. He felt terribly small and exposed and he wanted to hide somewhere, hide and curl up into a ball . . .

He looked frantically about him. The swimming-pool glittered under the big, high lights, and he imagined the man putting him in it and holding his head under the water until —

He ran to the wooden steps that led up to the balcony. He knew what was up there, there was a gym and a sauna and changing rooms, and maybe he could find a corner to hide in . . .

Just as he set his foot on the first step something caught his eye and he stopped. Down there behind the jacuzzi was a door, a brown varnished door with slats in it and one of those big metal handles like the doors at school. It looked like the door to a store cupboard.

It drew him. He wanted to get in there.

He ran to it, grasped the handle, heaved it open. He was inside, and the heavy door had swung shut behind him, before he realized that it was completely dark inside.

Jamie heard himself gasp; but before panic could overwhelm him completely some instinct made his hand go up and search the wall to his right. His fingers found what they were looking for and pressed it, and at the same moment as the light came on Jamie became aware of a deep humming sound.

It wasn't a cupboard. It was the basement area, with concrete steps leading down. The humming sound was coming from what looked like huge central heating boilers, except with their works showing.

Jamie descended the concrete steps. It was very warm down here, warm with a pleasant sort of mustiness, like when you were snuggled under the blankets. And now he felt guiltier than ever, he felt that he must be a very bad person indeed because in spite of all that had happened and all that still might happen and the man and Amanda and the darkness and the gun — in spite of it all, Jamie found himself getting interested.

Because this place, clearly, was what made it all work. This was what kept the swimming-pool clean and at the right temperature and made the jacuzzi bubble and the sauna heat up. There were pipes and pressure gauges and grilles and voltage boxes and switches galore and as Jamie walked among the thrumming machines he felt his old fascination rising up and pushing away even his fear.

And he knew that that was wrong, because the man might come back and he should be thinking about that instead of what this switch did and what this dial meant . . . But it was so warm here, so warm and nice and hidden, and he didn't want to think about the man any more, he just wanted to stay down here and play, play with these tempting switches and not have to think about it any more . . . oh, he must be a very bad person indeed . . .

41

"AH! Hear that."

Ewan held up his hand, concentrating for a moment on the heavy-limbed strivings of the music. A candle was smoking. The smoke seemed to drift upward in slow motion, as if it could hardly penetrate the congealed, nightmare air. The room was full of red eyes, peeking at her from wine-glass and fire-irons and TV screen and gun-barrel, winking as the firelight winked.

"There — hear it?" Ewan said. "The way the music refused to resolve, even at that highest moment of intensity — even then that cryptic chord recurs. The unanswered question. Balancing on the cusp between agony and ecstasy. So beautiful . . . Wagner was quite a bastard, really, but he knew about love. He knew its secret, its essence."

"No."

Amanda spoke, and in speaking she managed to break through the soporific spell that lay upon her, the gauzy enwrapment of beat and scent, the surges of drowning, deathly music. "No," she repeated. "It isn't like that, Ewan." She knew now that she was going to die anyway. She might as well say it.

"What, darling?" In the firelight his high-cheekboned face was a schematic mask, all angles, all shadows. "What isn't like what?"

459

"Love. It just isn't like that. It never is." She stirred in her chair, flexing her fingers which had gone numb from gripping the chair-arms. She spoke clearly and flatly. "All that supercharged transcendent stuff — it's just not real. Love's never like that. It would be nice if it was, but it isn't."

The hooded expression came over Ewan's bright penny eyes. "You're referring to us, I suppose," he snapped.

"No," she said. "Not just us. Anybody."

"Oh, darling, not even you and Mr Wonderful Nick?"

"No. Anybody. You and me, me and Nick, whoever . . . It's just not like that, Ewan. It's a part of life, and it can be good or bad, but that's all. It doesn't change life or uplift it or redeem it or any of that stuff. That's what you can't see."

The frown forming between Ewan's brows looked as deep and red as a wound. And then all at once he was smiling. Smiling sadly on her and shaking his head.

"Oh, my poor darling," he said, his voice softer than ever, soft as cats' feet stalking. "They've got to you, haven't they? What a pity. Oh, I don't blame you. It's hard to keep the flame alight in this shit-awful world. Hard not to get infected, corrupted. And then before you know it you're believing those things you just said. Before you know it, you've accepted the world's crappy, trivial, fudged values, or you think you have . . . Never mind. We're going to prove them wrong, darling. We're going to leave

460

all that shit behind, and we're going to leave it together." He held up his hand again. "Here it is! The *Liebestod* . . . "

He pressed the volume on the remote control. Over a bed of tremolo strings the horns took the yearning theme upward in sequences. Clarinet and flute sketched nervous arabesques as the groundswell of morbid longing gathered and thickened.

"Wonderful," Ewan breathed. "Just perfection . . . " He gave her a wry little smile. "Of course, there never is perfection, is there? Not in this world. Perfection would be if we could both go at *exactly* the same moment. But I suppose that's as impossible as both *coming* at the same moment. Get it?"

He uttered a single, high-pitched titter, and something turned over in Amanda. It was that hate. She found it had grown. She registered its presence gratefully; she wanted it with her when she died.

"Ah, well." Ewan rose slowly to his feet. The violins were glittering like shot silk high above the stave. He lifted the shotgun, cradling it. "I'm sorry it can't be exactly simultaneous, but it's near enough." He stepped towards her, smiling into her eyes, and lowered the shotgun so that the muzzle gently brushed her temple. She smelt oil. She tasted the imminence of death like choking copper. "First you," he said, stepping back and lifting the gun again. "And then me. I suppose this is the traditional way, isn't it?" He briefly touched the muzzle of the gun against his open lips. "Like that? Bit like a

461

blow-job, really. You should know about that, darling. I'll bet you give Nick plenty. They say if a man eats garlic it flavours his semen. Does Nick eat garlic, darling? Does he taste of it?"

She was silent. Suddenly she didn't fear death, not if life meant Ewan. She preferred it.

"But answer came there none," Ewan said archly. "Oh, well. I suppose I'll never find out the truth of that — Oh! darling, listen! This is it — this is the passage . . . !"

A solo oboe picked up the thread after a brief hush, and then the strings surged in, dashing the great love theme against rocks of timpani in a first, deceptive climax. No, not yet; the strings began their dizzy climb of sequences, up a shifting staircase of keys, mounting . . .

"Don't speak, darling," Ewan whispered. He lifted the gun again and held the muzzle an inch from her left temple. "Just listen . . . just listen to the end . . . "

The stairs of tonality levelled out for a moment, just a landing, then the ascent again, reaching upward, higher and higher, almost there . . .

The brass fire-irons at her side winked their goodbye to her. Then winked again, more brightly. Not with a red light, but a cold white flash. Her eyes flicked to the side in time to catch the same flash travelling across the curtains.

She couldn't be sure, daren't be sure; the suffocating volume of music shut out any other sound, like the sound of an engine . . .

Ewan swayed a little as the giant climax

462

gushed from the speakers, ecstatic streamers of string sonority with great underpinnings of brass, and as he swayed the muzzle of the gun kissed her brow. Beside her the fire-irons winked again. Just firelight this time. She saw something else winking too: the bunch of keys that he had taken from her, lying on the mantelpiece. She flexed her fingers a little more.

"Ahhh . . . " Ewan shuddered a little. The glory dissolved, and the music asked its yearning question again before diminishing to a long-held shimmer of strings and woodwind, the last, ethereal, dying cadence gliding towards silence. Ewan closed his eyes a moment, then opened them.

"Goodbye, darling," he said, and there was a thunderous knocking at the front door.

"Amanda!" Nick's voice, muffled, shouting. "It's me, Nick!"

Ewan's head whipped round, rigid, his eyes blazing. She calculated she had two seconds. It took one second to seize the poker from the fire-irons. It took another second to grip it in both hands and thrust it forward, coming up out of the chair with her whole weight behind it, and drive it three inches into Ewan's side.

He was roaring like a bull as he toppled and hit the floor. Her mouth was open, but she didn't know whether she was screaming. She knew there was blood on her. She knew that she had to step over him to snatch the keys from the mantelpiece. She knew that she had done it and that she was running for the door, running out to the hall, running to the front door, unlocking it, opening it . . . and she knew that that was Nick's astonished face and these were Nick's arms into which she was falling . . .

"Oh, my God, what the hell's been going on . . . ?"

"Madman. Killer." She had no breath. "Jamie . . . the little boy . . . don't know what he's done with him." She pointed up at the leisure complex. "There. He says he put him in there. Quick."

"Oh, my God," Nick kept saying in a stunned voice. "Amanda, what . . . ? God, the blood on you."

"I know. Killed him." A sob escaped her. "Please, Nick . . . the little boy . . . "

He didn't protest any more, just nodded numbly, white. He ran with her up the service road. By the time they got to the leisure complex her hands were shaking so wildly that she couldn't get the key into the lock. She had to give it to Nick.

"Please let Jamie be all right . . . " Her teeth were chattering. Nick unlocked the door and they went in. "Please . . . let Jamie be all right . . . "

The pool area was blindingly bright after the darkness outside. Bright, and empty.

"Jamie!" Amanda called.

Echoes mocked her.

"Oh, Jesus . . . the bastard, he lied, he lied . . . "

"What's up there?" Nick pointed to the galleried balcony.

"Gym — changing rooms . . . Yes, yes,

464

maybe he's hiding, he's frightened to come out . . . Jamie!" She ran to the steps, pounded up them, shouting Jamie's name.

"There's another door over there — "

"Yes, plant room — try that too," she called over her shoulder. "Jamie, it's all right, it's Amanda, come out . . . "

She had just reached the top of the wooden steps when a *boom* rang out through the whole building.

The main door, slamming.

"Jamie . . . ?"

She turned at the top of the steps, slowly. It wasn't Jamie.

Ewan, his eyes bulging, his lips drawn back over his teeth, came hunched and shuffling through the glazed doors into the pool area. He had blood all over him. He had a trickle of spit running down his chin. He had the shotgun.

"Amanda . . . " The voice that came out of him was like the whirring of a rusty clock about to strike. He had seen her, of course. That was why he was smiling. That was why he was lifting the gun and pointing it straight at where she stood like a brilliantly lit target.

"Hooooooy . . . !" Nick, who had been about to open the plant-room door, was running at Ewan, running the length of the poolside, running at him and shouting to distract him and to take the fire on himse —

oh my Jesus no

"*Nick* . . . "

She was screaming his name on a shrill,

465

agonized note as Ewan swung himself about and pointed the gun straight at Nick's oncoming chest. And it was just then that all the lights went out.

Amanda's scream cut off like a guillotine. The darkness was as complete as the light had been and she could see the flash as the gun, after an instant's pause, went off with an explosion that seemed to mash her eardrums. And in amongst the booming echoes that followed she heard the gasping and the sound of a body hitting the tiled floor . . .

"No . . . " She was muttering it under her breath like a prayer. "No . . . no . . . no . . . "

"Amanda!" Ewan's dragging, crumbling voice. "Amanda . . . it's over, darling . . . "

He can't see you yet.

Clenching her chattering teeth together, she stepped on to the balcony and began to move stealthily along, guiding herself by the gallery rail. The darkness was resolving, as her eyes adjusted, into a teeming screen of pointillist dots with here and there a denser blob. One of the blobs was Ewan, down below. He was standing on the poolside: listening.

Keep moving, slowly slowly . . . because past the changing rooms is the other set of stairs that lead straight out to the lobby, there's a way out if you can just . . .

Way out, there's no way out for you, he's shot Nick and he's done God knows what with Jamie and you've failed, failed, and there's no way out . . .

She bit down on her tongue to quell the

466

hysteria that was swarming up inside her, tasted blood.

One step at a time . . . one step at a time . . .

The fuzzy shape of intenser darkness that was Ewan was moving too. Circling slowly round the pool, towards the balcony. Hunting her.

She tried to move a little faster, taking her hand from the rail, groping ahead of her for obstructions —

Her shin collided painfully with something edged and heavy and before she could put out her hands to grab it there was an almighty clattering, something like a stack of steel dinner plates tumbling and crashing —

oh God oh God

The black shape of Ewan had frozen, head lifted.

Blindly and automatically her hands fumbled to still whatever it was she had disturbed, and touch supplied the information swiftly, irrelevantly: *weights, barbell weights from gym, Ben works out every morning . . .*

Suddenly the shape that was Ewan made a decisive movement forward and now she could see him more clearly and he was lifting the gun to his shoulder —

oh God oh God he can see me too — and her hands were moving of their own accord, ahead of her petrified brain, and gripping the dishlike rim of one of the weights and lifting it, shield, weapon, grab *something . . .*

She straightened as she hefted the weight. Ewan saw the movement. The gun swung,

467

pointed straight at her —

and with an audible *thunk* the lights came back on, searing and white, and showed her the gun trained on her like a compass needle to north and behind it with his finger on the trigger Ewan, dazzled and blinded by the spotlights directly above the balcony blazing down into the pool and straight into his eyes —

Now . . .

With something between a groan and a yell she flung the weight at him with both hands like a fisherman throwing a net. It flew like a grotesque wobbling discus and Ewan was still blindly blinking as it struck the side of his head. His neck snapped sideways and his feet went up into the air and like a footballer caught by a scything tackle he seemed to hang in the air for several seconds before he fell, slamming horizontally down right along the tiled edge of the pool. His head bounced with an indescribable sound as the back of his skull hit the tiles and then he was sliding, toppling inertly over the edge and into the water, the gun falling from his slack hands. There was a flat splash, a seething of bubbles, and then silence.

The water bloomed pinky-red. The rippling surface played glittering tricks with the colour, throwing reflections of it up to the pine ceiling, until at last it tired of it and grew still, became a mirror bearing a reflection of slowly moving red clouds.

A faint, high-pitched, almost inhuman noise was coming from Amanda's throat. She found that she was scuttling sideways along the balcony, back and forth, in a sort of crablike dance, clenching and unclenching her fists, unable to take her eyes from the red patch in the pool. It was only the groaning sound that broke her strange trance of hysterical triumph.

Nick . . .

He was lying on the floor on the other side of the pool near the wall. Her legs had gone hollow and she almost fell as she ran down the steps and then almost fell again on the wet tiles of the poolside and it was as if she was never going to reach him . . .

She flung herself down beside him. He was lying on his back. His breathing was fast and shallow. His eyes were open and they turned beseechingly towards her as she bent over him.

"Nick," she said, "it's all right . . . " And though for his sake she tried not to look at what was covering his jacket and staining the floor she could not help it and she thought: *so much blood, oh God so much blood . . .*

42

SO much blood that even the ambulancemen blanched a bit until Nick's jacket was cut away and they found that the shot had only winged him in the left arm. The sudden darkness had deflected Ewan's aim, and the resulting flesh wound had made a hell of a mess and hurt like, as Nick said, buggery and was nowhere near as serious as it had looked.

"I should think I'll get some time off work, anyway," he said as they were putting him into the ambulance drawn up outside the door of the leisure complex. Loss of blood and shock were making him light-headed; he sounded almost tipsy. "Oh, God, listen to me, typical Brit, being all joky under pressure, yuk . . . Amanda, I never did tell you why I came down here, did I?"

She held his hand. "It doesn't matter. I know anyway. And I feel the same."

"Do you?" He smiled dreamily as they started to close the ambulance doors "Magic . . . "

The WPC who had been hovering round her touched her arm. "We've found the little boy. Hiding down in the basement. He's OK."

"Oh! thank God . . . thank God . . . " Relief was too weak a word: it was as if she had been injected with some invigorating, exhilarating drug. A drug that made you cry, too. She stood for a moment with the WPC's arm around her, sniffing and blinking at the scene.

470

Upper Bockham was transformed, a world of blue lights, police vehicles, uniformed figures passing and repassing, the crackle of radio sets. Up at the cottages someone was having the hard task of telling a woman that she had become a widow while she slept.

Amanda scrubbed at her eyes. "Can I see him?"

The WPC nodded. "He's been asking for you."

Jamie was in the lobby, looking very small in the midst of a knot of police officers. Another WPC was holding his hand and as Amanda approached she said, "This is the little chap, is it?"

"The one who likes playing about with light switches," Amanda said, kneeling and hugging him to her. "That's him."

THE END

Other titles in the
Charnwood Library Series:

PAY ANY PRICE
Ted Allbeury

After the Kennedy killings the heat was on
— on the Mafia, the KGB, the Cubans, and
the FBI . . .

MY SWEET AUDRINA
Virginia Andrews

She wanted to be loved as much as the
first Audrina, the sister who was perfect
and beautiful — and dead.

PRIDE AND PREJUDICE
Jane Austen

Mr. Bennet's five eligible daughters will never
inherit their father's money. The family fortunes
are destined to pass to a cousin. Should one
of the daughters marry him?

THE GLASS BLOWERS
Daphne Du Maurier

A novel about the author's forebears, the
Bussons, which gives an unusual glimpse
of the events that led up to the French
Revolution, and of the Revolution itself.

CHINESE ALICE
Pat Barr

The story of Alice Greenwood gives a complete picture of late 19th century China.

UNCUT JADE
Pat Barr

In this sequel to CHINESE ALICE, Alice Greenwood finds herself widowed and alone in a turbulent China.

THE GRAND BABYLON HOTEL
Arnold Bennett

A romantic thriller set in an exclusive London Hotel at the turn of the century.

SINGING SPEARS
E. V. Thompson

Daniel Retallick, son of Josh and Miriam (from CHASE THE WIND) was growing up to manhood. This novel portrays his prime in Central Africa.

A HERITAGE OF SHADOWS
Madeleine Brent
This romantic novel, set in the 1890's, follows the fortunes of eighteen-year-old Hannah McLeod.

BARRINGTON'S WOMEN
Steven Cade
In order to prevent Norway's gold reserves falling into German hands in 1940, Charles Barrington was forced to hide them in Borgas, a remote mountain village.

THE PLAGUE
Albert Camus
The plague in question afflicted Oran in the 1940's.

THE RESTLESS SEA
E. V. Thompson
A tale of love and adventure set against a panorama of Cornwall in the early 1800's.